DEATH

IN A TIME OF

CONSPIRACY

GEOFFREY SEED

CRANTHORPE
MILLNER
PUBLISHERS

First published by Cranthorpe Millner Publishers (2023)

ISBN 978-1-80378-104-4 (Paperback)

www.cranthorpemillner.com

Cranthorpe Millner Publishers

TABLE OF CONTENTS

"One lie is a lie.
Two lies are lies.
Three lies – that's politics."

-     Jewish folk saying

those graveyards, all those masked gunmen firing salutes over coffins wet with drizzle or holy water. Each side surely had enough martyrs now, names cut in polished marble, never to weather away not even in a thousand winters.

But here, the sacrificial dead of the past spoke to the present. For their voices to be stilled and terrorism negotiated into history, the process of peace would require every faction to put aside all weapons and admit they'd sinned. Then might reconciliation stand a chance.

Yet if terrorism was political theatre, those directing it behind the scenes had little incentive to draw back the drapes and go centre stage themselves. Such figures moved only in the unlit wings.

And even in there were darker corners and other actors performing in a play few knew had been written. She had glimpsed some of them – those anonymous men and women she'd ferried to and from missions when conversation was not made, questions not asked.

If nothing else, that morning's job reinforced her suspicion of all not being well. Their agent was out of lies. If she hadn't arrived when she did, those he'd betrayed would have run him to earth. His naked, tortured body would've been found on some country road, head first in a black plastic rubbish sack, eight grams of lead in his brain.

Ginny knew that spiriting blown agents out of harm's way was dangerous enough, even if handlers had time to prepare. No plan survived first contact with the enemy, so one fly-by-wire job had to be expected every so often. Two in quick succession was more concerning.

But only the spooks in their bunker knew what might be amiss for they dealt in treachery. That was their trade – cross and double-cross. In such a dirty, irregular war as this, could they ever really play strictly by the law or convention?

Yet Ginny worried about what might have been done for the greater good in the name of queen and country. With an end to hostilities, could a captain like her come to be judged complicit in dubious operations over which they had neither say nor veto?

Her thoughts were interrupted by the crew room's secure phone. It was Kat Walsh, the staff sergeant from military intelligence and liaison officer with the funnies.

'I hope you've got a kilt with you today, Ginny.'

'That's an odd thing to say. Why would I need one?'

'Because they all wear them where we'd like you to go this afternoon.'

Ginny mistrusted Kat, felt her chumminess was as fake as her accent. This was a woman pushing up through the ranks, determined to prove herself equal to any man in that most masculine of worlds.

'I think you best just tell me what the job is.'

'Right, got a pen? OK, there's a little seaside place, Port Logan, due south of Stranraer—'

'In Scotland? So are things going wrong there, too?'

'Nothing's going wrong anywhere, ma'am. It's just that one of our lost boys needs a lift.'

'By my reckoning, we've already had two other lost boys this week.'

'But all's gone well, hasn't it? Anyway, if you could be on the plot at three thirty, we'd really appreciate it, ma'am.'

'So where is the pick-up point exactly?'

'OK, it's a stone causeway, like a harbour wall with some sort of old lighthouse at the end of it, and there's a bit of a beach alongside where you can put down. He says you shouldn't have any problems.'

'Anything else I should know?'

'Only that he's in the reserve from the troop.'

Ginny recognised the coded reference to her next passenger being ex-Special Air Service and said she understood.

'Please get him back to them quick as you can,' Kat said. 'They're expecting him at HQ.'

Kat might have added that he'd once been her lover but that would be a secret too far. For Ginny, it hardly stacked up that someone still operational from so feared and resourceful a regiment could not make it back to Hereford without outside help.

But he might be injured or cornered by the bad guys so couldn't leave his foxhole for long. In that case, a pilot had a right to break the convention of mission secrecy surrounding Special Forces ops and be given all available intelligence to assess risk.

Ginny now felt justified in having already made a written complaint to her flight commander about Kat's lack of trust on what she suspected – without proof – were deniable Special Forces jobs.

But Kat had fobbed him off with the standard defence of national security.

'The funnies sing from their own hymn sheet at morning prayers,' he'd told Ginny. 'Just remember that where you are now is where reputations go to die.'

'Don't I just know it.'

'But you'll be out of the place soon. Try to make the best of it, there's a love.'

2: PRIEST

"... whoever resists the authorities
resists what God has appointed and
those who resist will incur judgement."

-    Romans 13, verse 1

No soul living could remember a time when the portrait of a
nameless holy man in the ancient church of All Hallows had
not looked down upon them, eyes pleading, cheeks deep-
furrowed as if from the passage of tears at all the wickedness
in the world.

Waxy smoke from candles beyond counting had fumed
the image and intensified the strangely hypnotic quality of
the face.

Some parishioners felt the picture should be sold to raise
funds. Others disagreed and thought it a unique piece of
church history, one bearing a passable likeness to the cleric
who led them in prayer: the Reverend Ralph Hill.

Here was a scholar-priest, skin parchment pale, black
cassock dusting the vanishing names of those at rest beneath
the nave. He could seem formal sometimes, even austere, his
mind troubled by matters beyond the borders of his parish in
rural Herefordshire.

His congregation knew he carried great hurts in his heart

yet remained a good servant of the Lord for all that. Ladies who arranged flowers on the altar thought him still handsome, if slightly shabby in appearance. He ought to re-marry or engage a housekeeper, then his life wouldn't be so solitary.

But Ralph Hill was not a man who welcomed advice. Of the four churches in his ministry, All Hallows was the smallest but the one abounding in memories of those he had lost. Such intangible comforts would soon be taken from him.

Those in high office found his radical politics – and the unwanted publicity they inevitably attracted – intolerable. They were counting the days to his next birthday, when retirement could be deferred no longer.

Ralph Hill stared at his painted likeness wondering, as always, who this man had been and what purpose the trials of his existence had served. The face was an image of anguish, hauntingly preserved down the centuries. What tests had he endured along the hard road he'd chosen to travel? Had faith sustained him to perform good works in the life and death religious struggles of those times?

But he would surely have known that faith without action was hardly faith at all. Ralph Hill did. Prayer and pamphlets were insufficient armaments if the weak were to be protected from evil's powerful forces.

The clock in the stump of the All Hallows tower struck twelve. A prepared vegetarian curry awaited him by the microwave. He walked through the porch with its musty earthiness, then across the untended graveyard where the remains of moon daisies and cow parsley swayed in the wind amid grass too tall to be mown.

The vicarage was Victorian, a grand house built when

clergymen were grand people. Not any more. All was neglect and decay – timbers rotting, slates fallen from the roof. But the hallway showed evidence of partial regeneration.

A new staircase and floorboards had been fitted and the walls papered in a pink and white candy stripe design. None of this was Ralph Hill's doing or choice. He'd been in no fit state to decide anything when this work was undertaken.

It had been the scene of a monstrous crime, an act of calculated revenge for which he could not atone or rid himself of his survivor's guilt. He would remain forever afflicted by the memories of what happened on that ungodly morning five years ago.

*

'That sounded like the post, didn't it?'

'Yes, I'll get it.'

'No, you finish your breakfast, darling. I'll go.'

Her slippered feet cross the kitchen to the lounge then through to the hall. All goes quiet save for the postman's van driving away.

'That's nice, Ralph,' she calls back. 'Some kind person's sent us a book—'

How odd. He's told no one she was staying with him. He never did. Their discretion bordered on secrecy born of necessity. Another moment of silence. The fingers of the electric clock move to eight thirty-two.

He rises from the table and pushes back his chair. It scrapes across the red tiles. The cat looks up from its cardboard box in front of the Aga.

Something feels wrong. But what? And why?

'Let's see who it's from.'

These are to be her final words, the last time he'll ever hear her voice.

Then comes a blast of explosive energy, so fearful, so sudden and intense that it hurls him to the floor two rooms away. Dust billows through the open kitchen door and over his prone body.

The reverberating, thunderous noise finds no escape from inside his skull. Everywhere is chaos and confusion. He stumbles towards the hall. That's where she lies amid the blades of glass smashed from the mirror on the wall.

But she no longer has eyes to see.

Ralph Hill falls to his knees and holds her to his chest, rocking her with infinite tenderness, his tears, her blood, his remorse.

The shredded pages of a bible printed in Afrikaans are nearby and the remains of the package in which it was delivered. The word of God destroyed by those corrupting His message from a continent far away.

To Mrs Bella Venter, C/O the Reverend Ralph Hill.

He reads their names, typed on what is left of the padded envelope. It matters not who falls in this battle without rules or borders. Vanity and deceit inevitably come with a bill. Did he really think a dog collar was some sort of amulet against the enemy's agents, even here in this green and pleasant land?

All those covert missions, all his subterfuge. They'd surveilled him then and now, chosen when to strike for the greatest effect. Kill one, terrify a thousand. Isn't that what the Chinese say?

Ralph Hill is in shock. He cannot stop trembling. If the darkest hour is just before dawn, when will the sun ever rise on this most impious of times?

*

The phone rang in his study as he closed the front door on his way to the kitchen to make his lunch.

'Daddy… hello, it's me.'

He was taken aback, caught unawares by a voice he wasn't expecting and hadn't heard for almost two months.

'Virginia? This is a surprise.'

'I hope I find you well, Daddy.'

'Yes, I'm very well, thank you.'

'Run off your feet as usual, I suppose?'

'Indeed I am, still trying to do the Lord's work.'

'Not much of that where I am, I'm afraid.'

'No, well there wouldn't be… not in your line of business.'

Theirs was a mutually disapproving relationship, no longer warm. It had descended into filial duty, an acceptance by Ginny that he was getting no younger and by her father that she did a dangerous job. They were close, once. But that was before his world was blown apart, and lying in the debris was the truth about a man she thought she knew but didn't.

'Listen, Daddy, I'm coming down to Hereford later this afternoon,' she said. 'I could drop in and see you if you're going to be at home.'

'Are you on leave, then?'

'No, I'm working. There's one of our people north of the border who needs to get home.'

10

The Reverend Hill knew from this oblique reference what manner of person her passenger would be and where home was. He should have let it pass and only later would he come to regret that he didn't.

'Ah, I see… one of your killer friends.'

Ginny sighed audibly. She would ring more often were it not for his inability to ease off criticising her and sniping at the armed forces.

'It doesn't matter who he is. It just gives you and me a chance to meet, but only if you can bear to see me in my working clothes.'

For all the spiritual guidance dispensed, the injunctions to forgive and to be accepting of the ways of others, the priest was but a man, not always capable of applying his wisdom to himself.

'Yes, all right, you must come if that is the case. But how will you get here? Can you requisition a car or something?'

'I don't need to. I've got a helicopter.'

'Yes, I know you have a helicopter but there's no airfield near here.'

'There is… your lawn is more than big enough and it's on my way back to base.'

'No, Virginia, absolutely not. I positively forbid you to land here in your dreadful gunship.'

'It's not a gunship, Daddy.'

'It is still an instrument of warfare and I don't want it anywhere near the vicarage.'

'But I'm about to be posted back to Germany. This is my last chance to say goodbye.'

'Can't you get a taxi or use some other means of transport like normal people do?'

'You're saying you don't want to see me, are you?'

'That's twisting my words,' he said. 'Of course I want to see you but can't you at least respect what I've tried to stand for all my life?'

It was Ginny's turn to sneer then.

'Please don't give me any more of your love and peace routine,' she said. 'Try looking at your own hands for once, Daddy darling. They're far bloodier than mine will ever be.'

She put the phone down. The Reverend Ralph Hill stood in the silence that remained. His daughter was right, of course.

The charge against him was hypocrisy and he was guilty. As guilty as sin.

3: PASSENGER

"I am a man
with a cripple inside him.
He suffers so much I would kill him
if I dared."

-    Nearing An End by Norman MacCaig

There were evenings beneath velvet black skies when Robbo would stand wordless in awe at the mysteries of a cosmos of which he knew nothing beyond that his own blink of existence within it ultimately counted for nought. Had he been religious, he might have found comfort in the notion of an afterlife, some better place only an all-powerful creator could devise. Heaven would be out there, somewhere, amid a hundred million stars spinning above the dance of life and death below, a reward for blameless living or for those who found redemption. But where was he to find his?

Happiness and despair, honour and shame; the damp earth folds over all in the end, just as it had those he once knew, the ones whose faces he saw rising from their restless graves to deny him sleep.

Robbo would go into the night then, running through the witching gloom of the Galloway Forest until darkness gave way to dawn and the owls stopped shrieking. To run was to escape but he feared he never could, not until he himself had joined those who'd already gone.

For now, introspection had to wait. The bothy's log burner had gone out. His bare feet were chill on the stone-flagged floor as he prepared coffee for a new client, Ms Tilly Brown.

She'd arrived with her camera equipment four days earlier in a Volvo estate, silvery grey like her hair.

'I've never been so glad to leave London,' she'd said. 'Noise, traffic, I swear the place gets worse by the week. You can hardly breathe, the air's so bad.'

'So a few days trekking through the wilds is what you need, then.'

'It's great to be here but I wasn't sure if you'd still be acting as a guide.'

'Why's that?'

'Because the magazine I saw your advert in was at least two years old. I only rang on the off chance.'

He guessed she'd be in her mid-forties, toned at a gym, well maintained inside and out. Here was a woman, educated and at ease with who she was and what she'd achieved, but whose accent provided no clue to her origins.

Making assessments of all who came into his orbit was an unbreakable habit. They'd left base the following morning, camping along remote nature trails, over granite hills and through bogs and forestry for her to get shots of red kite, deer, otters.

'Photography always been an interest of yours, has it?'

'An interest, yes, but I've only just been able to devote more time to it.'

'But you're too young to be retired, surely?'

'Flatterer,' she said. 'No, I was a lawyer then there was

14

restructuring where I worked and I thought to hell with it, I'll take redundancy and do what I want for a change.'

They cooked over burning logs and brushwood, roasting cuts of rabbit and pigeon he'd shot then taken from the freezer before they set out. Eating meat he'd killed on a fire she'd made aroused the primitive within them both as they lay in separate tents listening to the cries of creatures that inhabited the night.

After supper on the second evening, she asked if he was married.

'No... I'm not married.'

'But you've been hurt, though?'

'Haven't we all? What about you... you married?'

She poked a stick in the sparking embers with her right hand and held out her left so he could see she wasn't wearing a wedding ring.

'I'm divorced. Never was meant to be a good wife... domestication and all that.'

'Why did you get married, then?'

'Good question... honest answer? Well, on the actual day, my wedding dress looked rather beautiful and everyone was waiting for me in the church.'

'Doesn't sound like the best of reasons.'

'No, big mistake. I walked out of the marriage six months later.'

'Children?'

'I never wanted responsibility for anyone other than myself. And you?'

'No, but we're wired differently, aren't we... men and women?'

'I always got asked if my biological clock was ticking and

I'd say no, I can only hear my bank balance getting bigger.'

'Sounds like you know your own mind.'

'Most of the time, but it took a divorce to prove that to myself.'

'No regrets about not having kids?'

'A little twinge in my thirties, maybe,' she'd said. 'Still, I have a cat but she's not a child substitute, she's just a cat.'

Now, on the morning of her departure, he took her coffee into the sitting room. She stood by his bookshelves wearing a fisherman's blue guernsey and patched hippie jeans. A moment of embarrassment passed between them. They'd paused outside her room the previous night, each close enough to see into the eyes of the other. But he'd turned away and gone to his own bed.

'I'll make some toast and scrambled eggs,' he said.

She went with him to the kitchen and watched. Places were laid for them at a gate leg table set with blue and white crockery, linen napkins and a sprig of heather in a plain glass vase. They ate together but not in silence.

'How do you cope with this reclusive life you've got here, cut off from everyone?'

'I don't find it that hard.'

'It must be pretty monastic, though.'

'People come to stay like you. I'm not completely below the radar.'

'I looked at your visitors' book,' she said. 'You've not had many this year.'

'It'll pick up.'

'Enough to pay the rent on this bijou little place?'

'I manage. I've been going almost three years and always have done.'

'Your advert said you're ex-Army. What regiment were you in?'

'No mob you'll have heard of. I was just a squaddie doing what I was told.'

'A squaddie? With Marx and Gramsci on your shelves?'

'They're only books, doesn't mean a thing.'

'It's interesting, though.'

He shrugged and cleared away their plates. Further interrogation was cut short by his pager. It was the message he'd been expecting from Kat since she rang two days before: *NW97240 45500. 15.30 today*. The co-ordinates were the grid reference for Port Logan, a coastal village on a hammerhead peninsular off Galloway, about a dozen miles south of the port of Stranraer.

'Something's cropped up,' Kat had said. 'No arguments, we have to meet. I'll send you details of where as soon as I can fix up the transport. Don't let me down again, Robbo… do you hear? Don't you fucking dare.'

The rope around his neck would never slacken. One tug from Kat and he'd be twisting in the wind. But then, so would she. Theirs was mutually assured destruction.

*

It didn't take much effort to persuade Tilly Brown to drive him to Stranraer though it was in the wrong direction for her. His Land Rover was having a new gear box fitted. He said a taxi wouldn't get him to where he had to be in time.

Besides, he intrigued her, not because of what he said but what he didn't. There was also something about him that his soldier's calm efficiency couldn't entirely disguise – some

17

conflict, maybe danger. She discerned it fleetingly as he'd looked at his pager.

For such a man, presentable but not handsome in any women's magazine sort of way, to have no female or family photographs in his home was strange. He was unusually tidy, too – books and CDs filed alphabetically by author or artist. This was a methodical individual, fond of order and neatness.

She'd paid his fee upfront and in cash as requested and when she had asked his name, he simply said Robbo. If he mentioned a surname, she didn't hear it.

They now drove west along the A75, tucked in behind slow-moving container lorries lumbering towards the ferry to Northern Ireland. Robbo's hands held on to the black canvas holdall she'd seen him take from a cupboard beneath the staircase. There was a distance between them. He was already somewhere else in his head.

'Are you meeting someone off the ferry?'

He nodded but kept looking at the road.

'Your girlfriend?'

'No, not a girlfriend.'

'Maybe I'll book in with you again,' Tilly said. 'I've enjoyed the last few days.'

'Yeah, do that. It'd be great.'

She dropped him beneath the clock tower of the Stranraer Museum on George Street. He said he'd walk to the terminal from there. For reasons she couldn't explain, Tilly didn't believe him. She found a parking space a hundred yards further on and watched him go into the hotel next to the museum.

Four minutes later, a taxi arrived. Robbo emerged into the weak sunshine and got in. Tilly held up the traffic in the narrow street to carry out a three-point turn before following on.

The cab was a navy-coloured Vauxhall Cavalier. It headed south down the A716 coast road alongside the waters of Luce Bay and fields of black cattle grazing beyond the march of a dry stone wall.

The tourist season was coming to an end. There were few cars on the road. She held back, worried in case Robbo turned around and saw her.

After the hamlet of Chapel Rossan, the Cavalier turned right onto the B7065 to Port Logan. Robbo had misled her. His affairs weren't hers, yet she almost felt cheated. But her sense of the clandestine and the unexplained was heightened.

So, too, were the fantasies she'd had when they'd slept under the stars, albeit separated by canvas.

They reached the village where she watched him pay off the cab driver outside an inn. It was a little after three twenty. Tilly parked and got her camera from its metal case. She screwed on a telephoto lens and steadied herself by the open window of the driver's door.

Robbo was walking the road, which curved round the beach towards the harbour wall, his jacket zipped up to the neck. At the end was a primitive lighthouse built in pale stone worn smooth by wind and rain. This was where he stood, silhouetted against the massing banks of storm clouds.

She got focus. His light brown hair blew about his face. And he still gripped the straps of the black bag he'd not trusted to the boot of her car.

Click. Tilly fired off a shot. As she did, a camouflaged military helicopter came in fast, and low, barely fifty feet above the sea.

Click, click. The pilot turned its tail landward and hovered just above an outcrop of rock and shingle beneath the lighthouse. Robbo clambered aboard.

Click, click, click. Then he was gone and the sky tumbled with gulls once more.

4: CRASH

*"Force and fraud are in war
the two cardinal virtues."*

-    Thomas Hobbes, 1588–1679

Ginny could see Port Logan's parallel streets of whitewashed cottages and guest houses set between ploughed fields and a picture-postcard bay lapped by the Irish Sea. Her objective was waiting on the causeway as arranged. He threw a bag on board and strapped himself in behind her.

'Put your life jacket on,' she said. 'We'll be flying over water.'

Ginny spun away before anyone could see what was really happening. The whole operation took less than thirty seconds.

She had already planned a route: south east over the Isle of Man, making landfall again near Colwyn Bay then skirting Mount Snowdon, the Berwyns and across the hills of mid-Wales to SAS headquarters. The weather forecast wasn't promising – rain spreading from the west. But she'd flown in much worse.

Ginny turned and motioned her passenger to put on his headset and mic. She didn't want to sit in silence all the way. Curiosity – and her mounting annoyance at Kat – had started

21

to out-muscle discretion.

'I'm Ginny. What do they call you?'

'Robbo.'

'That's your nickname, is it?'

'Yeah, my nickname.'

'OK, good to know you, Robbo. I haven't had to lift anyone out of Port Logan before.'

'No, don't expect you have.'

'I've done a couple of these trips in the last few days,' Ginny said. 'I might be wrong but I get the feeling there's some sort of flap on. What's happening, do you know?'

'Not a clue.'

'So you're another mushroom like me.'

'Sorry?'

'Kept in the dark and occasionally covered in shit.'

'Ours not to reason why,' Robbo said. 'So we're headed back to Northern Ireland, are we?'

'No, to headquarters, Hereford. Weren't you briefed?'

'Not as such, no, just given the RV for you.'

Ginny could only wonder why a one-time trooper from the SAS would be given a pick-up rendezvous but not told he was going back to base.

Robbo seemed older than the other two she had rescued – around forty, average height, average build, not much of a talker, self-contained. He'd a flat, nasal accent of people from that drizzly, mined-out coal belt between Liverpool and Manchester. Beyond this, he was unmemorable, an everyman who could pass in the street and be forgotten immediately. Maybe anonymity was his shtick, how he survived whatever he did for the funnies.

Ginny caught him looking at her before she could delve

further. His eyes weren't hostile, just blank and indifferent like those of a shark. It was obvious she'd got all the answers she was going to get.

Sixty minutes later, they were over the southern end of the Snowdonia National Park. Dense rain clouds were closing in. Ginny reduced height to fly beneath them but visibility was poor and forced her to keep close to the contours of the wooded hills. In front was a stretch of water. She knew then they were slightly off course and checked her bearings.

The map showed it as Lake Vyrnwy, a reservoir four miles long, half a mile wide. Ginny veered slightly east to follow its length. Jutting out into the water from the north side was a Gothic stone tower with a conical verdigris roof.

Had she not been wearing a helmet, she might then have heard a noise like a detonator exploding above the cockpit. It was only the instrument panel starting to flash red that alerted her to danger. Some malfunction had wrecked the rotor gearbox. All power was immediately lost. The fuel pipe was ruptured and they were on fire, spinning down like a sycamore seed.

Training took over. She fought to regain control, to auto-rotate and glide out of danger. But at five hundred feet, no pilot would have had time to avert the inevitable after such a catastrophic mechanical failure.

If Ginny had a scream in her throat, it died as the Gazelle smashed into the lake ten seconds after the explosion. The force of the impact snapped its back, and hers.

A photograph of her in green military fatigues, laughing, light brown hair loose to her shoulders, looking more like a catwalk model than a combat pilot, would be released later by the Army and appear on many a front page.

But for this moment, she and her aircraft sank towards the still-standing ruins of Llanwddyn, the village sacrificed to create the reservoir a century before. Her sightless eyes stared out from the Perspex bubble of the cockpit and through the emerald waters to where the three prim Davis sisters once welcomed guests at the Powis Arms Hotel.

Here and there were cottage walls where a Welsh dresser might have stood, polished and proud, heavy with a blue and white dinner service. In the streets of cobbles beyond, boys and girls had walked to Sunday school in boaters and knickerbockers and knelt in chapels where only fish now swam. And trespassing in this long-drowned arcadia was a machine of war from an unimaginable future. Strapped inside was Captain Virginia Caroline Hill, twenty-eight years old and unmarried.

Divers would later cut her free then swim her to the surface. Her remains were now the property of a coroner who would order a forensic examination and open an inquest.

Of Captain Hill's passenger, Robbo, there was no sign – dead or alive. But this information would not emerge in the confusion of the tragedy, for it had no place in the script that the Fates had decided to ignore.

5: NEWS

"Smoke and shadows are we."

- A Book of Sundials, T.N. Foulis, 1914

The Reverend Hill had read of artists working on beaches, building complex structures from sand and driftwood or intricate mandalas of pebbles. They laboured between tides, aware that their efforts would soon be washed away, if not by the next cycle of the sea then the one after. The shoreline would always revert to how it had been before man had the temerity to leave a mark. Thus, the ephemerality of human endeavour was illustrated.

To Ralph Hill, the parallel was all too clear. He lay on his bed after lunch, auditing his life's struggles as the end of his three score years and ten approached. Duties and obligations once performed without effort now tired him. Age was a factor but so was the heaviness in his heart that rest alone could not ease.

Ginny's call should have been an affectionate exchange of pleasantries between father and daughter. Instead, it was cut short by another row. They remained far apart still and he might never find favour in her eyes again. The young were not inclined to forgive for they had yet to discover any weaknesses in themselves and so realise how simple it was to fall from grace.

Time was passing. He sensed a sort of psychological trip switch activating within himself. Much of what he had held dear was slipping away. He was reminded of his own father. His deal with the devil was to survive the trenches of the Great War but thereafter, to relive in nightmares all he had seen and done on behalf of his king.

Ralph Hill the boy was often woken by screaming and swearing, his father lashing out at enemies he had already killed but who would never die in the battles still raging behind his eyes. All was terror and confusion, even when he regained consciousness, sweating with fear and uncertain where he was.

It was forbidden to ever speak of these harrowing nights. Only in his final days did his father talk about the Western Front and then, not as a rational human being but as the blind, demented soul he had become.

Random memories tumbled out from the fog in his head, of crow-picked bodies crucified on the wire, exploding shells hurling men in the air minus legs or arms or heads, and the avenging faces of his enemies, pursuing him until the last moments of his own release from that conflict without end.

Such tableaux of horrors were the foundations of Ralph Hill's conscientious objection to warfare and the sacrificial waste of men fooled into marching behind patriotism's drum by those always too far away to catch the foul whiff of death its beat foretold.

Virginia never accepted his deeply personal reason for being a pacifist any more than she'd shared his belief in God or socialism. At eighteen, she paraded her rebellion in khaki by joining the Army.

They made her an officer at Sandhurst then a pilot in the Air Corps. Her father was appalled. But his objections were dismissed as those of a naive idealist who failed to see the moral ambiguities of modern conflict and therefore, the obligation to intervene in the cause of a just war.

Yet however hard Virginia might search the mournful fields of Flanders now, she would find no moral ambiguities, only bones and buttons and the wind in the trees.

*

Ginny Hill's helicopter fell from the sky at four forty. The light was poor, the location remote. If any cottager or farm worker thereabouts witnessed the Gazelle spiralling down into the dark waters of Lake Vyrnwy, they did not report it.

Neither did anyone see her injured passenger swim to the shoreline nor the drift of blood he left in the water. Had they done so, they would have watched him strip off his lifejacket then stumble as if drunk towards the trees surrounding the lake.

Within an hour, a distress signal had been detected from the jacket's radio beacon by RAF Valley and a rescue mission launched.

At six thirty-five, Britain's national news agency, the Press Association, transmitted a one-line snap to alert subscribing media outlets to a breaking story.

Military helicopter believed crashed in or by a lake near Snowdonia. More follows.

The BBC's duty news organiser in London read this then rang Christian Moreley, newly dried-out ex-crime correspondent on a final warning and reassigned to less stressful general duties in Manchester. He could be on air from the location in two hours.

Moreley called home to say he'd probably not be back that night. The wives of hacks on a story, like those of cops on a case, learn that broken promises are covered in the small print of the marriage contract.

'It'll cost you a bunch of flowers,' his wife said. 'And not some half-dead daisies from a petrol station, either.'

Moreley headed south through Cheshire then on towards the Welsh border. The news organiser rang his car radio phone each time the PA filed an update.

Ministry of Defence say chopper based in Northern Ireland. No info yet on casualties.

The terrain became more hilly as he drove further west by fields of sheep and through dark plantations of towering conifers snatching at the shifting grey clouds.

Army and police activity near Lake Vyrnwy Hotel at southern end of lake.

The hotel was set on a wooded slope above the reservoir. Moreley parked and quickly befriended the PA's stringer from the local paper to catch up on what had happened.

She had already trawled the hotel bar and the few houses nearby for witnesses but hadn't found any.

They watched two soldiers crossing the roadway across the top of the dam's sheer wall of huge stone blocks but attempts to get information from a uniformed police sergeant were waved away.

Moreley feared he would struggle to get a voice piece on any of the radio bulletins that night. He was in the hotel bar when the receptionist came through to say she'd got a phone call for him. It was an officer from Army liaison.

'I can brief you about this unfortunate helicopter business if you want.'

'I do want, and as quick as you can. Where are you?'

'By that Gothic tower thing, pumping station or straining house, whatever they call it.'

'I'm on my way.'

'Good, but it'll be off the record, lobby rules and all that.'

'Fine, give me five minutes. I didn't get your name, by the way.'

'Tell you later,' the caller said.

*

The Reverend Hill's afternoon nap became a long, fitful sleep. When he woke, he felt stiff-jointed and barely rested. He went to his study for one last read of the hand grenade of an article he planned to lob at the Church of England's hierarchy via his local paper, the *Hereford Times*.

It would be picked up by the nationals and cause the row he wanted. He would not go quietly into retirement. A mitre or two needed knocking off first. Disarmament was never a priority for the self-interested cynics who sat atop the church.

Their failure to protest against the inherent evil of nuclear weapons made them as culpable as those who gave God's illusory blessing to men about to die in Flanders.

Ralph Hill's attempts to challenge the dangerous assumptions behind the present-day arms race had only ever been met with polite indifference.

He neither understood nor accepted how the Church could line up so cravenly behind whichever British government held power and thereby genuflect to the demands of the warmongering Americans.

His was the ethical case against his own leadership. Tomorrow could take care of the consequences.

It was time for him to pray. The church was empty. None of his flock was there to hear his final offices of that day in which he implored God *to give unto thy servants that peace which the world cannot give.* He offered other prayers, too, but silently: for Virginia that she might come to understand; for himself that he might find the inner strength to survive the controversy he was about to detonate in public.

A few candles still burned by the altar. These he blew out and watched their smoke curl away to nothingness. Then he set the burglar alarm and locked the medieval oak doors of the porch behind him. Such precautions offended all his beliefs. But without them, insurers would not cover the repair costs of any more spray-painted vandalism accusing him of being *commie scum*, or worse.

The path back to the vicarage passed near where his wife was buried, six years dead now, her stone marked by patches of yellowish-orange lichen, spreading like plague sores across her memory and the shame that never left him.

*

Moreley felt a shiver of menace walking alongside the lake. The wind rose chill from the water, on which a nail paring of a moon reflected here and there as it passed behind the clouds.

He saw the beam of a torch swinging through the wooded edge on the other side of the reservoir. Someone was looking for something amid the trees.

'Chris – hi, this way.'

It was the confident, home counties voice of the Army liaison man. He emerged from beneath the trees, hair over the collar of his waxed jacket, hand out to shake Moreley's.

'Freddie de Lanerolle,' he said. 'Good to meet you.'

He and a team of Army investigators had flown across from Northern Ireland in another Gazelle when news of the crash broke.

'Will you be able to put a piece together for the radio bulletins tonight?'

'If you mark my card, I might just about make the ten o'clock.'

'What about the TV boys tomorrow?'

'Depends what pictures they can get,' Moreley said. 'The chopper being lifted out of the water would make the news – unless something more horrible happens somewhere else.'

Moreley had trodden in enough blood to know how the world turns in far-off places, and in newsrooms, too.

'OK, understood.'

'Listen, I know it's early days but are you sure this is an accident and not terrorism?'

De Lanerolle maintained his here-to-help PR smile.

'With the best will in the world, Chris, I'd say that's bollocks.'

'But the Provos have mounted some elaborate stunts in the past.'

'Believe me, any terrorist trying to get near one of our helicopters would be in a body bag before he got his Semtex out.'

'But you can't know it's not sabotage till you recover the chopper, can you?'

31

'No, but everything here points to a mechanical failure.'

'Hand on heart and hope to die?'

'Absolutely, even in these unfortunate circumstances. Now, let me give you everything we have so far but there's something we'd much rather you didn't make public until tomorrow.'

'Go on, I'm listening.'

'It's an absolute racing certainty that the pilot's dead—'

'Poor bloke.'

'No, that's the point. The pilot was a woman, the only one we've got flying helicopters.'

'That'll please the tabloids,' Moreley said.

'Too right it will but if you report that this side of midnight then her family will know it's her before we've had a chance to tell them ourselves. Wouldn't be cricket that, would it?'

*

The Reverend Hill had started leaving his radio on overnight to trick would-be burglars into thinking he was not alone. The offensive graffiti on the church was unnerving and caused him to accept how vulnerable his anti-nuclear campaigning had made him.

It might be a badge of honour to have right-wing politicians accuse him of being a useful idiot, an unpatriotic crypto communist who'd readily swallowed Moscow's propaganda, but he'd be at physical risk if the oaf who'd daubed obscenities at a place of worship ever decided to confront him personally late one night.

Supper was a boiled egg and toast – comfort food for

widowers and bachelors alike. He would drive into the village the next morning and buy provisions. His larder, if it could be called that, was empty except for the last of his prepared vegetarian meals.

He undressed, brushed his remaining teeth and partial denture and stood at the loo, trying to pee. Maybe he would visit his doctor in the morning to ask about that problem, too. Once in bed, he thought of Virginia again, wondered where she was, what she was doing. Awful words had passed between them, words that could never be unsaid. Wounds might heal but scars always remained.

He drifted to sleep, vaguely aware of a woman's voice on the radio in the next room. Had he been fully awake, he might have heard her introducing the third story on the ten o'clock news.

The pilot of an Army helicopter that crashed into Lake Vyrnwy in North Wales is believed to have been killed. Reporting from the scene, Christian Moreley.

The Gazelle came down in the beauty spot reservoir that supplies water to Liverpool. An Army source said the pilot was flying solo, preparing for a training exercise about to begin this week. An air accident investigation is already underway and though terrorism hasn't been ruled out, mechanical failure is thought to be the more likely cause.

The pilot has not yet been named and divers will begin a search for a body at first light tomorrow. Work will then start to lift the aircraft from where it's thought it came to rest, about sixty feet down in what remains of the remote village that was flooded when the reservoir was created in the 1880s.

Soon after this bulletin ended, the Reverend Hill was woken by the repeated ringing of his front doorbell. It took a

33

moment to compose himself. Still the bell rang. Who was it? Could it be the graffiti artist come to teach the red rev of tabloid infamy a lesson he wouldn't forget?

He pulled back a corner of the bedroom curtain. On the threshold stood three men: a police constable, an Army officer in uniform and a padre. Ralph Hill went downstairs in his pyjamas and dressing gown. He opened the door but kept it on its chain.

'Yes, what is it? What do you want?'

'May we come in, sir?' the officer said.

'Come in? No, certainly not. It's the middle of the night.'

'Yes, I realise and we apologise but this is about your daughter.'

'What about my daughter?'

'Sir, I'm afraid there's been an accident.'

6: ESCAPE

*"Life is a passing shadow,
the shadow of a bird in his flight."*

- The Talmud

From high up in the swaying crowns of the trees beneath which he lay, Robbo would have looked like a victim of murder, sprawled face down in a patch of dead ferns and falling leaves.

Had a police doctor rolled him over, they would have noted a gash across his forehead and scalp consistent with a blow from something hard and sharp, hair clotted with blood, right cheek swollen and going as blue as the egg of a duck.

Bruising was also evident on the chest, indicating possible damage to the ribs. Both hands were cut and fingernails blackened by soil as if he'd frantically clawed his way up the steep bank in a failed effort to escape an assailant.

All his clothing was saturated – lightweight Berghaus hiking jacket, plaid cotton shirt, beige woollen sweater, jeans, leather walking boots, thick socks.

That morning's shave had been hurried. Two razor nicks were visible near the cleft in his chin. His complexion was lightly tanned, eyes green. Further examination would show pale longitudinal scars on the left forearm and on the upper right arm, possibly suggesting healed-up knife wounds from a life that had known violence.

Were this a homicide, detectives would immediately try to establish a name and an address then trace his next of kin. But this individual's pockets wouldn't reveal any clues. His wallet, credit card and driving licence were in a bag at the muddy depths of the lake.

Checks of missing persons files, criminal and fingerprint records or international police wanted lists would draw blanks. Without a name or a paper trail, no tax or social security inquiries could be made, either. The man in the woods was but a ghost glimpsed in the daylight.

Night had closed over Robbo. Distant voices came to him, real or imagined... he didn't know. But they were no more than whispers on the wind that disturbed the dead leaves by where he lay.

Dangerous... be careful... wits about you.

He could have called into the darkness for help. But his training – escape and evade, escape and evade – cautioned him to stay silent. Whose voices were these? Something felt wrong. He didn't know why.

Any wish to anaesthetise his pain with sleep fell to the urge to crawl deeper into the woods to hide. But to hide from what – a noise in his head, a feeling in his gut? For the moment, it was enough to still be alive, as it was when he'd rolled the dice with death those times before.

*

He is in the front passenger seat of a Lincoln Mark VII sedan, midnight blue and bullet-proofed, cleaving tight to the side of a mountain road with a ravine barely a car's width away. Bolivians call it El Camino de la Muerte – the road of death. There are no safety barriers, just wooden crosses to the memory of those who didn't make it home.

Behind him sits Frederico Molina, an overweight man of thirty-six. His useless legs are supported by callipers because of polio caused by a quack doctor's contaminated vaccine.

Frederico was an object of pity and ridicule in his village, the boy unable to run or kick a ball or ride a bike. He withdrew from public gaze, lived and studied in Miami to qualify as a keeper of accounts – a quipucamayoc, as the ancients would have called him.

'My books always balance in the end,' he'd say with pride.

But one debt demanded settlement over all others. It took almost two decades to call it in.

Frederico was still young but had already found favour with clients of power and influence. They tracked down the phoney medic to a dusty desert settlement called Villa Montes near the border with Paraguay.

Two men in chinos and navy-coloured cotton jackets intercepted him on his way to work as a janitor. They said someone wished to pay their respects. He looked puzzled, said he was busy. But they were quietly insistent.

He was escorted to a black Range Rover with darkened windows and driven to a makeshift airstrip in a wilderness where wild jaguars hunted their prey.

Frederico was already waiting, prickling with sweat in the shade of a Cessna. The charlatan was steered towards him. He was made to remove his check shirt, denim overalls, boots and the underwear he'd started to foul. He knew he was about to atone for a great sin and prostrated himself in the red dirt, begging, pleading, hands together in supplication if not in prayer.

It was an effort for Frederico to swing his heavy upper body between his crutches in such unforgiving heat, to finally confront the conman who'd taken his parents for fools and made him a cripple.

He found balance and pulled a Colt Super .38 from the holster over his heart. Barrel and grip were plated in gold such as the Incas would once have fashioned into exquisite jewellery. The trigger was solid silver.

The man's wailing changed to sobbing. Again and again, he kissed Pachamama – mother earth, the giver of all life. Frederico took his time in the exaggerated stillness of the moment. When he was ready, he fired at close range into the backs of the man's knees then through his ankles and both elbows.

Vengeance in that land of myths and evil spirits – observed since before the wheel and the horse were ever known there – was not a matter for the gods, however divine their rights.

To show weakness was to invite one's own destruction, not least for a man unable to stand on his own two feet.

The Range Rover drove away and the Cessna took off. The huckster writhed on his own Calvary, a bloodied puppet without its strings, his screams unheard by all but himself. The pilot banked so Frederico could look down and freeze the memory. Then they headed north, back to La Paz.

And as they disappeared into the empty heavens, a solitary condor began to circle on a thermal, its wings wider than a man is tall and barely seeming to move.

Frederico would recount this instructive parable about his life and times to all potential partners in the field of commerce wherein he now specialised. As he told it to Robbo, he concluded with a shrug as if to ask, who can we trust in this terrible world of ours?

He knew Robbo to be in the British Army and asked to see his passport. It was always advisable to establish a person's bona fides. He said this with a smile that came and went with ease. Robbo was shown to be Brian Oliver Roby, born in Warrington on 4 September 1951, making him thirty-four next birthday.

Port of entry stamps included those from America, South Africa, Canada, Belize, Angola and Zimbabwe. Both knew what he meant when he said he was scoping opportunities in South America. There was only one business in Bolivia for which travellers met middlemen like Frederico.

They continue to descend the rutted, twisting shelf of a road towards the town of Coroico. The verge is just scrub and scree then fresh air. Robbo tries to avoid glancing down but cannot stop himself. Fear is its own buzz. The remains of wrecked coaches, trucks, cars lie a thousand feet below, broken bits of rusting metal not yet claimed by the jungle. Maybe their one-time occupants are still down there, skeletons now, picked clean by insects, skulls grinning but unlikely to get the joke.

'Dangerous country, yours,' Robbo says.

'Only for fools, my friend. You are in good hands, believe me.'

Robbo trusts he means those of the driver who squints through the billowing dust thrown up by the petrol tanker in front.

Yet the odds against surviving El Camino de la Muerte are no worse than in the trade that brings the Englishman and the Bolivian together: the fabulously lucrative trafficking of cocaína. But Frederico has a word for the wise.

'There are many dangers, inglés – greed and envy,' he says. 'If you are successful, the product may bring you riches beyond all your dreams but you will also make enemies. Enemies who might have been your friends one day but who will kill you the next without a thought.'

Frederico, ever the accountant, says crystal generates a billion US dollars in Bolivia alone every year.

'Making it is illegal but it is our great export so you can say that our prosperity depends on criminal activity like no other country.'

'For jobs, you mean?'

'For those who don't have one, yes,' he says. 'The alternative for them is starvation, nothing less.'

'What about you, Frederico... professional people? You benefit, don't you?'

'Ah yes, we do, but not always choose.'

'What do you mean?'

'Let me explain our way of doing things, inglés... you are waiting at a bus stop and a man, a stranger, he smile is very nice and then from his pocket he takes a photograph of your wife or your beautiful children, and he says what a lovely family you have. You are immediately afraid but he smile even more and says you must not be worried, he only wants a little favour, a little co-operation. Yes? What would you do, inglés? You take his money or his bullet?'

'Everyone has a price, I suppose,' Robbo says. 'There is a point where everyone bends.'

'And when that point is reached, amigo, you are just a fish on a hook… that much I know and can tell you.'

So police officers, politicians, diplomats, bankers, lawyers, judges and accountants are caught and landed, but by way of compensation, share in the unimaginable profits being made by the cartels whose servants they have now become.

And so the world turns, the seasons change and those who make coffins and dig graves also give thanks to Pachamama for her most bountiful of gifts – the coca bush.

*

Frederico and Robbo had left La Paz early that morning, twelve thousand feet above sea level, streets drifting with wispy clouds, people bone-chilled and breathing hard in the thin air.

Robbo knew about altitude sickness from his Army training. He touched no alcohol after flying in from Miami and acclimatised for two days, resting up in Frederico's mansion in the affluent suburb of La Zona Sur far beyond the city's tin shack slums.

Apart from the cold, he might still have been in Florida – sprinklers on every razored lawn, luxury cars, boutiques, restaurants. But Frederico's house stood out even here. Entry was by electronic gates. Guards armed with Uzis patrolled the grounds and video cameras scanned the approach road. Frederico had much to protect, or to hide.

Inside, the floors and central staircase were of Carrara marble, off-white with blue-grey veins. Each bath and sink had gold taps. The Persian carpets were antique, wine-red

41

and hand-woven in Kashan or in silk from Nain. Apart from lurid modern paintings of naked women, Robby sees no evidence of a female presence, just conspicuous consumption assembled without moderation or style.

As they progress down from the Altiplano, the temperature rises. Heat and humidity envelop them. Frederico wants to stop at the next roadside hut for beer and food.

'But unless you want your bowels to explode, do not drink their water,' he says.

Robbo offers him help through a muddy yard where hairy black pigs grunt and grub by an open sewer, but Frederico needs none. The proprietor knows him and approaches as a peasant would a prince. He shows him to the best table on the verandah at the back with a view over mountains that fold away to the far horizon. They and the driver eat chuños, small freeze-dried potatoes served with eggs and cheese, and order bottles of lager.

'Much further to go, is there, Frederico?'

'Four or five hours, no more.'

'And he'll definitely be there, will he… your connection?'

'He will. But remember, inglés, you are going to the lion's den… not everyone can be sure to come out. Play your hand with care.'

He puts down a fifty-dollar bill to pay for a meal costing less than ten. The owner bows from the waist in humble gratitude at this Robin Hood gesture. As Frederico returns his wallet into an inside jacket pocket, Robbo sees something glint within. It is the golden gun with which the sham doctor's outstanding account had been paid.

Robbo leaned on a fence under a starless Welsh sky, confused, uncertain, still in pain. He was in a state of almost battlefield derealisation. His brain had shut off all functions except those needed to survive. But he was clear of the claustrophobic forestry and the voices that had sounded so threatening for reasons he did not understand.

It began to rain, softly at first, almost soothingly. Far across the valley, the beam of a car's headlights cut through the gloom. Robbo watched it slow down and stop. The lights went off and all became dark again. A new one appeared a moment later from the window of someone's home.

But it came to him that there was sanctuary, a place to feel safe and where his aching tiredness might ebb away.

How strange, being beckoned by a distant beacon of warm light, seeming to promise his itinerant self a haven of sorts. He'd never experienced that emotion before – a feeling of attachment. The Welsh of the diaspora would call it hiraeth, a longing of the soul to return from whence it had come.

For Robbo, nothing else mattered. He would stumble through nettles and brambles to reach his chimeric refuge. No obstacle would be allowed to get in his way, for driving him forward was a warning from some inner voice: *you may have just eluded the Reaper, comrade, but don't kid yourself that he's given up on you.*

But how could it be certain that the Reaper was a man?

7: GRIEF

"My God, my God,
Why hast thou forsaken me?"

-     Matthew 27, verse 46

The Reverend Hill closed the front door on his three visitors without a word, locked it then caught sight of himself in the hall mirror. It might have been a stranger staring back, a man wearied by time, eyes blank, skin drawn tight over the skull beneath.

He had anointed many like it in the past, bid them the holiest of farewells in the quiet dawn of a hospital ward or in the chintzy surroundings of a care home, curtained off from those whose own time would come soon enough.

The Army padre had offered to stay with him, two pious men to sit out the long watches of that most cruel of nights. Ralph Hill didn't respond. Grief had descended on him with the suddenness of a sea mist. But he could never let himself be guided out of it by a cleric in khaki giving religious justification to war.

Only two camps existed in the Reverend Hill's world of certainties: those of allies and those of enemies. Yet his prevailing emotion at that moment was anger... anger that had metastasised between him and Virginia when he learned of the career she intended to follow.

He begged and pleaded – for her own good – to consider the moral case against militarism, the righteous cause for which he'd argued from pulpit and soapbox all his life. But she ignored his entreaties, defied his wishes. Only one conclusion was available to him.

'You're still punishing me, aren't you?' he'd said during one of their final rows. 'You're taking revenge for your mother but who are you to sit in judgement? What did you know about our lives?'

And now this… if not a death foretold then one he had feared. Nothing that might be said or done could relieve the unbearable weight of this new cross the Fates had heaved upon him or silence the memory of the animus in Virginia's voice as she uttered her last words to him.

Try looking at your own hands for once, Daddy darling. They're far bloodier than mine will ever be.

No reconciliation could take place now, nor the giving of her as a bride, the holding of hands, the touching of cheeks or laughing at memories from before, that time of lost content. This was his end of days. Principles no longer mattered or had purpose. He leaned against the wall then slid to the floor, lacking will or strength to stand. Sprawled in the hallway where Bella had breathed her last. He had nothing with which to salve his pain but the gall of regret.

After the savagery of Bella's killing, he'd tried to rationalise it politically, condemned the wickedness of the forces behind it. But he knew in his broken heart that his was the original sin.

Five years on from her assassination in 1985 and in the deeper reaches of his conscience, the guilt he'd felt over

Bella's death was joined by remorse at Virginia's. He and he alone was responsible for their estrangement, just as he had been for breaking his marriage vows.

He beat his fists against his temples, unable to stop imagining how her broken body must look, trapped in that accursed war machine deep in the darkness of a lake in Wales. They'd said she would have died instantly, couldn't have suffered. But how could they know? What terrors might she have endured in the moments before?

Part of him wished he could swim down to her, free her from the wreckage and cradle her in his arms like the child he remembered and place her on the bank and kiss her sleeping eyes, then she might wake and smile and his sins would be forgiven.

At this, he began to weep. The road ahead would be strewn with sorrows. Yet he must somehow survive it a second time, care for Virginia in death as he hadn't in life.

Everything that needed to be done for the funeral he would supervise – the choice of coffin, the flowers, the music. But what had she liked and listened to? He had no idea, still less who her friends might be.

As for the service, he would officiate and to hell with anyone who advised otherwise. It was his daughter, his church. All proceedings, from the greeting of the coffin to the committal, would be at his direction. There must be a eulogy, but from whom? Anyone except a representative of the military. He would not allow Virginia's funeral to become an occasion to glorify her occupation.

Even as these notions came and went in the agony of the moment, he was aware that some might present as unchristian, selfish. In that instant, he didn't care. He had devoted his life to the God of all mercy and consolation but it didn't feel that way, just as it hadn't when he'd knelt in Bella's denatured blood. Why was he being racked by violent loss yet again? Hadn't the slaughter of dearest Bella been a sufficient ordeal? Did his only child have to be taken from him, too? Part of him, that preordination, the rational human being beneath the cloth, wanted to scream out in fury and demand that God give reason why, yet again, the meek suffered and evil triumphed.

For a priest, he was thinking the unthinkable once more: that God was no longer at his side. Where was God when Bella's killers constructed their bomb or when she opened the mail that morning or when Virginia fell from the heavens to her death? What had been the purpose of his life? Where had faith got him?

So many times he'd debated this with atheists and agnostics, had been taunted by them to provide evidence for God's existence or a scientific basis for his own faith. There wasn't any for either; there was no incontrovertible evidence for any of it. Yet millions accepted what they believed was real and did not demand evidence of its truth beforehand.

In the emotional aftermath of Bella's murder, he'd admitted such doubts to the sexton digging a grave. The sexton was an uncomplicated man.

He kept pigs and poultry, grew vegetables and had returned to the village after service in the Army to work on the land.

'Sir, it wasn't God who went and got that lady killed,' he'd said.

It followed that He didn't make or post letter bombs. Men were responsible for that. Ralph Hill had had to keep

47

reminding himself of his own spiritual guidance to those grieving occupants of some impoverished breeze block dwelling in a township who'd just lost a son or a brother in the fight for freedom from apartheid.

God isn't a dealer of cards or some puppet master controlling our destinies. What we have from Him is our free will to make our own choices in this life, for better or for worse. Whatever happens, He is with us in our tragedies, He is on the gallows with the condemned and at the graveside as we shed our tears as you do now. Even in our anguish, we must never forget that.

But with the death of Virginia, her father's trust in the Almighty was again being put to the test, if not to the sword. In the bleakness of his grief, the Reverend Hill had to cling to the belief that God had not abandoned him.

Yet his doubts were profound and called into question the very fundamentals of his life-long ministry. He had never felt more alone as he began the slow ascent of the stairs to a bedroom he'd not entered for years – Virginia's. If it hadn't been a shrine before, it would be from thereon.

*

Earlier that same evening, Giles Worth had shown his security pass to a blue-shirted Ministry of Defence guard in MI5's bunker in Curzon Street and walked up to his third-floor office in F Branch, from where domestic subversives were targeted and spied upon.

It was sparse and impersonal with a view through sooty net drapes over Bolton Street to the opposing tides of traffic along Piccadilly, the discreet gentlemen's clubs of Pall Mall and the plane trees of Green Park beyond.

He collected the John le Carré novel he'd left behind the previous day then went down to the floor below to start his stint as Night Duty Officer. The building was emptying around him with a virtual sigh like some sprawling creature settling down, tired from its exertions, eyes almost closed.

Those who attended to its bodily wellbeing during the day – typists of Section A2A who transcribed the tapped phone calls of spies, terrorists and subversives, Post Office engineers manning banks of recording machines on the fifth floor, those who ran agents, bugged buildings, followed suspects – were being exhaled into the evening to disappear like a winter's breath onto trains or buses or into pubs to drink more than they should, for theirs were burdens more heavy than most.

Worth was an Oxford man – a two-one in English but, as some noted, only from Pembroke. He was unmarried, starting to run to fat and, regrettably for him, lacking any dynastic family links to the security service to be a one-of-us insider.

His career should have been better starred than it was. But his operational tour of duty in Northern Ireland hadn't inspired confidence, according to a confidential report sent to management services in B Branch. This was the least of it. But the affair was covered up and Worth given pithy words of advice from his greybeard section head.

'Do yourself a favour and remember this,' he'd said. 'We're like doctors here. We can bury our mistakes but don't you start banging on about being made a scapegoat or someone'll dig up the bloody body as evidence against you. Got that, have we?'

Worth was transferred back to London and given a desk

to fly. He'd never been socially at ease with colleagues. Since Ireland, he suspected some knew about the foul-up. Why else would he sense such disdain in their eyes? But he was forbidden from telling them what really happened, that he wasn't to blame. Those who sent him there were. But that's the trouble with secrets. They're never supposed to get out. Worth withdrew into himself, kept his head down in the bundles of transcripts from all the tapped phones and spike-miked rooms he had to analyse each day.

The isolation of occasionally being rostered as NDO relieved him from the contempt of others. Shortly before six o'clock, Worth walked down the long corridor towards the Night Duty office at the back of the building. The section controller was waiting to brief him.

'Usual stuff's running,' he said. 'But we've had some cryptic message from a cuckoo in the military over the water who's heard a whisper that something might be going bang today.'

'In Ireland or over here?'

'Not sure but whatever and wherever it is, we don't know about it so we're not happy. Listen out for anything that fits the bill and do the necessary.'

The Night Duty office housed the brain of the beast during the hours of darkness. All the sinews of its clandestine functions were diverted there and monitored.

It had phone links to Special Branch at Scotland Yard, the Cabinet Office and Downing Street, in case Mrs Thatcher needed to be woken in the early hours with intelligence from MI5's twilight zones. A coded message might be rung in from an informer inside a terrorist cell or some extremist political party. Life and death information could pass through the NDO's hands. Worth was not immune to the addictive nature of being within this loop, of feeling special, that he belonged.

For those hours, more so than on day duties, he saw himself like a medieval priest who could read Latin. Only he could interpret the gospels of secrecy, what they meant and how they could be used to influence the illiterate, ignorant masses. It was power, albeit illusory. For Worth, what gave it added piquancy was that nobody out there was aware of what this anonymous, unmemorable man knew – not his family nor his neighbours in North London, not drinkers in his local pub, not the woman who coyly smiled at him in Shepherd Market and whose services he could pay for but never would. If such people thought about him at all, they would guess he was some sort of civil servant or banker, a man of sober suits, a brolly when wet, a *Daily Telegraph* from the newsagents on Holloway Road to read on the bus into his office. How they misjudged him.

Soon into his shift, Special Branch liaison rang to say that the Press Association was shortly to alert subscribers to a breaking story about an Army helicopter from Northern Ireland crashing in Wales. Was this what the cuckoo had warned about?

Worth put his copy of *The Spy Who Came in from the Cold* on the camp bed in the corner to read later. The real thing looked like making this a busier evening than expected.

*

Ralph Hill knew he wouldn't – couldn't – sleep that night. He lay on Virginia's narrow iron bed not to rest, not to pray,

51

but to think back to times and places wherein he could never go again.

The early light fell across the leaded window, pale and pink, slowly passing over the innocence she'd left behind: the doll's house bought from Hamleys when she was seven, a teddy bear in a tin pram decorated with rose buds, her little wooden desk and chair, and on the shelf above, story books in which everything turned out right in the end for all the boys and girls and their mummies and daddies.

They had been happy once, long ago. Virginia held them together in those early years, her hands in theirs, a Christian family united in God's sight by sermon and example. But what happens over time behind a front door when it is closed, even that of a vicarage?

Who can say, who can know, what conflicts stir within – and why? There are no victors to write the histories of personal wars, for no one wins, no one escapes harm when love is lost.

Virginia had been a gifted child, observant, insightful, his one arrow to the future. He'd always thought – or preferred to believe – that she was neutral during the years of attritional sniping between him and Cynthia.

He was deluding himself. In the bad-tempered disputes over Virginia joining the Army, it was plain that she and her mother were on the same side, and probably were on everything else, too. But Virginia's harsh words were spoken in anger.

What had been the deeper, more considered feelings she'd committed to her diaries?

Ralph Hill knew she'd kept one from starting grammar school in 1973 until enlisting seven years later. He'd seen

52

them once, lined up on a shelf in the cupboard by the side of the chimney breast.

But she'd shut the door quickly. These were her secrets. He also knew where the key was hidden: in a matchbox buried – as only a child would – amid a heap of pine cones she'd collected and put in the grate. Could he withstand punishing himself still further by reading her private thoughts from those troubled times? It had never occurred to him to pry like this until now. He began to rummage through the cones and twigs dropped by jackdaws making nests. As he located the key, a vehicle drew up below Virginia's window.

He looked down. A man in jeans and a waxed jacket got out of an estate car and rang the front door bell. The Reverend Hill opened the window.

'What do you want?'

'Sir, good morning. Sorry it's so early but I'm from Army liaison.'

'I don't want or need to liaise with the Army, thank you.'

'No, I understand, but we're afraid you're going to be pestered by the media very soon.'

'That won't be the first time.'

'I'm sure not but this will be different. It's going to be very unpleasant for you.'

'I can deal with such people.'

'But not alone, sir. My name is Freddie de Lanerolle and I've been sent to help you.'

'Help me? My God, you've got a nerve. You're the damned people who stole my daughter in the first place and now you've gone and killed her.'

The Reverend Ralph Hill pulled the window shut, trembling with anger and renewed shock. He felt a tingling by his mouth. This sensation moved up the left side of his face and he began to see double. He couldn't keep his balance.

Then he was flat on the floor, face against the cold green tiles of the hearth. And all he could hear was the doorbell ringing again and again.

8: REFUGE

*"Until lions write their own history,
the hunt will always glorify the hunter."*

- African proverb

Florence Rossiter's cottage backed into the hillside from where its dun-grey stones were quarried before Victoria became Queen of England. It was called Tan y Graig, meaning "under the rock" in Welsh, and gave a view from its four front windows across the valley to the wooded slopes of Lake Vyrnwy.

She'd arrived home cold and emotionally tired after helping out at a children's hospice in Shrewsbury, across the border in Shropshire. The wind was rising, the rain coming down harder. As a girl on nights like this, Florence imagined the cottage to be a ship battering through the giant waves that were the hills thereabouts. Here she felt safe and secure and always would.

She poured a glass of water to drink with her blood pressure tablets and sat in an armchair by the Rayburn. The grandfather clock measured out the minutes of another passing day. Florence never married and had no living relatives, just friendships from her time as a health visitor. She'd seen life given and life taken away and knew that happiness and sadness were but phases as arbitrary as existence itself.

Florence's own story was proof enough. Her feckless mother in Liverpool had trysted with a foreign sailor who'd come and gone on the Mersey tide before Florence was even born. Only by chance had she survived Hitler's blitz of the city's docks. When she was evacuated to live with a farm worker and his wife in Wales, no one could have predicted that they would come to love her, and she them.

After the war, she could make her own decisions and stayed at Tan y Graig with the people she called Mum and Dad, for they gave what she'd never had before. As they grew old and ill, she nursed each to the end. Then she'd grieved and put daffodils where they lay on a stony hillside under a stand of beech trees bowing to the prevailing wind.

Florence, coffee-brown skin lined now, frizzy hair gone white, knew the arc of her own life. There was comfort and tranquillity in being thought of as a wise if solitary woman who in another time, another place, would have been known as a healer.

She took her tablets, poured the remains of the water into the sink and went upstairs. Lying in bed in the dark, she listened to the gale cutting through a plantation of conifers not a hundred yards away.

Florence closed her eyes and was back below deck in that old coaster once more, bucking through the turbulent sea towards who knew where or who knew what.

*

Blood ran into Robbo's mouth from the wound on his head,

56

diluted with rain but still slightly warm. The sight of blood – and worse – never concerned him, yet the taste of it now made him retch. He wiped his face and eyes. When he regained focus, the speck of yellow light guiding him had gone out.

Panic wasn't in his nature but he sensed it in that moment. Only by getting to where it had been might he be saved. His mind had no space for any other thought – not the pain he was in, not why he was in it.

The body he occupied might have belonged to another save for the muscle memory of the beasting that had been his training and selection for special duties. He stumbled on down the sloping field.

Breathing became more difficult. A weird mass of pale shapes began materialising out of the darkness in front. For a moment, he thought he was hallucinating. But it was a herd of cows, disturbed at his approach. They stood and stared as he trudged on through their muck.

Ahead was a barbed wire fence. It tore at his pants as he climbed over. The ground beyond was boggy, spiked with reeds. His boots sank knee-deep into the ooze. One came off and he couldn't retrieve it. But his feet and clothes were already so wet and cold that it hardly mattered.

The land gradually rose out of the morass. Barely a hundred yards further on and there was the road on the other side of a five-barred gate. He headed west, exhausted but euphoric, towards where he thought the light would've been.

Neither rain nor gale slackened off. The rest of nature seemed drowned out – no owl shrieks, no sheep crying to each other on that blackest of nights.

A faint, insect-like droning noise came to him. It got

closer, louder. It was a chopper, flying low. The fear he'd felt on hearing those voices in the woods, that primal sense of being hunted by something unseen, something unknown, swept across him again like ripples on a pond.

And the words of that poor sod he'd left in the lake returned to haunt him… *I get the feeling that there's some sort of flap on. What the hell is happening?*

He didn't know then; he didn't know now. Finding refuge was his only concern. The animal within was taking over.

*

The call to Kat Walsh's hotel room phone came as night fell and the search for Robbo was being stood down until dawn. She recognised the patrician voice of DASP – MI5's Deputy Assistant, Political, Northern Ireland.

'So sorry to disturb your evening,' he said.

'That's quite all right, sir. I was only reading.'

'Good. Well, I was just wondering when you last had a day off?'

'Quite a while ago, sir. Is there a reason why you ask?'

It was far from being a secure phone so she knew to read between his lines.

'Because you're not too far from a wonderful old National Trust property – Powis Castle. I would think less than an hour from where you are now.'

'I'm afraid I don't know it.'

'Well, it's the sort of place that someone like you would find utterly absorbing.'

Standing by her window, she could see Lake Vyrnwy between the silhouettes of trees on either side. Somewhere beneath the black mirror of its surface, a corpse lay in unnatural repose amid the ruins of a drowned village. It could yet be the undoing of many, not least Kat herself. But DASP was aware of the implications.

'I think you'll particularly approve of the decor and furnishings upstairs in what's called the Oak Drawing Room,' DASP said. 'And also in there is a painting known as *View of Verona*, which I think is glorious and I'm sure you will, too.'

'Right, well I better go and take a look, hadn't I, sir. When do you think would be most convenient?'

'No time like the present, is there? I'd suggest tomorrow morning, getting there about ten.'

'I shall look forward to it, sir.'

'And who knows, you might meet someone with similar interests to yours and be able to swap notes, as it were, because I know he has a lot to learn from you.'

Kathleen Walsh, source handler, keeper of confidences, resolute in deed as in her regimental motto, knew that information shared was an advantage lost. But this elliptical instruction from DASP was intriguing. Would she be meeting friend or foe? Not everyone wanted peace in Northern Ireland, even now in the back end of 1990. There was much housekeeping still to do before the entrails of the conflict could be read by those who'd staked nothing but were coming to judge others who'd risked everything.

These outsiders – police officers from England – would never have stood in streets where gutters ran with blood and rain and broken glass. What remained of those who'd got in the way of yet another attack in the long war had to be brushed onto the shovels of road sweepers then tipped into rubbish sacks.

She was aware that these new enemies were circling, range-finding on their targets and armed with hindsight and questions as lethal as any bomb.

Kat went down to reception and retrieved her aluminium attaché case from the hotel safe. It contained her 9mm Browning, a clip of ammunition, another outfit of civilian clothes and a sealed white envelope stamped "Restricted".

Back in her room, she locked the door. From the minibar she took a can of Guinness. It frothed from the ring pull as she put it to her mouth and splashed beer onto her denim jeans. She swore to herself then took them off to rinse in the bathroom sink. They would dry over a radiator with the knickers and bra she'd already washed by hand. Even spies had unglamorous necessities to attend to.

For now, Kat lay on her bed, long legs crossed at the ankle, belly as flat as a board and just as hard. From the envelope she took a single sheet of typed paper, undated and unsourced.

It was the briefing note she'd written before the helicopter crash, setting out the limits of what could be released publicly. She'd given Ginny Hill's age and rank and hailed her as a pioneering female pilot in the Air Corps.

Of her passenger, it said:

A man in his late thirties also died on this training exercise. He was a civilian contractor to the British military in Northern Ireland, therefore no personal details will be released in order to protect his family from terrorist reprisals.

We should all be careful what we wish for. Kat tore the paper into pieces and took them to the loo.

She pissed on them and watched as they were flushed into the sewer with all the other shit.

Yet even she couldn't repress a rueful smile. Men make plans, God laughs; she owed those words of wisdom to Robbo. The bastard had outwitted her – survived. Where was she to find this most loose of cannons? And what would happen if she didn't?

Guys like him were part actor, part snake. They could ease into whatever role was demanded then slough off that character's skin to reveal another. Terrorists who'd been bribed or blackmailed to act as agents could never be fully trusted. They'd double-crossed their own cause and comrades for silver. If the day came when it suited, why wouldn't they betray their secret masters?

But Robbo was a professional with a criminal mind. It was just as his savvy troop commander observed about him in an annual confidential report:

A resourceful and brave soldier, quick-thinking and intelligent, but, I fear, somewhat amoral. I would worry about which route he would take should he ever come to a fork in the road.

For Kat and the other fishers of men in her unit, that was the very reason why Robbo was such a great catch. Yet the game moves on, rules change and suddenly, no one is safe. They needed to land him a second time. Until then, he'd be a danger to her like no other.

More pressing was how much background could be safely revealed to whoever she was to meet the next day. Kat had long since learned that it didn't matter who shared your bed, it was always wise to sleep with one eye open while remembering that no war was ever fought without deceit.

She sat at the dressing table mirror and considered the woman who stared back. Her mother always said she was striking, not pretty. Men enjoyed Kat's lusty company and she theirs. She knew they would all fuck her given half a chance. But Kat was rarely available, except when there was advantage to be had. Tomorrow, she would wear her vivid titian hair to the shoulder, use only a hint of lipstick, maybe some blusher. She must appear open and unthreatening, someone with nothing to hide. Robbo wasn't the only actor on this stage.

Whoever – and whatever – the stranger in the castle turned out to be, she couldn't risk trusting him any more than any of the other players in the cast.

*

Florence sensed something amiss even before she was properly awake. By that time each day, her black and white cat, Cilla, would have come home from a night's hunting, jumped on Florence's bed and be purring by her face for breakfast.

There was no Cilla that morning. It was a little after six o'clock. Florence found her slippers, put on her dressing gown and went downstairs. Cilla was more cherished companion than cat. But like her owner, she was getting old. She may have curled up somewhere warm in the kitchen or the living room. But she hadn't.

Florence, worried now in case Cilla was trapped or injured on the hill, went across to the back door. She would get her wellingtons and go outside to call her. As she did, she saw something dark wedged hard against the other side of the clear plastic cat flap. Cilla's way in from the porch had been blocked and she could be heard crying in the yard.

Florence unlocked the door and pulled it open. The body of a man who'd been slumped against it fell at her feet, head dark with dried blood, face greyer than a winter's dawn.

9: GUILT

"Whoever sheds human blood,
by humans shall their blood be shed."

- Genesis, chapter 9, verse 6

Where does a priest turn to obtain absolution for his sins?

What if these were not everyday wrongs but grievous transgressions that darken the conscience?

And were he to find his unholy secrets too shameful to admit, even to a fellow priest in the privacy of a confessional, would the only alternative be to take them to the grave?

Such questions troubled the Reverend Hill, lying between the shroud-white sheets of a hospital bed, assailed by mortality and a rare sense of self-doubt.

He had always convinced himself that his politics were motivated by the message of love in the gospels and a desire to apply it practically to the injustices of the world and thereby help to bring about God's design for the human family.

Clergy who stayed silent on the most profound moral questions of the age warranted only his contempt. This was never an option for him. But principles come with a price, more so now in the disorientating surroundings of an emergency ward.

Nurses, ancillaries, doctors moved around him in a blur between the sick and the dying, their stories unknown, their burdens soon to be set down.

Ralph Hill, fatigued by wounds no one could see, sins he was sure that no one could forgive, felt only envy. He wished to be like them, rid of the white torc of office and its responsibilities, to be just another face on a pillow making no impression.

Yet Virginia's last words allowed him no release. His own daughter had known the truth and surely despised his hypocrisy for which there could be no atonement.

If her death – and the murder of his lover before that – were tests set by God, could they equally represent punishment for His servant's display of righteous arrogance down the years?

This trait hadn't gone unnoticed by his bishop. They'd had many a tetchy inquest after some negative publicity resulting from his anti-war campaigning.

'It's not the doubters who worry me, Ralph,' the bishop said.

'Then who, Bishop? Who gives you cause to worry?'

'It is those of faith who are so confident of their own righteousness.'

'But faith has to be put into action or it is hardly faith at all, surely?'

'Total certainty in one's faith leads to fundamentalism, Ralph, irrespective of one's religion, and from that comes a willingness to kill in the name of your creed.'

'But that hardly applies to me, Bishop.'

'I'm sure it doesn't but it's as well to remember that doubt brings humility and respect for the points of view of others.

Doubt and faith are sides of the same coin.'

Ralph Hill's faith in God should have sustained him now, yet his own doubts continued to rise to the surface like shrapnel in the body of some old soldier.

He would get dressed soon, discharge himself whatever the doctors said and return home. Funerals did not arrange themselves nor should grief outrank duty. But whatever malaise had reduced him to this state, continued to claim the little energy he had left. He lay back, breathing through his mouth, watching the rise and fall of the cage of bones beneath the blue cotton gown they'd made him wear.

'We need to keep you in for a few tests,' a doctor had said. 'I'd say you've had a stroke, maybe a mild one but a stroke nonetheless, and your blood pressure is way too high.'

A nurse leaned over to give him two tablets. He began to feel drowsy, strangely outside of himself, beset by other questions needing answers he couldn't find.

He remembered the Army man, Freddie-something-or-other, driving him to Hereford Hospital. But how had he gained entry to the vicarage – which was locked – and known that its occupant had collapsed?

And why was this Freddie person still in the ward as if guarding a captured prisoner of war?

So much didn't add up, yet much else was clear. Unforgivingly and painfully so.

*

It begins innocently enough. The Reverend Hill is reading *The Guardian* in a corner seat on the day's first train from Hereford to London. It is mid-February 1983. Snow fills the ruts of ploughed fields; rivers are the colour of iron. In the world beyond the sleeping shires of England, the winter of the Cold War shows no sign of turning to spring.

The government of prime minister Margaret Thatcher – for whose soul and salvation he does not pray – reportedly plans to build five new nuclear submarines armed with the latest Trident missile system from America. The Reverend Hill swears out loud.

'That bloody woman. Insanity, that's what it is.'

An elderly man opposite looks up and shakes his head in silent rebuke, which Ralph Hill ignores. Thatcher's team is negotiating on the back stairs, away from the public gaze. Only when the ink is dry on the deal will it become official. Then she'll relish the great political and social controversy it'll cause.

Leaders of Britain's Campaign for Nuclear Disarmament see the possibility of revitalising their waning movement. Regional stalwarts like Ralph Hill have been summoned to the Quaker meeting house opposite Euston station to plot a protest campaign of civil disobedience and political lobbying.

Intensifying the nuclear arms race unites clerics and crypto-communists alike. The session is productive and concludes after three hours. He leaves the building, buttoning his overcoat and thinking about hailing a taxi to Paddington station and the train home.

But west-bound traffic is at a virtual standstill. It'll be quicker to walk. Other pedestrians are muffled up too, scarves across faces against the wind and the noxious fumes from engines idling along Euston Road.

Ralph Hill is already drafting an anti-Thatcher feature in

his head for the *Church Times* and doesn't notice a man falling in step beside him.

'Good afternoon, Reverend Hill.'

He looks to his right and sees a stranger not yet forty, pale and freckled, with the hair of an albino and wearing a green frock-like coat favoured by Scandinavians.

'I'm sorry, I'm not sure we've met. Were you at the meeting?'

'No, I was waiting for you outside,' the man says. 'My name is Tomas Bolund.'

His English is good but slightly accented so not his first language.

'I'm pleased to meet you but why were you waiting for me?'

'There is something I have been sent to discuss with you, something of importance.'

'To do with CND?'

'Not CND, no, but another issue which is of concern to all people of goodwill.'

'Sadly, we are spoilt for choice in our world, aren't we?'

'That is true but the one I wish to talk about is a great evil, in fact it is wickedly so.'

Ralph Hill waits politely.

'Our concern is apartheid in South Africa, Mr Hill, that most cruel of political systems.'

'*Our* concern… who has sent you to me?'

'I am a diplomat. I act on behalf of my government's ministry of foreign affairs.'

The Reverend Hill pauses, always wary of authority and its motives. He stares into the stranger's face and wants to know how an English country parson could possibly help any government, foreign or otherwise.

'I shall explain,' Bolund says. 'But in confidence – there must be absolute discretion.'

Even if Ralph Hill had looked across to an office building by Euston station, it's by no means certain that he would have seen the long lens camera at a window on the second floor. But he doesn't.

He and his companion walk on, two anonymous figures in a tide of others all with concerns and fears of their own. A few minutes later, they enter a Turkish café by Warren Street tube station. The diplomat orders coffee and baclava for them. Ralph Hill uses the café's pay phone to ring home.

*

Cynthia Hill returns from her husband's study to the warmth of the kitchen and her basket chair by the Aga. Yet again, Ralph would be back late. She is alone in the vicarage. It's dark soon after four o'clock in these dormant days. There is a gale blowing, too.

If more snow comes, it'll find a way under the slates and cause even more damage in the attics. The house is neglected and in need of care. She knows the feeling.

How she misses Virginia, misses her laughter and music and the passion of her opinions that caused such unchristian rows between father and daughter. At least the place felt alive then. There is only silence now.

Virginia has gone to the Army and is set on her chosen path. At eighteen, she was free to make her own decisions, wherever they might lead. Three years on, Ralph still didn't understand that parents don't own a child; they hold them in trust but for a short time only. Then their work is done.

For Cynthia, Virginia's departure has brought on a sense of emptiness and loss, a feeling of dissatisfaction with her life.

She has her art classes and good works in the parish, and she's always accepted having to share Ralph with God and the congregations of All Hallows and the other parishes. What she resented was the time Ralph spent peace campaigning or addressing meetings, writing articles. It's started again. Why else is he in London?

What have his efforts amounted to? Nothing but unpleasantness – unwanted press attention, summonses to the bishop for a ticking-off and her being stared at in shops in Hereford. People know who she is, and for all the wrong reasons. She hates them whispering and pointing at her as the wife of the vicar the tabloids love to taunt.

Not everyone approved of her marrying a clergyman. But she was on the shelf by then and just as wilful as Virginia would become. Like her, Cynthia wouldn't take advice, not from a father who knew about managing a bank but nothing of love. Or so she'd thought then.

It's not that late but Cynthia feels tired. She scribbles Ralph a note and leaves it on the kitchen table: *Ham/cheese in fridge. Having an early night. C.*

Cynthia forces the cork back into a bottle of cheap red wine. She must not drink a third glass. Sleep is a rare enough blessing as it is. The hall is draughty, their bedroom unheated. She gets under the duvet without undressing and draws her knees to her chest then lies in the dark, listening to the old house sighing to itself.

'I really am sorry I didn't manage to get home for supper last night.'

'Doesn't matter, Ralph, don't worry about it.'

'I had something to eat before I left London, a sandwich at the station.'

'That's all right, then.'

'My meeting went on for quite a while, by the way. People there from all over the country, thrashed out some really effective campaign ideas to work on.'

Cynthia loads her breakfast plate and cutlery into the dishwasher. She doesn't reply.

'Shall I tell you about them?'

'I don't have time, Ralph. I'm seeing the doctor.'

'The doctor? You didn't mention anything about being ill.'

'It's something and nothing, nothing to concern yourself with.'

'But I must come with you.'

'There's no need, honestly. You have church matters to attend to.'

'They can wait. Besides, I've got something important I'd like to talk to you about.'

'No, the surgery opens at eight thirty. We can talk when I get back.'

*

Why had he lied to Cynthia later that day? What synaptic impulse decided – without conscious reference to him – that it was best to protect her from the truth even before he knew what it would involve himself?

He'd only just been auditioned yet was keen to be in character as a man about to embark on a double life. Cynthia always accused him of being impulsive, quick to get bored without fresh stimulation. She would've preferred him to tread the easier paths in life, to stay clear of controversy unless preaching the authorised opinions of his church. But that wasn't his way. There were rows.

'Why don't you think of your family first?' Cynthia would shout. 'Just think of me for once.'

'I am the person I am. You knew that when you married me.'

'Yes, but not the size of your ego, what really was important to you.'

The memory of these attritional differences remained with him still, adrift in the somnolent warmth of a hospital bed. They required an acceptance that, amongst his many faults, was the sin of vanity.

Those who had sent Tomas Bolund to recruit him to their cause that afternoon on Euston Road must have stood in the shadows of his public life to observe the man within before making their move.

It flattered him to know he was judged equal to an assignment that could only succeed by subterfuge and a capacity to take risks in a fight against evil.

'There will be danger, I won't disguise that,' Bolund had said. 'But you will be helping to achieve the overthrow of a wicked system and all the oppression that goes with it.'

'Yes, I can see that but what you're asking me to do will be illegal.'

'But a greater good will be served by your mission.'

'By secretly helping those people the government in South Africa calls terrorists?'

'And whose plight we judge you'll be in sympathy with because of your own profound sense of moral purpose.'

Ralph Hill's strongest instinct was played as a weakness and another meeting agreed. Thus, kings and bishops and pawns were being moved around the board.

*

Cynthia doesn't return home until lunchtime. Ralph asks what the doctor said was wrong.

'She's not sure. She's making an appointment for me at the hospital.'

'What are your symptoms? You still haven't told me.'

'It's just that I feel exhausted most of the time, I'm losing a bit of weight. That sort of thing.'

Cynthia has no wish to go into detail, doesn't want to alarm her husband or herself.

'What is it you were going to tell me at breakfast?' she says.

'Ah yes, well I've been asked to take on some new work… for CND.'

'What sort of new work?'

'It's about Trident, getting our campaign ready for when Thatcher goes public with her latest plan to bring the end of the world that little bit closer.'

'So you'll be away from home even more?'

'Only a little, just co-ordinating with other peace campaigners overseas.'

'Where overseas?'

'Europe mainly, Sweden for sure, I think.'

'And you'll be able to fit in all this extra responsibility with your parish work?'

'I think so, yes. It'll mean my curate holding the fort every so often but I'll only be away for a couple of nights at a time.'

Cynthia has nothing to say, nothing that might persuade her husband that she needs him more than ever since Virginia left their lives. Her lunch is half-eaten. She gets up and takes her long, waxed coat from a peg in the utility room and walks into the garden. The sky is grey with clouds folding down from the Black Mountains, heavy with more snow.

Ralph watches his wife cross the lawn, still white with yesterday's fall. Her wellingtons scuff a path towards the gate and the two-acre wood of beech and cherry where she's taken to sitting, whatever the weather.

There is no thaw in the chill between them, no warmth in their togetherness.

Yet this makes it easier to mislead her, if only for her own good. How could he tell her he'd just been recruited as an unlikely agent of the Swedish government, a courier, a conduit to the enemies of the South African government's secret death squads that hunted them down like vermin. As he turns Tomas Bolund's card over and over, he does not realise there will be blood... more blood.

It will find its way onto the votive hands and vestments of the Reverend Ralph Hill, vicar of All Hallows in the county of Hereford. And he will never be able to rid himself of its stains.

10: SUSPICION

"As flies to wanton boys are we to the gods;
They kill us for their sport."

- King Lear, Act 4, Scene 1

Tilly Brown lived in that grid of Victorian streets between
the Holloway and Hornsey roads in North London. She
remembered such places from her post-war childhood, those
colourless days of rationing, kids playing on bomb sites,
Churchill back in power.

Wives stayed at home then, husbands worked as
labourers, railway shunters, porters, night watchmen, or did
anything – legal or otherwise – to feed their families.

The street moved up through the social gears in the
property boom of the 1980s. That's when professionals like
Tilly started moving in – civil servants, accountants, city
types – fitting bespoke kitchens, transforming dowdy rooms
with colour supplement style. SUVs became de rigueur for
the school run, Jaguars and BMWs commonplace.

Tilly attended one new family's housewarming, all
scented candles, Thai cuisine and John Coltrane playing free
jazz on a Bang & Olufsen deck. The talk was of second
homes in France, skiing in the Alps. Another guest, slightly
overweight and well into the chablis, leered her into a corner

towards the end of the evening. He said his name was Giles.

'Your glass is empty,' he said. 'Can't have that, this is supposed to be a party.'

Tilly smiled but said she was about to leave.

'You must let me escort you home. We could have a nightcap at my place, if you'd like.'

'That's kind of you but I shall be fine, honestly.'

'I had a really good architect, excellent builder too. I'd love you to see it.'

'Another time, perhaps. I'm leaving for Scotland early tomorrow.'

'I've got a four-poster, bought it in the Cotswolds.'

Tilly forced another smile and put her glass down, ready to go.

'I'm sure your wife must have been delighted.'

'But I'm not married, you see. We could take off into the night if you'd like.'

'That's a kind offer but no, I really can't,' Tilly said. 'But don't let me stop you.'

Tilly described the man's amateur chat-up lines to Mrs Nally, the neighbour who cat-sat for her and was one of the street's original residents.

'Ah, that'd be him, Champagne Charlie, the fella at number twenty-six.'

'Is that what they call him?'

'In the Half Moon, they do. Grandson's the barman, poured him into a taxi often enough.'

'I can't imagine how people like that work the next day. What's his job, do you know?'

'Something for the government, the grandson says.'

Two days after Tilly arrived home from Scotland,

Champagne Charlie came out of his house as she passed catch a bus on Holloway Road. He was dressed for Whitehall – dark overcoat, dark suit, white shirt, black brogues, well polished.

'Good morning,' he said, without first realising who she was.

When he did, he quickly turned back to his front door as if he'd forgotten something. Tilly saw the embarrassment on his face, slightly blotched in the uncharitable light of morning.

When it came, her bus was crowded and she stood all the way to Euston station. She caught a local train to Watford. Her mother lived in a care home there – ninety next birthday, frail, almost blind. Tilly visited every fortnight from a sense of duty.

The old lady had no idea who she was. She dozed in a fake leather armchair, mind confused, body hollowed out by age. Residents, male and female, muttered and shuffled around the dayroom, staring into a world only they could see.

Other lost souls sat watching a large television in the bay window, absorbed by news they couldn't understand from places they couldn't remember. Tilly was also looking at the TV.

What she saw jolted her – not the huge Chinook hovering thirty feet above a lake but the smaller helicopter being winched up from the airbags that had raised it to the surface, tail twisted, rotor blades bent, skids buckled.

The shot pulled back to a reporter doing a piece to camera. Tilly strained to hear his words above the shouts of carers herding residents into the dining room for lunch.

'... *killed three days ago... based in Northern Ireland...*

in Wales.'

⌐t her mother's hand slip from her own and moved
TV. A photograph of a smiling young woman in
⌐.⌐igues came on the screen captioned Virginia Hill,
Army Air Corps. She looked confident, attractive, a woman
at ease with who and what she was.

*Captain Hill was the only female helicopter pilot in the
Air Corps and was flying alone. Sources say terrorism hasn't
been ruled out but mechanical failure is the most likely cause.
Her father is the outspoken peace campaigner and CND
activist, the Reverend Ralph Hill. He was admitted to
hospital shortly after hearing of his daughter's death.*

Tilly gave her mother's forehead a kiss, which meant
nothing to either of them. She left for the station, preoccupied
by thoughts of the young pilot's violent death and the
coincidence of photographing a similar-looking helicopter on
the same day hers crashed.

Her train clattered through the sooty brick confines of
outer London, the marshalling yards, dreary suburbs without
end, tower blocks where washing hung limp on balconies
high in the sky. Her own life had become just as monotonous
and dull.

She'd taken redundancy from the Metropolitan Police
legal department and embraced freedom from work. But she
found she now lacked structure and purpose in her life, had
no professional challenges, little human contact. Wasn't it
said that normality was a paved road, comfortable to walk but
no flowers grew on it? If we are the sum of our experiences,
what was she doing with hers?

A feeling of discontent assailed her, of being unfulfilled.
She was barely home from taking pictures and wild camping

in Scotland yet the idea of going back without delay was tempting. It'd be displacement activity but give her space to think about the future. Time ambushes all in the end. She didn't need to visit a care home to realise that.

There was also another reason, but one she'd not readily admit: the prospect of being with Robbo again. The redoubtable Mrs Nally would advise against taking any such interest in so unreachable a man, and an untruthful one at that. But herein was his appeal; that sense of him being someone who'd be dangerous to know.

'And there's you, almost on the change,' Mrs Nally would surely observe with womanly wisdom. 'Tricky time of life, that much I can tell you. You're not in control of the head. Just you mind yourself or mark my words, you'll take a fall.'

Mrs Nally would probably be right. But it still niggled Tilly that she didn't know who or what Robbo really was. Why hadn't he dropped more hints about his private life during those nights under the stars, eating and talking together when it would have been most natural? Why hadn't he tried to take her to his bed? Most men in that situation would've made a move. And had Robbo done so, she'd have smiled and gone willingly.

Once home, she would look again at the Port Logan material in her darkroom in the cellar. She was especially proud of the image of Robbo fighting to stay on his feet in the helicopter's downdraught then throwing his canvas bag on board and scrambling in after it.

Here was intrigue, the drama and mystery of a moment captured against a threatening sea and a gathering of moody clouds.

She would print off an enlargement but in black and

white. This would bring out its most haunting quality – that of something appearing to be real and tangible, yet at the same time, illusory and beyond reach.

It would please her to have it framed and hung on her bedroom wall. She could then go to sleep looking at it, wondering what was written in the margins of Robbo's story.

*

Kat Walsh had only disdain for the reporters and camera crews feeding on the carcass of the downed Gazelle like the parasites they were. But de Lanerolle's guiding hand was keeping them on message. For now, neither he nor they knew about the more sensitive operation running amid those lonely hills. Even as Kat drove south to Powis Castle, Robbo was being hunted by a four-man brick of SAS trackers she had badgered out of the training wing in Hereford. She knew he'd be dug in somewhere, invisible, a tree in a forest. Only those with his skills and training could run him to earth.

No one could have survived a crash like he had without injury. Wherever he'd lost blood or rested, broken a twig or made a footprint in a field, the trackers would find it. It wouldn't be straightforward but the books could then be tidied up.

Kat headed through the wooded deer park surrounding Powis Castle. Its reddish-brown gritstone walls towered from an outcrop of rock. It was the grandest of fortified houses, fabulously rich in history and treasures bought – or stolen – by those who'd dwelled within for the past seven centuries.

She parked her car – an Astra hired in de Lanerolle's name – and walked up a steep path to the gatehouse.

Kat paid the entrance fee by cash not credit card. It was second nature never to leave a paper trail.

The Oak Drawing Room was on the first floor, reached by a set of back stairs whereon only the boots of servants had once trodden. An elderly guide – white hair, pink face, blue blazer – asked if she needed any assistance.

'Thank you, but no,' she said. 'I'm happy just to look around and take it all in.'

The ceiling was a vast relief of moulded plasterwork, ornate and delicately achieved. Light from a central chandelier reflected on the linen-fold panelling, oak polished with beeswax. On one wall hung a full-length portrait of Robert Clive – Clive of India – whose descendants lived in the castle and inherited his collection of priceless antiquities plundered from the subcontinent. And in an alcove nearby, Kat saw the painting mentioned by DASP.

The guide appeared at her side without a sound.

'Beautiful, isn't it?' he said. 'You probably won't have heard of the artist, Belotto, but the work of his more famous uncle will be known to you, I'm sure… Canaletto, yes?'

'Of course, Venice and all that.'

'Well, Bernardo Belotto was a considerable talent in his own right. He painted this view of Verona from the Ponte Nuovo between 1745 and 1747, which was about twenty years before we believe the picture was bought by Robert Clive.'

Kat nodded but moved away from this well-meaning but intrusive man before whoever was to make contact arrived. She feigned interest in other portraits and an inlaid grandfather clock. Its brass face showed ten fifteen. It would look odd if she stayed in the same room much longer, but she couldn't leave the RV just yet. There was no back-up plan.

The guide was already looking at her a little suspiciously. He hovered nearby, doubtless wondering why she didn't move through to the next room. Kat had to buy time.

'I'm sorry,' she said. 'Would you mind if I sat on your chair for a moment?'

'No, not at all. Don't you feel well?'

'Just a little bit faint, that's all.'

'Please, come, sit here. Can I get you some water?'

'No, I'll be OK. I didn't eat much for breakfast.'

'Ah, most important meal of the day, breakfast.'

'If I can just sit quiet for a few minutes…'

She leaned forward, elbows on her knees, to shut off any more conversation. A group of visitors entered, talking knowledgeably about what they'd seen so far. The guide greeted them and launched into his spiel about the room's art and history and its sumptuous furniture and furnishings.

Kat continued to stare at the floor. What the hell was going on? Could the funnies be watching her, testing her? Was she being set up?

Paranoia is the default position for those who conspire. But a minute later, a hand touched her shoulder.

'Not feeling ill, are you?'

She looked up. The man standing in front of her had the roseate complexion of a drinker and wouldn't see seventy again. He wore a grey suit with chalk stripes, had thick silver hair brushed back and oiled. His manner was blunt and within his accent was a trace of its origins in the industrial midlands of England.

'No, I'm fine, thanks,' said Kat.

An introduction was hardly needed. He was recognisable

from television. This was Sir Frazer Harris, the Labour Party's combative ex-Secretary of State for Defence, now absent from frontline politics since losing his seat three years ago in the 1987 election.

So he was DASP's man. Curiouser and curiouser. But intrigue was what Kat had signed up for. Nothing gave her a bigger buzz.

'Come, follow me,' Sir Frazer said. 'We need to talk. There's a lot to get through.'

*

Robbo began waking from an ordeal that could have been a nightmarish dream were it not for the real enough aches in his head and upper body.

He lay motionless on a couch of soft cushions in front of a fire of logs in a hearth heaped with embers and ash. The logs sparked and popped; the shadows of flames flickered across a ceiling kippered yellow by years of woodsmoke.

Slowly, gradually, Robbo regained more consciousness. He felt safe, though from what, he still didn't know. In that moment of amniotic awakening, it was enough not to sense danger. But where was he? How had he been saved from the night? He tried to sit up but fell back because of the pain in his chest. It took a moment for him to breathe without discomfort. Then, did he hear a voice... a woman's voice, humming to herself a short distance away?

It came again, simple and rhythmic like a song to send a child to sleep. A door opened behind him. He wasn't alarmed. The woman came and stood by him. She carried a tin tray, bright with painted flowers and bearing a bowl of soup.

'So, we are awake, are we?' she said. 'I was starting to think you'd be needing the undertaker and not the doctor.'

She had a kindly Caribbean face and spoke with an unlikely soft North Wales accent. Robbo, confused and uncertain, asked if she was a nurse.

'No, darling,' she said. 'You were left on my doorstep like a bundle of clothes but I've patched you up best I can.'

'So this isn't a hospital?'

'No, you're in my home but here, take this, it's vegetable. I made it myself. You need to eat up to regain your strength. You hear what I'm saying?'

'Yes... sorry to put on you like this. Can't seem to remember things.'

'Then don't try. Time enough for that, just you clean your plate.'

She took two logs from the wicker basket by her easy chair and dropped them into the dog grate. Sparks showered up into the void of the chimney. She watched them disappear then turned her gaze towards the man who'd fallen into her world.

'They call me Florence,' she said. 'What about you, darling? What is your name?'

Robbo would have answered but they both heard a noise from the yard at the back. Someone – or something – had knocked against a metal rubbish bin. Florence saw the sudden fear in his eyes. He rolled off the couch despite his hurts and took hold of a brass poker from the hearth.

'Easy, crazy man, easy,' she said. 'It'll be a fox or a sheep wandering off the hill. I'll go and look, you stay where you are.'

84

She peered from behind the curtains at her kitchen window and saw several men in the mid-afternoon gloom. They wore dark berets and camouflaged smocks as they emerged from the Dutch barn beyond her gate. They were carrying rifles.

Now it was Florence's turn to be afraid, for reasons she didn't understand either.

11: RECKONING

"Fast flits this scene of woe and crime,
And soon the whole shall close."

-    Traditional hymn, Henry Francis Lyte

A spade… digging. That's what woke him. It had been another unsettled night. Then he heard the sexton, toiling hard as always, cutting into the gritty brown earth of the graveyard, rhythmically, methodically.

The Reverend Hill saw him in his mind's eye: jacket off, sleeves rolled up. And on the right forearm, an image of his Mary, tattooed in some backstreet dive during shore leave coming home from whatever war he'd just survived. Its colours were fading, the black of her hair, the red of her lips, losing a little potency each day. But the same was true of the living canvas from which she smiled.

The sexton's was an ageless task, as familiar to Ralph Hill as the words he'd intoned so often over the dead and those who grieved at the edge of eternity. Hadn't he always tried to give comfort, to assure them that there was a time to be born and a time to die and beyond this capricious life was the kingdom of heaven? How fraudulent, how baseless this all seemed now when the next coffin on which he'd be required to cast a handful of symbolic dirt would be that of his only

86

child.

Again and again, he demanded to know of himself by whose unholy writ had one so young been taken. God's servant had no answers when he needed them most.

He sat on his bed, hands together but not in prayer. On the bedside cabinet was his fountain pen and the notebook in which he scribbled ideas for sermons.

Night falls slowly when sleep doesn't come. His last entry, made soon after discharging himself from hospital, was an attempt to find words to convey the depth of his grief and remorse.

If I am happy, you will be the sadness behind my eyes.

If I am in pain, you will be the hurt they cannot find.

When I am buried, you will be in what remains of my heart.

Reading the lines again, he knew the underlying sentiments should have been spoken in life, not death. His days of atonement would be without end, the guilt for his failings never assuaged. Yet what he had written, imperfect and self-pitying though it was, expressed undeniable feelings.

They were raw and honest and therefore worthy of forming his ex-voto testament to Virginia, a penitential devotion that he would secrete deep into a crevice in the stones of the churchyard wall by which she would lie.

Only he would know it was there and in time, paper, words and author would be no more. It'd remind him of his gentle Latin master's advice to those he sent out into the world with plans and dreams: *Pulvis et umbra sumus* – we are but dust and shadows.

Ralph Hill stood in his pyjamas in the bedroom that had been his daughter's since childhood. It was exactly as she'd left it on what was to be her final visit home. A corner of the duvet was folded back, the pillow disarrayed. There was nothing to suggest that she hadn't just woken up and gone downstairs for breakfast.

He knelt, put his face where she had been and submerged himself in her scent until he might have drowned in her memory. On the wall above was a wistful portrait of Virginia aged ten and forever innocent, painted in oils by the accomplished artist who had been her mother.

In the churchyard beyond, the sexton dug ever deeper into the earth. The Reverend Hill rose and forced himself to observe like a man condemned to witness the building of his own gallows.

Could he hold himself together on the approaching day, down there where the very stones required those who gazed upon them to account for their lives and the sins committed therein? Would he remember his words, play his part or, weak in body and spirit, be unable to set aside his guilt and pray not for the soul of the dear departed, but only for himself and her forgiveness?

Yet he did not have to sup from this chalice. He could be the grieving parent, sitting alone in one of his church's antiquated box pews, a victim of circumstance deserving of compassion. But he knew this would be an act of cowardice, a final betrayal.

In life, they had been lost one to another because of his purblindness to those closest to him. In death, he had to make amends. His duty was clear. And he would find the strength to perform it.

The sexton was already standing waist-high in the grave, shovelling displaced soil onto a black tarpaulin at its side. Ralph Hill turned away and went across to the fireplace. The matchbox in which Virginia kept the key to her secrets was still there, hidden among the pine cones gathering dust in the cast iron grate.

He would unlock Virginia's cupboard, read her diaries, know her private thoughts. Nothing she had written could cause him greater distress than that he was already enduring. He had a need to understand her opinion of him, even as her grave was being prepared. She was a witness to the slow death of his idealism, had watched him discard the habit of holiness. The urge to know her was a means to confront himself and the sins he wished to expiate.

*

Wednesday, 24th March 1983:

Home on leave. Mummy doesn't look well, I'm sure something is wrong and not just because Daddy is away again but she will never talk about her health. She says Daddy is overseas on some 'peace' mission but she has no idea where or when he will be back.

Thursday, 25th March 1983:

I used to think it was my fault, me living at home and having all those rows with Daddy, and Mummy taking my side, that this was the cause of the trouble between them, but from what she says, they are just as unhappy now if not more so. Was there ever a more inconsiderate husband than my father? Not only that but he is still so politically gullible and incapable of seeing Moscow's hand manipulating his peace movement to the advantage of the Soviets. That's what they do, they work through front organisations and useful idiots like my father.

Friday, 26th March 1983:
A postcard has arrived from Daddy. He is in Sweden and says he has several meetings to attend and he doesn't think he will be back for another week. So, Daddy's search for utopia goes on while the rest of us face up to what's happening in the real world and try to defend his freedom to continually criticise our bit of it.

*

He is flying above a slew of little wooded islands in the Stockholm archipelago, its dark blue waters criss-crossed by the wakes of ferries and yachts. Amid the trees are wooden houses with red-tiled roofs, jetties for dinghies and tended lawns where wispy smoke rises from the fires of barbecues.

The plane continues to climb and enters cloud over the Baltic. Ralph Hill settles back, eyes closed. The briefing he's just had is still front and centre in his mind – that and the assignment from which he cannot now turn back, not that he wishes to.

On his lap is the scuffed leather attaché case he's had since theological college. Inside are shirts, socks and underwear for three days, a toilet bag and in a money belt, more cash than he's ever handled or seen in his life.

But he'll be at no risk from muggers. Tomas Bolund says his people will shadow him from the moment the plane lands in Johannesburg.

'You will not even know they're there,' Bolund said. 'We take care of our own.'

Ralph Hill is awash with adrenalin, every sense heightened by the prospect of danger. He feels alive, exquisitely so, freed from his world of structures and hierarchy, his purpose on earth renewed.

The war against apartheid is a battle between good and evil, a single issue with a single enemy, fought with blood and bravery in the here and now. Thousands have been martyred in its name, even more tortured and jailed. To play a part, however peripheral, in the overthrow of such a cruel regime is to put the injunctions of Christ's teaching to work.

He'd flown to Stockholm the previous night. Bolund had booked him a room in a hotel near the airport. After breakfast, Ralph Hill took a taxi to Stortorget, the ancient square in Stockholm's old town. Its tall, Dutch-gabled buildings were decorated in greens, reds and pinks and thronged with passengers off cruise ships looking for gift shops and coffee.

At ten o'clock, as instructed by Bolund, he'd sat on a bench opposite a café once painted bright vermilion but muted now by the snow and winds of many winters. Some of the medieval streets leading off the square were so narrow the sun would struggle to shine within. He checked his watch. Bolund was late.

A woman approached, thirty-something, jeans, jacket, short dark hair and with the deep tan of someone who went sailing or skiing. She smiled, inclined her head as if to ask if he minded her sitting alongside. Ralph Hill returned the smile and gestured for her to join him.

'Thank you,' she said. 'I wasn't sure… you being a priest, you know—'

'That I might be afraid of women?'

She laughed and rummaged inside her shoulder bag for a pack of cigarettes.

'Would you…?'

'Thank you but I don't smoke.'

The square milled with young tourists burdened with backpacks, cameras, maps, and talking in a babel of languages.

The woman's English was excellent but he couldn't quite place her accent. It seemed to hint at French but he wasn't sure. She asked him where he was from.

'England, a county called Herefordshire near the border with Wales. Do you know of it?'

'Yes, I have heard it is very beautiful there, very historic.'

'It is, yes. Christians have worshipped in my church for almost a thousand years.'

'Goodness,' she said. 'And what are you doing here, so far from your flock?'

'I'm just on a short holiday, seeing some of your interesting places in Stockholm.'

For the Reverend Hill, this was the palest of white lies, and practice for the role he would soon assume.

'Something interesting happened right by where we sit,' she said. 'Something horrible.'

'What was it? What happened here?'

'There were many noble families of Sweden put in this square a long time ago by the king of Denmark and they were executed.'

92

'How dreadful, but most of history is soaked in blood, isn't it?'

'But in modern times, too, blood is being spilt,' she said. 'It is a dangerous world, still.'

'Made more so by the politicians, I'm afraid. So few of them possess the virtue of disloyalty to the regimes that support them and their careers.'

'Aren't priests like you supposed to be above such comments, to stay clear of politics?'

'Yes, and sadly, most do,' Ralph Hill said. 'But what should be done in the face of those regimes that are sustained by brutality and terror and where the moral order is inverted and good becomes evil and evil becomes good? Where is a priest's true duty to his congregation and to God in those circumstances?'

'Goodness, forgive me for saying so but you look such a mild man, not like you have so much passion inside you.'

He shook his head, embarrassed. His heart was never far from his sleeve. Beyond the square's huge stone water fountain, a girl with golden hair was playing a guitar. She sang about love and peace, and teenage boys sitting at her feet moved their heads in time to the music, maybe dreaming of how to find it.

The Reverend Hill's new companion had gone quiet. He asked where she was from.

'I live in Geneva in Switzerland.'

'And what do you do, what is your profession?'

'I am an administrator, I work for an international organisation.'

'That sounds important. Which one, may I ask?'

'It is the World Council of Churches.'

'Ah, so that is why you sat with me – you would know I am just a harmless country vicar.'

She smiled once more then dropped the butt of her cigarette onto the paving bricks beneath their bench and ground it out beneath the toe of a black slip-on.

'I have enjoyed talking to you but I must leave,' she said. 'I must be somewhere else but I hope your visit to Stockholm will be to your benefit.'

'It will, I'm sure. You go safely, now.'

She stood up to go and gave him a final smile.

'Oh, by the way, Tomas will be a little late but he asked me to give you this.'

She reached inside her bag again and handed him a thick white envelope.

'I'm sorry, I don't understand. Who are you? What is this package?'

'Tomas will be along in a minute. He will explain some more. Goodbye, Mr Hill.'

*

Tomas Bolund didn't speak when he arrived. He just beckoned Ralph Hill to follow him across the square to a café in one of the sunless side streets.

It was quite dark inside. Bolund found a back room with even less light and ordered coffee. They talked quietly, head to head, across a square table.

'I must apologise for our surroundings, Mr Hill, but we behave discreetly, it is important.'

'I understand that but who was that woman you sent to sit with me?'

'That is Jana. Jana Kuper. It is her organisation that is supplying the funds for our work.'

'You mean the World Council of Churches?'

'Yes, they are our partners in this.'

'But you said it was your government behind everything, the government of Sweden.'

'This is a very sensitive matter, politically and diplomatically, so my government cannot be seen to be involved.'

'So you are using cut-outs like me, is that it?'

'We have to operate in self-contained cells to minimise the risk of exposure.'

'Does that mean you expect things to go wrong in South Africa?'

'No, it does not. But the South African government employ their spies in both the political and armed wings of the anti-apartheid movement, so we have to take every precaution.'

'If the worst happens then I am an Englishman and the World Council of Churches is in Switzerland so your government will be kept at a safe distance from any controversy.'

'Please understand, Mr Hill, we would not be having this conversation if we felt you were not equal to this task. We trust you... completely.'

'Then why did Jana need to meet me in that rather odd way? Our conversation barely amounted to a few pleasantries.'

'That may be so, but it was sufficient for her to confirm our judgement about you. Besides, it is the WCC's money she gave to you and she has to account for it.'

'So it is money in the envelope?'

'Yes, it is Dutch guilders to the value of twenty thousand pounds sterling.'

'Then it's fortunate for you that I am a man of the cloth.'

*

A stewardess offers him tea or coffee. He takes tea and a pack of three digestive biscuits. The businessman in the seat next to his asks for wine. A child is crying somewhere behind him. The seat belt signs ping off and a woman gets up to walk to the toilet cubicle. The engines throb and thrust them southwards at five hundred miles an hour. It is a flight like any other: random strangers bundled together with their secrets. And far below, the sea and the tides roll their pebbles ever smoother, ever smaller and the world turns as it must.

12: POLITICS

"The past is very hard to predict."

- Old Marxist joke

The MI5 file on Sir Frazer Harris, Labour's one-time Secretary of State for Defence, described him as an ex-communist who, according to confidential sources, spoke of putting opponents against a wall in the class war that was surely coming.

He was a young comrade then, inflamed by the spectre of pre-war fascism. For him, the only option was a long march towards utopia by way of the Soviet Union. But the true believer – religious or political – faces many a temptation on the hard path of virtue and righteousness.

By the time this solipsistic schemer against the evils of capitalism reached high office, he no longer opposed trade union reform, nor did he argue in Cabinet – as expected – for Britain to unilaterally abandon its nuclear weapons and quit NATO.

And those he'd once lionised as freedom fighters before he fattened into late middle age were condemned as terrorists who should hang for their murderous crimes.

Few could spot the difference between him and his Conservative predecessor. Military men and spooks would wryly observe, in the privacy of their clubs, that Sir Frazer might once have been Moscow's useful idiot, but he was now theirs. Yet his shift to the ideological right presaged defeat in a general election. The blow was only softened by directorships and consultancies. He'd hoped for a seat in the House of Lords but was granted a knighthood. Thereafter, his socialist ideals, threadbare as they'd become, were worn under suits from Savile Row.

Kat Walsh considered Sir Frazer's life and interesting times as they took Earl Grey tea in the orangery at Powis Castle. She settled back, more ready to listen than talk.

'What you have to understand is this,' he said. 'I've still got a friend or two in the darker corners of the Establishment and they continue to talk to me.'

'That's why we're having this meeting, isn't it?'

'Indeed it is, because we have a problem, you and me. A problem that's getting more difficult to resolve as each day passes.'

'Sir, there's nothing that isn't under control.'

'Miss Walsh, please, having had to deal with the mandarins of Whitehall for years, those who saw me as some sort of milk-in-first oik who couldn't see he was being soft-soaped, well… I can assure you that I can.'

'Sir, I didn't mean—'

'I'm sure you didn't but don't, because it won't help either of us.'

Sir Frazer drank with incongruous gentility, saucer beneath cup to prevent any drips staining the finest tailoring Gieves & Hawkes could provide.

'With respect, sir, I'm only here to reassure you that the matter that concerns us all is being dealt with.'

'But not very effectively,' he said. 'Let's take stock, shall we? You and the intelligence lot are in the mire for reasons I'm not entirely clear about, but I'm being told that you've got a rogue agent on the loose and you can't find him.'

'Sir, as I said—'

'Let me finish because if this all goes to rat shit, it won't be the likes of you who's nailed to a cross, it'll be me because I was supposed to be in charge.'

'I can see that, sir.'

'Let's understand each other. My area was policy, everything else was operational.'

'But you still had ministerial responsibility, didn't you?'

'When it was convenient, yes.'

'Would you like to explain what you mean, sir?'

'Well, let me do just that. I remember a meeting with only me and three others present so that meant four coffee cups on the table, four biscuits on the plate, but when the minutes came back, there were only two names on the circulation list – me and a civil servant. So who were our absent friends and what were they up to?'

'I wasn't there, sir. I couldn't say.'

'Then I'll tell you. They were the bastards getting me to give them political cover. It's like the Americans would say, they were covering their arses.'

'But what were you giving them political cover for, sir?'

'Whatever they were planning to do in Northern Ireland, of course. The minutes were written so as to say I approved as the minister so I could be seen as driving the policy.'

'I'm sorry, sir, but what had you approved?'

Sir Frazer ran his right forefinger between collar and neck. Sunlight poured through tall sash windows and onto the lustrous leaves of citrus bushes in terracotta pots. It was getting warm in the orangery, uncomfortably so.

'I'd made a speech once... talked about taking the fight back to the terrorists, taking the gloves off. They wanted to put it into practice.'

'You mean fighting fire with fire, shooting to kill?'

'I didn't say that. I didn't know what was being done and I still don't, not really.'

'Sir, all I can say is nothing of this will leak from us. We'll put it to bed quickly and quietly.'

'You need to,' Sir Frazer said. 'You must know there are English detectives starting to dig up the past over there... cleaning out the stables for this bloody peace process.'

'We are very aware of them, yes.'

'Then you must realise if the very existence of this missing man becomes known to them then God help us all. If he starts talking—'

'He won't, sir. He'll not get the chance.'

Sir Frazer looked at her over half-moon glasses and breathed in through his nose. The air was humid, scented with red and yellow kaffir lilies. The orangery was closed to the public for that morning. Two folding chairs and a round metal table had been brought in and set with a white cloth, bone china crockery and assorted pastries.

Kat had to take any hint of conflict out of their conversation. She asked how he'd managed to arrange such a private – and splendid – meeting place with the National Trust.

'I'm one of their regional trustees,' he said. 'I told the manager you're a journalist.'

'In the circumstances, I'll not take that as an insult, sir.'

'No, please don't. I've been at war with those buggers for years.'

Sir Frazer stood up, suddenly twitchy, unable to sit still.

'Come on, let's go for a walk,' he said. 'I don't think anyone's found a way to bug the trees, not yet anyway.'

*

Across from the medieval castle, dusty rose-red and high on its escarpment of rock, was a hill of ancient oaks and silver firs, tulip trees and rhododendrons, which, in season, had flowers like gouts of blood. They'd gone there from the orangery, along an Italianate terrace hung with purple wisteria wired against walls of soft mellow brick and by statues of dancing shepherds and mythical figures.

The path led them to a dark tunnel through a monumentally tall yew then down to formal gardens and the woodland beyond.

Sir Frazer, brawny shoulders slightly hunched, walked with his hands clasped behind him as if he were a statesman on a photo-op.

They sat on a Lutyens bench to look back at the ancient home of Welsh princes, to regard in awe what the hand and mind of man could achieve, at his history, his empires and at nature, beauteously reordered to his will.

'Don't think I shall ever tire of this view,' Sir Frazer said.

'Stunning, isn't it?'

'I always make sure I've the time to sit here whenever I visit Powis,' he said. 'It's a bit different from where I started out in life, I can tell you.'

His best days were long gone – no chauffeur-driven limo

now, no bodyguard, no access to the secure phone system for secret conversations with the prime minister and others. His purpose had become ever more obscure. But he'd enjoyed the illusion of power. And powerful men become addicted to taking risks. As they get away with one, then another, so a sense of immunity replaces that function in the less privileged brain that sees danger and cries halt. Sir Frazer had played by big boys' rules in Northern Ireland and now knew – or feared – this might have been a gamble too far. Kat saw how vulnerable he was. But did he realise it fully himself? She waited, didn't waste the advantage of the silence between them. He was there for the taking.

'Tell me about the helicopter crash,' he said. 'What happened... what really happened?'

'That's being investigated, sir.'

'I know it is but it wasn't an accident, not according to my sources.'

'We don't think so either but helicopters aren't fitted with black boxes so we're reliant on the air accident investigators for the answer.'

'So what are the chances of it being the work of the terrorists, the IRA?'

'That can't be ruled out, sir. It's the most likely possibility and you may find that confirmed publicly before long.'

'How? In what way?'

'We've a safe and reliable conduit in the media.'

'You'll leak something, you mean? That's playing with fire, isn't it?'

'Not in this particular case, sir, no.'

'God, what a blasted place Ireland is. Don't those buggers ever want peace?'

'Apparently not, but then they're not the only ones who don't want it, either.'

The wind blew from Long Mountain and bent through the trees around them. Kat saw a shiver pass through him.

'This agent, the runaway, what's the story about him? Tell me what you know.'

She took a small black notebook from the pocket of her Barbour which, worn with jeans, was an off-duty Army uniform in itself.

'Sir, I shall try but I will be breaking the Official Secrets Act.'

'Listen, I know all about keeping secrets. Are you with me?'

'Yes, sir. Well, he's ex-Green Jackets, then Special Forces, highly trained and extremely resourceful, and he was on board the helicopter when it crashed.'

'And we're absolutely sure he survived, are we?'

'Our frogmen carried out an extensive search of the lake and they're confident there wasn't a second body. Besides, we found his life jacket in the reeds by the shore.'

'And the team you've got searching for him, you must have briefed them. Can they be trusted? I mean, will they keep everything confidential?'

'They were told we had a man on the run who had to be apprehended, nothing more,' Kat said. 'But please understand, sir, in Special Forces, we do favours for each other; we don't ask why or what and we never speak out of turn. It's the only way we know how to work, to be effective.'

Sir Frazer seemed puzzled. That was hardly the style in Westminster. Kat reassured him that surveillance was also being carried out on the missing man's former wife.

'So there was a wife, was there? Is she likely to shield him?'

'She's a civilian, sir. The marriage didn't last long and it ended extremely badly so we think that's highly unlikely.'

'Any children to complicate matters?'

'Not that we know of. There's nothing on file.'

'Right, now tell me why he was on that damn helicopter in the first place, because you've kept all that secret, haven't you?'

'The plan was to fly him to the SAS headquarters near Hereford.'

'And then what?'

'That's above my pay grade, sir. I don't know.'

'Then how was the problem going to be solved, Miss Walsh? How were they going to bring him back inside the tent or is this something else you don't know about?'

'Sir, you know full well what this agent did against the terrorists for the common good, so with respect, let me ask you a question: how do you want this matter to end?'

For the former Secretary of State for Defence, this wasn't some political hypothetical, it was a question of the here and now, of the threatening and contemporary moment.

It went to his visceral anxiety that all he was, and all he had been, was no longer his to preserve but in the hands of others, and potential enemies.

'How do I want this matter to end? Good question,' Sir Frazer said. 'Put it this way, I don't want to be left in a situation where I'm showing any ankle on any of this. Are you with me?'

*

Later that morning, Kat Walsh parked in a lay-by on the way back to Lake Vyrnwy and checked the tape she'd made. The wind had caught the mic hidden in her jacket every so often but she'd got his balls in her hand now.

If it came to it – God forbid – he couldn't play Pilate and claim clean hands, not now. Nor could the spooks upstairs. She drove away, smiling.

*

Just before lunchtime, visitors to Powis Castle began leaving the terraced gardens and stately rooms for the café in the courtyard by the statue of Fame and Pegasus. In the woodland walk, a young couple remained on the Lutyens bench, from which a glorious vision of arcadia could be seen. They'd been there for ten minutes or so, kissing and embracing. Other people strolled by, too discreet, too embarrassed to stare.

Had they done so, they might have noticed the lovers removing something from its curved backrest, something small, a piece of equipment, maybe. But nobody did. Whatever it was went into the woman's National Trust shopping bag.

Then she took her companion's hand and they walked through the oaks and giant firs, by the ice house and the pond where mallards swam and fish broke the mirrored surface every once in a while.

They made for the orangery. Here, the man took something from beneath a powder blue ceanothus standing by a round metal table. That went into the woman's bag, too.

Later, others would also listen to Sir Frazer's wish not to end up showing any ankle on this most uncomfortable of matters.

But in a game without rules and fought in that most tenebrous of worlds, all that mattered was never being on the losing side.

13: HUNTED

"He who lives with the devil
becomes the devil."

- Yiddish saying

Florence hurried back to her parlour, alarmed, uncomprehending.

'That noise, it's some men, they've got guns—'

Her words were alien in the innocence of such surroundings, in a room of ornaments from seaside holidays and coronations, of a Sunday best tea service with pink and white flowers on a dresser polished until it gleamed.

Yet Robbo understood. His body stiffened. In that moment, the nightmarish sense of being pursued became real.

'They're in uniforms like soldiers. What are they doing here?'

Robbo couldn't know for sure. But what had been a refuge now felt like a trap. Florence stared at his injured face and saw in his eyes that same look of bewilderment she'd witnessed in patients close to death.

'Are they something to do with you?' she said. 'If they are, I want no trouble with no one, not with guns. You hear me? I don't want it.'

'Keep your voice down. Did they see you?'

'No, they're across the yard, by the barn.'

'How many are there?'

'Three, I saw three of them.'

'Listen, these aren't nice people, Florence. They mean to harm me, do you understand?'

She clearly didn't but how could she know the ways of a world that had collided with hers without warning?

'Why would they harm you? What have you been doing?'

Robbo ignored her question.

'They mustn't find me, Florence. There's a place I've got to get to. Will you help me?'

A fist began banging against the door of her kitchen. It could only be them. Nothing in life had prepared her for such a moment.

An unhealthy heart beat beneath her apron and the green cardigan she'd knitted last year. The doctor said worry was bad for her. Yet here were men with rifles and a badly hurt stranger and it all seemed as if she'd been caught up in something violent on television. Men could be heard talking outside. The unseen fist hit against the door again.

'Anyone at home? We just want a quick word.'

Florence's Samaritan impulse to help was struggling against an inbred fear of ever crossing authority, not least when it appeared in uniform. Robbo could only watch as she turned from him and went to open her door.

*

Frederico sleeps in the back of the Lincoln. He snores quietly, as if not to wake himself. The driver chews a plug of coca leaf. He does so slowly, methodically, then works it around his mouth to form a lump in his right cheek. The habit is turning his teeth brown.

Robbo stares into the desert of shale ahead, shimmering beneath the hammering sun. There is no shade, no trees, no grass, just the illusion of driving across a vast lake of yellow mud.

The Lincoln starts to slow down. Something has been seen by the driver. It's another car, black and bobbing in the watery mirage. Frederico stirs. The gun beneath his jacket is clear to see. But it won't be needed.

The two men with Uzis who start to check the Lincoln and its occupants are on Lucho's payroll. This is the third time they've been stopped on the way to his ranch. Frederico had already warned him of Lucho's paranoia about security.

'Gringos can be welcomed here with a bullet in the head,' he'd said earlier. 'But you are with me today so I think you be safe.'

'You *think* I'll be safe? What's that supposed to mean at this stage in the game?'

'Lucho survives because he's a suspicious man and he know how much his enemies want to destroy him.'

'The other cartels, you mean, his rivals?'

'No, the CIA and the American drug agency. Those are his real enemies.'

'But you've vouched for me, haven't you? He knows why I'm here?'

'Yes, and he's very interested,' Frederico said. 'But Bolivians have much reason to hate the *yanquis* and those who would collaborate with them.'

'But I'm a Brit. You've seen my passport, I'm here on my own, no Yanks.'

'Tranquilo, my friend.'

Frederico eases himself into a more comfortable position on the back seat.

'I am just, how do you say, the middleman. Lucho is the big boss so I say again, have good answers to the questions he asks you and everyone will be happy.'

*

Robbo shakes Lucho's hand. It feels like leather. He is short, five six at most, broad-shouldered and muscled where it matters.

His pants are denim jeans cut off at the knees and worn with a green sweatshirt, soiled by engine oil and the shit of the cattle he breeds.

Lucho's is the emotionless face of a peasant in late middle-age, eyes harder than pebbles, wary, missing nothing from beneath a wide-brimmed hat of woven straw. He displays neither watch nor jewellery, no heavy gold chain, no rings, nothing to flaunt wealth. His appearance is that of a *cocalero*, a subsistence grower of the crop he processes into the champagne of drugs and on which his empire is built.

Anonymity is further protection – should armed bodyguards not be enough – against those who would descend from gunships to abduct him to stand trial far beyond the lawless land where his writ now runs.

Only with caution and ruthless guile does Lucho survive and prosper. His influence seeps like groundwater below the foundations of society, through government, the judiciary, the military and police. Within these offices are those who accept Lucho's patronage, for the alternative has little attraction.

'Find the weakness, find the man,' Frederico observed on their long drive.

Robbo is aware of this. Information is currency in itself. And through his own sources, he is rich with it. He's examined aerial images of Lucho's compound – his house, workshops and extensive farm buildings, the hangars for his twin-engine Piper Seneca and an ex-military Huey – a Bell UH-1 Iroquois – kitted out with M60 machine guns either side.

He knows the locations of his host's secret cocaine kitchens, the pits of chemicals where coca leaves are stomped into paste by workers who thread their way to and fro along jungle paths like armies of ants.

But most important of all, Robbo has a portal to the future, and knows just how damaging it will be to the barely literate billionaire who is waving him into his villa.

'Come,' Lucho says. 'We eat.'

The soldier from across the sea has only his wits between himself and the scavengers circling the cloudless sky.

He is strip-searched by Lucho's men. His shoes might be bugged; he might be armed or wearing a wire. Robbo doesn't object. This is business, nothing personal. He would do the same.

*

Children can be heard playing upstairs. A maid mops the kitchen's dusty marble floor. She swills water around her bare brown feet and doesn't look up from her task. Not every room is plastered yet. Bare wires hang out of holes in some of the walls. It's a modest house, Spanish in style, terracotta roof, pink bougainvillea shading the veranda.

Lucho does not approve of the *narco-arquitectura* of those who show off their illegal opulence by building Floridian mansions in Cochabamba or La Paz. It attracts attention and envy. Neither benefits the wellbeing of those within.

He leads Robbo into a dining room. Frederico swings behind on his crutches. They sit on high-backed chairs at a long table made of dark wood and drink beer from bottles.

Two bodyguards allow a young woman in to serve chicken with a spicy yellow sauce and onions. Maybe she's twenty, with a pale gamine face and yellow hair. She doesn't speak, doesn't meet anyone's gaze.

Lucho seems content for Frederico to lead and interpret if necessary. He prefers to listen and watch, to sniff the humid air for deceit in the sweat of those who answer to him. Robbo suspects he understands English better than he lets on.

'So, inglés,' Frederico says. 'Are you tired, you want rest or we talk now?'

'I'm fine, thanks.'

'I have told Lucho what I know about you but he wants to hear it for himself.'

Robbo sets down his drink. He makes eye contact with Lucho. To show fear would be to show weakness and thus be despised.

'OK, right, I'm in the Army, the British Army, and I'm on special duties.'

'What sort of special duties? Secret work?'

'You could say that, yes.'

'We will come to this but what Lucho don't understand,

112

why you have made it your business to come here, just to him.'

'There are two reasons: first, my current mission directly affects him and second, I want to make some serious money.'

'Serious money means serious risks, inglés.'

'Taking risks is what I do, what I've always done.'

Frederico looks across at Lucho, whose face remains unreadable.

'But what if you got caught, Señor Roby? Do you think about that, about being locked in prison and losing your reputation, your family?'

'I'm not married, I don't have a family. Anyway, how I see it, risk is always a calculation. Do your research and if the odds look good, you go with it; if not, you don't.'

He takes another pull of his beer. Persuading Frederico to set up this meet was the easy part. But the point of no return is long gone. They can't figure out if he's a madman or a spy – maybe one with balls of steel, but a spy nonetheless. Either way, they're intrigued.

'How you know about me, inglés? How you learn about Lucho?'

Robbo takes a beat before answering, only partly for effect. He would play their paranoia.

'I have access to information, to intelligence.'

Lucho doesn't blink. His gaze remains fixed on Robbo. The silence is broken only when Frederico makes a self-evident observation.

'That is a dangerous thing to say, Señor Roby. You need to tell us more.'

'I am a British liaison officer. I work with the Americans, their drug enforcement officers.'

'And what is this work?'

'We are planning new operations for our governments and our military forces against the traffickers of drugs.'

'What do you mean, new operations? Why is this?'

'Because the political pressure to do something about cocaine is growing. There's a lot of crime and social damage that it's causing in the inner cities of America and Britain.'

Lucho, arms crossed over the barrel of his chest, speaks for the first time.

'We only supply a demand,' he says. 'Is it not what you people call capitalism?'

'That's not how it's seen in Washington and London,' Robbo says. 'It's now like a war to them and they're going to fight back soon like it's a moral crusade.'

'And you say you know these plans?' Frederico says.

'In broad terms, yes. I've read the logistical reports.'

'Why we believe you, Señor Roby? Why do we trust what you are saying?'

'That's up to you, but why would I come here, alone and unarmed, if I wasn't serious about what I'm proposing?'

'Maybe you have a death wish.'

'No, what I've got are the American reports, which you can see if we reach a deal.'

'But why do we want to? We don't need new markets, our business is good.'

'That's not true, is it? Your American market's collapsing. You've flooded the States with cocaine and you're only getting about thirty thousand dollars a kilo now but three years ago, back in '82, you got sixty.'

'That is what you say—'

'No, that's what the CIA say. I've seen their figures and

114

they're going to get worse.'

Frederico doesn't reply and bats his empty beer bottle over the table between the thumb and forefinger of his right hand. Robbo presses on.

'You've got men who've lost their jobs in the mines at Potosi, there are teachers, unemployed, all moving here to the Chapare, slashing and burning the forest and planting coca bushes where there's already about fifty thousand hectares under cultivation. It's massive overproduction and that's what's causing the prices to fall. You need a new market and that's in Europe, and I'm offering you a foolproof way into it.'

Lucho stands up. He's heard enough. He says something in Spanish to Frederico that Robbo does not understand then gestures for them to follow. His two bodyguards are to come, too, sidearms tucked into the backs of their jeans.

*

They're in a cellar beneath the basement of Lucho's house. He leads the way, for it is more like a bank vault – locks, keys, codes. It takes a moment for Robbo's eyes to adjust to the semi-darkness. The air gets chillier the deeper they go. Lucho opens a steel door for Frederico and Robbo to enter. His bodyguards wait outside.

The room is a concrete box, twelve feet square. Against the left-hand wall, a plain kitchen table. And on it is Lucho's monthly income from America – more than a cubic yard of US dollar bills. They are arranged in packs an inch thick in see-through plastic sleeves. No bill has a face value of less than five dollars. They were delivered by plane earlier that week.

'Christ,' Robbo says. 'How much is this?'

'I don't know, not yet,' Frederico says. 'But maybe this money serious enough for you, inglés?'

Robbo nods and grins and looks across at a second table opposite.

On it are calculators, ledgers, notebooks, a money-counting machine. But any likeness to clerkish accountancy ends there.

Taped to the wall above is a sequence of colour photographs, A4 size, taken at the same bend in a river. They show peasants watching the progress of several bodies floating down with the current. Some of the corpses are caught by rocks or in the branches of overhanging trees. On each body is crouched a vulture, ripping into the decomposing white flesh of its host. Every image is a visual reminder, a word to the wise, to whoever might be counting Lucho's money in this oubliette or anyone being shown the rules of engagement in his particular line of commerce.

'Loyalty is very important, inglés, don't you think?' Frederico says.

Before Robbo can reply, Lucho adds a little wisdom of his own.

'You give a pig a chair, he try and climb on your table.'

*

They emerge into daylight. The sun is still high and harsh. Later, it will slip behind the Andean mountains where evil spirits are said to dwell in the ravines and chasms beneath the snow line, three miles and more above. Lucho leads them towards the airstrip where his Huey is parked. Pilot and navigator hunker over a map in brown cotton fatigues, helmets upturned on the red earth beside them. Two gunners unload belts of dull brass bullets from a large tin box and feed them into the Huey's M60s.

They work silently, handsome men with proud, primitive faces and Donna Karan T-shirts and Patrick Cox loafers bought in Florida.

'Where are we going?' Robbo says.

'To see parts of Lucho's operation more closely.'

Robbo buckles himself in. The crew begin their instrument checks, flicking switches, marking charts. The blades of the Huey start to spin, slowly.

Its gunners squat with their legs either side of their fearsome, snouting guns. There are many enemies in the world they inhabit. But they joke between themselves. They have no fear and need their boss to know this. He sits with his back to the pilot and navigator. All is noise and oily heat. Robbo catches something quite alien in such a deadly, masculine machine. It's a drift of perfume, something cheap but feminine nonetheless.

He turns and sees the yellow-haired girl who'd served lunch being pushed onboard. Her spotted red dress has risen up her left arm. There are healed cut marks, an inch long, paler than the surrounding skin. She's a self-harmer. Robbo is puzzled by this. Why does she need to come on the trip?

She takes the seat next to Frederico, facing forward. The Huey's engine builds to a thumping whine. They lurch forward and are airborne, powering up until they are but a bobbing shadow on the canopy of the dark green jungle far below.

Robbo inclines his head to Frederico's.

'Does this mean our deal is on? I haven't even told Lucho about my route yet.'

'There is time for that,' Frederico says. 'First, you must pass a test.'

'Still suspicious of me, is he?'

'I have told you already, he is an instinctive man – he follows the feelings in his gut.'

'So he's not convinced I can open up Europe for him?'

'No, not yet, but I'm sure he could be.'

'But what if he isn't?'

Frederico manages a pitying smile.

'Then, inglés, maybe you will never suffer the indignities of old age.'

*

Robbo crept upstairs to Florence's bedroom where the window gave him an angled view across the concrete yard to a barn stacked with hay and a row of tumbledown tin sheds, scabby with rust.

The living wasn't easy on hill farms. They mended and made do. He peered from behind a curtain, plain blue and utilitarian like the utility wardrobe and brown chest of drawers where Florence moth-balled her clothes.

Robbo now saw the faces of his pursuers, those who'd only existed in his sixth sense until then. They were troopers, keen-eyed and attentive, following orders. Florence stood facing them, listening.

Rain drifted in with the mist from the mountains. It spilled from a broken gutter, dripped off the soldiers' tunics and the stubby little snouts of their submachine guns. Robbo was no stranger to these weapons – compact MP5s, perfect for close combat. So did that mean they were prepared to use lethal force to take him? But why, and on whose authority?

A strange, out-of-body feeling passed through him, of being absent yet present, as if what he was witnessing was someone else's life unravelling, coming to an end.

He felt cornered, weak, momentarily unsure about what was real, what was imagined. But he knew he must fight any urge to curl up on the eiderdown of Florence's bed and wait for her door to be kicked in.

Then he saw the soldiers turn around quickly. A tractor drew into the yard, an ancient Massey Ferguson, noisy and grey with bald tyres and a sheepdog yapping from a trailer. The driver had muddy overalls, boots tied at the ankles with baler twine and a sack around his shoulders to protect against the weather.

He jumped down from his seat, leaving the engine clattering away. Something had made him angry. He reached into the trailer for his rabbiting gun, an old bolt-action .410. The soldiers levelled their weapons as he came towards them, waving his gun above his head. Robbo heard the farmer loudly screaming at them in Welsh.

'*Be dech chi'r diawled yn gneud ar fy nhir i*?'

The soldiers looked confused.

'What the hell are you talking about?' one of them said.

'He wants to know what you devils are doing on his land,' Florence said.

'*Does gennych chi ddim hawl i fod'ma. Roes i ddim caniatad i fusnesa ar fy fferm.*'

'Calm down, sir. Just put your gun away then we can talk.'

119

'No,' said Florence. 'He won't calm down. He says you've no right being here, you've no permission to come snooping around his farm.'

'Tell him we're only doing our duty, just making some inquiries in the area.'

The farmer was getting more agitated, redder in the face. He started shouting again.

'*Rwan cer oddi yma a phaid a dod 'noi neu fe ddanfona i'r ci arnock chi.*'

'I think he's telling us to fuck off,' the soldier said.

'But more politely,' said Florence. 'And if you don't go, he'll set his dog on you.'

The soldiers nodded one to another. The farmer might be off his head, his gun loaded or not. If he put it to his shoulder, they could kill him in self-defence.

But that would expose their mission. Retreat was the smarter option. They kept him covered and walked towards the road, slowly, backwards.

Florence returned indoors. Robbo guided her into the parlour and sat with her. She said she was fine, didn't want a cup of tea. He asked what she'd told the soldiers.

'Nothing, I didn't get a chance. Emrys came to get some feed for his sheep before I could say anything.'

'He did seem pretty annoyed, didn't he?'

'Doesn't like the English, Emrys doesn't. Never has, bit of a Welsh nationalist, you see.'

Robbo smiled. But his was a problem postponed, not solved. Not yet.

'Florence, can I ask you... what were you going to say to the soldiers if he'd not arrived?'

She looked away and plucked an imaginary piece of fluff

from her apron.

'If they'd asked me about you, you mean?'

'Yes, about me.'

'I would have said I hadn't seen any strangers, I didn't know anything.'

'You'd have told a lie for me?'

'Yes, darling… but don't say anything to them down at the chapel.'

Robbo put an arm around Florence and drew her to him. He felt relief, of course. He knew now that she'd help him to escape. But greater than that was the salve of human contact, its undemanding innocence and its promise of a tomorrow he'd not been sure he would see.

14: CLUES

"Ars est celare artem.
The art is to conceal the art."

- Latin quotation

Some images have the power to haunt the subconscious, to inhabit those parts where fears go to hide, and so it was with Tilly Brown, walking up the ramp to the concourse of Euston station from the charcoal light of the platforms below, all noise and fumes from idling engines.

Her mind was in neutral, thoughts adrift between the demented stranger who'd once been her mother and her own unsatisfactory life and what, if anything, could be done about it. She and others newly arrived from Watford headed, herd-like, onto a concourse already stiff with thousands of would be passengers delayed by a signal failure.

Tilly was jostled onwards by people behind. They forced her ever deeper into the waiting crowd, which parted then quickly absorbed her into itself. Her claustrophobic dread of enclosed spaces took hold. She couldn't breathe. It felt like being dragged down in an airless cave of legs and shoes and suitcases. Then she blacked out.

*

'You all right, love?'

'Here, drink this. It's only water.'

'You'll be OK, just sit tight for a minute or two.'

Tilly stared up at a circle of kindly faces from a bench they'd cleared for her.

'I'm sorry—'

'Nothing to be sorry about, love. You just came over dizzy, that's all.'

*

Euston Road was cool and windy. She needed air, however polluted. Her bus arrived and she found a seat towards the back. There was still dirt on her coat from the fall and she'd be bruised the next day.

She knew exactly why she'd succumbed to panic, albeit the reason would probably only make sense to her. It was those photographs, the ones she'd assembled for the prosecutor's evidence bundles at an Old Bailey trial, not against ODCs – ordinary decent criminals – but IRA terrorists who'd blown up a department store.

They were scenes-of-crime pictures, unsparing images of those who'd been sacrificed to the gods of others: women buying skirts or scarves, returning an unwanted present, or just browsing until it was time for coffee and cake.

How pink our flesh, how pale our bones.

For Tilly Brown, these were graphic illustrations of life reduced to a throw of the dice. Decisions people took that morning – to have an early breakfast, to chat to a neighbour or not, to catch this tube, not that – were made without thought.

They weren't on a Roman road but one which could switch right or left on a whim and thereby continually change what happened next. Break the sequence at any point and it wouldn't be their blood pooling in the dust and debris.

But they didn't. So each mundane action led to that shop, that floor, that rucksack and the final blinding flash that tore apart everyone the Fates had contrived to put in its path.

Tilly knew it might so easily have been her. She often shopped there, could imagine hearing the sigh of a ghost being given up in the brief silence after the blast and seeing that hand reaching out from beneath a heap of garments, a hand with liver spots and raised blue veins and a wedding ring still shining till death us do part.

These photographs and all their malign detail burned in her mind. Terrorism terrorises. That is its function.

She came to dread large crowds in public places for we were all now enemies in a long and covert war. Her bus edged into the luminous night through rush-hour traffic. It began to rain, lightly but enough to lacquer the pavements of streets where, in some rented flat or a cheap hotel room, more bombers could be holed up, watching and planning, clammy with tension and a fear of informers and the SAS and of dying for their cause as they had condemned others to do.

*

The cat mewed to be fed the moment Tilly opened the front door. She collected her mail and monthly photographic magazine from the mat then hung her coat to dry above the hall radiator.

Supper was two slices of pastrami beef and an avocado salad eaten at a cluttered kitchen table as she read the *Evening Standard*. She drank iced water, not wine, conscious of holding her pre-menopausal figure in check.

All was vanity and conceit but she'd read her Vizinczey. A carefully conserved older woman held many attractions.

The *Standard* filled most of page five with what she'd seen on the lunchtime TV news at her mother's care home – a dramatic picture-story showing the huge Chinook hauling a smaller helicopter from a lake.

The helicopter that crashed in a North Wales reservoir, killing the Army Air Corps' only female pilot, Captain Virginia Hill, 28, was recovered in a major military operation today.

It was floated sixty feet to the surface then winched by Chinook onto a flatbed lorry. Captain Hill was on an exercise from a base in Northern Ireland.

The wreckage of her Gazelle will be taken to Boscombe Down for Ministry of Defence experts to investigate how it came to ditch in the water. An MoD spokesman said mechanical failure, not terrorism, was the more likely cause. Captain Hill had been due to be reassigned to Germany. An Army spokesman said she was a talented and experienced pilot and her death was a tragic loss.

Amen, thought Tilly Brown. She shivered, projecting her private terrors into the pilot's final moments, trapped in her aircraft, now as broken-backed as her body must have been.

The cat leapt onto the draining board to lick the sink's dripping tap. She would normally shoo him off but it didn't seem to matter that evening. Tilly went to the cellar instead and set up her darkroom equipment to print enlargements of her pictures from Scotland – those she'd snatched of the enigmatic Robbo.

She stood in the subdued red light, waiting. Seeing a picture or a face slowly appear in the developing tray as the bromide swilled over the photographic paper always fascinated her. It was a sort of magic, the summoning up of a memory from nowhere to preserve it, to make it real once more until it, too, fades. Robbo emerged... those cautious eyes, his hair blowing in the chopper's downdraught, the canvas bag he'd carried so tightly, thrown on board.

Tilly pegged the blow-up to dry. It was at head-height so she could look straight at it. In so doing, her lawyerly instinct to check small details took over. And one in particular caught her eye.

On the helicopter's tail close to the rear rotor, was its number: XV648. That combination of letters and numbers registered with her, and so it would. She'd seen it barely an hour before.

She hurried back upstairs for her *Evening Standard*. There was the photograph of the crashed helicopter being pulled from the lake.

And on the tail was its number: XV648. Her helicopter and the dead pilot's were one and the same.

So many thoughts came into Tilly's head. She already knew she must have photographed the helicopter on the same afternoon as the accident. But nothing had been reported in the paper about a passenger being killed.

Robbo could only have been dropped off somewhere between Scotland and Wales. Should she phone him, book another few days' trekking in the wilds and say how relieved she was that he'd had such an incredibly lucky escape?

Or maybe post him a copy of the enlargement with a note sufficiently intriguing to have him call her? Either way, she had a perfect excuse to renew contact.

She was about to return to the darkroom when her front doorbell rang. It was gone seven o'clock. No one was expected, or wanted. She peered down the hallway and behind the door's glass panels, could make out the silhouette of a man.

*

In another house in another place, it was the telephone that rang. Chris Moreley went to answer. If it was the news organiser in London with some damn fool tip about Shergar pulling a milk float in Barnsley, they could fuck off. He was fraying at the edges after working six days – and most nights – without a break and was only just about clinging onto the wagon.

He and Angela rented a semi on an estate of executive homes in Cheshire where streets were named after dead artists and populated by couples who were dull even when drunk. They drove company cars, played golf and made remarks like 'cash flow is king'. There wasn't a second paragraph in any of them.

Their Pinot Grigio would doubtless be as palatable as the next guy's but Moreley's post-clinic determination to stay dry was reason enough to feign a contagious illness should anyone else in Holbein Way invite them round for drinkies.

'Yep, Chris here.'

'Ah, Mr Moreley. Good to hear your voice.'

'I'm sorry, who is this?'

'It's Eamon… you remember Eamon, don't you?'

'Of course, but his voice is nothing like yours.'

'No, well that's because I'm the new Eamon. He's moved on and I'm his replacement.'

'Fascinating, but why are you ringing me? What do you want?'

'Just to check that you and your wife are still going out tonight.'

'Are you lot listening in to me again because if you are—'

'Come, Christian, only doing my job. We've got something for you, a bit last-minute but we think you'll be able to find a good home for it.'

'But I'm going out tonight—'

'Yes, Chinatown, the Peking Garden, we know that, so we can see you there.'

'No, don't do that, don't show out in front of my wife.'

'It's all right, we'll wait till you go to the gents.'

'I don't have a choice, do I?'

'Oh, but we do, Mr Moreley. The choice is always to do what's in our best interest.'

The phone went dead. Moreley closed his eyes, shook his head in impotent anger. But Eamon was the piper and this was just another tune.

He looked around but knew he'd find more booze in a temperance hotel than in his living room. Angela shouted down from the bedroom to ask who'd been on the phone.

'No one, nothing important,' he said. 'Are you nearly ready? Table's booked for eight.'

'I'm coming, you get the car out and I'll be right with you.'

They drove into central Manchester with barely a word between them.

'You are going to cheer up a bit, aren't you?' Angela said. 'It is my birthday, you know.'

'Yeah, sorry. Something's on my mind, but it'll be OK, we'll have a good night.'

They'd tapped him up fifteen years before, in the mid-seventies. He was crime reporting in Fleet Street then, matching cops pint for pint because that came easy.

Someone must have talent-spotted him at a promotion party. He got a call in the office next day.

'There's a wine bar down at the end of Villiers Street by Charing Cross station,' the voice had said. 'It's called Gordon's. Get there about seven tonight and I'll have something useful to tell you.'

The caller was a lowland Scot, his accent gentle, his manner assured.

'Don't get me wrong,' Moreley said, 'but newspapers are always getting calls from cranks who say they know who shot the sheriff. You need to tell me who you are.'

'I'm just someone who could help you in your work.'

'In what way could you help me?'

'With access to information that's not in the public domain, the sort of stuff our elders and betters would rather keep quiet.'

'Is that so? Well, give me an example.'

'All right, if you wish. I can tell you that the security services—'

'MI5?'

'Yes, them, they keep a file on our prime minister, Mr Wilson.'

'They've got files on every MP. They start them the moment they're elected.'

'Yes, but Wilson's is filed under the name of Harold Worthington. That's not terribly original I know but Wilson thinks the security services are plotting against him so access to this file is highly restricted and only allowed where it's kept in Sir Michael Hanley's office.'

'I know the name but who's he?'

'He's the director general, the chief spook.'

'OK, this is all very interesting but why would you talk to me about it?'

'You're a journalist, aren't you? Aren't you supposed to cultivate sources?'

'When I know who they are, yes,' Moreley said.

'Then think of me as a conduit, a back channel.'

'But if you're really in a position to know about Wilson's file then you'll have signed the Official Secrets Act so I don't understand why you'd take a risk in talking to a newspaper reporter like me who you don't even know if you can trust.'

'If I may say so, you'd be far better off concerning yourself with what's in this for you, not worrying about me.'

Thus, Moreley met the first of three men he only ever knew by their code name: Eamon. But as there was no such thing as a free lunch, any hack partial to the products of the Rhone Valley should have known he'd be singing by suppertime. To misquote a line from Dylan's My Back Pages, he was so much younger then but wiser than that now.

*

'Hello, I know I'm not expected so forgive me, but I simply

130

had to come and apologise for my rather tipsy behaviour the other night.'

It was Champagne Charlie, Tilly's neighbour and would-be suitor from the far end of the street, delivering flowers and chocolates and a word-perfect little speech he must have rehearsed.

'That's very kind, thank you,' she said. 'But you really shouldn't have bothered.'

'I would hate for you to think ill of me.'

'I don't think ill of you.'

'I took a drink on an empty stomach that night, not a good idea.'

'Parties are parties. No bones broken as far as I am concerned.'

He smiled, said he was sorry once more, then made to leave her doorstep. Tilly went along with the act. He'd clearly bought the gifts after work then gone home and changed into what, for him, would be casual clothes – light tan leather jacket, blue shirt and jeans in which an unfashionable crease had been ironed.

'Look, do come in, have a coffee or something.'

'Are you sure?'

'The place is a tip so you'll have to take me as you find me.'

'There's absolutely no need to make any excuses, honestly, no need at all.'

Maybe he was fifty, pinkish cheeks and crinkly laugh-lines around eyes with bags so fleshy that no haemorrhoid cream would ever shift them. She led him into her front room and moved last Sunday's papers from the settee.

'Right, what would you like? I've decaf coffee, Earl Grey,

or there's wine, red or white.'

'Well, if you're having one, I'll have a glass of red, thank you.'

She was halfway out of the room when she turned back.

'Look, I'm so sorry but I don't know your name. Isn't that awful?'

'No, of course not. I'm Giles Worth, really pleased to meet you, and properly this time.'

'And I'm Tilly. Good to meet you, too.'

They both smiled and she returned a minute later with a bottle of Châteauneuf-du-Pape, two glasses and a corkscrew.

*

To enter Gordon's Wine Bar was to return to a vanished London, an underground drinking den that Dickens would have recognised, haunt of actors and theatre people, writers and trysting lovers whispering in the candlelight until their cover stories ran out of time and those they betrayed expected them home.

This sweaty, smoky, crepuscular setting, walls plastered with newspapers from the Great War onwards, was also favoured for other discreet assignations: those between detectives from the Special Branch and their snouts. It was too dark to see whatever was transpiring between shadowy figures in a barrel-ceilinged area cut from the bedrock alongside the Thames.

Moreley stood near the better-lit bar that night, making sure he could be seen. He'd walked to Charing Cross, still puzzling over his caller's motives. Of all the hacks in Fleet Street, why him? No one knew about the approach. It might still be a con and he'd no wish to look gullible and naive to the news desk. Enemies were never in short supply in Fleet Street.

He got to Gordon's early, had a couple of glasses on his own. Booze he could take; a joint made him puke. Drink gave him an inner confidence, that fuck-off-I'm-better-than-you feeling he needed to survive. He hadn't been found out yet.

Some old down-table sub once cornered him and asked why an alcoholic was like a vampire. Moreley said he didn't know. Back came the reply: because neither can see themselves in the mirror.

If there was a funny side to this bit of hard-won wisdom, he didn't get it, nor would he until it wasn't a laughing matter any more.

Moreley wanted another wine – his third. It would've been cheaper to buy a bottle. The man in front was ordering a glass of house white and a platter of cheese – mature Cheddar with a black wax coating. He had a mild Scottish accent and a pleasant, engaging manner with the woman who served him. So this was his caller.

He turned and gave Moreley a slight nod of recognition and made his way to the dark end of the bar. What was a hack to do but follow?

15: TEMPTATION

"Now tell us all about the war,
and what they fought each other for."

- Robert Southey, 1774–1843

On the night before his daughter's funeral, the Reverend Hill had her coffin wheeled down the nave of All Hallows on a bier built in the workshop of the undertaker's family firm in the 1880s. She would remain in front of the altar, lit only by candles and watched over by her father, until the dark gave way to the dawn.

Grief would displace anger in its own time, for no amount of self-loathing could atone for the life he'd lived and what had become secondary in the process.

He sat within touching distance of her casket, limed oak with brass fittings. To his right, the roundels of the south window depicting the implements of Christ's torture – scourge, hammer, spear. Above him on the chancel arch, the portrait of the unknown holy man painted in a time of martyrs, his face as anguished as his likeness below.

Ralph Hill's vigil was a meditation on the nature of suffering. He could have prayed to God for comfort but didn't. He'd tried this when his wife lay on the same bier as their daughter now. But guilt was no more susceptible to divine intervention than cancer. It had to be borne alone.

*

He walks down the steps from the cool confines of the aeroplane into the wrap-around warmth of a South African afternoon. Two stewardesses wait at the bottom, smiling, pointing him towards the terminal building.

His thanks are expressed with exaggerated politeness. Here is an Englishman abroad, a model of clerical rectitude, above all suspicion.

'You must think like an actor giving a performance on the stage,' Bolund had told him.

'Or a clergyman in the pulpit.'

'Yes, if you believe in your character, that he is real, then so will your audience believe.'

In Ralph Hill's left hand is the bible he'd read during the flight; in his right, a briefcase with his passport, a history of the Boer War, a letter of introduction to a senior figure in the Dutch Reformed Church and various samizdat articles on religious repression in the Soviet Union. These are but props. The wad of banknotes he's to deliver are in a body belt. His suitcase is one of the last to appear on the carousel. He wonders why and tries not to infer anything from this. Ahead is passport control.

An obese, unsmiling man sits in a glass booth by a terminal linked to the National Intelligence Service computer. If the Reverend Ralph Hill has ever come to notice, his name will flash on the screen like those of anti-apartheid supporters, communists, foreign journalists or

135

anyone else whose thoughts, words and deeds might subvert white rule and thus warrant surveillance.

'Good afternoon, sir. What is the purpose of your visit to South Africa?'

'I'm on a short holiday, just a few days.'

'Have you friends or family here?'

'No, I haven't, but I'm hoping to meet some fellow churchmen.'

'For any particular reason, sir?'

'Well, I suppose South Africa's always in the news so I want to be better able to explain the situation from a religious perspective to my own congregation when I go home.'

'Yes, do that but just you make sure you tell the truth about us, you understand?'

The officer stamps Ralph Hill's passport. He passes along a corridor from airside to the public meeting area. The secret police will be watching him – and every new arrival – from behind windows with one-way glass.

A man stands before the exit. They make eye contact. It's as if he's been waiting for him.

'Step this way, please,' he says.

'Is there something wrong?'

'No, it's just a random check.'

Ralph Hill is led to a side room. The door is closed behind them. A second man stands by a table. Neither is in uniform. He thinks they must be detectives.

'Open your bag, please.'

'Yes, of course, but you know it's already been through Customs, don't you?'

'Your bag, sir. The briefcase, not the suitcase.'

He does as requested. The contents are spread over the

table, the pages of the book and bible flicked through, the anti-Soviet propaganda noted. Then all is returned to the briefcase. He isn't searched. His body belt is not found.

'Is that it?' Ralph Hill says. 'Can I go now?'

'Yes, thank you for your patience. Enjoy your holiday.'

*

Bolund had briefed the Reverend Hill to be in the ground floor lounge of the Empire Hotel in Hillbrow at ten thirty each morning for his first few days in Johannesburg.

'Someone will approach you once we're sure you're not being watched,' he'd said.

'How will I know it's the right person?'

'Because he will ask you where you are from, you will tell him then he will ask you something about the Mappa Mundi in the cathedral in Hereford.'

'Couldn't I just give him or someone else the money without all this intrigue?'

'You're not getting nervous, are you?'

'Maybe a little, but I'm concerned that what we're doing is all a little over elaborate.'

'Mr Hill, we are engaged in a guerrilla war. We have to be as cautious as the enemy is cunning and vicious.'

He'd nodded and dismissed his second thoughts.

'So what will happen when this man makes contact?'

'He will give you some more instructions, which you must follow.'

The Empire Hotel is a short walk from where he is staying in a family-run guest house. The owners are white and sycophantic, the maids black and deferential. They address

137

him as master and try as he might, he cannot persuade them to do otherwise.

No one makes contact on the first day. He takes coffee and waits almost two hours, reading – with mounting anger – the Johannesburg Star's account of more brutal conflict in South Africa's border war with Namibia. Yet again, more blacks will die fighting for their independence from the apartheid state.

He returns to the Empire the next morning, through a crowded street market, breathing in the foreign scents of pawpaw and aubergines, pomegranates, marrows and sweet peppers being sold, others discarded and trampled underfoot. Hillbrow is noisy, vibrant, colourful, a neighbourhood where language and boisterous culture collide. But it can sometimes be dangerous. The desperate and the damned hustle hereabouts – unemployed migrants, drunks, knots of emaciated addicts stinking of piss and vomit, eyes blank yet able to seek out the weak and the vulnerable, for on them does existence depend.

He takes the same table at the Empire. The lounge is busy but the black waiter remembers him from yesterday and the decent tip he left.

He comes across with coffee on a silver tray and bows as he backs away. Ralph Hill feels uncomfortable in his white skin, by the presumed entitlement of his race.

'Is anyone sitting here?'

The Reverend Hill stares up from his newspaper. The man in front of him is in his fifties and looks ill. His face is creased and papery, yellow like old newsprint, his dark polyester suit hanging on him, a size too big.

'No, please sit, be my guest.'

The man nods his thanks. He waves to the waiter who takes his order for a glass of amasi. It looks like liquid yogurt and smells of cheese.

'Forgive me for asking,' Ralph Hill says, 'but what is that drink?'

'Amasi? Got a lot of vitamins and minerals in it, helps the immune system.'

'Sounds very healthy. I must try it.'

'You do that, man. They say it puts muscles in your spit.'

His Afrikaner accent is harsh; his consonants come out hard. *Man* becomes men and *spit*, speat. The Reverend Hill returns to his newspaper. His companion lights a cigarette. The first two fingers on his right hand are stained smoky brown from nicotine. He coughs into a white handkerchief and looks at what he's expelled.

'So where are you from, vicar? You from London?'

'Not London but England, yes.'

'I've never been there, too expensive. You on church business here?'

'No, more of a holiday, really.'

'The weather's not so hot right now. It'll be our winter soon.'

'Well, whatever it's like, I don't suppose it'll be as cold and wet as a British winter.'

'That's a fact for sure, man. What's the place where you're from in England?'

'You mean where I live? It's near Hereford. Do you know of it?'

'I've heard of it. Isn't that where there's that old map of the world, the Mappa Mundi?'

'In Hereford Cathedral, yes.'

Ralph Hill's smile of covert recognition is only partially returned.

'Welcome, comrade,' the stranger says.

'The pleasure's mine, I can assure you.'

'Look, time's not on my side. You've got a letter of introduction to a guy from the local church?'

'Yes, that's right.'

'So here's what you do. Go back to your guest house, phone him and see him this afternoon. The secret police'll be listening so this'll keep up your cover story.'

'I understand.'

'But be back here in the lounge by six o'clock, no later.'

'Will you be here?'

'No, but my boss will.'

'Right, who is that?'

'The man who just served us our drinks.'

'The waiter... you mean he's in on all this?'

'More than you can imagine.'

'So what should I do at six o'clock?'

'That's when he's off duty. He'll leave by the main door. You just follow discreetly but don't wear your clerical collar. Play the tourist and he'll lead you to where you must be.'

'What's his name? Can you tell me that?'

'Abraham. Brave guy. Disowned by his family.'

'Why have they done that if he's fighting for such a righteous cause?'

'He can never be honest about what he's doing, it'd be too dangerous for them and for him. They think he's a traitor who's sold out to the whites.'

'You mean he's leading a parallel life? That must involve considerable risks.'

'Let me put it this way: if a man in perfect health can be taken into a police station in this country but for reasons no one can explain, he becomes ill as he's being questioned, so ill in fact that he has to leave in a coffin, then yes, Abraham's life does involve some risks.'

*

Night falls suddenly in the southern hemisphere. Dusk doesn't linger. One moment there is a blood orange sunset then above the bush and scattered kraals, in wild places untouched by time, stars start to gleam, sewn into the threads of heaven, and fragments of cosmic debris shoot across the milky-blue galaxy for an instant and are no more.

But in high-rise commercial cities like Johannesburg, the night sky is obscured, washed in an unnatural sodium glow from all the street lights, office blocks, shopping malls, factories and apartments in the teeming streets below.

And those within, those who toil like termites in a mound, are confined to their ordained places by the inverted logic of a system where violent oppression is the policy of the state but resistance to it is terrorism.

Ralph Hill keeps this in mind, no more than fifteen paces behind Abraham, a slight figure in a pale green singlet and jeans, never a conventional warrior, never important enough to be remembered by those for whom he fetches and carries at the Empire Hotel.

He is a fighter of a different order. This would condemn him in the eyes of the minister from the Dutch Reformed Church Ralph Hill had met that afternoon.

'Unfairness is to be found in every society,' he'd said. 'I

141

doubt that Jesus thought that revolution was the means to bring about a just society. Good Christians are unwise to involve themselves in politics.'

He'd meant black Christians but didn't need to say this in terms. Thus, his church remains blind to the central, sinful injustices of political and economic exploitation on which the regime it upholds is founded. Abraham moves through the shifting crowds of Hillbrow, a fish in a sea of others, past the Friendship Supermarket and brightly lit liquor stores, by the buyers and sellers of shoes and second-hand clothes under canvas stalls.

Here and there are sweaty little bars throbbing and thumping with dance music and never once does he turn around to make sure the English priest is keeping up. There are bananas and apples in the plastic bag he carries. His identity card is in his back pocket in case the police stop and search him. But he and everything about him is in order. A quiet, quiescent black man, respectably employed, law-abiding.

Then he disappears from view without warning. Did he go into a store or cross the street? Ralph Hill walks faster, looking everywhere, gripped by a sudden panic. His concentration must have lapsed momentarily. He's on his own, a white man with a fortune strapped round his waist where street robbery is commonplace. Bolund said he'd be shadowed, so where are his minders?

He pushes through women dragging tired children by the hand and languid young men in groups, smoking and drinking beer from bottles. Car horns blare out at jaywalkers, a huge truck delivering Coca Cola blocks the intersection.

He feels his arm being tugged and spins around, fearing a

mugger.

'This way, comrade.'

It's a teenage girl, hair braided with multi-coloured beads, smile full of reassurance.

'Abraham is in the pharmacy. Go, he waits for you.'

And there he stands, at the far end of the counter. Ralph Hill moves closer and sees Abraham holding the 'staff only' door open for him. They climb a flight of concrete stairs. Someone is waiting at the top. It's a woman, white, well-spoken, sounding more English than Afrikaans.

'Welcome,' she says. 'In here, quickly.'

They step inside a storeroom-cum-office. Its shelves are loaded with boxes of medicines, pills, toiletries. It all smells of pink ointment remembered from childhood. There is a desk. The woman leans against it, arms folded. She's 44/45, thick chestnut brown hair showing a little grey, wearing a chemist's white coat, unbuttoned over a pleated blue skirt and a pale satin blouse.

'So you're the Reverend Hill, with us at last,' she says. 'I'm delighted to meet you.'

She has flecked brown eyes and a fine facial bone structure that will maintain her strikingly handsome looks well into old age.

'I'm Bella Venter,' she says. 'You have my personal thanks for all you're doing for us.'

The Reverend Ralph Hill knows full well that he has a wife at home, a daughter in the British Army and that as a minister of religion, should never entertain such thoughts as are passing through his mind at this moment.

But he is a man and they do, and from then on, his soul is lost and cannot be saved.

16: WATCHING

"Ab hoc momento pendet aeternitas.
On this moment hangs eternity."

\-   Motto

Florence Rossiter was unlikely to have known the Italian word *dietrologia*, conveying the need to examine what truly lies behind that which is said, especially in official versions of events. It's also doubtful that the African term *ubuntu*, describing the nature of virtuous humanity, was often heard in the isolated hill country of North Wales where she lived.

But after Robbo fell at her door like an exhausted bird, blown off course and injured, both could have meaning for her.

Why had she felt suspicious of what she was told by the soldiers who came looking for him with guns? Why was she not afraid of the stranger whose hurts were unexplained and of whose story she knew little and could find out less?

Whether she recognised it or not, the reason lay in her affinity with outsiders, for those caught up in the winds of conflict – as she had been – and set down in a distant place, damaged and alone.

Florence had known loss and struggle yet found a way out of despair. She was prepared to help Robbo but wished he'd open up about who and what he was.

'Are you a soldier?' she'd asked. 'Is that why those Army men came for you?'

'I can't tell you, Florence. I'm sorry, I really am.'

'But you must have some idea, darling.'

'It's better this way... safer all round.'

He'd not be drawn further, wouldn't even say if he had a wife and family or where he came from, though she thought his accent slightly Scottish. Florence had the wit to know to leave him be, for he had greater concerns on his mind now.

'They'll be back, those men,' he said. 'I can't stay here, I've got to get away.'

The soldiers had all but housed him. He knew they'd be out there somewhere, dug in, watching. A plan was forming in his head.

But for it to succeed, an elderly spinster without even a parking ticket to blacken her name had to break the law and assist an offender. If she didn't play her part in his subterfuge, he'd be cornered by those who wanted him dead.

*

The *Daily Mail's* new night lawyer leaned back, shoes on his untidy desk, and read the next day's page-three lead.

'Interesting story... not overburdened with any named sources though, is it?'

'But nothing wrong with it legally, is there?' the news editor said.

'Not legally, no, but I sometimes worry about stories that have to be taken on trust.'

'You'll get used to it. The guy behind this never lets us

down.'

'Who is he, just to set my mind at rest?'

'He's a reporter.'

'One of yours or a freelance?'

'Neither, he's with the BBC.'

'Then why isn't he doing it for them?'

'That's it, you see. The Beeb can get a bit twitchy over stories like this.'

'But it's an exclusive, isn't it?'

'Yeah, but it's about spooks and terrorists.'

'So?'

'So there's no one to go on mic so he pitches stuff to us first and if it checks out, one of our blokes writes it then our mate piles in with all his other background for the Beeb.'

'And you've done this before and it's not come back to bite you?'

'Never. Everyone's a winner.'

*

The call came after breakfast as Kat Walsh packed to leave her temporary quarters in the Lake Vyrnwy Hotel. This part of the job was over; the caravan had moved on. There was nothing more to see there. The trackers had a bead on Robbo so she must now link up with them.

But Sir Frazer Harris demanded a sit-rep first. He rang from a payphone in his gentlemen's club, the East India, in the elegant building in St James's from where the Prince Regent announced Wellington's victory at Waterloo in 1815.

Life in Westminster had imbued Sir Frazer with nothing if not suspicion and wariness. He'd had an unexpected lunch invitation from a new club member who, coincidentally, now worked for his replacement as Secretary of State for Defence. Sir Frazer did not want any shocks to upset his digestion while dining with a civil servant whose motives he didn't yet know.

'You've been keeping me in the dark, young lady,' he said. 'I won't have it, do you hear?'

'That's not the case, sir. We're making good progress and you'll be hearing about it.'

'Like what, for instance?'

'I'm sorry but I can't go into detail, not on this. It's an open line.'

'That's as may be, but I'm picking up whispers from my contacts.'

'What sort of whispers, sir?'

'About this outside police inquiry that's going on, those unsolved cases over the water.'

'Anything specific that's concerning you?'

'The whole bloody thing concerns me and it should be terrifying you lot.'

'Go on, tell me why.'

'You've got a leak, must have.'

'I doubt that very much, sir.'

'And I'm telling you, these outside investigators, they're homing in on your man on the run.'

'Sir, we're taking care of that situation. Believe me.'

'You need to because these bastards are digging away, demanding records and God knows what else.'

'Our files have been well tended, that much I know.'

'They better be because good people could end up behind bars if they're not.'

'It won't come to that, sir.'

'And that's supposed to reassure me, is it?'

'With respect, we've got eyes on the suspect even as I speak to you.'

'You have? And that's definite, is it, not more of your bullshit?'

'Yes, it is. I'm just about to join that part of the operation myself.'

'Then make damn sure you put this matter to bed. Are you with me, young lady?'

'Of course, sir, yes,' Kat said.

Beyond her window, the black lake stretched far into the distance under lumbering clouds, as grey as Welsh slate, filling the air with the smell of rain.

Sir Frazer-bloody-Harris could swing in the wind a while longer. She would cover him but only so far as it protected her. He wasn't to be trusted, and not just because he was driven by self-interest. That was the way of all politicians. The good knight did not need to know that the watchers had been in contact. The old lady was on the move. They'd bugged her car with a tracker. She was driving across country, probably towards Shrewsbury, forty miles away.

Kat paid her hotel bill and set out for there, too. She hoped Sir Frazer had read his *Daily Mail*, sitting in a plush armchair beneath portraits of illustrious men in the home-from-home that was the East India Club.

And were it ever necessary, its attentive staff would doubtless provide a bowl of water to wash his hands of the grubby business of carrying out his wishes.

The Mail had other loyal readers, too. Florence Rossiter was one of them. She would buy a copy later that day and see from a photograph how beautiful Virginia Hill had been and read how tragic her death was. Such a pity she'd never come across the word *dietrologia*.

*

IRA terrorists did sabotage the military helicopter that crashed in a lake last month killing poster girl pilot, Captain Virginia Hill, 28.

A confidential report seen by the Daily Mail overturns earlier suggestions that her Gazelle suffered a catastrophic mechanical failure while she flew solo on an exercise over Wales. Investigators now say shrapnel found embedded in Captain Hill's helmet could only have come from a bomb.

'The force and direction of this damage is consistent with an explosion, not a malfunction, in the aircraft,' they concluded.

An urgent security review is now underway at the Army Air Corps base in Aldergrove near Belfast to establish how the IRA was able to get access to Captain Hill's helicopter and plant their bomb.

'This is a highly embarrassing failure,' according to a Daily Mail intelligence source in Northern Ireland.

'The shrapnel came from the gearbox above and behind the pilot's seat,' according to the report by air accident investigators at Boscombe Down, where the wrecked helicopter was taken after being winched out of Lake Vyrnwy in Powys. They suggest the device was quite small, maybe made from a watch with a timer, a battery and a detonator or a blasting cap, placed near the main fuel line.

An ex-Special Forces officer told the Daily Mail that such a device was easy to make.

'But hidden in the right place, it can cause devastating consequences as in this case.'

Captain Hill was the AAC's only female pilot and had starred in recruiting drives to attract more female recruits. She was unmarried and the only child of controversial peace campaigner, the Reverend Ralph Hill. Her funeral will be held today at his parish church in Herefordshire.

It's understood her father has refused to allow the burial to take place with any military overtones. A parishioner said, 'It's doubly ironic that a father so against militarism should not only have a daughter in the Army but then lose her in this terrible way.'

*

'OK, ma'am, still got eyes on the car.'

'Target Two still inside the building?'

'Affirmative. Twenty minutes now.'

'Any chance of accessing the vehicle?'

'Negative. Parked by a window. People working inside.'

'What's she doing in there?'

'No idea. It's a kids hospice.'

'We still think Target One's in the car, do we?'

'If he is, he can only be in the boot.'

'So he might never have left his hideaway?'

'Doubtful. We've been inside since Target Two left and there's no sign of a visitor.'

'And the outbuildings?'

'Ditto.'

'So he has to be in the car?'

'That's favourite but who knows?'

Kat stood on the top deck of a multistorey car park, plumbed into secure Army comms and looking down into the swirling muddy eddies of the Severn coiling, noose-like, around the half-timbered town of Shrewsbury.

'You there, ma'am?'

'Something happening?'

'Target Two's coming out... on foot... not going to the car.'

'You with her?'

'Affirmative... walking towards a street called... wait one... Frankwell.'

'Got it... leads up to the river.'

'Approaching a bridge over the river... making to turn left into... Smithfield Road.'

'She'll be coming towards me, then.'

'No... wait one... Target Two's crossing the road... to a street called... Mardol. Got that?'

'Yep... I'm heading there... not far... OK, I've got visual.'

'So you'll take it now?'

'Affirmative. You stick with the car.'

At a distance, Florence could pass for a farmer's wife, shopping in town as she haggled at market. At close quarters, she was an elderly woman with Caribbean heritage, dressed in a shabby green overcoat buttoned to the neck, brown ankle boots and a red cloche hat that would've been fashionable in the fifties.

Kat crossed Mardol and stared into a shop selling pottery and gifts to watch Florence reflected in the window, passing behind her.

Target Two carried on up the street. Kat stayed twenty yards behind and saw Florence enter the NatWest Bank. She reported in to the watchers.

'Target Two's drawing out cash… a wad of the stuff, tens and twenties.'

Florence put the notes in her purse and walked outside. It was starting to rain. She walked more quickly and made towards a pedestrianised street of department stores.

But she didn't stop at any of them. Kat got ahead of her, stood out of the worsening weather in the entrance to a jewellers and waited. What was the bloody woman up to?

The watchers couldn't be deployed much longer. Hereford would want them back. She needed a result, and quickly. Florence came nearer. Kat had to stifle the urge to grab her by the lapels and demand to know where the hell Robbo was.

*

Florence, head down against the rain, mind elsewhere, was starting to wonder if she'd done the right thing. Last night, it had seemed like an act of Christian charity to help a stranger in distress for reasons he wouldn't explain but which, if she was honest, were mysterious and exciting.

Nothing like this had ever happened to her. She'd not slept, worrying if she could carry off the secret role he'd persuaded her to play. With the dawn came more doubts, a fear of the unknown and the consequences of trusting a man who didn't trust her – not fully, anyway.

'Is what you've done very bad, Mr Robbo?' she'd asked him.

'It's best if I don't answer that.'

'But it would be the truth and they say it's the truth that sets you free.'

'No, Florence, in my case the truth would do exactly the opposite.'

She sensed his growing detachment, his uncompromising determination to outwit whoever was pursuing him.

'Would you go to prison for whatever it is you've done?'

'The state can turn on its own, Florence, when a sacrifice is needed to appease the gods.'

She'd looked puzzled, didn't – couldn't – understand his answer to a simple question.

'But will the police come here? Will they be next at my door?'

'I think that's unlikely.'

'Yet those soldiers came after you, didn't they, darling?'

'Yes they did, but those behind them will want to keep things in-house, under their control.'

She'd looked at him with disquieted eyes.

'I am what I've become and I've only got you to help me to get to where I have to be.'

'And where is that, Mr Robbo?'

'Again, forgive me, but it's best you don't know.'

So now she was in Shrewsbury with a list of items he'd asked her to buy with money he didn't have and for a purpose he wouldn't reveal.

*

Rain bounced up off the slicked black cobbles in front of Shrewsbury Station, built by the early Victorians more in the style of an Oxford college than a place to catch a train.

It had leaded lights and mullioned windows with carved stone heads either side of each. And into this fake Tudor building went Florence Rossiter, face drawn and anxious.

Kat kept up her commentary for the watchers.

'Target Two entering the station... she's in the ticket queue.'

'What if she gets a train?'

'I'll busk it.'

'Where's Target Two going?'

'I'm by the door, can't hear her... wait one... she's paying cash... she's leaving.'

'To catch a train?'

'No, thank fuck. To go back into town.'

Kat made a half-turn so Florence couldn't see her face. Newly decanted passengers sheltered under the veranda. Water cascaded from a blocked gutter.

Taxis left and arrived but Florence stayed put. Kat took a gamble and moved alongside Target Two.

'Can you believe this weather? Awful, isn't it?'

'Yes, it's getting worse,' Florence said. 'They said it'd be like this on the forecast.'

'You've just arrived, have you?'

'No, I've been getting a ticket.'

'Ah, lucky you, getting away somewhere warmer and dryer than this, I hope.'

'No, just to Scotland, seeing an old friend but not till next week.'

'Have you got far to get home now?'

'Yes, quite a distance. Over in Wales, that's where I am.'

'That's where I'm going. Where do you actually live?'

'You'll never have heard of it but it's near Lake Vyrnwy if that means anything to you.'

'What a coincidence, that's where I'm staying, in the hotel there.'

'I know the hotel well enough. It's lovely. I had a meal there once.'

'So are you just sheltering or waiting for someone to pick you up?'

'No, I have a car but it's on the other side of the river. I've got some shopping to do first.'

'Me too. Let's hope we don't get drowned doing it.'

Kat stepped slightly away from Florence to search her bag for something she knew wasn't there. She now had a direct connection to Robbo's guardian angel. She'd bet the farm that the train ticket was for him to get back to Dumfries. Moments like this were almost sexual to Kat. She luxuriated in intrigue – intrigue and conspiracy that fed on themselves in the darkness of their immaculate conception, for darkness was all they needed to thrive.

'I've made contact with Target Two... the line's open but don't transmit to me. OK?'

'Affirmative, ma'am.'

*

An hour later, Kat watched Florence leave a charity shop then walk down a narrow alley of medieval buildings with huge oaken frames, raised in the time of Henry IV to house butchers and fishmongers and families who threw shit from their jettied rooms into the offal in the street below. Now, it was coffee shops and little boutiques selling knickers and perfumes and dresses for brides.

The sun came and went through leaden clouds bringing more rain. Florence turned right into Fish Street, lugging two bags of shopping up a flight of worn stone steps to shelter in a café. Kat gave her a couple of minutes then followed.

She bought coffee at the counter then caught Florence's eye as she looked around for a table.

'Oh, hello again,' Kat said. 'Do you mind if I join you?'

'Of course not. You look very wet.'

'I got caught in that fresh downpour.'

'I thought you'd be on your way to Lake Vyrnwy by now.'

'Ah, I wish. No, I've hit a problem.'

'What's happened?'

Kat said that the car of a friend who'd promised to meet her had a flat battery.

'What a nuisance. Will you have to get a taxi?'

'Between you and me, a taxi would cost me more than I can afford, going all that way.'

'Oh dear, I don't think there are any buses that go there from here.'

Kat sipped her coffee, waiting – hoping – for Florence to take the bait. But she didn't.

'Forgive my brass neck but can I beg a lift with you? I'll pay something towards the petrol.'

'You don't have to, my dear. I'm going there anyway so I'd be happy to take you.'

'Really? That's so kind, I'm so grateful,' Kat said. 'Have we got time for me to get us another coffee? The cakes look nice, too. Would you like one?'

*

156

They walked through intermittent showers to Florence's car, parked a mile away.

'I'll dump my pack in the boot,' Kat said.

'You don't have to. It can go with my shopping on the back seat.'

'No, it's soaking, it'll mess everything up.'

'It's only some old stuff I've been buying, things from Oxfam.'

'I thought I saw you coming out of there. What were you after?'

'Just a couple of suits, a few shirts, shoes, that sort of thing.'

'For you?'

'No, no, not for me. It's men's clothing.'

'For your husband?'

'I'm not married. It's for our local theatre group. I help out with the costumes.'

Florence opened the boot. Inside was a garden spade, pair of shears, spare tyre and brown woollen blanket in case of a break down in cold weather. There wouldn't be space for a cat, still less a man.

'Must drop off these clothes first,' Florence said. 'We're rehearsing our Ayckbourn comedy tonight... Chorus of Disapproval. Do you know it?'

She drove them towards the Welsh border, by swollen rivers and hills smoking in low cloud. They arrived in Llanrhaeadr, a straggling village of stone cottages, and stopped by what'd been the National School, converted now into the headquarters of the Tanat Theatre Club. Florence took her bags and unlocked the door. She emerged a few moments later and returned Kat's smile, not with any sincerity or warmth but a rare degree of satisfaction. There'd been no sign of Mr Robbo inside. He must have ghosted his way out as he said he would.

Before she'd left, he'd warned her about a woman who might cross her path. A woman with hair the colour of flames and bewitching eyes, deep enough for a man to drown in their treachery.

'She is never to be trusted, Florence… she's poison,' he'd said. 'Be on your guard.'

He spoke with an emotion he'd not displayed previously. Thus Florence had known of Kat before their encounter in the rain. For her own part, she'd sensed what an easy mark Kat had taken her for – not only a hick from the back of beyond but black, too.

'Right,' said Florence. 'Let's get you to the hotel.'

And behind the latticed window where children once learned of kings and queens and the heroes of empire, a figure moved further back into the shadows, his enemy outflanked if only for that moment.

17: FAREWELL

"Pray for those who died violently
(and) went to the grave unable to tell their stories."

-   Russian kontakion for the dead

What if a man's existence was no more than a spark between two oblivions?

What if religion really was the opiate of optimism which atheists said, dispensed to gullible souls by clerics like the Reverend Hill?

What if, therefore, he'd been no more than a huckster at a country fair, peddling tonics and cure-alls, readily discredited by science?

At such thoughts as these, his vocation's solid foundations became sand, shifting with doubts that had disturbed his mind since Virginia's death. Nothing could ever be certain for him anymore, not his faith, not his wider beliefs.

Despite all his peace campaigning, the world still stared into the nuclear abyss, arms dealers prospered, governments waged war. And on the north aisle of All Hallows, a memorial to men from thereabouts who'd fallen in conflicts from Balaclava to Belfast had space for many a new name to be picked out in gold leaf.

For Ralph Hill to have thought – or even dreamed – that

his feeble efforts might remotely help to turn such bloody tides of conflict was a measure of naivety and arrogance.

His vigil for Virginia was almost over. It was coming dawn. Some vestigial colour began to appear in the panes of medieval stained glass above him, a hint of French blue in the Madonna's gown, the gentle rouge of her face.

The night had been tranquil but a wind was passing through the mourning yews in the churchyard. The Reverend Hill felt cold, his joints stiff. He'd not eaten since yesterday lunchtime, hadn't taken his tablets. He stood up but sat down again quickly, dizzy, grabbing at one of the poppy-head bench ends to steady himself.

In the dissonance of the moment, he wasn't entirely sure where he was and construed the look on the face of his painted likeness above as one of distaste, as if the unknown holy man knew of all Ralph Hill's manifest failures as husband, father, priest.

The great door from the porch creaked open on hinges of iron hammered into branches and tendrils, all clenched tight into the thick oak planks by a blacksmith's nails. Two of the altar ladies entered, backlit and silhouetted by the coming day. They saw him and hesitated.

The Reverend Hill wanted only solitude, not the flowers and sad smiles of those who would now interrupt the final moments of his vigil.

He turned away. Had he not done so, he would have seen a third figure, that of the Army's representative, Freddie de Lanerolle, walking in dressed as a civilian – dark suit, white shirt, sombre tie – and carrying a leather briefcase.

'Sir... Reverend Hill?' he said. 'Time's getting on. We have to make a move.'

'Why? What is time on such a day as this?'

'Sir, forgive me. I understand how you must feel but we have a document you must see.'

'A document? What do you mean?'

'It's from your daughter.'

'I don't understand.'

'We write them, sir. Personnel in the armed forces write letters for our commanding officers in case we become casualties.'

'How very proper. Part of the contract you killers make with each other, is it?'

'Sir, it sets out what your daughter wants to happen today.'

'It's very clear what is to happen today. I shall take her funeral and there's an end to it.'

'No, sir. That's not what she wanted.'

'She was my daughter.'

'Yes, but she was also an Army officer and she has left us instructions as to how she wants her funeral to be conducted and how her affairs are to be put in order.'

The Reverend Hill got to his feet.

'This is outrageous. Why have you only told me this now?'

'Because you have shut yourself away, sir. You've not been answering your door or your phone however many times we have called.'

'Show it to me. Show me this document.'

De Lanerolle unlocked his briefcase and took out a single sheet of handwritten paper from a white envelope.

'I haven't my glasses,' the Reverend Hill said. 'Read it to me.'

De Lanerolle tried not to show how uncomfortable he felt, standing by the coffin of the woman whose words he was about to deliver to her father.

'Are you sure you want me to do this, sir... here in the church, now?'

'Yes, just get on with it.'

'Right, well sir, this is what your daughter says... *"I wish for my funeral to be held at the church of All Hallows in Herefordshire where my father is the vicar. I wish the service to be led by my very good friend, Martha Whitten, who is my executor and also a lay preacher.*

'Out of respect to my father's views, I wish for there to be no uniforms worn by any of the mourners and for there to be no overt military symbolism on display. I wish for the religious side of the ceremony to be kept to a minimum and for there to be just one piece of music played.

'I have given Martha Whitten the details of it. Finally, I wish to be buried in the churchyard of All Hallows, as close as possible to the grave of my mother".'

The soft echo of de Lanerolle's voice died in the dustier reaches of the nave. He'd no desire to see into the old clergyman's rheumy eyes, to trespass further into his pain, so looked away as he handed the document to him.

'You'll see it's signed and witnessed, sir, and dated. This is your copy.'

The Reverend Hill folded it once, twice, then slipped it within his cassock and made to leave. An anxious de Lanerolle reminded him that the funeral was due to start at ten thirty.

'Do you need any help getting ready, sir?'

Ralph Hill shook his head.

'No, not from you or anyone else.'

He let the fingers of his right hand run along the bevelled edge of the coffin as he went out. She'd defied him to the end, got her own way even at the edge of the grave.

*

Martha Whitten was older than Ginny, coming forty, broader in the beam, mousy hair cropped as short as a boy's. Whereas Ginny had cut a glamorous, woman-at-war figure, Martha did not.

But as friend and civilian counsellor, she knew of Ginny's damaged childhood, her warring parents, and could bring calm and reflection to her risk-taking world when military action so often got pinned down in the moral and political ambiguities of conflict.

The Reverend Hill refused to take any part in the service. He sat at the back, alone and unreachable. In front of him, in box pews patinated by age and use, were two distinct groups: villagers Ginny had known since childhood, and outsiders whose dangerous calling she had shared.

The service might have been conducted in a religious setting but its tone was humanist save for when Martha addressed the congregation and her own beliefs showed out.

'As Christians, we believe that Jesus went through the deep waters of death for us... all is not lost, even in this most bleak of times. We can be certain that Ginny will be redeemed.'

She paused on the chancel steps of All Hallows, her own loss apparent.

'It was my privilege to know Ginny well,' Martha said. 'I

witnessed her great emotional intelligence, her professionalism and that commitment to do what was right and in the best interests of the country she loved and served, at whatever personal cost.'

It was beyond tragic, she told the congregation, that someone so young and brave had died doing her duty.

'She abhorred those who thought human life was cheap, that people could be written off as collateral damage in pursuit of one cause or another.

'Ginny's work in Northern Ireland helped to save many lives, including, ironically, some of those who would have seen her as the enemy because she wore the uniform of a British Army officer.

'The political conflict in Northern Ireland has now claimed three thousand lives – police, soldiers, men and women and children – there and here on the mainland. We owe a huge debt of gratitude to Ginny and many in the Army like her who are all that stand between us and the terrorists who would—'

Martha stopped mid-sentence. She saw Ginny's father get to his feet. Some of the mourners turned around, unsure if he'd changed his mind about officiating. He had, but not in the way they expected.

'Stop this, stop this now,' he shouted.

The Reverend Hill stood in the aisle, grey and gaunt like some agitated old evangelist. He began to walk unsteadily towards his daughter's coffin.

'I'll not have my church used as a recruiting office for the military.'

People moved uneasily in their pews, acutely embarrassed but unable to look away.

'And I won't have my little girl's funeral exploited by you warmongers, do you hear me?'

Two parishioners went to his side and led him to a vacant seat, holding a hand each.

He could then be heard sobbing, broken by grief. Martha cleared her voice.

'Ladies and gentlemen, I think it's probably best if we end now with Virginia's chosen song for this, the saddest of days. It's based on a Sufi poem and is rather beautiful.'

She nodded to the verger who'd lined up the track on the CD she'd given him.

This is a strange affair
The time has come to travel
But the road is filled with fear...

The voice of June Tabor rose like a mournful wind, brushing the petals of lilies and roses on its angelic ascent, by the painting of the long-dead holy man then ever upwards on the scent of candles to fade in the smoky darkness of the Saxon bell tower.

Oh where are my companions?
They're prisoners of death now and taken far from me
And where are the dreams I dreamed in the days of my
youth
They took me to illusion when they promised me the
truth...
This is a strange, this is a strange affair.

*

A photographer was banging off shots from behind the cemetery wall, so Kat stood apart from the mourners around

Ginny's grave. She'd no wish to be smudged, not there, not anywhere. The undertakers let the coffin down into the deep red earth. All was silent save for the handfuls of dirt cast upon it by Ginny's father then Martha Whitten.

Kat didn't know her personally, only that she'd pitched up in Northern Ireland. Yet she saw Martha looking across at her several times. Why was she doing that? What little sins might Ginny have revealed to her very good friend?

Bloody dykes. That was the rumour.

They'd been seen having breakfast in the snooty Culloden Hotel outside Belfast. This proved nothing, of course. But its spook habitués noted such irrelevances, put them by in case they should ever come in handy.

Kat was about to leave when Whitten cut across the long, wet grass towards her.

'Hi, I'm sorry but you're Staff Sergeant Walsh, aren't you?'

'Yes, I am.'

'Good to meet you. I just wanted to say there's no wake as such but there will be coffee and biscuits in the vestry so you're very welcome to join us.'

'Thanks, but I'm about to leave. I'm working.'

'Ah, I see. I understand.'

'How did you know who I was, by the way?'

'Just by asking around.'

'Really? Why would you do that?'

'Because wasn't Ginny on a mission for you when she died?'

'No. Don't you read the papers? She was on a training exercise.'

'Is that right?'

'Yes, why would you think otherwise?'

'Only because of something Ginny said to me. I must have misunderstood.'

'She shouldn't have been discussing operational matters with you or anyone else.'

'No, she wasn't. I'd just asked her if she was free for supper that night.'

'And that's all?'

'Yes, that's all.'

'Glad to hear it,' Kat said. 'Careless talk and all that...'

Kat's parting smile wasn't warm.

She went to find her car, her mind taken up with the past and the present and all that remained to be covered off. The watchers still hadn't located Robbo. She'd ordered them to stake out the village where Florence helped with the theatre club.

Kat knew in her water that he'd still be in that area, hiding up until it was safe to make it back to Scotland. Why else would the old lady buy that train ticket? But he'd not elude her that way. Even so, time was against her. Hereford wanted their men back in twenty-four hours.

Robbo's great asset was the ability to blend in, to be prince or pauper. He'd carry it off. This she knew from their days posing as husband and wife in rented properties across Northern Ireland.

These were different safe houses from where to meet agents and touts, gather intelligence and carry out surveillance, despite Robbo being in a wheelchair in one of them. Their cover story then was that he'd been injured in a car crash in South Africa. Kat was now his driver and carer. But when each day's covert work was done, they retired to bed and became the most energetic of married couples.

It was when they were assigned new duties that Kat dreamed up an audacious plan. It required only that Robbo forfeit his life if it went wrong. Such was his obsession to win Kat that he thought it a gamble worth taking. As she flew to Belize for a jungle training course, Robbo was posted to the British Embassy in Lima, Peru as part of an international anti-narcotics campaign.

He crossed the border into Bolivia alone and unarmed, thinking on his feet, refining Kat's plan as he went. But something happened to him on the mission, something life-changing and so profound that though he succeeded, he failed her. And in so doing, what was in his head would become a threat to Kat. Like the spider who copulates then kills her mate, so Kat would proceed as her nature intended.

As she began to drive away from the car park, a figure ran towards her. It was de Lanerolle. She wound down the window.

'Something wrong?'

'You need to know this. Two guys at the back of the church during the funeral, not military, I thought I recognised them.'

'Reporters?'

'No, I ran their car number through the system to make sure. They're the English cops.'

'What the hell were they doing here?'

'Don't know for sure but I knew I'd seen them before,' de Lanerolle said. 'They were at police headquarters in Belfast and our Int Cell says they're in the team that's digging into the unsolved murders over there.'

Kat closed her eyes and pushed back in her seat. She

thumped the steering wheel with the palms of her hands.

'Fuck, fuck and fucking fuck again.'

'Anything I should know about?'

She shook her head and drove away. It was right what the Bard said: sorrows and troubles never came as single spies.

18: SPOOKED

"A man is not honest simply because
he never had a chance to steal."

-    Folk saying

The first light of a London day fell across Tilly Brown's dressing table, over her Baltic amber earrings, the crimson beads in a Yemenite necklace and the heap of filigree silver brooches and rings piled in a cigar box of Spanish cedar that once sat on her father's desk in his chambers.

Beneath Tilly's mirror were tubes of creams to moisturise and firm her body, to remove make-up and nail polish and relieve pain in ageing muscles. A woman's face at twenty was a gift from nature but, as Coco Chanel wisely observed, in her forties, it was her responsibility alone.

Tilly was barely awake and swung her legs from under the duvet and walked the three paces, naked, to her en suite bathroom. She yawned and pissed as noisily as a horse. The door remained slightly ajar.

Only when she looked up did she notice something – someone – in her bed.

'Christ!'

Then she remembered just how neighbourly – and drunk – she'd been with Giles Worth the night before.

*

'So, I've told you about me,' Tilly had said. 'What about you? You're a bit of a mystery to people round here.'

'I can't think why.'

'Off to work each morning, all poshly spoken, smart suit but no one has a clue about who you are or what you do.'

Giles smiled at this. He refilled her glass – unasked – then his own.

'There isn't much to tell. I'm just a humble civil servant, shuffling papers from desk to desk.'

'Go on, then... tell me about the papers you shuffle.'

'Policy reports, feasibility studies. That sort of thing. All quite boring, really.'

Tilly was slowly adjusting her view of him, range-finding. At their first meeting, he'd come across as gauche and inexperienced as far as women were concerned. For whatever reason, he was better company now, unassuming, self-effacing in an attractive sort of way.

But she'd not been a lawyer for years without sensing when someone was being evasive.

'OK, so which department are you in, Giles? Which ministry?'

Her guest took another drink. Tilly half expected him to play for time and ask to use the loo. But he answered without hesitation.

'I'm with the Ministry of Defence.'

'Ah, so is that why you're cagey about your work... because it's sensitive?'

'In a way, I suppose it can be. We're always encouraged

to be discreet.'

'So what exactly are you working on at the moment?'

'Well, that's the thing. I can't really talk about it.'

'What, not even to a taxpayer like me?'

'Sorry, no. Please don't think me rude but official secrets and all that.'

Tilly nodded tactically then went to get another bottle of Châteauneuf-du-Pape from the rack in the kitchen. She handed it to him, content to cede the job of opening it to a man and his ego.

'Do you know what I think?' she said.

'No, do tell me.'

'I think you're ever so nicely trying to mislead me, to put me off the scent.'

'What scent? I've told you, I work for the Ministry of Defence.'

'I accept that but I can't help thinking that it's what you do there that's interesting.'

'I'm sorry, Tilly – I can call you Tilly, can't I?'

'Of course, we're neighbours.'

'Well, the work is really quite routine, well, my role in it, anyway.'

'So you're not a spook or engaged in cloak and dagger sort of stuff, then?'

'Good God, no,' Giles said. 'Just look at me... overweight, wrong side of forty, not in the least bit handsome, and there's no Aston Martin parked outside my house, either.'

Tilly laughed as she was meant to. But when she'd worked in the Met Police legal department on terrorist cases, several similarly ordinary men would materialise in the

172

office, supposedly from mundane jobs in Whitehall, just like Giles. But, as she told him, they were secret squirrels from MI5.

'Well, I can assure you I'm not one of those,' he said.

Tilly didn't respond immediately. Her silence spoke for itself. It was she who refilled their glasses this time. The second bottle was almost empty. Giles was becoming more pink in the face.

But he showed no sign of wanting to leave or being discomforted by her questions. In fact, he seemed to find it all rather enjoyable.

'Are you hungry, by any chance?' Tilly said. 'I was about to make myself some supper and you're welcome to join me if you wish.'

'How kind. I will, if I may.'

'I'm on a vegetarian kick at the moment. Is that all right for you?'

'Of course. It'll be delicious, I'm sure.'

He joined her in the kitchen, glass in hand, and watched her stir-frying bamboo shoots, water chestnuts, Chinese cabbage and other vegetables in a wok.

'I can make us some China tea, if you'd like?' Tilly said.

'Thanks, but wine is just the ticket for me.'

He opted for a fork, not chopsticks. As they ate, Tilly changed tack. She was already figuring out how Giles could be enlisted to her cause.

'When we first met at that party, you told me you were unmarried.'

'That's right, professional bachelor, that's me.'

'There must have been girlfriends, though?'

'Oh, yes. Plenty of those, but I never seemed to find the

right one.'

'Maybe they wouldn't keep your secrets—'

'I told you, I don't have any.'

'I know, I'm only teasing. But tell me about yourself. I take it from your accent that you had a rather privileged upbringing?'

'Then you take it entirely wrong,' Giles said.

And so he began to describe his childhood, led her to the sooty brick heartland of industrial Staffordshire, to streets of two-up, two-down terraces named after great battles – Alma, Inkerman, Mafeking – by chip shops and struggling businesses like the Lunch Box Café, Pam's Pantry, Eric's Wireless Repairs. Fixed in lachrymose memory were overweight women in floral pinnies hanging out washing, tiny gardens with lupins and clumps of London Pride, outside toilets and racing pigeons flying up into the smoggy air from backyard lofts of planks and wire netting. And somewhere in this cribbed and cramped maze of houses and factories was Trafalgar Street, where he lived at number 17 with his nan, for his mother suffered with nerves and her husband laboured in a blast furnace. Besides, he'd no idea how to cope with the clever little boy he'd fathered.

'What is your very earliest memory from there?' Tilly asked.

'Of looking over a wall at the other children playing in the street.'

'Not of playing with them, just watching?'

'Yes, because I was always wearing my best clothes. Nan insisted on that.'

'What, you never were allowed to play out, you didn't get dirty or get bruised knees?'

174

'I suppose I must have done sometimes but I can't remember doing so.'

'So your nan kept you indoors most days?'

'I suppose I was rather sheltered.'

'A bit like a disabled child who had to be protected from mockery?'

'Do you know, I'd not thought of it that way, that being clever could be a handicap, but you're right. That was me.'

'Maybe your nan was being cruel to be kind.'

'Yes, I suppose she was.'

'She must have seen something in you, recognised that early spark that, with the right encouragement, could lift you out of the back streets.'

A far-away look of almost wistful gratitude came across his face.

'She wanted to give you a better start, better than she'd had, or your parents.'

He said his nan had paid for his piano lessons, taught him to play chess and not for a moment had he ever resented the cloistered life she'd imposed upon him. Then he made a telling confession.

'I think Nan was the only person I've ever loved, truly loved, I mean. I know she loved me.'

Tilly softened her tone of voice and asked what had happened to her.

'She died... long time ago, now. It was me who found her body.'

Tilly put down her glass on the kitchen table.

'No, really? How old were you?'

'Thirteen. Came home from school and there she was, in a heap in the kitchen.'

'So what did you do?'

'Sat with her for quite a time. She felt very cold… it must have happened that morning. We didn't have a phone, of course, so I went to the corner shop, Horton's, and told them.'

Tilly didn't interrupt. What he was recounting was obviously still raw.

'It was a heart attack. They wanted me to go to the funeral but I wouldn't… couldn't bear to, so I got a bus into Wolverhampton and just walked around till it went dark.'

In the circumstances, a third bottle was called for. They returned to the front room. He took the easy chair by the Edwardian fireplace, tiled with images of colourful birds in climbing plants. She sat on the sofa, knees tucked beneath her, and changed the subject.

'You went to university, I suppose?' she said.

'Yes, I read English.'

'Where, which university did you go to, Giles?'

'Oxford.'

'Wow, Oxford… that's a world away from the Black Country.'

Giles Worth, getting more maudlin by the minute, closed his eyes.

'Was it hard to fit in? I mean, it must have been a bit daunting at first for you.'

He told Tilly about his first day, that walk down the narrow cobbled street off St Aldate's across from Christ Church and Christopher Wren's Tom Tower, through the great carved gates of Pembroke, under the vaulted stone ceiling by the porters' lodge and into the medieval calm of the Old Quad.

It had the feel of a monastery, tranquil and learned, a wide

176

lawn, window boxes of flowers against walls of honied Cotswold stone. Dark, cool passageways leading up stairs with worn wooden treads that creaked.

Dons worked in panelled rooms cluttered with kettles and toasters, armchairs and books, all in junk shop disorder. Every flagstone, every bannister, every handle bore the patination of age, of people who'd gone that way long before.

'I was somewhat prickly at first,' Giles said. 'I felt inferior in the company of those public school types. They're all so naturally at ease, aren't they? Success is a given for them.'

'So what did you do to survive?'

'I bought a tweed jacket and a pair of brogues and even started smoking a pipe, then I got active in the junior common room and in politics, too.'

'On which side of the political fence were you, left or right?'

'Oh, definitely the Tory side, but with my background, I suppose I should be Labour. '

Tilly made no comment but sensed Nan still guiding him, even in the voting booth. He had enlisted in the Officers' Training Corps and got a commission as a second lieutenant.

'That wasn't very student-like,' Tilly said. 'Not in the late sixties when there was revolution in the air.'

'I know, then there was terrorism, hijackings, weak governments here, the oil crisis. It was awful, seemed like the world we'd known was falling apart and looking back, I think I was searching for certainty in an increasingly uncertain world.'

As if to demonstrate his need for order, Giles joined the Catholic Church. He admired its tradition and was drawn to the authoritarianism of the Jesuits.

'You're a man who wants structure in your life, aren't you?' Tilly said. 'And I suppose the Church is much like the Army but with prayers and incense.'

Giles didn't answer but asked where the bathroom was. Tilly was getting drunk but not as sloshed as her guest. She might yet wheedle a favour from him. This was a man who needed a confessor. There were tensions inside him, loneliness, insecurities.

He was giving her the truth, but not the whole truth. Another bottle should do it.

Giles came downstairs, face and hair damp as if he'd thrown water on himself to freshen up. Tilly patted the sofa to indicate he should sit by her. She filled his glass again. They talked about him getting a disappointing second at Oxford, going to Germany to teach English in a school near Essen, coming back unhappy then passing the civil service exam.

'That's when you joined the Ministry of Defence, was it?'

'Yes, been there ever since.'

'So you'll know about military matters, that sort of thing?'

'A little, why?'

'Because I've come across something really intriguing.'

Tilly led him – unsteadily – down to her darkroom to see the blow-ups of Robbo climbing into the same Army helicopter that would crash in a lake soon after and now featured in that day's *Evening Standard*.

'That's quite a coincidence,' Giles said.

'But the *Standard* makes no mention of a passenger, dead or otherwise.'

'So he probably got dropped off along the way, lucky blighter.'

'No, I've done a rough timing between the take-off I photographed and the reported time of the accident and I don't believe he could have been.'

'But it'd only take a minute or so for the pilot to put down for someone to disembark. Not sure you can base anything on your guesswork.'

Tilly sensed him becoming a sober civil servant once more.

'You may be right but having spent a few days with the passenger, there was something decidedly odd about his manner when we parted, something very distracted and secretive then this happens straight after.'

'Like I said, he's probably still thanking his guardian angel.'

They returned to the sofa in Tilly's sitting room. The last bottle of wine was almost empty. It was getting late. She had to make her pitch before he went.

'Might it be possible, Giles, for you to ask around about the crash, discreetly obviously, anything about what might have happened to the man in my picture?'

'No, couldn't possibly do that. The Ministry of Defence isn't some little office. It's a huge organisation and I'd have no idea where to ask around.'

'But you agree something doesn't add up here?'

'No, I don't, and you as a lawyer will know that suspicion is no substitute for evidence.'

Before Tilly could counter-argue, a car backfired immediately outside her front window. The noise was like a single shot from a handgun.

As it penetrated right into the room, Giles hurled himself to the floor and curled into a ball, hands over his head.

'Hey, it's only a car,' Tilly said. 'No need for this.'

Giles lay on the carpet, shaking, his face no longer flushed.

'Come on, Giles, get up. What's the matter with you?'

But he lay rigid, like a child woken from a frightening dream.

'Ireland,' he said. 'Ireland.'

'No, it's London. What's Ireland got to do with anything?'

'Can't tell you, can't tell you.'

'OK, but calm down. You're safe here.'

'I can't go outside, I can't.'

He was reliving some past event, something too vivid for memory to delete. For Tilly, it made him more intriguing... more useful.

'You don't have to. I've a spare bed, you can sleep in that.'

She guided him upstairs. Sweat ran down his left temple. The spare room was next to Tilly's. She went to open the door but he held her arm.

'Please, no, I can't be on my own.'

'There's nothing to be scared of. You're just a bit drunk, you'll be fine.'

'I won't. It can get like this. Let me be with you... please.'

So she sat him on her bedside chair to undress. She'd no concerns about sleeping by him. His fear wasn't an act. It was tangible, real. But apart from this, she was now more sure about the true nature of Giles Worth and why he'd made a fool of himself to her at the neighbour's party.

They lay in the dark, neither asleep. It'd been a while since a man had shared her bed. Had Giles reached out,

180

stroked her hair or begun the first gentle moves towards that *petit mort* in which love and lust are exquisitely indistinguishable, she would have played a willing part.

But he didn't, and nor would he.

'Tell me, Giles... tell me the truth.'

'The truth about what?'

'The truth about you,' Tilly said. 'You don't like women, do you... not sexually, I mean?'

'How can you say that? You hardly know me.'

'We're sharing a bed, aren't we?'

'Only because I'm drunk and incapable.'

'But even if you weren't, you wouldn't want to fuck me, would you? Wouldn't even try.'

Giles didn't reply. It was his turn to answer with silence.

'I'm not in the least bit offended,' Tilly said. 'In fact, I'd be happy to be your beard if the social need ever arises in the future.'

Still Giles said nothing. It wasn't long before he was asleep. As her own eyes began to close, Tilly thought of the past, how it walked alongside us in the present, a companion faithful unto death whether wanted or not.

What had happened to Giles in Ireland? Why was he even there? Trauma can rise from its own grave, unwittingly summoned by a sudden recollection, a gesture, a picture, or something as mundane as a backfiring car.

*

The embarrassment of the next morning quickly passed. Giles showered but declined breakfast. He had to go but took coffee first. They stood facing each other, cups in hand.

'Look,' he said. 'About last night. You will keep my little secret, won't you... that personal matter?'

'Of course, I'll not be saying anything to anyone.'

'Thank you so much. My life is complicated enough as it is.'

'You've no need to worry, Giles,' Tilly said. 'But you'll not forget to ask around about the man and the helicopter, will you? Discreetly...'

19: DEAL

"Pale death... knocks at the cottages
of the poor and the palaces of kings."

-    Horace, Odes

Robbo could have been crouching in a sap during the Great
War, cold and dark in a claustrophobic seam beneath enemy
lines, not knowing if those who wished him ill were above,
listening for any sound that might give him away.

He lay amid a heap of hessian sacks in the crawlspace
beneath the stage of the village theatre club where his
unlikely co-conspirator, Florence, had left him food, clothes
and money. That wasn't all.

She'd cut out a story from her newspaper about the
helicopter crash. It was her way of saying he didn't have to
admit anything. She'd always suspected a link between him
and what had happened at the lake. Here was confirmation.

Florence was right, but the official report quoted in the
article wasn't. It maintained that the only person onboard was
the pilot, killed by an IRA device, while she flew solo on an
exercise in Wales.

For Robbo, slowly recovering, thinking more clearly, here
was a misleading report, leaked to frame the IRA as saboteurs
to cover up what was now starting to look more like a

conspiracy. Kat would benefit and the funnies, too. Ginny Hill hadn't been flying solo, wasn't on an exercise. Crucially, and with a vengeance, Robbo now believed he'd been the prime target that day, that it was him – and the knowledge in his head – that they'd meant to eliminate. The pilot was collateral damage.

She'd hinted at smelling a rat after all the fly-by-wire rescues she'd been ordered to undertake. He could have told her more, that the funnies were tidying up, doing a bit of housekeeping.

Hostile outsiders were at the gate, detectives from the mainland asking questions, seeking witnesses like Robbo, who knew the answers.

But those whom the gods once praised were destined to disappear out of harm's way, somewhere over the rainbow – or under the water – where their voices couldn't be heard.

For now, all Robbo had to do was to stay alive. Those who wished to see him buried should have a care, for he could drag them under the earth with him.

Florence would arrive soon. They had a plan but with no guarantee of success. She would back her car close to the theatre club's front door. With the boot open, Florence had to load in a few old props and pieces of scenery large enough for a man to hide behind. The hope was to make any watchers think Robbo was escaping with her.

She'd then drive to Shrewsbury to catch the train connections to Dumfries. While this was happening, Robbo would leave by the back door, wearing the brown suit and other clothes Florence had bought from a charity shop. He'd have a ten-minute walk to the garage of Tanat Valley Coaches to catch the next bus out of the village.

184

But for those few minutes, he'd be exposed, out in the open, gambling his life against those who would take it from him. They might try to abduct him, force him into a vehicle. He would fight dirty. He'd taken a screwdriver from the props room.

But if he made it to the bus, he would find a bed and breakfast place in wherever it went, lie low, work out how best to get to where he next needed to be. Florence knew nothing of this. What she didn't know she couldn't reveal. He felt bad about not returning her almost maternal trust.

But Kat would turn every trick on the old lady. The desire to win, to overcome whoever or whatever the obstacle, was Kat's way. Didn't he just know it.

Hers was a trait needed to survive in children's homes, which was then exploited by the military, who gave her the family she never had.

Robbo was aware of all this and more. They hadn't just shared a bed in Northern Ireland but each other's secrets, too. How naked we are in love, how unprotected we leave ourselves.

In those nights when the subconscious decides to replay images encrypted by memory, a man might wake, crying out, wet with sweat for he cannot delete what he has done, and thus undermined by remorse, confess his sins to the one person who won't understand or forgive.

And so it was with Robbo.

*

The gunner's long black hair flails in the warmest of winds. He's seen something below. He sights down the barrel of his

185

M60, pans left then right and mutters inaudibly into his neck mic. The pilot rolls the Iroquois starboard and gains more height.

Whatever the danger, it passes. It could have been the *leopards* – not wild animals but the heavily armed anti-drug police who wear spotted camouflage on raids.

Robbo feels that wondrous terror of being close to sudden, savage death, knowing that shrapnel might rip into him at any second, dicing his guts to pieces of tissue to fall through the air and lie like orchids on the soft damp floor of the jungle, to rot and stink where sunlight can barely reach.

Ahead, the Andes, range after range of great folds of rock forced ten thousand metres high by the collision of continents millions of years ago.

The girl with the yellow hair glances across at him from beneath her fringe. He smiles. It's a human reaction, even between strangers.

Her eyes are almost colourless, seawater blue if anything. But she looks down again, seems afraid. She makes pleats in the hem of her spotted red dress like a child in disgrace.

'You all right?' Robbo says. 'Not feeling sick or anything?'

She shakes her head. So she understands English. Her features could be Scandinavian in origin, skin almost translucent, freckles over prominent cheekbones.

But who is she? What is she doing with these most dangerous of men?

'Where are you from? Not Bolivia, is it?'

'Leave it, inglés,' Frederico says. 'You get to know her good later, OK?'

They descend towards a ledge on a steep ravine. From the

air it looks like a hurricane or some other natural disaster has just struck. Many hundreds of trees have been stripped out from the virgin rain forest to form a wide channel of bare earth down towards the foot of the valley. In the space and sunshine created, peasant farmers have planted a new and fabulously profitable crop to sell to Lucho: poppies.

Uncountable thousands of the grey-green pods await scoring with knives for the opium gum inside to seep out then to be harvested to make heroin for the needles of junkies across America and Europe. Lucho will have to buy more planes to fly in his profits.

The Iroquois drops to land. The poppies are flattened in its downdraught. A sudden side wind bucks the helicopter before it hits the ground hard. The gunners get out first, eyes hidden behind mirrored shades. Each unhooks an M60 from its mounting and cradles it in muscled arms, tense and alert even in this remote and uninhabited clearing. They and the flight crew take the girl and move away, out of earshot. They know that what is to be discussed is not for them.

Far in the distance, beyond the bare blue shoulders of the lower mountains, it's possible to see different weather systems at the same time: rain to the south, clear skies and sunshine in the west, clouds gathering from the north.

'So, inglés... you see what we have here?' Frederico says.

'You're diversifying. Smart move.'

'Big profits. You want some of this?'

'I think we need to discuss your other product first,' Robbo says. 'That's what I've come for. If that works out, we can shift some of this other stuff then.'

Frederico nods in apparent agreement. The sloping terrain and the matted undergrowth of dead lianas and clustered epiphytes are difficult for a man on crutches to navigate.

Their progress is as slow as Lucho's face is unreadable.

'You must start from the beginning, inglés,' Frederico says. 'We must know your plan.'

'It's simple,' Robbo says. 'When I fly back to England from Belize in a military aircraft, we land at an RAF base in the countryside but I'm not searched. I can carry in anything I want so long as it's not an illegal weapon or ammunition.'

'How can this be?' Frederico asks.

'Because I'm an intelligence officer, I am trusted.'

'So you can take in our product, but not very much?'

'I want to buy three kilos from you, the pure stuff, not cut with anything, then I can test the system and if it works, it can become a regular supply line into Europe and we both profit.'

'Three kilos is nothing,' Frederico says. 'It is a sample, nothing more.'

'Yes, but once I've organised the route and the soldiers to work it regularly, could be over a hundred kilos a year, and doing it my way, there'd be no Customs officers poking about at the other end.'

Not for the first time, Lucho asks why they should trust him. Robbo can only repeat his previous answer and says his offer of passing them secret American documents about planned anti-drug operations is further proof of his good faith.

'When can we see them, these documents?'

'Once I have tested that your product is pure,' Robbo says. 'You can have them and the twenty thousand dollars for your product, in cash or banker's draft, I don't care.'

'This could be a trap, inglés, a sting against us by the

188

CIA,' Frederico says. 'It has been tried before.'

'It isn't a trap and to prove it, I will stay with you or your people until you are satisfied that the documents are genuine, and don't forget, I can bring you more such information if we build trust between us.'

They pause. Frederico needs to take a breath, to mop his forehead. Lucho whispers something to him.

'Wait here, inglés,' Frederico says.

They move away, slowly, talking head to head. One of the gunners approaches them. He is given instructions and fetches the yellow-haired girl. She looks frail and bewildered, lost in the physical enormity of the setting. Frederico waves to Robbo to join them.

'Inglés, we have been talking, Lucho and me,' he says. 'You take her for a walk. She needs the company of a man.'

He leers at Robbo as if to make sure he's understood. The girl looks down at her canvas gym shoes, hands together almost as if praying.

They reach the edge of the jungle, by palms and aromatic shrubs then deeper into the green-hued shade of the quina and eucalyptus trees sighing high above them. Robbo stops. Somewhere amid all the serpent roots of the undergrowth live creatures they cannot see but which could kill them, for there are no rules in this place, only the instinct to survive.

He turns to the girl and asks her name.

'La hippie, that's who I am round here.'

'You're an American, right? Where from, exactly?'

'That doesn't matter. We haven't much time, do you want to do it here?'

She leans back against the flaking trunk of a pale eucalyptus and hitches up her dress. She's not wearing any pants. Robbo sees track marks on her inner thighs leading up towards her golden pubic hair.

There is a child's innocence about her nakedness, that absence of shame or propriety that is only learned later. Yet there she is, inviting a stranger to take her where she stands, coarse and grotesque like a hooker in an alley behind a backstreet pub.

'You want to fuck me, don't you? Isn't that what you want?'

'No, cover yourself up, it's not what I want.'

'But they said you would.'

'Then they're wrong. Who are you? What's going on here?'

She moves away from the tree, slightly agitated. Maybe it's coming time for a fix. There's a look of hurt and rejection in her eyes. But it could be fear. She hasn't done what she was ordered to.

'Listen, I'm sorry,' Robbo says. 'This is not personal, nothing against you. You're very pretty but I don't understand what you're doing with these guys.'

'Because I belong to him now, that's why.'

'You mean Lucho?'

'Yes, him. I'm his property, I belong to him. I have to do what he says.'

'But you're not his slave, why do you stay?'

She shakes her head at his naivety. The sun catches her yellow hair as they emerge from the jungle.

'It won't be forever,' she says. 'My boyfriend, he's coming back, you know. He said so.'

'Where is he, then? Why's he not with you?'

'He went to Europe but he'll be here any day now, then

we're outta here.'

Lucho and Frederico are waiting. One of the gunners takes the girl through the poppies to a rocky bluff on the other side.

She stands alone, the junkie and the crop she craves framed in one telling image. Frederico's blue shirt is dark with sweat by his armpits and under the tight leather strapping and holster in which his gold-plated Colt rests.

'Inglés, we have a problem with you,' says Frederico.

'Why? What problem?'

'What you tell us, what you say you can do, this is all good... but maybe too good.'

'So let me take the product and you'll see the route works. There's no risk or cost to you.'

'No, that we cannot do.'

'Why not? It seems simple enough to me.'

'Lucho, he don't believe what you say. The Americans have many spies against us and you are one of them. That is what he believes, I am sorry.'

'Then ask yourself why would I offer you their plans, their operational secrets, which you can check out, if I was one of their spies? It doesn't make sense.'

'Because you an agent, inglés, you cannot be what you say you are.'

One of the gunners approaches, M60 held ready. Robbo is cornered. There is to be no Hollywood escape, no grabbing a gun and flying the helicopter to safety. He's screwed. All soldiers know they could die in action. But not like this, on a desolate mountainside in a war few even know is being fought.

Frederico heaves himself back to Robbo's side.

'There is one way to prove yourself, inglés, a way to show

191

us you are not a spy.'

'What's that?'

'The girl over there—'

'What about her?'

'She gave you pleasure, yes?'

'Not in the way you mean, Frederico, my amigo.'

'That is for you but for us, she will not go back.'

'You're leaving her here? You can't do that, she's just a kid.'

'No, she betray us and there is a debt to pay.'

'You're going to kill her?'

'Not us, inglés... you. You will kill her then we know you are not a spy.'

'You can go and fuck yourself, Frederico. I'm not your hangman.'

'Listen to me, inglés. This girl, her boyfriend, cheat us. He take our product to Italy and we wait for our money a long time, he never comes back and now the time is gone.'

'You can't do this. She's another human being, not a bloody deposit on a drug deal.'

'But that is what she agreed.'

'Then she wasn't in her right mind, for God's sake.'

'But our business is this way, it has to be like this for us to have trust.'

The gunner is eyeing Robbo. He's waiting for any signal from his boss. This is the jungle. What price principles here? The girl is a heroin addict. She will never make old bones. Who will know, who will care, if he lays down his life for someone who is already as good as dead?

'Come, inglés,' says Frederico. 'We must join the girl. You have then to choose if you want to be in business with us or not.'

Lucho walks behind them with the gunner. Frederico's progress through the red soil of the poppy field to the place of execution is difficult. They approach the girl. Her breasts make hardly any impression beneath her dress. A slight breeze lifts a few strands of her yellow hair. She turns to look at them, her back to the ravine. Does she know, does she realise, what is about to happen, that whatever dreams and hopes she might have had will end here, where natives believe that if trees are cut down, evil spirits are released?

Frederico pulls out his Colt and hands it to Robbo. He looks at it with distaste, at its gold and silver vulgarity. Lucho's guards level their weapons at him. Robbo drops the Colt into the dirt and kicks it away. He becomes depersonalised as if he is watching someone else carrying out his actions.

He walks to the girl's side, embraces her. She puts her thin white arms around him and they kiss like parting lovers, long and deep and with a passion engendered by the closeness of death.

The men in the semi-circle around them do not move. They are not sure what it is they are witnessing. Then the girl appears to faint. She goes limp in the Englishman's arms and he lays her down on the rocks at the edge of the ravine with great tenderness. Her head lolls to one side, unnaturally.

Frederico swings himself forward. He looks at the girl's body and lifts her dress with his crutch to see what he can never enter. Then he levers her onto her side, onto her front then into oblivion for raptors to find and feast upon later. Robbo stares into the face of Frederico as he passes. What goes around, comes around. They have a deal now but there will be a reckoning for him, and for Robbo himself. Trauma always presents its bill.

*

Six days later, Robbo is on a tourist bus for the four-hour journey from La Paz to Puno, across the border in Peru. It's an old Dodge, painted in phosphorescent green stripes with orange flames coming up from the front wheel arches. Most of the passengers are young – Australians, Europeans, Yanks, backpacking to the glassy expanse of Lake Titicaca then on to the glories of Machu Picchu, eight thousand feet up in the Andes.

He's older than the kids around him. He looks hardened by whatever life he's led. That's not their business. He is left alone.

Robbo feigns sleep, despite the adrenalin rush at being just a few minutes from safety. He's pulled off an outrageous, off-the-books mission against the odds. He nurses his kitbag on his lap but is already feeling the psychological burden of his success.

They should arrive at the border crossing soon. He has a twenty-dollar bill in the top pocket of his thick plaid shirt should some official prove awkward. The bus draws into the Customs area.

Passengers file off to have exit stamps put on their passports. Robbo's shows he is Professor Adrian Bradshaw and folded inside are letters of accreditation on the stationery of the anthropology department at the University of Manchester.

Further down the dusty mountain road, they get entry

passes at the Peruvian Customs post and the bus rumbles on into the afternoon. Robbo, hair newly darkened, wire-rimmed glasses, will lose himself among other tourists passing through Puno, find a bed for the night then catch another bus for the long haul to Lima. He will attend the British Embassy and write a detailed report on the intelligence he's gathered in Bolivia for the ambassador and the anti-narcotics team. Kat will arrive on a regular flight from Belize City and stay with him in his hotel. They will go sightseeing, drop into cafés in the colonial splendour of the Plaza de Armas and take photographs of Lima at night from atop Cerro San Cristobal.

She'll notice his reluctance to talk about anything that happened in Bolivia. He's not ready yet, and may never be. But his nerve is to be admired and so is her audacious cleverness in planning such an operation.

Two days later, Kat will put on her British Army uniform, pack Robbo's three packages in her hand baggage and board the plane back to Belize City.

From there, she will make her way to the jungle training camp where SAS troopers sprawl under canvas watching video tapes of football games or feeding live mice to their pet snakes.

As Robbo dozes on the bus and anticipates all this, an English-language weekly is rolling off the press in La Paz. It carries an intriguing but rather incomplete story.

'*Police are investigating the mysterious death of a prominent La Paz accountant, Señor Frederico Molina, whose body was discovered in the Hotel Cadiz last night.*

Señor Molina, who suffered from polio as a child and used crutches with callipers on both legs, was retained by several leading commercial and political figures.

A police source said Señor Molina had been found in a bath but hadn't drowned.'

Asked what he meant by this, the source refused to comment further or on a rumour that they had already opened a formal murder investigation.

One line of inquiry is to discover why Señor Molina was staying in a hotel when he had a palatial home in La Zona Sur where armed guards were much in evidence last night.

A spokesman for the Hotel Cadiz declined to say who had booked the room. Asked when Señor Molina had arrived and if he was alone or accompanied, the spokesman said this was a police matter and he could add no more.

20: FATE

"Power corrupts and there is nothing more corrupting than power exercised in secret."

- Daniel Schorr, veteran journalist

It was, according to Samuel Pepys who witnessed it, a *malicious bloody flame* consuming all in its incendiary path on that Sunday morning in 1666. Taverns, shops, the houses of the rich, the hovels of the poor – the Great Fire of London spared nothing and no one. And in this apocalyptic ruination would have smouldered the ancient city church of St Andrew-by-the-Wardrobe, so named because Edward III had kept his royal paraphernalia nearby three centuries before.

Christopher Wren rebuilt the church only for it to be destroyed a second time in another biblical – if unholy – firestorm, unleashed by the Dorniers and Heinkels of Hitler's air force in the blitz of 1940.

Giles Worth pondered such twists and turns of fortune, good and ill, as he hurried along Queen Victoria Street to St Andrew's, late for practice with MI5's office choir, the Oberon Singers. He took the steps up to its panelled double doors two at a time. The old red bike of the choirmaster, Austin Dellow, leaned against the stone quoins of Wren's brick tower, which, with the outer walls, had survived the Luftwaffe raids.

His choir was already warming up, rehearsing *Videte miraculum*, a glorious motet for six voices at Candlemas written by Thomas Tallis in the days of the Tudors. Dellow had a polymathic intelligence and an infectious passion for medieval church music, plain song and liturgical drama.

Worth sang tolerably but knew he'd not make the final cut. He'd rarely got into any first eleven at school and so it continued through life. But he had another, more purposeful reason to attend St Andrew's that evening.

The Oberon choirmaster was head of A Branch and therefore, MI5's chief burglar. He wasn't entirely a law unto himself but could bend and break it under a charmingly anodyne provision known as the *third direction*. No lawmaker would ever be advised to set it down in actual legislation.

Thus, by custom and practice, Dellow possessed many secrets. He also owed Worth a professional debt. It was Dellow who'd overseen the mission in Northern Ireland that went so badly wrong and for which Worth was recalled to London, his record blotted with blood thereafter.

He'd thought of inviting Dellow for a drink in the Pig and Eye Club, the spooks' own bar on the sixth floor where they sold beer from the wood.

But a meeting in a church might induce more candour. Dellow was famously discreet. His politically sensitive – and legally dubious – work in the national interest was carried out by a loyal crew of ex-cops, ex-cons and blaggers. As he once remarked, *swans never swim in sewers*.

So Worth stood at the back of the church, listening to a

run-through of the responsory at First Vespers of the Purification. He smiled to himself. Here was irony, for so much that crossed Dellow's desk was beyond any such cleansing.

*

It was a woman who answered when Tilly Brown rang Robbo's number in Scotland to say she'd like to register for another course.

'I'm sorry but we're not taking any bookings at the moment.'

'But I was only there the other week. What's happened?'

'It's the man who runs the place, he's having a break, I'm afraid.'

'You mean Robbo?'

'Yes, that's right. I'm not sure when he's going to be back.'

'But the place isn't closing down, is it? I had a wonderful few days there.'

'I'm really not sure to be honest. Robbo didn't leave us any information about his plans.'

'But if you're answering the phone for him, you must know something.'

'Sorry but I don't. I'm just a friend but if you give me your name and phone number, I'll pass it on to Robbo if he rings in.'

'Right, well I'm Tilly Brown, I'm a photographer and all my contact details should be in his system from when I stayed.'

'OK, I'll dig them out.'

'Could he have gone back to Northern Ireland, perhaps?'

The woman paused momentarily before answering.

'Did he mention that he might do that, then?'

'Not in so many words but that was his drift. I know he's got links over there, to the Army.'

'Then you know more than me. Doesn't normally talk about himself, Robbo doesn't.'

'No, but what else is there to do when you're sitting around a campfire for a few nights?'

'Sounds like you and he got friendly. Hasn't been in touch with you, by any chance?'

'Of course not or I'd know what was going on, wouldn't I?'

'True enough. OK, if I hear from him, I'll tell him you've called.'

'I'd really appreciate that. Thanks for your help.'

Tilly Brown couldn't know that all calls to Robbo's business number were being diverted to Army intelligence and the phone of Kat Walsh, his former lover who wished him dead.

And Kat Walsh couldn't know yet that Tilly Brown was already in Scotland, applying the first principles of detective work: start digging in the centre and move outwards from there.

*

The living room in Dellow's apartment was ordered, uncluttered. Two chairs of pale Scandinavian oak with sheepskin seats were placed either side of a fire surround of cloud grey Carrara marble in a chimneypiece painted apple green.

He'd four shelves of operatic records, CDs of Tallis, Byrd, Taverner, books about Rossini, Shostakovich, Mozart, Beecham. No ornaments were displayed, no pictures, no photographs of loved ones. Every surface in the kitchenette was clear, not a plate in the sink or a spoon on the draining board.

Worth felt sure it was a security services property. Dellow kept it warmed until it was needed as a safe house or to debrief a source. Maybe he met his burglars there, set them their tasks, took possession of whatever they'd stolen, copied or photographed.

There would be bugs hidden somewhere, a video feed, too. He must mind what he said, remember that his disarmingly laid-back host majored in deviousness.

Dellow hadn't wanted to chat in St Andrew's or in a pub. He suggested they walk towards Holborn and the mansion block where he lived alone during the week.

'If it's an office matter, we'll be more private there.'

He'd stowed his bike in the hall then taken Worth up in the wheezing wire mesh elevator to the fourth floor and shown him into the flat. Dellow took a bottle of Bushmills from a cupboard but only one glass.

'I'd join you but I'm on some tablets for my heart, you see.'

'Not anything serious, I hope, sir.'

'Probably not but the MO has forbidden me any firewater for the duration.'

They settled themselves in the Swedish chairs. Dellow crossed one long leg over another and jiggled it up and down as if to the beat of a song only he could hear.

Worth felt like a student again, one needing to impress his tutor, to get his approval.

'So, Giles… what's troubling you?'

'Well, this could be something or absolutely nothing but I thought it best to run it by you.'

'Even though you're not in my branch?'

'Yes, you're more likely to know if this is a matter that could concern the service.'

'Concern us in what way?'

Worth took a breath.

'If what I'm about to tell you amounts to anything, it's best that the service is forewarned and prepared for whatever fallout there might be… if there is any, that is.'

'Understood, Giles. You just fire away.'

He refilled the younger man's glass. Worth said he'd been NDO when an Army source in Northern Ireland had warned of something going bang that day.

'I'd hardly been told this when Special Branch rang in to say that an Army helicopter from over there had just crashed in a lake in Wales.'

'But that wasn't reported as terrorism at first, was it? Mechanical failure was what they said.'

'That's right,' Worth said. 'But it was also reported that the only person onboard was the pilot who was killed, a young female.'

'Yes, I read that, too. Tragic business.'

'Right, please bear with me because this is where it gets speculative,' Worth said. 'There's a woman who lives near me who photographed that same helicopter in Scotland barely seventy minutes before it ditched in Wales.'

'Really? What an extraordinary coincidence.'

'It is indeed, and her pictures show it hovering over the beach at a tiny place called Port Logan and picking up a man before flying south.'

'How interesting. Go on.'

'My neighbour had just spent three days with this man at some centre he runs in the wilds. She actually gave him a lift part of the way then followed him to the rendezvous with the helicopter without his knowledge.'

'Why would she do that?'

'Because he intrigued her. He's ex-Special Forces, you see... Northern Ireland and all that.'

'So what's being suggested here, then?'

'I'm not sure she rightly knows herself but she's clearly suspicious as to why the official version of this event doesn't make mention of a passenger, dead or alive.'

'Isn't that obvious, Giles? He was dropped off somewhere en route.'

'My thought exactly but for whatever reason, she thinks otherwise.'

Dellow leaned forward and topped up Worth's glass again.

'Does it matter what she thinks? I mean, what locus does she have in this matter? She sounds a bit infatuated, if you ask me, like she knows the soldier in a biblical sense.'

'That could explain why she's so fixated, I suppose.'

'Not sure you should be wasting your time on this, Giles.'

'But there is a reason, sir. She was a senior lawyer with the Met Police for years, handled lots of terrorism cases. She's very level-headed and no fool. Got useful connections, too.'

'Has she now? Anyone we know?'

'I couldn't help seeing a rather affectionate card on her mantelpiece from a commander in the Met.'

'Goodness, Mr Worth, we might make an intelligence officer out of you yet.'

'You'd better get a move on, sir. I've rather been out of favour of late.'

Dellow looked over his glasses and held Worth's gaze for a moment. Neither needed to add anything. Dellow wanted to know the name of her commander friend.

'You may know him, sir, or know of him... Laurie Benwell.'

'Yes, I know of Benwell. Running that inquiry into those murders our friends across the water didn't solve.'

'A good connection, then?'

'Certainly is,' Dellow said. 'Takes no prisoners, Brother Benwell doesn't. They say it's best to wear a tin hat when you cross his path.'

'I wouldn't know. But will we need one... the service, I mean?'

'Better give me your neighbour's details. I'll see if our insurance policies are up to date.'

'By the way, she's back in Scotland, digging up anything she can on the soldier.'

'Then you keep breaking bread with her and report to me, no one else. Understood?'

'That's my intention, sir.'

'Good man. Now, one for the road. Can't have you thinking I'm inhospitable, can I?'

*

The cold night air heightened the potency of the Bushmills. Worth made his unsteady way to Holborn tube station with other late-night travellers, some less able to walk a straight line than him.

He bought a ticket for Archway and changed at King's Cross to the Northern Line. His train howled in like a banshee. The carriage was warm and stuffy, his head confused by whisky and sudden self-doubt.

Had it been politic to tell Dellow about the crashed helicopter and the soldier? Did it matter that he'd potentially compromised Tilly Brown, or was this – and every other consideration – subsumed in the bitterness of being scapegoated for that damnable episode in Ireland?

The tunnel entombed him and all else. He closed his eyes and in that darkness was a more threatening blackness in which the moonless night closed around hunter and hunted alike.

Neither knew of the approach of the other.

*

'Catch yourself on, son. What we're being ordered to do is fucking insane.'

'Yes, I realise it's not without risk,' says Worth.

'Not without risk? That's fucking rich, that really fucking is, yeah? Do you and those other cunts in London know what we go up against here? Do you?'

Worth kept quiet, allowed himself and MI5 to be berated by a comparatively junior Special Branch constable.

But that was irrelevant when confronted by the uniquely informal camaraderie between SB officers of whatever rank.

The feeling against Worth at the briefing was laden with dislike and mistrust of the outsider.

The constable knows he isn't going to be reined in by his inspector. Here was another case-hardened man who'd seen too much incompetence not to know the colour of blood.

'You don't, do you?' the constable says. 'None of you do, not a fucking clue between you.'

But now the three of them are crawling on their bellies across fields and open countryside. Politicians in Westminster want the fight taken directly to the bad guys.

And the spooks who bankroll this dirty little civil war are demanding action and results. They are the pipers to whose tune all must dance, for lives depend upon keeping up with the music.

Their target is Jo Jo Ryan from the IRA's northern command – a collator of intelligence, a planner of murder around his kitchen table.

He'd known he was a target for the security forces, so grubbed out every hedge and tree around his remote smallholding to make it harder for the surveillance teams of E4 Alpha to dig in and spy on him. Jo Jo is fifty-eight, a widower built like a bull, has swept back silver hair and a farmer's weather-reddened face. His Special Branch file is thicker than a gatepost.

Worth had read it, the white and blue SB50 reports typed out in triplicate by handlers who run agents inside the IRA, those hated touts who inform for wads of MI5's limitless cash until they get caught and tortured then shot.

Some are brave, some weak or pliable, greedy or mad. Special Branch have a source close to Jo Jo. His SB50 information is rated B2, indicating he's well placed and reliable. This is why SB on the ground argued that this mission was dangerous and unnecessary.

But their agent had discovered a date when Jo Jo would be away, his farmhouse empty if only for two hours. MI5 seized on this heads-up as a rare opportunity to get a further drop on a terrorist godfather.

London put a plan together. Worth was handpicked for his eagerness despite a lack of operational experience. He'd done all the courses. He was to get into Jo Jo's house and photograph the legs of the big pine table in the kitchen from every angle and take precise measurements.

These would be used later to create a replica leg, fit it with a bug then break in again and use it to replace the original.

'Is this All Fucking Fools' Day?' the SB constable says. 'Because if it isn't, you're a bigger head-the-ball than you look.'

'Come on, old chap. We can do this,' Worth says. 'It'll give us priceless intelligence, get everything in real time about what's being planned around that table.'

'Dear Christ, get it into your fucking head that we already get priceless intelligence. We've got a man on the inside, remember? Your firm pay him enough.'

But a decision has already been taken before the briefing. And now Jo Jo's house is in sight, Worth's enthusiasm for the mission is less than it was. He has a backpack with cameras and lights and a moody key for the front door from the MI5 department that specialises in such items. He's not armed.

The SB inspector and constable, faces streaked with camouflage grease, carry MP5s with night sights and handguns for close-quarter killing. Worth gets safely inside.

His minders lie tight against the earth wherein they may yet end up if this job goes to rat shit.

Worth has been told their radio communications are secure but to keep them to a minimum. There's a sudden flash through the darkness from the kitchen window. Worth hasn't drawn the curtains. He'll be seen. The inspector orders Worth to close them.

'Why the fuck did they send us this joker?' the constable says. 'He'll get us all killed.'

They wait, ten minutes, twenty. Cloud cover is low. Rain is forecast. An owl wafts from its barn to a telegraph pole, silent and creamy white. Only the owl can see them, each as still as a corpse but watching the night like him.

The headlights of a car sweep along the road as if making for the village a mile away. There have been others. This one turns into Jo Jo's drive.

But it can't be him. He's not due for an hour at least. Yet it is him, his Shogun's headlights illuminating the pebble-dash frontage of the house, its garish Spanish-style porch and the terracotta pots of box bushes either side of the door.

And it's then that Worth chooses to emerge in a blind panic, pissing himself as he runs away. Jo Jo leaps out of the car and follows him. He has a weapon and fires. Another man steps from the Shogun and gives chase in the darkness.

It's the last thing he'll ever do. He is shot from the shadows by the inspector. Jo Jo turns back, fearing an ambush by loyalists. He gets no further than his car. The inspector's second round hits him in the right temple. He spins, spraying an arc of blood across the windscreen and bonnet of the Shogun.

The constable catches up with Worth, who is shaking. Jo

Jo is confirmed dead. They have to leave immediately to RV with their back-up team.

'Where's the other guy?' the constable says.

They find him on the drive with a hole in the back of his head. He's rolled over and a torch beam put on his face. It's studded with bits of gravel and there is blood coming from his nostrils. He's forty or so, a hard-looking man even in death. The constable recognises him even if the inspector doesn't.

It's his agent – the eyes and ears of Special Branch in Jo Jo's camp.

21: CONFESSION

"I will sing of mercy and judgement:
unto thee, O Lord, I will sing."

-    Psalm 101

It was Bunty Mainstone, one of the altar flower ladies at All Hallows, who saw the vicar walking barefoot in the graveyard an hour before midnight. She'd been going to bed and looked out into the starlit night from the landing window before drawing the curtains.

Her friends thought Cemetery Lane an eerie place for an elderly widow to continue to live. Yet she felt grounded in that house, watching the seasons come and go, the spring brides and their bouquets and the long shadows of mourners against the snows of winter.

The figure she saw that night appeared like an apparition by the gate from the vicarage lawn. Her hand went to her mouth. It could be a burglar. She thought of phoning the police then recognised the Reverend Hill's stoop and was immediately worried about his state of mind.

Everyone in the village knew how stricken he'd been by his daughter's death. He wasn't taking services and some even said he'd turned against religion and no longer believed in God.

Whatever the truth, Bunty Mainstone felt a personal sense of responsibility towards the priest who'd guided her spiritual life for so many years. She hurried downstairs for an overcoat and put on the green wellingtons by the door.

The vicar was standing by Virginia's newly dug grave, muttering to himself, or to the memory of all he had lost.

'What are you doing out here in your pyjamas, Reverend Hill?'

He looked up but in the confusion of the moment, seemed not to recognise who she was.

'Come on, let's get you indoors,' she said. 'You're coming home with me.'

She rekindled the fire, sat him in what had been her husband's easy chair and put a woollen blanket around his shoulders. Then she poured him a brandy and made sure he drank it as she washed his feet in a bowl of warm soapy water.

Not a word did he say, not of thanks or explanation. Mrs Mainstone settled back and watched over him in the light of the fire, his mouth open, denture missing, face as marbled as a corpse. God's representative revealed himself to be just another man that night, old and weak and weary. He'd not asked for a lighter burden in this life, only broader shoulders. But this wish had been denied him.

In the morning, she would ring the curate. He would know what to do for the best.

*

The emotional legacy of bereavement wasn't unknown to Ralph Hill – all its pain and anger, and the mood swings that followed. He'd observed these stages often enough, praying in the homes of others. He also knew that acceptance usually came eventually. Yet he feared that for him, there would be only self-recrimination for a life he'd thought well-lived as a steward of the mysteries of God, but which, by any test, had failed the person to whom he owed the greatest duty of care.

It had taken Virginia's death for him to recognise that all his endeavours on behalf of good causes had really been driven by ambition and vanity, albeit beneath the vestments of the church and held to be for a higher purpose.

Lying in Mrs Mainstone's spare bedroom, he recalled the advice he'd once given to a mother whose child had died from leukaemia: *some events you don't get over. You just have to find a way to live with them, to put them in a place where they don't hurt so much.*

So heal thy priestly self, he thought, find comfort in your own words and when you fail, as you surely must, there will be little option but to scream at the arbitrary brutality of fate.

The doctor had called and diagnosed physical and mental exhaustion. Complete rest and regular meals were advised. Mrs Mainstone was happy to provide both. Then the curate arrived, an assertive man, tall and bony, scrubbed until he shone, bearing plans from a higher authority.

'The bishop's private secretary has telephoned me,' he said. 'The bishop has every sympathy with your loss and he'd like to know what more we can do to help.'

The Reverend Hill shook his head and said nothing.

'Ralph, I think the bishop is saying he would appreciate knowing what your intentions are.'

'My intentions? What can he mean by that?'

'You're not at all well, Ralph. I'm coping as best I can on

my own but another full-time priest needs to be appointed to come and work here.'

Ralph Hill would have shrugged had he the energy or inclination. Instead, he closed his eyes. His visitor pressed on with his allotted task.

'The truth is you should have retired years ago but they let you stay on and now, with all that's happened and this terrible burden you're having to bear over Virginia—'

'Spit it out, for God's sake,' said the Reverend Hill. 'What you're really saying is the bishop has always wanted to see the back of me, now he's got the perfect excuse.'

'No, Ralph, that's completely unfair. You must know yourself that we have a situation here which cannot go on indefinitely. The parish is suffering, everyone's aware of that.'

'Then what am I being required to do by His Grace?'

The curate poured himself a glass of water from the carafe on the bedside table.

'I've been speaking to Virginia's friend... Martha, the counsellor.'

'Who?'

'Martha, you know, she led the service... she says Virginia brought her to see you once.'

'Did she? I don't recall.'

The curate's imperceptibly raised eyebrow suggested he knew that Ralph Hill hadn't the slightest desire to remember.

'Be that as it may, Martha's father is the dean at Wells Cathedral. He's a widower like you and he's told her that you're very welcome to lodge with him for as long as you want.'

'Why should I want to decamp to Somerset and stay with

a complete stranger?'

'But you're not a complete stranger, Ralph, not to him, anyway.'

'How can you say that?'

'Because he knows a great deal about you and admires all the peace campaigning you've done over the years.'

'And that's supposed to make me feel better about being turfed out of my home, is it?'

'The dean's a good man, Ralph. He's got the approval of his bishop and the Cathedral Chapter for you to help out with services, maybe do some pastoral work in the community.'

'I haven't a choice, have I? All this has been cooked up behind my back.'

'Ralph, you've no relatives to go to and for your own good, our bishop thinks you shouldn't be living on your own at a moment like this but in a religious community where you'll have all the support and spiritual understanding you'll need while you recover. There are too many sad associations at All Hallows for you.'

There was a time when the Reverend Hill believed we were more than a handful of dust at the end of life's struggle, that the almost sacred nature of suffering – as in the passion of Jesus – brought one closer to the heart of God, in whom total trust was placed. He would also have argued vehemently against anything in conflict with his personal wishes.

But he was in retreat, whether he liked it or not. He sank back into the depression in his pillow, white cotton like the flag he now had no option but to fly.

It was, as the French say, a *faute de mieux* – for want of anything better.

214

They sat on plastic chairs in the cabin-like waiting room inside the workshop of a garage, Martha Whitten and Ralph Hill, drinking coffee in styrene cups from a vending machine covered in oily fingerprints. Sweet wrappers, cigarette packets, empty sandwich boxes had all blown across the draughty concrete floor and into a corner.

Two mechanics in dark blue overalls could be seen through the window in the chipboard wall, working on a red Peugeot to the thump of pop music on their radio.

Martha's car, an early 1960s Morris Minor estate, had just been winched off the flatbed truck that had recovered it from the hard shoulder of the M5 north of Bristol.

They'd been heading down to Wells with his books and few possessions when her nearside front tyre burst. The garage didn't have a suitable replacement in stock so there was another delay while calls were made to suppliers.

Martha asked the Reverend Hill if she could get him another drink.

'Thank you, Martha, but no,' he said. 'When do you think we'll be on our way?'

'Not for another hour at least, maybe longer judging by what the manager said.'

Ralph Hill, elbows on his knees, chin in his hands, stared down at the floor.

'Not the most pleasant of places to be stuck, is it?' Martha said.

Her companion didn't reply. But he'd used her name for the first time. That was positive. He'd said little since they left Hereford after breakfast, doubtless conscious of all he

215

was leaving behind. Martha had sensed his mood and made no attempt at small talk.

But now, in this most unlikely of confessionals, he began to unburden himself. It might have been because she was an unthreatening matryoshka of a woman or because she'd been Virginia's closest friend.

Whatever the reason, it mattered little. What he was about to tell her would be the truth and come from the heart.

*

Kat was alarmed at the panic in Sir Frazer Harris's voice when he rang.

'Got to see you,' he said. 'I've been given another gypsy's warning.'

'About our little problem?'

'You can call it little, missy, but it's keeping me from my sleep, that much I'm certain of.'

He was in Walsall for a meeting at an engineering firm that paid him as a director and exploited his name and title on the company's notepaper. He wanted Kat to come to a service station on the M6 immediately.

'Sir, you're saying this is serious enough for me to drop everything else I'm doing?'

'Yes, I bloody well am. You be in the café at Hilton Park at eleven. Got that?'

She arrived early to cast an eye over the RV. It was crowded with families, sales reps eating the breakfasts they'd foregone earlier, giddy school children, pensioners on coach trips.

Nobody stood out. But those who were invisible for a

living just wouldn't, anyway. Kat bought coffee and cheesecake then found a table in a booth. She'd wired herself for sound but would struggle to get much of the noble knight over the piped-in music and all the other ambient noise.

Frazer Harris worried Kat, a politician double-dyed in all that trade's foibles, and with scant understanding of the cat and mouse complexities of a world he'd notionally overseen when in office, but only ever from a convenient distance.

As Robbo's handler, Kat had responsibility over the search for him but knew beyond doubt that if anything went wrong or became public, she'd be on the scaffold, not Sir Frazer, despite his claims to the contrary. It was a comfort, if only of sorts, to know that nothing about Robbo or his activities was ever written down on a contact form, filled in every time a handler met an agent. But Robbo was more a subcontractor doing what had to be done, according to those who, like her, were never obliged to account in public for their actions.

Kat had already been tipped off that Commander Benwell's squad of English detectives investigating specific unsolved killings in Northern Ireland were combing through Army CFs. For Kat, some alleys were more uncomfortably dark than others.

Sir Frazer was suddenly in front of her. He sat down heavily on the chair at her side and exhaled theatrically.

'I'm absolutely cream-crackered. Get me a coffee, love.'

'Is your secretary not with you, then?'

'I no longer have a secretary.'

'Then, sir, with great respect, I'm not here to act as one.'

'What did you say?'

Kat's skills in diplomacy were worn thin by the mounting

strain of knowing that if Robbo wasn't found, only disgrace and incarceration awaited her.

'I'm saying I'm not here to take orders for drinks or anything else.'

'Listen to me, young lady—'

'No, you listen to me. I'm working night and fucking day to sort out the little difficulties you and your pals created, so I don't take kindly to being treated like a waitress.'

'You seem to forget who I am,' Sir Frazer said. 'Your lot exploited this situation, whichever way it was caused.'

'Yes, we did, to get bloody politicians like you the bodies on slabs you wanted.'

'Keep your voice down,' he said.

'You need to remember what the Yanks said in Vietnam... once you've got people by the balls, their hearts and minds usually follow.'

'What the hell's that supposed to mean?'

'That you need to recognise that it's not you who's in control of this situation.'

Sir Frazer gave her a hostile stare but knew in his dyspeptic gut that she was right.

He rose and returned a few minutes later with coffee for them both.

'Thanks,' Kat said. 'Now, ruin my day with your bad news.'

*

Martha knew that when counselling someone whose guilt could no longer hold back conscience, it was obviously important to listen to the words being spoken but also to let

218

the silences breathe and not interrupt with too many questions.

She'd sat with traumatised policemen, soldiers, men who'd witnessed or taken part in horrifying acts in zones of conflict that broke the laws of warfare. In the end, remorse and culpability demanded a day of reckoning, whatever the consequences.

So it was with the Reverend Hill in the stale air of that squalid box of a garage waiting room, assailed by the banalities of Radio 1 coming at them through the thin walls. The turmoil within him was obvious, the absence of stillness. When he began to talk, it wasn't to Martha directly but as if to himself, his words escaping in an ill-ordered jumble at first.

'I knew it was wrong... I can't say I did not know that... yet I let it happen... I knowingly sinned against every precept I had lived my life by up to that point.'

His right hand was balled into a fist. He kept hitting it into the palm of the left. His knuckles showed through, pale beneath mottled skin.

'And Cynthia... dying hour by hour, alone... and there was I, thousands of miles away, in the disguise of a priest... what a fraud... what a weak and shameless fraud in the sight of God and man.'

One of the mechanics dropped a wrench into the inspection pit and shouted an obscenity. Ralph Hill didn't open his eyes. He was elsewhere, if only in his head.

'It was Bella who insisted I return home... it wasn't me, it wasn't my sense of obligation to do what was right... no, not at all... it was Bella's.'

Martha knew that Bella must have been his lover, the

South African political activist assassinated by letter bomb at his vicarage five years ago in 1985.

The killing made the papers for days but Ginny was reluctant to revisit that time with Martha except for one session when she got maudlin drunk and allowed her bone-deep anger to show out.

'Daddy betrayed us,' she'd said. 'Mummy and me, betrayed us without a thought but that treacherous little bitch, Bella… Christ, she betrayed everyone.'

Only later would Martha learn from Ginny's father just what she had meant.

*

However conciliatory his tone, the news Sir Frazer Harris delivered over cakes and coffee in the motorway service station did spoil Kat's day.

He had a connection in the Cabinet Office whose task was to ensure the prime minister was never wrong-footed by anything politically sensitive coming out of the civil war in Northern Ireland.

Sir Frazer said the Met Police detectives under Commander Benwell seemed to be putting great efforts into one particular unsolved murder.

'He must be spoilt for choice,' Kat said. 'Which one's he gone for?'

'The Army intelligence officer, the one blown up outside Ballymena three years ago.'

Kat tried not to let her reactions show. The game still had to be played. She finished her drink and dried her lips with a napkin.

'That was an IRA kill. What's Benwell going over all that again for?'

'Maybe because the Provos never claimed it.'

'Why would anyone take notice of anything those murdering shits say?'

'Maybe because they didn't do it.'

'Oh please, don't be so naive.'

Sir Frazer let this further insubordination pass. He seemed to savour Kat's growing discomfort.

'Tell me, Miss Walsh, the dead man had been on a surveillance operation with you... yes?'

'He was our driver on that night, true enough.'

'And the other man on the job was your missing agent, that's right too, isn't it?'

'Yes, and he gave a statement to the police but the two of them parted well before the bomb went off so he couldn't tell them much.'

'But he's vanished so he can't be re-interviewed about what happened.'

'Why do they need to talk to him again? Can't they just read his statement?'

'Of course they can, but something's missing from the timeline that Benwell's trying to establish and he's not happy.'

'Sorry, I'm being dense here but what exactly is missing?'

'According to what I've been told, Benwell's trying to find out where the man's car was parked before the surveillance operation began, where the bomb could have been placed.'

'I can't understand why, out of all the murders in that damned place, he's majoring on one with the IRA's fingerprints all over it.'

Sir Frazer sipped his coffee as if deliberately taking time to reply.

'Do you know of a double agent high up in the Provos command with the codename Navoi?'

'There isn't such a person.'

'Ah, so this must be something else above your pay grade.'

'I'd know about him if he existed.'

'All right, let me ask you if you know why this source is called Navoi?'

'Obviously not, but you're going to tell me.'

'Navoi is a region in Uzbekistan where they mine for gold,' Sir Frazer said. 'And that's what he's been giving the funny people for years... gold. Now Benwell's getting some.'

Kat was suddenly unsighted in her own little wilderness of mirrors.

'But what's in it for the funnies to allow Benwell access to him?'

'Because peace will come to Northern Ireland one day, Miss Walsh, and when it does, everyone who matters will want to be on the right side of it.'

Kat hardly needed to hear more. If any single operation of hers had an exposed flank, it was this one. And MI5's deep throat of a source would know that whoever put the bomb under the intelligence officer's car, it wasn't the IRA.

22: SINNERMAN

"Applaud, my friends, the comedy is over."

-    Ludwig van Beethoven, quoting the dying Augustus

'You know, Martha,' the Reverend Hill said, 'there is a painting in my church, it's a very old painting, the artist is unknown, but it shows a man in holy garb and we don't know his name either, so his life is lost to us and yet when we look at him, we make certain assumptions, that here was a man of God and principle, a priest worthy of our esteem because that is the impression which the image conveys. But we were not of his world, we cannot know it or him, therefore what we are seeing should not be taken at face value.'

'Yes, I remember this picture from the funeral. I thought it rather haunting. Why do you say this about it?'

Ralph Hill's only answer was a smile as bleak as it was ironic. They were finishing a delayed lunch of soup and rolls at The Lamb in the ancient town square of Axbridge. The cathedral city of Wells wasn't far but they'd not eaten waiting for the tyre to be replaced.

'I can't imagine how unbearable these past weeks must have been for you,' Martha said. 'I have known grief in my family and from my work but not to the same order as yours.'

Ralph Hill held the gaze of his dead daughter's closest

223

friend, her face sad and sincere, full of her own loss.

'Fathers and priests are meant to protect their flocks,' he said. 'If Virginia strayed from mine, it was because I was an indifferent shepherd.'

'No, I can't believe Ginny ever thought that.'

'Believe me, Martha, I have had more than enough time of late to reflect on my failings and I will take the truth of what I say to the grave.'

'I don't know why you feel this way but aren't you being hard on yourself?'

'Hard on myself... when I am the author of all the misfortune that's befallen me?'

This time, he looked through the window to the medieval town house across the narrow street, its oak jetties and gabled frame silvery in the afternoon sun. Martha waited until he returned to the room.

'Do you want to tell me why you have such feelings?'

'Now there's a question... that really is.'

'It's to do with South Africa, isn't it, with whatever you were doing there?'

'So Virginia told you something of this, did she?'

'A hint here and there but it was obviously something she didn't want to discuss in detail.'

'No... of course not. Why should she?'

A waitress cleared their table. Coffee was ordered. They were the only customers in the bar, theirs the only voices. Martha was anxious for him to carry on talking and not to break the confessional spell.

'Ginny did tell me once that you were a brave man... you took risks with your safety.'

'Maybe I did but not just with my safety.'

'Were they big risks... were lives at stake, for instance?'

'Yes.'

'People were killed, you mean?'

'Yes... murdered, tortured, put in jail for years. That all happened.'

'And could you have suffered any of these fates?'

'Had I been in the wrong place at the wrong time, it's possible, yes.'

'So why did you put yourself in such jeopardy?'

'Because fighting apartheid was a just war.'

'But it wasn't your war... not as a country clergyman in deepest Herefordshire.'

Ralph Hill didn't answer immediately. Absolution could only be achieved by going through truth, discomforting though the process was.

'What you say is correct. But I have to confess to something completely irresponsible here. Taking those risks energised me, made me and my ministry feel much more relevant to the extent that I came to want to face the dangers that were inherent in South Africa then.'

'Always needing a bigger and better hit... a bit like a drug user?'

'I suppose that's one way of putting it, though I am ashamed to admit it now.'

Martha refilled their cups from the glass coffee pot. The Reverend Hill took his white with sugar, two spoons. A cleaner began vacuuming the carpet in another bar. They would have to leave for Wells soon. But Martha pressed on gently with her advantage.

'When Ginny said you were brave, she also said you'd been a sort of courier in South Africa. What did she mean by that?'

He took a sip from his cup then set it down precisely on their table.

'I smuggled money in, large sums of money, to support the people fighting the government in Pretoria.'

'Wow, no wonder Ginny told me you were brave,' Martha said. 'Weren't people like that seen as terrorists by the regime?'

'And as subversives who would turn South Africa into a client state of Moscow.'

'So you were leading two lives... parish priest one day, undercover agent the next?'

'That's rather glamourising my role.'

'But there was a moral aspect to what you were doing, wasn't there?'

'Of course, but you mustn't discount the sheer exhilaration I got from it—'

'Being a world away from church fetes and tedious parish affairs?'

'Yes... instead of all that I was having secret meetings with political activists, eluding the regime's spies... it was hugely exciting and as I freely admit to you, very addictive.'

'But this all meant you being away from home a lot, I suppose...'

Ralph Hill looked away yet again, fixed on some atemporal memory, his body seemingly reduced within his sombre black suit. She wasn't there to judge but knew that Ginny had done so. Martha wanted him to justify himself, to understand a complex, contradictory man. She changed tack.

'How did you come to be so active on the ground in South Africa in the first place?'

226

Ralph Hill allowed himself the hint of another remorseful smile.

'It is one of my character defects that I get bored easily,' he said.

He twisted his wedding ring round and round and spoke as if giving evidence against himself as an expert witness in court.

'I'd attended one particular meeting of CND in London early in 1983 and afterwards in the street as I set off for home, a stranger approached me with a proposition that I should have declined... but of course I didn't.'

'And why didn't you?'

'Because another of my unfortunate traits is that of conceit.'

Martha listened to him, intrigued, setting out his recruitment as an undercover agent by a Swedish diplomat and an attractive young Swiss woman from the World Council of Churches.

'It sounds so cloak and dagger,' she said. 'I can see why getting involved appealed to your nature.'

'But politically, I was in total sympathy with them, Martha. I saw the magnitude of the evil of apartheid... a dehumanising system based on brutality and terror... blacks kept docile and if they rose up, be they men, women or children, they were shot down.'

'So the money you smuggled to them, what was that used for?'

Again, Ralph Hill took a moment to respond.

'I was told... no, I was assured, that it was to help to develop civil society out there.'

'And was it, did that happen?'

'That's what I wanted to believe.'

'You sound doubtful, like you can't be certain.'

'Certainty about anything or anyone couldn't be taken for granted in that conflict, Martha.'

'So the money you smuggled in might have had a less than peaceful purpose?'

'Given what I later found out, that is certainly the case, yes.'

'But Ginny told me you were a pacifist,' Martha said. 'That you considered all war morally wrong and futile and this was why you two fell out when she joined the Army.'

'Yes… but black people couldn't hold to a policy of non-violence indefinitely. The apartheid state was using overwhelming force against them and it would've been tantamount to being complicit in their own deaths to do nothing.'

'So your conscience as a priest wasn't troubled, knowing that the money could bring about more deaths, more blood being spilled?'

'Of course it was troubled,' Ralph Hill said. 'But as the Jews discovered in the last war, there comes a time when you have to fight your oppressors if you want to be free… that's if you can find the courage to face your own brutal death.'

'And in South Africa, could you do that… did you?'

'I felt sure I could, yes,' the Reverend Hill said.

It was a reflective Martha who turned away this time.

'I read once about a German soldier,' she said. 'He wouldn't look at the letters or the photographs on a French soldier he'd killed in the Great War.'

'Why was that?'

'Because had he done so, the dead man would have a

name and a family and wouldn't just be an anonymous enemy. Is that how you absolved yourself from the killings you helped to bring about... by not seeing the bodies of the victims as individuals?'

'No, no, it wasn't like that at all,' he said. 'I came to learn and accept that not all violence is sinful, that it can be the right course of action if all others have failed.'

'That sounds like a profound change of heart. Who was responsible for bringing it about?'

Ralph Hill looked at the cradle he'd made of his hands. His reply was barely more than a whisper.

'Bella... Bella did.'

The silence between them filled the bar. Martha waited for him to break it.

'When I first met her, it was as if every step I had ever taken in my life had led me to that moment... as if she had been waiting for me to arrive.'

'How could you possibly know that, Ralph? I can call you Ralph, can I?'

'Of course,' he said. 'I was never a romantic so I can't describe what I felt as love at first sight but I believe whatever it was went deeper... that every part of me knew this was meant to be, that I was meant to meet her and our lives would join together.'

'And yet you must also have known you had a wife and daughter back in England?'

'Yes, a sick wife and a daughter who, I am distraught to say, was a stranger to me—'

Martha had never taken a session like this. It was too personal for her to be dispassionate about what was being revealed. The relationship she'd shared with Ginny was intimate, without secrets, save for those she was hearing now from her father and which Martha guessed were the cause of the pain her friend suffered.

'A stranger who would never understand the quandary I was in during the days of complete turmoil in my mind after I met Bella.'

Martha would have asked what right he'd had to expect Ginny's understanding when her unfaithful father was about to break up their family, but the manager of The Lamb came across and tactfully said a coach party was due and tables had to be prepared.

They took the hint and gathered their coats. As they made for the car, Ralph Hill explained his dilemma a little more.

'I dared not tell Virginia about my double game in South Africa,' he said. 'To trust her with that information would have put the lives of many people in jeopardy, and what made all this more dangerous and complicated was when Bella told me she was playing an infinitely more deadly game than me.'

*

They headed through a wide marketplace in Wells, by stalls of vegetables and flowers, jewellery and art, and entered the cathedral gatehouse known as the Penniless Porch. Alms had been begged there for centuries. A homeless man, eyes bloodshot, kept up the tradition with his tin whistle. Martha put a silver coin in the cap by where his mongrel lay, ribs pale beneath its creamy brown fur.

The Reverend Hill strode ahead towards the wide swatch of lawn from which the sublime facade of Wells Cathedral rose up to the glory of God, a monument to the genius of medieval man's capabilities.

Sun and shade, honeyed stone and dark marble, statues in niches cast like actors in the magnificent drama of the piece.

To look upon it was to be humbled, to be put in one's place in a scheme of creation in which we assume centrality but are little more than the shadows of clouds passing over the earth, as the labourers who had quarried the stones now were or those who'd conceived the structure or preached the word of the Lord within it. Yet for Martha, this view of the cathedral always reinforced her faith in both God and man.

'Wonderful, isn't it?' she said. 'Takes my breath away every time I see it.'

Ralph Hill agreed. But he looked tired, frail almost. Daylight wasn't kind to a man not sleeping much and caring even less. His bags and books had been left at the house of Martha's father, the dean. He'd be back on Friday but until then, she would stay around, grieve together. They paused once inside the cathedral, awed by its numinous splendour as the pious must have been seven hundred years before when, master or peasant, this glimpse of the heaven their obeisance promised was first revealed.

Martha offered to show the Reverend Hill its many treasures that had survived the religious upheavals of the ancient world and the wars of this.

'That's kind,' he said. 'But I'd like to be on my own, if you don't mind. I still have much to reflect upon and in such a place as this, well... you understand, don't you?'

Martha smiled and said she did. She would wait for him in the north transept, beneath the pitiful figure of Christ crucified, carved out of yew. Ralph Hill passed down the vaulted nave alone, shoulders hunched, the weight of his own cross all too evident.

*

He slept with Bella Venter that first night, fell naked into her bed, lay with her without a thought for his wife, his vows to her or his church. Now almost sixty-three, the Reverend Hill had come late to sexual fulfilment.

He'd married Cynthia when he was forty-one. She met his conjugal expectations out of duty, not pleasure. Virginia arrived nonetheless a year later in 1962. But their infrequent coupling thereafter was a passionless business for which Cynthia made it clear she had neither wish nor desire.

Bella, on the other hand, was lustful, earthy, a woman almost twenty years younger than him and who, like soldiers in wartime, was aroused by the nearness of violent death, for she knew, like them, that life was but a loan and could be called in at any time.

'Tell me about yourself, Ralph,' she'd said.

They were in the storeroom above the backstreet pharmacy in Johannesburg. Abraham had left and they were alone.

'What's driving you to take such a risk with your own safety and freedom for us?'

'You have a just cause,' he said. 'The poor and the oppressed need to be given hope.'

'Yes, but don't forget that causes and ideas can have consequences, Ralph.'

And so did infatuation. His with Bella bordered on the irrational, impaired all judgement and sense of responsibility.

He could still hear the warning he chose to ignore, hear the intonations of her acquired English accent overlaying an Afrikaans heritage. And in the flames of the votive candles by where he now sat, he imagined her face, that wry, quizzical look she had, smiling at his devotion.

Yes, he had loved and been loved. But at what price?

Had this or anything he'd done been worth the sacrifices he'd made? Or was it a case of when a hand is taken out of water, there is no evidence that it was ever there at all?

*

'I have attended the death beds of many people, Bella,' Ralph Hill says. 'It's my experience that they rarely regretted the risks they'd taken during their lives, just the ones they hadn't.'

'And that's why you're helping us, is it?'

'No, not entirely. I believe in what you're doing and if by assisting you in some small way that entails a degree of risk to me, so be it.'

'So you subscribe to the theology of partisanship?'

'If you mean Christians having to take sides then yes, I do. There can be no compromise with apartheid, the killing of children and all the other horrors of this system.'

'Which makes you a dangerous troublemaker as far as our government is concerned.'

'Or a priest who has come to believe that liberation movements are the embodiment of the gospel, of its message of love and justice.'

Bella smiles at this. She's already locked the money he's smuggled inside a wall safe. Twenty thousand pounds sterling in Dutch guilders. High denomination notes.

'Thank you,' she'd said. 'Our work cannot continue without the generosity of others.'

She takes off her white coat. He sees the sway of her back beneath her satin shirt, the black strap of her bra, the curve of what it contains. She knows he is watching. She half turns and smiles. He should look away, feign embarrassment, but doesn't. He can't.

'Come,' she says. 'You must eat and so must I.'

There is another side entrance. It leads through a narrow alley smelling of animal piss, rotting fruit, beer. The heat of the windless day is compressed between high walls. Bella hurries on ahead as Abraham had done. Little children stop playing and stare at them. A baby cries somewhere. Bella reaches the steps of an apartment block. Washing hangs in colourful swags along the walkways. They make it to the second floor. Bella unlocks a protective barrier of welded steel rods then an inner wooden door. The room is dark, the air within is still. She switches on a ceiling fan.

'Would you like a drink?' she says. 'I have iced tea, beer, wine if you'd prefer.'

'Might it be in order to have a glass of wine?'

'Of course. White OK?'

'Perfect, yes.'

She takes two long-stemmed glasses from a shelf and a bottle of Bon Courage from the fridge. He feels as awkward as a teenager.

Is this her flat, has she a husband somewhere, children? Already in his head he knows where this might lead – where he wants it to lead. But she can't possibly feel the same about him… can she?

'Cheers, comrade,' she says. 'Welcome to the revolution.'

They talk politics, apartheid, the armed struggle, his almost communistic views and sympathies. She asks about his parish, his wife, his family background but gives away nothing about her own.

The wine keeps coming. It's more than pleasant, hints of peaches, oranges. He feels slightly drunk, light-headed. They're side by side on Bella's sofa. She lights candles and joss sticks.

'You're a good man, Ralph, but not a happy one.'

'That obvious, is it?'

'Your heart is heavy for some reason, isn't it?'

Bella opens another bottle and brings flatbreads, cheese, olives on a plate from the kitchen. It's like having a picnic in the twilight. She puts on a Nina Simone tape, sultry and soulful.

'Do you like dancing, Ralph?'

'Not something I've done in many a year.'

'It'll come back to you... just hold me round the waist and shuffle your feet.'

So he does and Nina wants to know where the sinnerman will run to. The song becomes more intense. Bella's eyes close. Her hands link behind Ralph's head. Her breasts, cupped behind satin, press against his priestly black shirt.

She kisses him. It is Bella who is in control, Bella who leads him to where he's never been and never wants to leave.

And in a minute more, they are in her bedroom, their clothes where they fall. He is without and within her, and she him. There is nothing in his mind save a primitive, all-consuming urge to possess her. Then it is done. It is over. Nothing in his life has prepared him for how he feels, how to emerge from this let-me-die-now moment.

Bella gets out of bed, pale in the half light, unashamed. She parts the curtain an inch or so and looks down into the alley. She's checking for something... but for what, for whom? The Reverend Hill doesn't notice. He lies back, as if in some far-away place, by an ocean of satisfied peace.

He feels no guilt, only contentment.

'Ralph? Ralph? Don't go to sleep.'

'Why... why not? Come here, by me again.'

'No, I can't. There isn't time. We have to get you back to your hotel.'

Bella somehow sounds different. Her manner towards him seems to have changed, albeit subtly. He sits up, concerned.

'Are you all right? Have I done something wrong?'

'No, Ralph... of course not. Come, we must leave here. It's not safe.'

They dress hurriedly. Outside, the rhythms of urban Africa beat through the night air. Voices, laughing, shouting, traffic horns, juke boxes. It all comes at the Reverend Hill, confused enough already. What has just happened? And why?

Bella halts at a corner, her face close to his.

'Ralph, listen to me,' she says. 'I want you to go back to England as soon as you can.'

'Go back? Why on earth are you saying that? I've only just arrived.'

'Yes, but it's too dangerous for you here.'

'I'm aware of all the risks. They've been spelled out to me and I accept them.'

'No, you're not listening to me,' she says. 'There's a war

going on here, a nasty, brutish war and it's too dirty for an innocent like you.'

'I'm sorry, Bella. No. I'm staying and I shall come back and carry on helping.'

She took both his hands in hers.

'I'm going to tell you something I shouldn't, Ralph... we're in the third phase of our armed struggle this year... that means more violent attacks than ever on military bases, power stations, on economic targets. The enemy will fight back... there will be retribution.'

'I understand all that, I accept it.'

'No, Ralph... what you don't understand is me.'

'What are you talking about?'

'I am not what you think... I am not what you see,' Bella says. 'Be wise, my honourable friend. Go home and stay with your family and your flock.'

She kisses the first two fingers of her right hand, puts them to his lips then is gone into the night. And so are her words of advice.

*

Martha worried when the Reverend Hill wasn't in the north transept to meet her as arranged. She asked one of the guides to help her look for him. They found him in the chapter house where canons would once have met to discuss cathedral business beneath a delicate tracery of vaulting ribs, springing across the ceiling like a fountain from a central pillar. He was asleep and seemed not to know where he was.

23: DISCRETION

"The world is a narrow bridge
but (do) not fear."

-     Rebbe Nachman of Breslov

After breakfast on the last Friday of every month, Sir Frazer Harris took a taxi from his club in St James's to Victoria station and paid cash for a ticket to Bognor Regis, the south coast town that, rather like him, had seen better days since the ailing king convalesced there in the 1920s. For these visits, the former defence secretary invariably wore an old tweed jacket, matching waistcoat and cap, and bottle green corduroy trousers.

It was a disguise of sorts. Though it was a while since his was a face on TV, people sometimes stared and bolder ones would ask who he used to be. But his seaside trips were private affairs. He wished only for the anonymity of crowds.

From Bognor Regis station, he walked down towards the promenade and turned right at the Royal Norfolk Hotel, all palm trees, lawns and the gilded crest of royal patronage shining in the sun. He'd stayed there once during a by-election.

So had the melancholic entertainer Tony Hancock, to film a dark comedy about a Punch and Judy man with marital problems. Sir Fraser could identify with this. His own wife was dead and not mourned.

A few hundred yards further on was a road of large villas, late Victorian with well-maintained front gardens behind hedges of beech and hornbeam.

The seventh house had its name, Woodside, cut into the gate's stone pillars. A Jaguar and a Jeep were parked outside. Sir Frazer strode up the path, not to the front door but towards the basement flat at the rear of the property. For once, there was a smile on his face.

*

The clock showed it was nearly eleven. He was due soon. The irises he'd sent the day before were an agreed code for how the afternoon should play out. Roses would've meant an entirely different performance.

She put the flowers in the art deco vase on the mantelpiece by the framed photograph of him and his dead mother near the House of Commons. The chintzy tea service from his family home was set on the table with slices of Battenberg on the cake stand. Clean towels hung in the bathroom and she'd made the bed with virgin sheets of crispy ironed Egyptian cotton. The props were in place, the set dressed.

And so was she – floral pinny, hair gathered in a headscarf like factory women favoured in the war, no make-up. She waited for his entrance on stage but with little need to rehearse her lines.

'Hello, Ma,' he will say and she'll reply, 'And how's my lovely boy today?'

They'd met at some theatrical party in the West End. She

was younger then – had an agent, got regular bookings, even did a few weeks in Coronation Street.

It was only a cough and a spit of a part but it was how the old boy recognised her. He came across as a man-of-the-people fan of Corrie so each hit on the other… in a manner of speaking.

She'd no idea who he was or what he did, not at first. All the goings-on in Westminster went over her head and she rarely read a newspaper unless she was in it. It was more important that he had an apartment in the Barbican, dressed well and waiters in pricey restaurants bowed and scraped to him.

But her world of make-up and make-believe couldn't always be relied upon to pay the rent. For a woman on her second divorce, his was a smile to return, an arm to link. So she got to know him and the Barbican rather well, and The Ivy and Rules and the Savoy Grill.

By then she'd discovered he was a politician, an MP for some industrial town without a playhouse so she didn't know it.

Her ex was a one-time showbiz writer who, like all the hacks in Fleet Street, couldn't lie straight in bed. His earnings, such as they were, either went up his nose or down a urinal, so her divorce settlement was south of nothing.

It was around then her phone stopped ringing. Work was drying up. She needed an angel, even if he was overweight and not at all handsome. Yet he was the one who came to appear on telly more often than she'd ever done.

He wasn't her only beau, of course. But in her calling, some roles had required she spend half the shoot with someone else's tongue in her mouth so what was the difference?

It's all an act, sweetie… just an act. Didn't mean a thing.

She heard a quiet tapping at her door.

'OK, you're on, love. Get out front and knock 'em for six.'

And there he stood.

'Hello, Ma…'

*

The story is told of a Jewish mama whose young son was unhealthily close to her. A psychiatrist warned about this relationship, to which she replied with some exasperation, 'Oedipus, schmoedipus, what does it matter so long as a boy loves his mother?'

But later in life, observe the damage done, the psychological wounds open up, if not on a shrink's couch then in the bedroom of a whore.

Sir Frazer looked around the room approvingly. Totemic memories in place. Tea was drunk, cake eaten, cups and saucers and plates put on the draining board to be washed later. They moved to the couch and sat side by side.

'How are things with you, Ma? All well, are they?'

'Yes, they are, sweetie,' she said.

'It's so good to see you again.'

'And you, my lovely. It's been too long, far too long.'

'I've been so busy, you see… seems like I never get a moment to myself.'

'No wonder you look so tired. Why don't I run a nice bath for you, get you relaxed?'

'Will you, Ma? I'd like that… I really would.'

241

She went to the bathroom, staying in character, keeping to the script. The bath was a creamy white roll top tub with claw and ball feet and brass taps. She tested the water with her elbow. Her boy mustn't get scalded.

This was all he wanted from her physically these days. He'd changed after losing his seat in parliament, wasn't the same man, became fearful of sex. And now this infantilism, this oedipal crisis that she found weird and pathetic and ludicrous, all at the same time.

But isn't that just like life itself, darling?

If it is, it's a bit off the wall, even for me.

Still, he must trust you with his most secret self, mustn't he?

Only because he holds all my bloody cards.

She called him in. He sat on the loo and removed his shoes and socks then his shirt.

'I better help you with the rest,' she said. 'Stand up for me.'

He did as he was told.

'Right, let's get all this off, my lovely… these trousers and pants.'

The knight of the realm who'd once directed the armed forces of a nuclear nation and been a powerful voice in Cabinet, now stood in wistful silence, remembering a time and a place long gone but where, in the deepest, most repressed reaches of his being, he desired to return, to return through the mystery from whence he'd arrived in the world and the safety of the grave-like womb within.

'Now, let's get you in the bath, shall we?'

He stepped into the water and sat amid the frothy bubbles, arms around his knees, head bowed. She took a flannel and

242

began to wash his back and rinse his hair.

'Now your private parts,' she said. 'Stand up again.'

He did so and faced her. She rubbed a bar of soap in her bare wet hands until they were lathered and began to massage his thighs, his backside and pot belly, then down through his wiry pubic hairs to his unresponsive cock and the shrivelled balls beneath.

His eyes were closed, his hands above his head, gripping the rail of the shower curtain.

'That feel OK, does it? Are we a clean boy, now?'

He didn't reply nor would he. She towelled him down slowly, his front and back and between his legs then his thinning grey hair.

'Shall we put your pyjamas on, now?'

He shook his head. So she led him by the hand, naked, into the adjoining room and the cool expanse of white linen that was her bed. He got in and pulled the sheets up to his neck. She took off her pinny and lay beside him. They were in semi-darkness, lit only by the scented candles on her dressing table.

'Do you want me to read you a story?' she said.

Again, he shook his head and put his face to her breasts.

'Ah, so this is what my lovely boy wants. Well, good boys deserve nice presents, don't they?'

*

Trains north from Bognor Regis to Victoria in the early evening were rarely overcrowded. Commuters were heading the other way. Sir Frazer found a seat well away from the few other passengers in his carriage. He had an *Evening Standard* to pretend to read as he mentally relived the day. There was a calmness about him, a feeling of wellbeing, of warmth.

The train pulled out and he felt himself drifting towards sleep.

'These seats aren't taken, are they?'

He opened his eyes to see a man standing over him, grey overcoat, black hair, unsmiling, pugnacious face. Behind him stood a younger man in a dark blue suit.

'No, they're not,' Sir Frazer said. 'But neither are any of the other empty ones.'

'You'd rather we didn't sit by you, then?'

'Not at all. You sit here and I'll move.'

'No, please, stay where you are, Sir Frazer... we'll not disturb your peace for long.'

He became fully awake. They knew who he was. Were they terrorists? They'd South London accents, not Irish. Christ, why hadn't they let him keep his armed protection officer? Even as he tried to look unfazed, the younger man sat next to him and the other in front. He was boxed in.

'There, that's cosy, isn't it, sir?'

'Who the hell are you? What are you up to?'

The man leaned forward, put his face close to Sir Frazer's. His breath gave off a hint of the strong mints that disguise the smell of alcohol.

'We're not up to anything, sir. We're detectives from the Met Police.'

'I find that hard to believe.'

'This is my warrant card... see? I'm Commander Benwell of the Major Crimes Unit and this is Inspector Roach.'

Sir Frazer would have written this down but he'd neither pen nor paper.

'The thing is, Sir Frazer, we'd just like a quiet word.'

'Then make an appointment through my solicitor.'

'Not a good idea, sir. We're trying to keep this informal... like this conversation never took place. You understand, I'm sure.'

'No, I don't understand, not for one minute do I understand. Why have I the unwanted pleasure of your company?'

'It's about a murder, sir... you could call it an assassination, I suppose... and our duty is to find the man responsible.'

'I know nothing about such matters.'

'Of course you don't. Politics is your game, isn't it? Giving cover to those doing the dirty work but keeping your own hands clean. That's it, isn't it?'

'I've no idea what you're talking about but I find your manner deeply offensive and I'll be making a formal complaint to the commissioner.'

'I think you know exactly what I'm talking about, sir. Ireland, Northern Ireland. Who killed who and why, that's what interests us.'

'I can't help you with any of this but the way you're going about your inquiry wouldn't encourage me to assist you even if I could.'

'No? Well let's try this, then. You've just left a house called Woodside, which you bought through a company in the Isle of Man after you got kicked out of your constituency. Right?'

Sir Frazer's display of righteous anger was giving way to fear – a fear of what this policeman knew.

'Anything I have to say I will say to the commissioner.'

'You go ahead, but indulge me for a moment more,' Benwell said. 'Woodside is split into four flats, not counting the basement flat, which is occupied by a Miss Poppy Nelson who describes herself as an actress but in real life, manages the property for you in lieu of rent. I'm still on the button here, am I not?'

'I've no idea where all this is leading or what it's got to do with murder or Northern Ireland.'

'You're being really patient, Sir Frazer, and I appreciate that so let's grab the bull by the bollocks, shall we? Miss Nelson is a hooker, a lady of the night who sells her body to men for money. OK?'

'What she does in her own time is a matter for her.'

'I suppose that's one way of looking at it, sir, but I could build a case against you of living off her immoral earnings.'

'That's insane, ridiculous. No one'll listen to you.'

'Well, you say that but I think the Crown Prosecution Service would give it a run.'

The former minister stood up, puce with impotent rage, but Inspector Roach sat him down, firmly, without fuss. Benwell asked if he remembered the Profumo sex scandal back in the early 1960s.

'Christ, didn't the media smack a few bottoms back then, Sir Frazer? Old Profumo's mate, the osteopath, getting stung with the same charge as we could pin on you.'

'You're blackmailing me, you bastard.'

'Not blackmailing, sir, I'm trying to save you from the Establishment and from Fleet Street.'

'Where a little shit like you will have friends, no doubt.'

'They'd certainly chase Miss Nelson, that's for sure. Quite a story hers, isn't it? It'd be a battle of the tabloid

246

cheque books to sign her up... you know how these things work, sir.'

There is a moment when a rabbit becomes quiet in the jaws of a ferret. It has squealed and struggled all it can, then goes limp. It knows it's as good as dead already.

Sir Frazer Harris slumped back in his seat. No one said a word, not until he asked what the deal was. Benwell set out his terms for taking no further action.

He knew about the undercover ex-soldier who'd gone AWOL, that something stank about the killing of an Army intelligence officer, that Sir Frazer had met with the agent runner, Kat Walsh.

'Right, understand this,' Benwell said. 'I want this guy found. The job I've been given to do is a poisoned fucking bucket and they're setting me up to fail. But I'll not be doing that so I want you into Walsh like a bloody Tampax. Make it your business to find out the moment she knows where he is then tell me. OK?'

Sir Frazer nodded. He'd no choice but to agree.

'And make no mistake,' Benwell said, 'if I get fucked on this, so will you.'

Sir Frazer stared at the detective's card in his hand. The train slowed into East Croydon station. Benwell got up to leave with Roach but had time for a final parting shot.

'Fond of your mother, were you, sir? I'm a Barnardo's boy myself... didn't ever know mine. Still, what you never had you never miss. Isn't that what they say?'

24: HIDING

"Farewell all joys.
O death come close mine eyes."

- From Orlando Gibbons' first set of madrigals, 1612

It took less than half an hour's research and a few questions in Stranraer library for Tilly Brown to establish that Robbo must have rented his cottage from the area's biggest landowner, Blair-Cameron Estates.

She arrived without an appointment at their headquarters in a converted stable block amid a complex of stone farm buildings near the ruins of Glenluce Abbey. The estate manager was a small, plump man with thinning, slicked back hair, skittering around his office in a black suit, tie and shoes, rather like a crow in a cage.

'I'm going to a funeral,' he said. 'What do you want?'

Tilly explained that she was a retired Met Police lawyer trying to trace the person who ran a trekking centre from one of Blair-Cameron's properties.

'Ah, him… the amazing invisible man.'

'What do you mean by that?'

'We can't find him. He's done a bunk without paying his rent for the last quarter.'

'Oh dear, so you've no idea where he is?'

'No, and neither have our debt collectors.'

'I see. Presumably he paid by standing order so can't he be traced through his bank?'

'No, that was the thing with him, always paid us in cash, which was a bit unusual.'

'Especially these days,' Tilly said. 'But tell me, what name did he use to rent the cottage?'

'You think he uses an alias?'

'Can't be ruled out, that's why it'd be helpful to know what he called himself round here.'

The manager opened the top drawer of a metal filing cabinet and pulled out two sheets of paper from a manila folder.

'This is our agreement with him, called himself Brian Oliver Roby.'

'Right, that figures,' Tilly said. 'Is there anything else of interest, any previous addresses or personal details?'

'No, nothing like that but he gave a reference for himself from the Army... says he had an excellent record, was resourceful, an honest man with leadership qualities.'

'What's the name of the person who signed it?'

'The signature's unreadable and it's not typed underneath, either.'

'But is it on official notepaper?'

'Yes, Ministry of Defence... Old Admiralty Building, Archway Block South, London SW1.'

'Any reference number, anything like that?'

'No, nothing.'

Tilly then asked if Roby ever had a female, maybe a friend, to help to run his business.

'Not to my knowledge. I doubt if he could've afforded to

pay anyone.'

'So no one's been answering the phone at the cottage in the past few weeks?'

'Absolutely not, no. We've changed the locks – no one can get in since he disappeared.'

'And what's happened to all his possessions?'

'The cottage was let furnished so there was only his shotgun and a few paperbacks and they're stored away safe here.'

'I take it you two must have met... what were your impressions of him?'

'My impressions... well, I was never a military man but I'd say there was something about Roby that made me think he might have seen things he wanted to forget. But what do I know?'

'Or any of us, come to that,' Tilly said.

'Can I ask why you're asking all these questions? What else has he been up to?'

'I'm sorry... you'll understand, I'm sure... security and all that, but I'm grateful for your help.'

Tilly kept a straight face as the manager made ten out of two and two.

'Look,' he said. 'Go and see Phil Prentice who runs a garage on the road to Newton Stewart. It's not far, just out of Glenluce, and he might fill in a few gaps for you.'

'OK, I will. Thanks. Were he and Roby friends?'

'If they were, they're not any more.'

'Why is that, then?'

'Because Phil didn't get paid for some big job on Roby's vehicle so he's seized it and has a mind to sell it if he can.'

'His Land Rover, you mean?'

'Yes, a big tank of a thing but it could make enough to cover the outstanding bill.'

*

The taxi dropped Robbo five miles from Petersfield on a country lane leading over the South Downs. He'd been picked up from a guest house in town and wore an ill-fitting brown suit and blue shirt and carried an imitation leather overnight bag. His forehead still bore traces of cuts, bruising and reddened scars. He told the driver where he wanted to go but his look and manner discouraged further conversation. Once the cab had left, Robbo set off towards the village of Chalton.

It was a chill morning. Spiders' webs sparkled with dew in the hedges on either side. The ragged remains of a late autumn mist were still caught in the branches of distant trees, all shedding their leaves now.

It had been a tiring journey by bus, train and hitch-hiked rides from mid-Wales to Petersfield but he'd got away with it. He was almost there, almost at his next staging post.

He'd read about this place in a magazine, logged it mentally for a rainy day. The weather was never certain in Robbo's world. But where better to hide in plain sight than on a stage such as this?

Just before ten o'clock, two coach parties of children and teachers arrived followed by other visitors – pensioners, amateur historians and the curious on trips out. Robbo joined the queue for tickets then walked into the past, back almost three thousand years to a faithfully reconstructed Iron Age settlement.

Here, the business of archaeology wasn't digging up bits of pot from the earth but was carried out as a living experiment above ground. The tools and methods of building and farming were employed to understand how Iron Age people actually existed. Robbo stood by himself admiring one of the roundhouses. It had a conical thatched roof and cob walls painted with liquid clay then covered in swirling designs in ochre and hematite. A young woman in Iron Age costume – wrap-round woollen skirt and a muddy yellow cloak pinned at the shoulder with a silver brooch – came over to him.

'Hi,' she said. 'This your first visit to us?'

She looked every inch a freckle-faced Celt – gingery hair in fly-away ringlets, eyes as green as the Irish Sea.

'I hope you're enjoying what you're seeing.'

'I am, yes,' Robbo said. 'Everything's so authentic, really impressive.'

'Do you want to see inside? I can show you if you want.'

A log fire burned in an open hearth sunk in the middle of a floor made from crushed chalk. Smoke filtered up to – then through – the thatch of water reeds, leaving a golden sheen on the underside.

Around the drum of a room were animal skin beds, stones for grinding corn, cooking utensils, a domed clay oven for baking bread.

'You can really imagine how it would've been, can't you?' she said. 'Cauldrons of porridge or stew hanging over the fire, kids running about, men coming in from the fields…'

'Are you a volunteer here, a student?'

'Yes, final year archaeology at Southampton so this is like fieldwork with a difference.'

'Is it easy to become a volunteer?'

'We're always looking for people in my team. Are you interested, then?'

'I could be.'

'Seriously, dressing up in gear like this?'

'I've got the legs for it and I can take off any accent you want.'

She smiled. He was old enough to be her father but attractive in a world-weary sort of way.

'Don't tell me, you're an actor between parts, resting. Am I right?'

'I'm whatever you want me to be.'

It was his turn to smile, to disarm, to co-opt to his cause.

'Tell me your name,' he said.

'Mags, short for Margaret. And you?'

'Robbie, short for nothing.'

'Well, Robbie, you won't be needing any make-up, will you?' she said. 'You already look like you've been in a battle with a rival tribe.'

'Ah, my scars you mean...'

'Sorry, didn't mean to be personal.'

'That's all right... a car accident.'

'Me and my big mouth.'

'Don't worry, it's OK.'

'Was it a bad one, the accident?'

Robbo paused for effect, to let his face cloud over.

'Bad enough... my wife didn't survive it, I'm afraid.'

'Oh God, I'm so sorry. I wouldn't have said anything if—'

'You weren't to know.'

'Yes, but—'

'Look, I just need my mind taken off things... doing something like this would, you know...'

'You don't have to say any more, I understand,' Mags said.

'Thanks, I appreciate that.'

'Look, I'm due a break about this time. Do you fancy a coffee and I can tell you about what our volunteers do?'

*

Phil Prentice's garage was a weathered shed the size of a small village hall, built of planks, and where they had rotted or fallen off, patched up with corrugated iron. A line of second-hand cars awaited buyers on the concrete forecourt. Tilly Brown parked and went inside the workshop. A man with a face as oily as his overalls was under the bonnet of a pick-up truck with a spanner and a flashlight.

She asked if he was Mr Prentice.

'Yes, I'm him,' he said. 'But I'm booked up, can't take on any more work.'

Tilly explained why she was there. Prentice listened, wiping his hands on a rag, not at all surprised that a lawyer from London was on the tail of a man who'd cheated him.

'Four hundred pounds... that's what he's done me out of... four hundred pounds.'

'That's a big loss for any business to take.'

'Reconditioned gearbox I fitted. Parts and labour, not cheap... not cheap at all.'

'Was that for his Land Rover?'

'Aye, and I've kept the damn thing and if I get the paperwork for it, it'll be out on the front there and I'll sell it.'

Tilly asked how long Brian Roby had lived and worked in the area.

'Let me see… two years or so, maybe more. Did a service for him then he would bring it in if there was something he couldn't fix on his own.'

'Did he ever tell you anything about what he did in the Army?'

'Not one to talk about himself, he wasn't, but I got the feeling he didn't trust anyone that's why he lived the life he did, up in the hills, on his own.'

'Do you think he was making a decent living doing what he was round here?'

'Well, if he couldn't pay his debt to me then he couldn't have been, could he?'

'Would you mind if I looked inside his vehicle?'

'No, you go ahead. It's round the back but there's nothing to see inside it… everything's been cleared out.'

'You mean there were personal possessions in it?'

'Bits of paper, litter. Nothing of any value.'

'Do you still have it, the stuff you found?'

'It'll not help you but if you want to go through *my* rubbish bin, it's all in there waiting for the bin men next week.'

So Tilly dug through it, and that's when she found the envelope.

*

It was a night of stars and stillness. Robbo had completed his third day as a volunteer and was resting amid a scatter of fleeces on a crudely built bed. Blue-grey smoke rose from the open hearth. The only sounds were the hiss of logs burning to ash and a vixen's shrieks on the hills beyond. He was still wearing his costume: leather sandals and trousers called *braccae*, and a long linen tunic.

His dyed red cloak hung from a peg. He'd told Mags he wanted to stay in the roundhouse to really get into the character of an Iron Age man.

As Robbo took on his new persona – that of *Brennus*, meaning raven – so some of the traits of his old self fell away and he began to notice the absence of fear, to sense that he had less need to be hypervigilant.

He wasn't threatened, wasn't prey to those transient fugues when he seemed to be just a witness to what he himself was doing.

Maybe such times were a psychological consequence of culpability, the price of the guilt one paid knowing that some action taken had been wrong and irreversible.

His penance was the recurring nightmare in which he saw himself taking the young woman in Bolivia in his arms again, putting his lips to hers, his tongue in her mouth, his hands over her breasts and up to the soft whiteness of her throat. Their faces part, just long enough for one to look into the eyes of the other and then that final kiss and the sudden, brutal wrench of her head.

Such was his anger and shame that day, he wished he'd joined her, tumbling down that ravine to eternity. This wasn't war or conflict or what he'd been trained for. He'd been used as the instrument of another, one who'd exploited his venality and his dog-like devotion.

With the girl's killing – which could not have been foreseen – what had been a daring if risk-laden caper schemed up by Kat to make them a fortune would be re-enacted in his head until his own eyes closed forever. Yet he'd proved himself worthy of trust to the cartel and thus to life itself. But he determined then that even in the jungle, there had to be justice. And so it was that Frederico's neck proved no more robust than that of the girl with no name.

*

Robbo snared a rabbit that afternoon. He'd lived off the land – and his wits – long enough to survive the notional rigours of a fake Iron Age settlement.

The rabbit was skinned, its floppy purple-brown guts buried and the body jointed to be roasted over the fire. These cooked pieces were then put in a vegetable stew. After a day hauling timber and labouring for the carpenter to make uprights for a new longhouse, it was a satisfying supper.

Mags dropped by later to check he was OK. She wanted to talk; he didn't. It was sufficient that she'd seen the scars on the surface of her new volunteer. He remained in uneasy remission.

That didn't mean he was in denial about his life or situation – no unconscious defence mechanism was at work on his psyche, saving him from the unbearable and all that he knew was beyond atonement. His would always be a restless sleep.

*

Tilly Brown's drive back to North London from Scotland was exhausting, despite pit stops at several motorway service stations. She slumped on her couch to open the bills and circulars that Mrs Nally had left on the hall stand after letting herself in to feed the cat.

Only the envelope Tilly had fished out of the bin at Robbo's garage concerned her at that moment. She'd make a cup of tea then begin discreet inquiries about the addressee, one Sally Tobin. Robbo had written to her but someone scrawled "return to sender" on the envelope. Whatever had been inside was missing.

It was possible the woman had moved from the address in West Sussex. But at least it was a start in getting a fix on the intriguing Robbo.

Was Sally Tobin a friend or a lover, or, if he'd lied to Tilly in Scotland, his ex-wife?

She switched on the kettle and went down to her darkroom in the cellar to check that her dehumidifier hadn't overflowed. All was fine, all her equipment as it had been when she left.

But she sensed something missing. It took a moment to realise that her blow-up of Robbo getting into the helicopter was no longer on the desk where she'd left it for framing. She was sure that's where it'd been. The cellar was only small. It couldn't be anywhere else.

And when she looked for the negatives of him and the Gazelle, they were missing too. She ran upstairs. Nothing else had been taken. Her TV, video player, radio, jewellery and every other item a burglar might steal were all still in place, nor could she detect a single sign of forced entry at any door or window.

Tilly sat down at the table, hand to her mouth. Someone had been in her home, violated it. But who, and why? The kettle whistled and steam filled the kitchen around her but she ignored it. She was in shock and couldn't move.

25: ASSASSIN

"... truth will come to light;
murder cannot be hid long."

- The Merchant of Venice, Act II, Scene II

'Welcome home, my hero,' Kat says. 'We've done it, we've fucking done it.'

She's smiling, laughing, red hair aflame in the morning sun. Robbo has just cleared Customs at Heathrow after a slog of a journey from Lima with a transfer in Miami. His white slacks are creased, shirt undone at the collar.

But if Kat is overjoyed at seeing him, Robbo is coming across as detached, preoccupied.

'What's up, lover? Still jet-lagged?'

He is but that doesn't explain his mood.

'It's great to see you, anyway,' she says. 'What a star.'

Robbo doesn't reply. His eyes are tired. He can never sleep on planes. Kat links his arm as they walk to the car park. She's buzzing, barely able to contain her excitement.

'My buyer just needs the nod about an RV to collect—'

'Keep your voice down,' he says.

'OK, sorry. Anyway, he reckons we'll clear a hundred thousand each, you and me, and that's just for starters.'

'That's what he's saying, is it?'

His tan leather suitcase is stowed in the boot of Kat's car.

They pick up the M4 and head west. Robbo tips the passenger seat back and stretches his legs. England looks luridly green and peaceful, a world away from the one he's just left and all that he did there.

'It shouldn't take us long,' she says. 'You'll like where I've booked… right little love nest.'

Kat had arrived back from jungle training three weeks earlier and rented a cottage in Wiltshire for the leave she was due. She'd flown into RAF Lyneham from Belize via Gander on a Special Forces C-130 – a *Black Herc*. Security checked her kitbag but only for unauthorised weapons and ammunition. That's all they are ever concerned with. Nothing else. She'd banked on that.

But even if she'd been caught with the three bricks of coke, she would say she'd been testing the system for weaknesses. Kat was never short of solutions to problems.

'Do you want to stop at a service station… get a coffee or anything?'

'No, let's push on,' he says.

'You sure you're all right, Robbo? You seem on edge.'

'Goes with the territory, doesn't it?'

'Yeah, but we've got away with it, lover. It's over, you can ease up now.'

'Can I? You sure of that?'

'Absolutely. Everything's cool this end.'

'So you think it's all plain sailing from here?'

'Why wouldn't it be? Come on, what's on your mind? Tell me.'

'No, can't talk now… don't want to.'

'OK, that's all right, I understand. Long flight and all

that.'

'Yeah, just put your foot down.'

'You'll feel better after a shower and there's a big soft bed. Everything else can wait. You just relax.'

The cottage is a homage to how an urbanite pictures a place in the country – hunting scene prints on the walls, floral-design curtains and carpets, and horse brasses on the mantelpiece above a log burner.

Robbo doesn't notice any of it and heads straight to the bathroom. He strips off and in the mirror catches sight of someone he once knew, burnt by the sun and much else. After Bolivia there will be no medals for this soldier, for there is no honour due to him.

Wasn't there a line in the bible asking what profit would be had by gaining the whole world while losing your soul in the process?

A shower washes away all traces of sweat and grime from his travels. The inner man will have to wait. Kat enters as he dries himself with a white towel.

'Feeling better now?' she says.

He ignores the question.

'How about something to eat? I can do us some smoked salmon, scrambled eggs, a glass of fizz?'

'Nothing for me… just sleep.'

He gets into bed, still naked. Kat, conscience untroubled, wants to fuck him; if she only realised, she already had. She undresses, crouches beneath the sheets and tries bringing him to life with her fingers, her mouth. He does not respond. Maybe it'll be different later. So she lies curled up close behind him and bides her time.

*

Robbo wakes, unsure where he is or if it's day or night. He's alone in a strange room. There's a strip of light showing beneath the door. Someone is moving about on the other side. Plates, glasses, cutlery are being set on a table. Then he remembers. He gets up, has a pee, washes his face. Kat calls through the bathroom door.

'Hi, Robbo,' she says. 'You must be hungry by now.'

'Be with you in a minute.'

He goes back to the bedroom and puts on fresh clothes – jeans, white silk shirt, blue cotton jacket.

'There's champagne in the fridge, lover. You open it and I'll serve.'

Kat proposes a toast to their triumph and future success. They clink glasses, drink then eat the promised smoked salmon but mostly in silence. It's nearly ten o'clock when they finish supper and move to the armchairs in the sitting room. There's still some champagne left. Kat puts the bottle on the coffee table between them. Then she empties the log basket and takes out the three sealed blocks of cocaine she's hidden within. She lines them up on the table, smiling, pleased with herself.

'Wow, Robbo, he who dares and all that,' she says. 'It must have been a hell of a buzz, getting this stuff out of Bolivia.'

He doesn't reply. His eyes are fixed on the vulture printed on the packaging around every kilo of product Lucho exports. This is his personal trade mark. Its significance will never be lost on Robbo.

'Now, tell me the full story,' Kat says. 'How you did it,

all the details, I want everything.'

This was a path he'd no wish to take again. But he has no choice. Kat has to know, to understand. He'd left bodies lying at the side of the road on his journey from being a soldier to a murderer. His sense of who and what he was had been stolen from him. For a man who played so many parts, his loss of self was to have his nakedness exposed.

'Come on, lover,' Kat says. 'No holding back.'

Robbo takes a beat then in a low, quiet voice in that twee little cottage in pastoral England, gives her edited highlights of conning his way into Lucho's presence.

'It was like any undercover role at first... you live, breathe and sleep the part. If you believe your own lies totally then so will your target.'

'Why did you say at first?'

He makes sure they have eye contact. She must see into his soul.

'Lucho set me a test... if I didn't pass, it was goodnight Vienna.'

'Christ, Robbo. What sort of test?'

'Some American girl, barely out of school... a junkie... left as a kind of deposit on some coke by a boyfriend who never came back with Lucho's money.'

'And so...?'

'I had to kill her. That was my test.'

'Kill her? But why, for Christ's sake?'

'To prove I wasn't from law enforcement, so they could trust me, do business.'

'God, Robbo... that must have been horrendous.'

He looks away, looks into a face that isn't there but will never leave him.

'Her hair, you know... so, so soft, yellow... such a thin kid, but her eyes... no hope in them.'

'And did you...?'

'I gave her a kiss... kissed her and she knew then, I know she did.'

'You broke her—'

'Yes... Judas fucking Iscariot that I am.'

Kat realises now why he's seemed so elsewhere since arriving back. But he's still another sin to confess. And this one will spin her into a red-haired rage. He reveals that he took revenge on Lucho's crippled middleman, Frederico.

'You did what?'

'I did to him what he'd made me do to the girl.'

'Tell me you're lying, Robbo... tell me you're winding me up.'

He shakes his head. He's serious. All that is going to be smuggled out of Bolivia now are the three kilos on the table in front of her.

'You're saying you risked your life, did a sensational job then lost your cool at the last knockings?'

'Yes.'

'To avenge some junkie who was as good as dead already?'

'There has to be justice, justice even in a hell hole like that.'

'Bollocks, you fucking bonehead,' she screams. 'Have you any idea what you've done? You've messed up everything we planned—'

'You planned. I was just the mutt daft enough to go along with it.'

'So you wouldn't have wanted the millions we could've

265

made?'

'Not after Bolivia, no.'

'I can't believe it… you killed a big player in the cartel. Were you out of your mind?'

'No, I was very rational about it.'

'So it's rational to make yourself a marked man, is it?'

'Do you know what, Kat? I suddenly don't give a damn.'

'No, you don't, not about me, not about yourself, but some little junkie comes along and you jeopardise every fucking thing to settle a score.'

'Christ, just listen to yourself,' Robbo says. 'Do you not understand what all that with her's done to my head?'

Kat pours the last of the champagne into her glass and drinks it in one.

'You're a selfish shit, Robbo, do you know that? Just a hired hand, no ambition to make something of yourself.'

'Out of the deaths of others? No. But people have never meant much to you, have they?'

'I care about what's important in this life.'

'Yeah, yourself.'

'Fuck off, Robbo. You can get outta here now. Go on, just get out.'

Robbo looks at her with distaste. He dials the number of a local cab firm from the card pinned on the wall above the phone.

Then he goes upstairs, gets his clothes, toilet bag and suitcase and returns to the kitchen. Kat is washing plates at the sink, angrily, noisily. He locks the cocaine in his case.

'Where the hell do you think you're going with that?' she says.

'I should've chucked this stuff in the jungle where it was

made.'

'I've got a buyer lined up, I told you.'

'Then you'll have to disappoint him, won't you? There's enough blood on it already.'

What he isn't to know then is that there will be more.

'Half of it is mine,' Kat says. 'I put up half the money.'

'Yeah, and I'll pay you back.'

He opens the front door and waits on the roadside for the taxi, suitcase in hand. Kat, ever the pragmatist, relents.

'Look, Robbo, don't go, not like this. Come back in, let's talk all this through again.'

'There's nothing for us to talk about.'

'Of course there bloody is. We can still work something out and make a few bob.'

'You've not been listening to me, have you? I'm done, I'm finished.'

Her anger erupts again.

'Then if you get caught, I'll deny everything, you little shit.'

'Good job I've got you on tape, then.'

'What tape? What are you talking about?'

'You're not the only one who gets wired up for little chats,' he says. 'Nothing personal, you understand, just a bit of insurance.'

*

The taxi drops Robbo at RAF Lyneham just before midnight. He shows his security pass to a guard and is given a bed in transit accommodation. After breakfast, he recovers his Land Rover from the car park and drives cross country through

267

Wiltshire and Hampshire then to the coast of Sussex and a bolthole by the running tide where all his secrets are safe.

*

In ancient Greek, the word *kairos* meant an opportunity, a critical moment for action to be driven through with force.

And so it was when the stars aligned to have Robbo and Kat working together in Northern Ireland again, soon after his return from Bolivia. They were to carry out a politically sensitive operation from a safe house in Ballymena.

'I don't like this turn of events any more than you,' Kat says.

'Too bloody right, I don't.'

'No, but we've no choice but to make a fist of it.'

'I'll sleep on the couch,' Robbo says. 'And just so you know, I've put in my return to unit request.'

For now, they've a surveillance to carry out. The target is a commander from the psychopathic Ulster Volunteer Force with the codename Pirelli.

Loyalist paramilitaries fear a republican future. They want to wreck peace talks between London and Dublin. If they kill even more Catholics, the IRA will retaliate then any brokered ceasefire will fail. UVF gunmen have to be arrested – or ambushed and shot dead – for the greater good.

Intelligence suggests Pirelli is tupping the wife of a terrorist comrade in jail. Kat plans to video him leaving the cuckold's house before breakfast. Starring in his own little movie will make him amenable to Kat's friendship... that and a briefcase full of cash every month.

For Robbo's new cover story, he's a builder's labourer.

His Army code name is *Laurel* and Kat's is *Hardy*.

The Transit van outside bears the name Little & Tucker Construction with a phone number that rings in military intelligence if dialled. It's stacked with tools, bags of sand, a cement mixer, building equipment, all just about visible through two dirty back windows. What cannot be seen is a hide of black drapes in the middle and from under which Robbo and Kat will film Pirelli.

Their driver will be O'Brien, a volunteer to the Int Cell from the Royal Corps of Transport. He arrives at the safe house and parks his Citroen estate on the grass verge in front.

He's late twenties, greasy-haired, scruffily dressed for the role. Kat introduces him to Robbo.

'Kat and me just met in Belize,' O'Brien says. 'In the same jungle warfare cadre.'

'And we flew back together.'

'I'm keen to move on, move up into intelligence work.'

'That's why I put in for him to join us on tonight's caper,' Kat says.

She leaves to do a final check on the camera equipment. They set off soon after midnight.

Within an hour, they're at the location – a loyalist stronghold in Belfast. O'Brien locks the van and walks to a prearranged RV to wait. Kat and Robbo share a flask of coffee in the hide, but not too much. Their loo is an empty paint can.

The hour before dawn comes. It is neither dark nor light. Slits in the drape allow a view through the windscreen down a sloping street of terraced houses. It's like watching an old black and white movie. They feel part of the unfolding drama yet strangely detached from its reality so in no danger.

A man drifts through their line of sight, wraith-like in the mist rising from the river at the bottom of the street, slicked wet from last night's rain. Who is he? Who is an enemy in this place... who is a friend? God alone knows.

Pirelli will soon emerge. The camera will not lie. And neither will Kat's new informant.

*

Next morning's midday news on BBC Radio Ulster leads with another terrorist atrocity.

A soldier was killed instantly this morning when a bomb exploded under his car. He was driving on a remote country road near Randalstown when the device went off, destroying his Citroen estate.

The alarm was raised by a farmer who heard the explosion. The area has been sealed off while the police and Army carry out a search.

A police spokesman said the attack looked like the work of the IRA dissident republicans who, like some loyalist paramilitaries, are opposed to the current peace talks between Mrs Thatcher's government in London and her opposite number in Dublin, Garret FitzGerald.

*

Robbo is packing to leave Ballymena. His request to be reassigned has been granted and he's to return to HQ, Northern Ireland. Kat doesn't want him outside the tent. But he's clearly fraying at the edges, becoming unstable, unreliable. That makes him a threat, not least to her. She needs more time to talk him round, to get her share of the gear he'd brought out of Bolivia and which he'd told her was safely stashed away.

'You really sure about leaving the team, Robbo? You could just apply for extended leave, post-traumatic stress and all that.'

'I don't think there's a pill for what I've got.'

'Look, we've been good together in the past... we can still be again.'

'After Bolivia?'

'Forget Bolivia. That was then, this is now,' she says. 'I'm pissed off with you for sure but come on, this life of ours... never boring, is it? What else would you do?'

He doesn't reply. Just for two or three seconds, it's as if he's derealised himself to escape whatever's in his head.

'I can't keep going on like this,' he says at last. 'I'll run out of luck one of these days.'

'Like O'Brien?'

'Who's O'Brien?'

'The guy who parked us on the plot to get Pirelli,' Kat says. 'Sat on eight ounces of Gadaffi's Semtex this morning, now he's all over the place.'

Again, Robbo seems disconnected, disinterested. His suitcase is almost packed. He's ready to leave.

'Still, he's no loss to us, Robbo.'

'Plenty more where he came from... isn't that what they whisper over our coffins?'

'Listen, you need to know something,' Kat says.

'Make it quick, I'm late.'

'That bastard O'Brien was trying to blackmail me.'

'Blackmail you? Why, what about?'

'You know I told you we flew back from Belize together, him and me, well I think he had a poke around in my kitbag while I was asleep.'

'What makes you say that?'

'Because soon after we got back, he dropped a fucking big hint that he knew what I was up to.'

'What, spelled it out, you mean?'

'As good as, remarks about snow and Charlie and drug runners rolling in money.'

'Did he, now? So what did you say?'

'He told me he was being posted over here so I made sure he was assigned to me. He was a threat, Robbo, a threat to both of us.'

'Did he know about me?'

'No, but he would've found out then doubled his price.'

'And what was that?'

'Thirty percent of the street value.'

Robbo reflected in silence for a moment.

'So we're in debt to the Fates, are we, Kat… getting the Provos to do our dirty work?'

'The Lord works in mysterious ways.'

He drives away, ever more preoccupied. There was no kiss, no touch of cheeks, no acknowledgement of the intimacy they'd once had. Everything was over. Robbo didn't believe in coincidences. But he had great faith in the IRA's stock of oven-ready car bombs, not least those that had unaccountably gone missing in raids carried out by the Army.

26: BETRAYAL

"... what is seen passes away;
what is unseen is eternal."

-    II Corinthians 4:18

The Reverend Hill stood looking up at the great astronomical clock of Wells Cathedral, built by a monk seven centuries ago and still marking every irretrievable hour and day. It was a masterpiece of medieval engineering showing the phases of the sun and moon but with the earth at the centre of this pre-Copernican universe.

Such certainty – or arrogance – of man and Church alike was both a lesson and a warning to those with unshakeable beliefs. This wasn't lost on a repentant Ralph Hill as he waited for his young confessor, Martha Whitten.

Over supper the night before, he'd begun to reveal more about his affair with Bella. But he held back, sensing that Martha – unlikely to ever be the object of male desire – had scant understanding of what had driven him onto the emotional rocks, to risk everything for a woman he'd only just met.

It was insane, but was it not said that to be madly in love was to be shackled to a lunatic?

'Sorry to have kept you,' Martha said. 'I had to make a

phone call.'

She wore a denim jacket over a floaty black kaftan disguising the belly fat she couldn't seem to shed. Her hair looked as if she'd cut it with kitchen scissors. Such a contrast to the fashionably chic Virginia, he thought. Attentive and shrewd though Martha was, what else did they see in each other to sustain their improbable attachment?

'How about a coffee, Ralph?' she said. 'And maybe a piece of cake?'

She led him out into an October morning threatening rain from clouds blowing hard over the Mendips. Ralph Hill hugged his jacket around him until they reached a teashop at the bottom of the market place.

Inside was fuggy and warm. To other customers, they could've been a father and daughter engaged in a serious conversation. Somewhere in his subconscious, it was possible that Ralph Hill was trying to explain – or justify – himself to Virginia, albeit now through her closest friend. A waitress brought their order. Martha cut into a Danish pastry and offered him half. But he declined. She reminded him of something he'd said at supper.

'Bella gave you a sort of warning, didn't she? Said you should go back to England.'

'Yes, she and her comrades were stepping up their attacks so I should leave right away before the regime retaliated with even more violence.'

'But then you told me she said something you didn't quite understand... something about her not being what she seemed.'

'Ah, yes... the enigmatic Bella.'

'What did she mean by that, Ralph?'

He stirred his coffee slowly as if to gain time to gather his thoughts. Without doubt, Martha must have already known that he was an indifferent husband and parent, but not that his actions had helped to bring about Bella's horrific murder.

*

He returns to the Empire Hotel and asks to see Abraham, the waiter. But he's told that Abraham's child has been taken ill so he won't be on duty for several days. Ralph Hill paces the marble floor of the reception area, uncertain what to do next. He doesn't notice he's being observed by two white men at the bar. All that concerns him is why Bella would take him to her bed one minute then say he should hurry home to England the next.

It's getting late but he decides to try and find his way back to her apartment. She must explain herself on this, the most unsettling of days. But Abraham had led him through so many busy streets to the pharmacy then he'd followed Bella down a rat run of alleyways to her place. Nothing looks remotely familiar.

He's going round in circles, starting to panic. Two girls appear to be following him. They could be prostitutes wanting business, or worse, to set him up for a mugging. The older one shouts across the street.

'You lost, mister?'

The Reverend Hill ignores them, wishes he'd worn his dog collar, which might have afforded some protection. The girl asks if he wants a taxi. He looks across at her, clearly afraid. She goes into a shop. A minute later, she emerges, smiling.

'My cousin, he is coming. He takes you.'

And so the cab arrives and to his shame, Ralph Hill doesn't thank the girls. All he wants is the safety of the guest house. And when he arrives, he finds a scribbled message from the manager with his room key.

Your daughter telephoned and said your wife is not well, you should fly back to England as soon as possible.

That such a day had yet another twist was hard to believe. But can he be sure it was Virginia who'd rung, not Bella wanting rid of him? Either way, he's no option but to phone home. He places a call through the international operator but gets no reply. Cynthia could be asleep. God forbid that she's in hospital. If only Virginia didn't live in an Army barracks, she'd have a number he could ring.

The hours until dawn pass slowly. He is consumed with anxiety and indecision and an overwhelming desire for what he's never had and which might still be snatched away for he has no power in these matters. Others will decide what happens next.

It's six o'clock when he places another call home. Cynthia should be awake. She is. She answers the phone.

'I've had a message from Virginia,' he says. 'She says you're none too good. Is that right?'

'I've had better days, that's a fact. When are you coming back?'

'I'm not sure. Aren't you due to see the consultant soon?'

'Yes, next week.'

'So you'll be telling him that you're a bit under the weather?'

'God almighty, don't you ever listen to me? I've got cancer, Ralph. Cancer in my bowels, in my bloody bowels, Ralph, so I'm not just a bit under the weather.'

*

He declines breakfast and asks only for a pot of tea. The waiter returns and says someone's asking for him in reception. Even as he looks around, Bella is walking towards his table. He stands up, napkin in hand.

'Hi, Ralph. How are you this morning?'

'I'm well… yes, good, thank you. I wasn't sure if I would see you again.'

'I thought you might be packing so I came early to say a proper goodbye.'

Bella orders black coffee from the waiter. If anything, her presence simply adds to Ralph Hill's confused state of mind. She senses this and gives him a lover's knowing smile to put him at ease. It doesn't work as well as she hopes.

'Ralph, tell me that you are booked on a flight out, aren't you?'

'Not yet, no, but I will be.'

She leans forward, lowers her voice.

'Ralph, please… I'm not supposed to be here but I shall worry myself sick until I know you're safely away.'

'Yes, but you must understand how much I don't want to leave you.'

Before Bella can reply, the manager approaches, almost bowing to the Reverend Hill.

'I'm sorry to interrupt, sir, but there's a telephone call for you.'

'For me?'

'Yes, it's your daughter again,' he says. 'Would you like to take it in my office? Save you having to go all the way back upstairs.'

Bella sips her coffee, tries not to catch Ralph's eye as he follows the manager out of the little dining area.

She certainly doesn't see herself as the other woman but is acutely aware of the damage she might yet inflict on the clerical peace of his family. He comes back after three or four minutes. His face is set, grim.

'Not trouble, I hope?' Bella says.

'My wife... she's ill. Our daughter is insisting I should be with her.'

'What's wrong with your wife?'

Ralph Hill sits knees apart, hands together between them, head down.

'She has cancer of the bowel,' he says. 'Our daughter is growing concerned about her.'

'Then you have no choice. This is another reason why you must return home without any delay.'

'But Bella, my marriage is over.'

'But she's still your wife. She's every right to expect your support at a time like this.'

'But you must promise me that if I go back to England, you'll still be here when I return because I am coming back.'

'I can't stop you if that's what you want,' she says. 'But nobody can predict where any of us is going to be next week, next month. You must understand, Ralph, we're in a war here and it will only intensify.'

'Will the diplomat be contacting me again? What do you think?'

278

'I'd say he's sure to, but you could always refuse to help any more. You've got the perfect excuse now with your wife being ill.'

'I don't want an excuse, Bella. That's the last thing I want.'

Bella looks at her watch. She has to go. He begs her to stay just a few more minutes.

'Why did you say you're not what I think?' he says. 'What did you mean by that?'

She looks at him hard, eye to eye.

'Ralph, I can't say any more... I can't, not for your safety or for mine.'

'But why not... after yesterday, why not?'

'Because what you don't know you can't reveal.'

'But that leaves me completely in the dark. I don't know what to believe or trust or anything.'

'Listen, you might look and sound like a priest but inside, you're a comrade. We're kindred spirits, you and me. We have orders and we must carry them out.'

'I understand your political leanings. They're obvious, so what else is there to explain?'

'Ralph, Ralph, please don't press me further on this.'

He is worried now, adrift in the uncertainty of events he could never have foreseen.

'Here's some advice,' Bella says. 'Go home and do normal things. Minister to your parishioners, be with your wife and don't think about the future or what may happen tomorrow. Take little steps and let the future come to you and do not weep without cause.'

Once again, she kisses the first two fingers of her right hand and puts them to his lips, then leaves without another word.

*

'So you flew back to England, none the wiser?' Martha said. 'You'd still no idea what Bella had meant?'

'Not at that point, no.'

'And was Ginny right to be worried about her mother?'

Ralph Hill nodded but was looking away. Outside, market traders were hurriedly anchoring their canvas stalls against the rising wind. Rain began to hit against the café window like grapeshot.

Martha left her companion with his thoughts and went to fetch a second pot of coffee and a tea cake with jam and butter for herself.

'Do you not want to talk about your wife, Ralph? I can understand it if you don't. It must have been so emotionally distressing for you.'

She poured fresh coffee for them both, aware that this confession still had more sins in it. The Reverend Hill began with a blunt truth.

'We should never have married,' he said. 'It was expected of us, of course. It was what her parents wanted but we were an ill-suited couple... no common goals. I was never even convinced she believed in God, for instance, but who knows, she might have been right about that if nothing else.'

'So she didn't share your commitment to CND and the peace movement, then?'

'No, she did not. Maybe I wouldn't have involved myself

280

in all that if Cynthia and I had been more compatible… if I'd had something to stay at home for.'

Martha thought this sentiment self-serving in the extreme but let it pass without comment.

*

Ginny has been given compassionate leave and meets him at Hereford station. It had been a long flight then a tedious train journey. He was tired, irritable, dreading the recriminations and bickering ahead.

'How is your mother bearing up?'

'I'm sorry but that's a damn fool question, Daddy.'

'There is no cause to be rude, Virginia. I'm as concerned about her as you are.'

She all but snorts at his assertion then bites back.

'There's got to be a first time for everything, I suppose.'

'Please, can we stop this constant sniping? It's exhausting.'

'All right, if you want,' Ginny says. 'But swanning off to South Africa while Mummy's so ill hardly suggests you're showing concern for her.'

'I'd no choice. Arrangements had been made and your mother wasn't begging me to stay.'

'That's as may be, but you now need to realise that we've got a big problem with her.'

'A bigger problem than her cancer?'

'It's all connected, because she's refusing to have the operation the consultant says she needs because the scans show the cancer is in a very awkward place and the only chance she stands is for her to have major surgery.'

Ginny pulls up at traffic lights. Her father looks at her.

'She's defying the medical advice? I don't understand.'

'It's psychological, in her head, her being obsessive compulsive about hygiene.'

The Reverend Hill hardly needs reminding of his wife's fastidious habits, constantly washing her hands, cleaning surfaces, vacuuming, all annoying in the extreme. Virginia says her mother has been told that if she has the operation, some of her colon will be cut out so she'll have to wear a colostomy bag.

'Her mother did, too,' Ralph Hill says. 'I remember there were terrible scenes about that.'

'Mummy says it was awful, just watching her try to cope with it, and she says she can't bear the thought of that happening to her, having to handle all that mess.'

'But even so, isn't that better than dying?'

'Only if you have something to live for.'

'She has plenty to live for, surely?'

Not according to Ginny: 'Then why has she written out the instructions for her funeral?'

*

The weather improved and the sun came out. Martha suggested a drive into the countryside for him to see his new surroundings. He agreed but would have gone along with whatever she'd said. If life is a battle, Ralph Hill was at the margins of the field, slowly dying from his wounds.

They passed through meadows of grazing sheep and pollarded willows, by dykes of still black water and here and there, squat stone farmsteads with rusted corrugated iron barns. She parked in a lane by a gate with a view towards Glastonbury Tor, rising conically from the Somerset Levels into a sky rinsed of its rain for the moment.

'So there is Avalon and all its mysteries,' Martha said.

'I don't follow.'

'This is it, this is Avalon, the place where King Arthur came to die but never did, and also according to legend, where the Holy Grail is buried.'

'Ah yes, I see – the Arthurian fairy stories.'

'People come to Glastonbury from all over the world because they're fascinated by them.'

'I suppose that organised religions like ours have created enough myths of our own to sustain our followers, so who are we to judge?'

'You must know that it's said Jesus came here with his uncle, Joseph of Arimathea?'

'Was that before or after He rose from the dead?'

'No, Jesus was a boy according to the story, and was with Joseph on a trip to the Cornish tin mines because that's what Joseph traded, tin.'

Ralph Hill allowed himself a hint of a smile.

'I can only think the crafty old monks of Glastonbury wanted to attract more wealthy pilgrims.'

Martha laughed, encouraged by this rare flash of lightheartedness. A cloud covered the sun. The alder and birch trees shed more yellowing leaves onto the marshy ground.

'Shall we take a stroll?' Martha said. 'The rain should hold off a little longer.'

They walked along the lane from which all the swooping swallows had gone back to Africa long since. The only sound was the wind through the telephone wires where they'd rested in the warmth of summer.

Martha had to prompt the Reverend Hill to resume his confession.

'It can't have been easy, that first meeting with your wife.'

'No... it wasn't. It was as if each of us resented the other for what we'd become.'

'But I take it she looked ill, so that must have provoked some sympathy in you.'

'In truth, I found myself dealing with her like I would a sick parishioner. I was attentive and showed my concern but when Virginia left us on our own, we might have been strangers.'

'You'd fallen out of love with each other.'

'If we ever were in the first place.'

'Did you try to persuade her to have the operation?'

'Yes, I did, very much so, but it was no use.'

'She'd made up her mind?' Martha said, stating the obvious.

'I got to thinking this was her way of punishing me.'

'For what, exactly?'

'Marrying her, my politics, the Church, her discontent at the life we'd had. Take your pick.'

'But she would've known that by not having the operation, she would probably die.'

'Yes, and by doing so she would bequeath me a degree of responsibility for her death thus all the guilt that would follow and also the enduring animus of our daughter.'

Martha saw this defence for what it was – convenient and beyond corroboration.

The more the Reverend Hill revealed, the harder it was to remain objective about the sincerity of his admissions. For his wife, cornered in a loveless marriage to an obsessive, selfish man, obliged to smile and publicly support him on matters she didn't wish to, divorce hadn't been an option, financially or socially. Martha couldn't help but feel Ginny's presence at her side.

'But you went back to South Africa, despite everything, didn't you, Ralph?'

'Only once more and only for a couple of days.'

'To smuggle more money?'

'Yes, the diplomat contacted me and made all the arrangements.'

'So this meant you could continue your affair with Bella?'

'I was infatuated with her... what else was I to do but follow my heart?'

Martha could have answered his question but chose not to. Instead, she suggested they find somewhere for lunch.

*

Looking out of the window of a vegetarian café in Glastonbury, Martha noted the similarity between the new-age patrons of shops selling crystals to cleanse the soul and the medieval faithful making pilgrimage to cathedrals to buy the bones of saints to help to secure their place in heaven.

Spiritual beings have always searched for the self, looked for answers to life's mysteries: why are we here? What is the purpose of it all?

For Christians of the ancient world, hell and purgatory were physical places and the devil, a constant presence tempting the ungodly.

For some of the Afghan-coated scions of the Woodstock

285

generation, existence itself was a kind of illusion. The devil was still real but now running the military-industrial complexes of the super powers or Big Pharma.

Martha and the Reverend Hill ate pumpkin dhal at a bare pine table.

The cat piss smell of weed being smoked by another diner took away from the more pleasing aromas coming from the kitchen.

A young man with dreadlocks brought peppermint tea for Ralph Hill and a dessert of white chocolate cheesecake for Martha.

'Do you think Ginny suspected you were having an affair, Ralph?'

'If she did, she never voiced anything of that to me.'

'But it would've been quite uncomfortable, wouldn't it… a daughter asking her father to confirm or deny he was being unfaithful to his wife?'

'Well she didn't. Besides, dry old sticks like me aren't meant to have a sex life, are we?'

Martha was content to let that observation pass. Instead, she told him how heartbroken Ginny had been after her mother's death, albeit that it was expected.

'Yes, I know she was,' Ralph Hill said. 'However much we may prepare for a loved one's passing, it's always a shock when it actually happens. There's always pain.'

'That must have been true for you when Mrs Hill died…'

'Of course it was. I grieved for her… privately, in my own way.'

Martha left this statement unchallenged as she finished her cheesecake.

'But you were with her at the end?'

'Yes… it wasn't safe to go back to South Africa afterwards.'

'Because the situation there was getting too dangerous like Bella said it would?'

'That was a factor,' the Reverend Hill said. 'But there were others… just as threatening.'

'Do you want to tell me what they were?'

He drew a long breath before answering.

'I'd been set up all along… an unworldly country clergyman out of his depth… so easy to trick, wasn't I? Such an easy mark.'

'You were set up? What do you mean? Why were you set up?'

'To discredit the church organisations in Europe of course, to show their hypocrisy, their readiness to send money to South Africa, whether it was to buy arms for terrorists or not.'

'To smear the churches?'

'Yes, because the fighters were getting all the weaponry they needed from the Soviets.'

'So the money you were smuggling—'

'Was to create bad publicity for the churches who were condemning the evils of apartheid.'

'But what about the Swedish diplomat who recruited you?'

'He wasn't Swedish and he wasn't a diplomat. He was an intelligence officer in the South African National Intelligence Service whose plan this all was.'

'Dear God. Did Bella know any of this?'

'Of course she did. She was in on it from the beginning.'

'No? Really?'

287

'Bella also worked for NIS. She was also an intelligence officer.'

'I can hardly believe what you're telling me. You mean she was really spying on you?'

'Yes, her job was to ensnare me, to get me in a compromising situation so I could be blackmailed. It's what spies the world over call a honey trap.'

'That's unthinkable, but you did go to bed with her,' Martha said. 'That could have been used against you, couldn't it?'

'Only if it'd happened where NIS had their cameras. But Bella made sure it never did.'

'But why put her career in jeopardy to do that and keep warning you to go home?'

'I'd like to say it was love at first sight but the more prosaic truth was she saw the communist in me, a fellow-travelling socialist whose ruination she couldn't face bringing about.'

'So was she a member of the Communist Party herself?'

'Absolutely, she was. NIS put her in there. She was their mole on the inside but she grew to loathe the regime and knew it had to be overthrown by any means possible.'

'So she double-crossed the intelligence people?'

'Leaked their secrets to the anti-apartheid fighters, warned them about arrests and operations that were being planned against them, anything to hamper the government.'

'That must have been as dangerous as it was brave.'

'There could be no forgiveness for her betrayal,' the Reverend Hill said. 'That's the reason she had to die.'

*

288

Even had Martha's car radio worked and they could've listened to the BBC's three o'clock news, the last item would only have been of marginal interest.

News just in. It's being reported that the body of a man recovered from Chichester Harbour in Sussex late last night was that of Sir Frazer Harris, the former Labour defence secretary. Police have yet to comment on local accounts of gunfire being heard shortly before the body was spotted in the water. We'll have more on this later.

27: DECEPTION

*"Let your plans be dark
and impenetrable as night."*

- Sun Tzu, The Art of War

Tilly Brown's house was a crime scene without evidence to prove it. Yet someone had ghosted into her darkroom. They'd found the camera roll of negatives from Scotland and removed all the shots of Robbo clambering on board the Army helicopter before it crashed. Her enlargement of the one for framing was also missing. She would've felt less menaced had something of obvious value been stolen. That it hadn't was unnerving. Yet Tilly tried to remain calm, to assess the situation objectively as she would have done in the Met's legal department.

How had the thieves gained entry? Why had they only stolen those specific items? On whose behalf were they acting – their own or a third party?

There were rational explanations for everything, yet she was struggling to find one in this case. The theft should be reported to the police but she'd sound foolish, telling them of a break-in that was all but invisible.

She would, however, inform her detective friend, Laurie Benwell. The lawyer in her wanted an independent record logged of what had happened.

The grandfather clock in the hallway struck eight. Benwell didn't keep regular hours so she rang his office. He was away on an enquiry – probably in Northern Ireland but this wasn't revealed – and not contactable. A message would be passed on.

Tilly's supper was poached egg on toast with a gin and tonic. It was that sort of night – nothing went together, the dots weren't connecting up.

She made a list of what she could establish:

1. The helicopter she'd photographed in Scotland was the one that crashed in Wales.

2. She'd found no public mention of a passenger being injured, killed or even on board.

3. Only Giles Worth knew about the photographs and therefore Robbo's presence on the helicopter shortly before it came down.

4. Giles had agreed to ask around in the Ministry of Defence about the helicopter.

5. When she'd phoned Robbo's business number, a woman answered despite the man managing the property saying it was closed up.

6. Her negatives and an enlargement were stolen while she was in Scotland.

Tilly then wrote three additional questions:

1. Was Giles Worth in any way connected to, or mixed up with, the burglary?

2. Could she trust him with any more information?

3. If some element in the MoD was behind the break-in, what reason could be advanced to sanction an illegal operation to steal something so seemingly trivial?

She hadn't any answers. But tomorrow, she would drive sixty miles south to the old Roman town of Chichester and visit the address of Sally Tobin, the woman who had returned Robbo's letter.

Even as Tilly decided this, the bell of her own front door rang. It was, strangely enough, Giles Worth, all smiles and casual clothes, carrying two bottles of wine in a plastic bag.

'You've been away,' he said. 'Thought we might celebrate your return.'

Tilly hesitated a full second before stepping aside to let him in.

'Sorry, I've had an exhausting journey. I'll take a glass with you but no more. I'm bushed.'

'OK, that's fine, this won't take long.'

She moved her supper plate to the sink and they sat across the kitchen table.

'I've been snuffling around in the undergrowth as requested,' Giles said.

'And?'

'And someone's told me something I think you'll find interesting.'

Tilly saw his eye go to the notes she'd been writing in her diary. She put it back in the dresser drawer.

'Go on, Giles, I'm all ears.'

'You need to talk to a woman who lives close to the lake where the helicopter ditched.'

'Why, how can she help?'

'That's for you to find out, but I'm told you'd not be wasting your time if you went to see her.'

He gave her Florence Rossiter's name and the address of her cottage.

'That's a long way from London,' Tilly said. 'Come on, give me a clue, just a hint, anything about why I should shlep all the way up to North Wales just on your say-so.'

He smiled but shook his head.

'Sorry, no can do. Seek and you will find but I say again, you'll not regret it.'

'Why are you telling me this, Giles? Sorry to put it like this but what's in it for you?'

'Nothing's in it for me. We're friends and neighbours, aren't we? You asked me to help and that's what I'm doing.'

Try as she might, Tilly hadn't the guile to prise anything else from him. If he was expecting her to mention the break-in, he didn't show it nor did he prompt her in any way. She was glad when he went and took the opened bottle home with him.

*

'Is that Christian... Christian Moreley?'

'Yeah, who's this?'

'Don't you recognise my voice?'

'It's Eamon, isn't it? Don't tell me, you're wanting another favour doing.'

'No, quite the reverse,' he said. 'Get your notebook, I've got some red meat for you.'

Within forty minutes of this phone call, Moreley had persuaded the BBC's news organiser in London that he'd a tip-off on a story that could lead any bulletin. He chucked a grab bag of kit and warm clothes in his car and kissed his sleeping wife. Ahead, the long drive through the night to Sussex where, in some subterranean hospital mortuary, the body of Sir Frazer Harris lay beached on a porcelain slab, awaiting a pathologist with a scalpel.

*

Tilly rang phone inquiries to ask for Sally Tobin's number at the address on the envelope. Nothing was listed. She'd either moved or was ex-directory.

But Florence Rossiter's was available. Tilly only wanted it to confirm where she lived, not to make a call. On the phone, Florence could hang up without feeling rude. Standing at her door, it'd be very different.

It was unfortunate that Sally and Florence lived hundreds of miles apart. Tilly would have to make separate trips. She'd drive to Wales first, but only because the infuriating Giles Worth assured her it'd pay dividends. But who told him this, and why?

She remembered Laurie Benwell's advice on informants over a boozy supper they'd once shared.

'It's always about their motive, Tilly love,' he'd said. 'Could be money, revenge, the buzz of being in the know, feeling important or something that you can't work out.'

'Never the mutualism of the public good, then?'

'Christ no, not in my experience. But always you have to listen to what they're saying then ask yourself, why's this bastard bothering to give me a leg up?'

Tilly had yet to divine her neighbour's motivation. But she was acting on his information, for he obviously had sources she didn't. Their rationale was even more opaque, puzzling. No matter, not for the moment.

She was still blindly stumbling around in her search for Robbo, but at least now she had a guide dog at her side.

*

It was almost dawn. Moreley, stiff and bone cold in his Saab, had a breakfast of flavoured milk and the last of the sandwiches bought at a garage when he'd stopped for fuel. A gale was blowing in from the English Channel. Oyster boats rocked to and fro, awaiting the crews who were starting to arrive in their Transit vans.

Eamon had rung Moreley's car radio phone on the journey down.

'Make sure you're in position early,' he'd said. 'The detective will be there about eight.'

It was pointless asking Eamon how he knew this – or anything else he passed on. There must be a reason why he – they – wanted the cop fronted in this way by a BBC hack. But he'd probably never find out what it was.

Moreley had arrived at Itchenor in the early hours and parked in a narrow street leading down to Chichester Harbour. Either side were red-tiled cottages of brick and flint, once the dwellings of fishermen, boat-builders or the littoral poor, but now more likely to be the fabulously priced second homes of weekend sailors.

He needed to stretch his legs, find a place to pee. The wind tore at the Union Jack above the harbourmaster's office. Beyond was a boatyard then a plantation of conifers. Fine rain began to fall. It clung to the fur around Moreley's hood and trickled through the stubble on his chin.

The cop would want the harbourmaster's best guess

regarding where Harris first entered the water for the tide to deposit him onto the marshy shoreline where he was found.

'He clearly didn't die at that spot,' Eamon had said. 'So where did the shooting take place, where is the weapon and who pulled the trigger?'

Moreley didn't need telling about the difference between what one might know and what one could show. Suspicion was not proof, whatever the source. But how was he to get corroboration for Eamon's sensational inference to fly the story by the Beeb's lawyers?

'Listen… Eamon… I have to deliver. I've sold this tale bloody hard to London.'

'And you won't regret it.'

'Yeah, but what if you and your lot are wrong, what if it really is suicide, no terrorist link, just some washed-up politician who's blown his brains out, what then?'

'You have to trust me.'

'So I can trust you to pay my mortgage when my contract's not renewed, can I?'

'I'll make sure it doesn't come to that,' Eamon said. 'Listen, this detective you'll meet… get cosy. He'll see it's better to have you inside the tent urinating out than the alternative.'

'What can you tell me about him? Have you got a name?'

'He's called Roach, a detective inspector but there's something else you need to know.'

Roach was deputy to Commander Laurie Benwell, now reviewing several unsolved murders in Northern Ireland.

'But what's any of that got to do with the death of Harris?'

'Some of them happened on his watch, when Harris was the Minister of Defence.'

'So what? Harris wouldn't know what was happening on the streets of Belfast.'

'No, of course he wouldn't,' Eamon said. 'So Roach couldn't possibly have any interest in this matter, could he? I mean, why on earth is he wasting his time at the seaside?'

'OK, OK, I get it.'

'Remember this, Christian, words spoken behind closed doors or a signature on a piece of paper… these can be lethal, too.'

'Like I say, I understand,' Moreley said. 'Look, you don't need me to tell you how legally fraught this is. I really have to have a way of getting back to you. A contact number, anything, just this once.'

'Sorry, it has to be like this, but here's something else to chew on. When you get down to Itchenor, look across Chichester Harbour.'

'At what? What am I looking for?'

'Thorney Island on the other side. It's an interesting place.'

'You mean there's a connection to Harris's death?'

'Keep digging, Mr Moreley, keep digging.'

Then Eamon had rung off.

Moreley zipped his flies. Eamon's information rarely went beyond hints and nods. Those were the scraps he was thrown, his rewards for supping with the devil. He was only ever told precisely what they wanted him to know. But apart from the riddle, his steer on the Harris story was different, much meatier.

He'd only ever met the first Eamon and then just the once, years ago. He'd never had a drink with any of them or formed a friendship as he did with cops and other sources. The spooks kept to their script, kept their guys from going off piste.

On some level, Moreley resented being used in this way. He was a hack, not a hooker, though the difference wasn't always obvious to outsiders. But he was too compromised to quit. He'd sold his journalistic soul – thus, his integrity – long since.

His fear was of outliving his usefulness, of crossing them in some way. *Private Eye* could get tipped off that he'd been a long-term spook asset. He'd no alternative but to toe Eamon's line. Besides, the Harris story could be a cracker.

Moreley looked across the harbour as advised. It was difficult to discern anything.

The weather, bleak enough for early winter, was closing in still further. All was mist and drizzle and the eerie shrieks of unseen gulls being carried on the gathering wind. It looked – and felt – like a place that clung to its secrets.

It'd done just that since 1956 when a headless corpse found in these same waters created a Cold War mystery like few others. Was it that of Buster Crabb, the MI6 frogman sent to spy out hidden equipment on two Soviet warships docked along the coast at Portsmouth? The body had been in the water too long to identify for certain. Fleet Street was still obsessed with the story, three decades and more later. This much Moreley knew.

The funnies weren't strangers here. But for now, he made his way back to the Saab to wait for Detective Inspector Roach.

*

The lamb had been tender and Welsh, pink like the Domaine Tempier that went with it. Tilly, strained by another long drive, deserved a treat. It was late afternoon when she'd arrived at the hotel. From her room, Lake Vyrnwy was just about visible in the foggy distance.

She could imagine how beautifully peaceful it must be in summer, shimmering between wooded banks with the hills and mossy green mountains of North Wales beyond. But now, in the dying light of the day, those same deep waters looked sinister.

Tilly tried not to think about Virginia Hill, trapped in that helicopter and condemned to die in the ruins of the drowned village far below. Such a terrible fate.

But what of Robbo during this tragedy? Had he been with her – as Tilly suspected – and how did the elderly spinster, Florence Rossiter, fit into their story?

Tilly had spied out her cottage en route to the hotel. Florence was pushing a barrow of logs from a load dumped on her front yard. She looked a tough and self-reliant old soul, kitted out in a long gabardine coat and woollen hat. A good night's sleep was needed before taking her on.

A waiter brought Tilly's coffee from the dining room to the bar, where she sat in a wingback, trying to see faces in the open coal fire as she'd done as a child at home. She should have felt relaxed but didn't. An element of self-doubt had wormed its way into her thinking. Professionally, she'd only ever assessed evidence gathered by others. She dealt in facts, signed statements, legal certainties. What if Giles and his contacts were right, that Florence did know something important, but when it came to it, Tilly wouldn't have the wit or experience to draw it out of her?

And what, as Laurie Benwell would say, was her own motivation for continuing to pursue the elusive Robbo? Might it be no more than displacement activity, a desire by a retired divorcee to ward off the tedium of life as it had become, to grab some excitement while she still could?

Yet when that had happened – if a burglary could be thought exciting – she'd dissolved in a funk. These uncomfortable musings were cut short by a farmer in wellingtons and dirty working clothes, entering the bar and loudly announcing his intention to warm his backside by the fire.

'I'm so sorry,' Tilly said. 'Here, let me move out of the way.'

'No need. You stay where you are.'

He'd thinning black hair and a face redder than a robin's breast.

'Nasty night,' he said. 'Raining terrible, it is.'

'Yes, I'm glad not to be out in it.'

'Not here on holiday, are you... not at this time of year?'

Tilly smiled and said she wasn't. She imagined he must be a big landowner, blunt but tolerated because he was probably worth a fortune and drove a Range Rover.

'Why have you come to these parts, then?'

His tone suggested he was suspicious of outsiders but intrigued by them, too.

'Because I'm on my way to somewhere else,' Tilly said. 'But I thought I'd have a night here and look at your lake, the one where the helicopter crashed.'

'Why? What's it to you what happened?'

Tilly tried to avoid breathing in the smell of sheep and their shit as his thick blue corduroy trousers slowly dried out.

She continued dissembling, albeit modestly.

'Nothing, really. But I'd watched it on the news so I wanted to see where that poor young woman died, the pilot.'

'We get planes coming over all the time, jets, Chinooks, all sorts. Low level flying... they train for it round here, see.'

'Did you see the helicopter that crashed?'

'No... heard plenty about it afterwards, though.'

'A lot of talk, was there?'

'Bound to be, wasn't it? All those strangers... swarming it was, military men, people from London. Are you from London?'

'That's where I live, yes,' Tilly said. 'I suppose the soldiers were helping with the rescue.'

'Yes... that'd be it. Can't see why some of them had guns, though.'

'Some of them had guns?'

'Yes, whole team of them, trespassing... going on farms where they'd no right to be, poking about in buildings.'

'Maybe they were searching for something that fell from the helicopter, something that might have caused it to crash?'

'But they were looking in places away from the lake... and they had guns. Why did they need guns? Frightening for people, it was... terrifying.'

He'd said his piece. Without another word, he left her and joined a man at the bar. Tilly Brown signed the receipt for supper and went upstairs to her room, her mind unexpectedly easier, tomorrow's meeting with Florence suddenly less daunting.

28: FEAR

"The man bitten by a snake
is always afraid of a rope."

-    Folk saying

No one is promised tomorrow; nothing is written, nothing is certain. This was axiomatic for Robbo whose life had so often turned on risk and chance. But being below the radar as Brennus, the Iron Age farmer – someone who would also have known that existence could be short and brutal – had put the future on hold. And yet he must break cover soon. Winter was closing in. It'd be December before long. Heavy snow and widespread travel disruption was forecast.

He must forego the solace he'd found in the roundhouse each night, alone with the shadows from the fire moving like memories across the walls. It had only ever been conditional and came with its own terrible logic for the life he had lived.

His sense of an ending had never been more acute, that soon, there would be no one left to deceive, not even himself.

Supper was a pheasant that flew into Mags's car that morning.

'Waste not, want not,' she'd said. 'I'll drop by tonight if I may.'

'I'll be here.'

'I need a little chat in private.'

What a coincidence, thought Robbo. So did he.

He tipped the greasy remains of the pheasant in the fire. It flared up brightly as Mags appeared with a bottle of red and two glasses. Unlike him, she'd changed into her own clothes – jeans and a windproof jacket over a knitted jumper with a polo neck.

She poured their wine and sat by him on his bed of animal skins stretched tight across a frame of poles.

'Cheers, Brennus,' she said. 'Nice place you've got.'

'Yeah, needs a duster here and there—'

'And a bit of hoovering wouldn't come amiss, either.'

They both smiled in the semi-darkness, clinked glasses. Then she told him the settlement was shutting down for three months.

'I'm so sorry. The management thanks you for everything but you'll need to find new digs.'

'That's OK. Don't feel bad about it. It's about the right time to be going, anyway.'

'You've played the part of Brennus so convincingly, like it came naturally to you.'

'Thanks for that. It's good when a performance gets decent notices.'

'You are an actor, aren't you? Come on, you can tell me now.'

'We're all actors, Mags, all of us… pretending to be something we usually aren't.'

'Stop teasing me, admit it. What's your stage name? What will I have seen you in?'

She looked at him too warmly for her own good. He saw the fire dance in her eyes. How young she was, how innocent.

In another life, he might've taken her hand, drawn her to him, for that was what he felt she wanted, to lie with him in that primitive place until the logs burned to ash and the sun rose once more.

'All you need to know, Mags, is that if I have to, I can put on an act.'

'You're so infuriating, Brennus,' she said. 'I've a good mind not to tell you someone's been asking questions about you.'

Robbo showed no outward sign of concern, waited for her to explain.

'One of the volunteers wanted to know more about you and that accident you were in.'

'Which volunteer do you mean?'

'The Scottish guy, that bore about the Roman Legions and their weaponry. I think he might have been a policeman in London before he retired.'

'What's my accident got to do with him?'

'Nothing, but he asked me when it happened and where it was, that sort of thing.'

'Why doesn't he just ask me if he wants to know how my wife died?'

'Maybe he feels a bit wary of you, suspicious even.'

Robbo leaned back, his feet to the fire, an adieu even more urgent.

'What about you, Mags, are you suspicious of me?'

She took a moment to consider her reply.

'If I'm honest, I'd have to say there's more to you than you'll allow to meet the eye—'

'Like everyone else until you get to know them.'

'Yes, that's true but in the time I've known you, you've

304

only told me about the accident, nothing else, not even your full name or where you're from.'

It was Robbo's turn to pause before answering.

'Mags, in my experience, it might look like someone is carrying a burden well enough but that doesn't mean it's not heavy or they're not only just about coping with what's in their head.'

The fire died a little more and the fox on the hill called for a mate.

'You're not going to tell me about yourself, are you?'

'What if I did and you disapproved of me? What then?'

'I don't get the feeling that you care much about what other people think.'

'Not entirely true, that,' Robbo said. 'Opening up to someone is always a matter of trust. How do I know I could trust you with what I might tell you?'

'Friends don't betray the trust of each other, do they?'

'Is that what we are, Mags... friends?'

'I would like to think so, yes... good friends. I'd like that very much.'

'And as a friend, would you help me, do me a favour or two before I leave here?'

'If I can, of course I will. What do you have in mind?'

*

The commissioner of the Metropolitan Police, Sir Graham Silvey, recognised in Laurie Benwell a most enviable attribute: that of being a lucky general. Nothing stuck to him, not complaints about his insubordination or his methods, just his successes.

By anointing Benwell, Sir Graham could navigate the treacherous Whitehall Triangle of Scotland Yard, Downing Street and the Home Office as confident as he could be that his man would get the result required if not the glory.

Sir Graham rarely turned down a chance to appear on TV. He performed well and looked magisterial in bespoke Henry Poole suits with a youthful coiffure by someone in South Kensington. There were those – like Benwell – who remembered it being grey.

For now, they stood at the baulk end of a snooker table in the opulent calm of Sir Graham's club, the Oxford and Cambridge, in Pall Mall. He tossed a coin to see who might cue off first. Benwell called heads and won.

He put side on the white ball, which spun back off the far cushion and gently settled against the reds, leaving nothing on for his opponent. Sir Graham, a tall, angular man, formed a perfect rest for his cue with the upturned thumb and splayed fingers of his bony left hand. He played away from the reds but went in-off with his first stroke.

'Sod, bugger and sod,' he said.

The game was cover for Benwell to brief his boss at a distance from those on the upper floors of Scotland Yard whose loyalties weren't always guaranteed.

'So, Northern Ireland, Laurie... who's in your cross-hairs?'

'This blighter on the run, he's the key to the whole inquiry.'

'The missing agent?'

'Sit that bugger down and he unlocks Pandora's Box for us.'

Sir Graham potted a red then a pink but left himself

banjaxed behind the black.

'Dammit. Not on form today, Laurie.'

'Decent pink, though.'

'Are you any nearer to housing him?'

'We're working on it.'

'What about bringing his handler in, that woman, shot across her bows and all that?'

'Walsh? No, she's more use to me out there. I've got a big ear on her phones.'

'With a warrant, Laurie? Tell me you've done the paperwork on this one.'

'Sure I have.'

'So what are you hearing?'

'That she's as desperate to find her man as we are. Calling in all sorts of favours.'

'Any I should know about?'

'Yeah, one from a phone engineer who owes her.'

'Christ, she's not doing illegal taps, is she?'

'Yep, but like I said, mine's kosher so we're getting her naughties for free.'

'You wouldn't ever say that bloody woman's risk averse, would you?'

'If we were at war, she'd cause fucking mayhem behind enemy lines.'

'What the hell's she really been up to, Laurie?'

Benwell potted red, brown, red, blue then left his boss snookered behind the green.

'I want to know how and why her oppo, O'Brien, came to get blown up by a car bomb. The funnies and their gold source swear blind it wasn't an IRA job.'

'Has Mrs O'Brien bought the official version of events?'

'Roach saw her. Not the brightest but she'll have to be told if all this goes the distance.'

'But why would Walsh want to stiff one of her own, another Army bod?'

'Can't say... not yet,' Benwell said. 'But I'm as sure as I'm gonna win this game that the dead guy's motor was outside Walsh's safe house the night before it went bang.'

Sir Graham played another foul shot from behind the green leaving Benwell with a simple red and an easy black.

'But anyone could've put the bomb on it after the target left, Laurie.'

'That's why I want that agent found and contemplating the meaning of life.'

'But Thatcher won't welcome her Army being discredited during these peace talks,' Sir Graham said.

'She wanted an independent inquiry and that's what she'll get.'

'Yeah, but all I'm saying, Laurie, is don't rush it.'

Benwell's concentration lapsed. He misjudged his next shot and left the commissioner on the last red with the yellow, green and brown all on offer. Sir Graham sank the lot but missed the blue. Benwell got it then dropped the pink and black to win. They shook hands and walked to the library.

'Anything else on your radar, Laurie? I can't afford to be blind-sided on any of this.'

'Sure, well there's a BBC reporter digging into the unfortunate death of our late and unlamented ex-Minister of Defence.'

'So all that dirty laundry's going to come out, is it?'

'Don't know his angle but he collared my staff officer early doors the other morning and we suspect this guy knows more about the old pervert's death than he's letting on.'

'Someone leaking to him, then? Not from your team, I hope.'

'Never, tight as a drum, my lot. It's someone else stirring the pot but don't ask me why.'

'Noises off in the media won't help us at all, Laurie. But you still think Sir Frazer topped himself?'

'I did till forensics dug the bullet out of his brain.'

Two more members entered the library but sat away from them. Benwell lowered his voice.

'Frazer wasn't happy. We knew about his mother and toddler sessions and I'd put the squeeze on him about Kat Walsh,' he said. 'But the gun used... here's the crippler.'

'Go on, how so?'

'The round that killed him was fired from a Browning Hi-Power, nine mil. But it's the same gun that was used to kill two IRA men in Belfast in '85.'

'Christ almighty.'

'We've got three possibilities. One, he shot himself, but we've no idea how he acquired that weapon. Two, it was a revenge hit by the IRA on the minister who let the SAS off the leash to whack a lot of their blokes, but that makes no sense because this wasn't an IRA gun.'

'No, obviously not but the third option, Laurie? What's the third?'

'If I had to guess, I'd say Frazer worried the solids out of Walsh... flapping on the phone to her he was, told her about my chat with him on the train and all the while, he's making himself a bloody liability to her.'

'But shooting a former government minister? That's not a runner, is it?'

'That Walsh is a mad bitch. Bloody psychopath.'

'Has the gun been recovered yet?'

'No, could be anywhere. Depends on where it was fired and how far the body floated.'

'I'll have to brief the funnies and Number 10 about all this.'

'Yeah, they'll need to get their lies straight,' Benwell said. 'Anyway, I'd best be off. I've still got a few more toes to stamp on.'

'OK, good to see you, Laurie. Thanks for the game.'

'You're welcome but you need to up yours.'

*

The first flurries of winter snow blew sideways off the peaks of the bare hills beyond Florence Rossiter's cottage.

Belches of wood smoke came back down the chimney of her open fire, where a visitor sat with smarting eyes.

'I'm so sorry,' Florence said. 'It's always like this when the wind's from the north.'

'Please, there's no need to apologise.'

'I'll open a window, shall I?'

'No, I'm sure it'll clear soon. You mustn't concern yourself on my account.'

Tilly Brown had made it into Florence's parlour. Little else mattered. The old lady had answered the door as expected. Tilly, dressed in a pinstripe skirt and jacket with a pale silk top, carried the leather briefcase she had had since law school. She'd deliberately spoken quickly as she produced an expired Metropolitan Police pass.

'But please understand, Miss Rossiter, I'm here more or

310

less in a private capacity.'

'Come in,' she'd said. 'It's too chilly to stand here.'

Florence took her best blue and white china from the dresser and seated her guest by the smoky fire while she made tea.

'From London?' Florence said. 'Just to see me. Heavens... I can't think why, really.'

'Let me explain, then. Yours is one of the few houses not too far from Lake Vyrnwy and I'm gathering information about the helicopter that crashed there.'

'Yes, terrible that was. Poor woman, so young... all her life ahead of her, she had.'

'Did you hear the helicopter come over or see it?'

'No, nothing. I'd be in the house. Late afternoon, wasn't it?'

'Miss Rossiter, can I take you into my confidence... woman to woman?'

'Well, if you like but I really don't know how I can help you.'

'Let's see about that,' Tilly said, holding the old lady's gaze. 'I believe there was someone else on the helicopter... a passenger, a good man, Miss Rossiter... served his country as a soldier. Robbo... that's his name—'

At that, Florence averted her eyes from Tilly's. She began to fasten and unfasten the bottom button on her cardigan.

'And I think he might have come by your house after the crash. Am I right, Florence? Is that what happened?'

Only the gale at the window disturbed the silence between them. Tilly now knew the tip-off from Giles was well sourced and her own suspicions well founded. She was swept by an exultant rush of adrenalin, that of the patient hunter scenting

311

prey.

Florence would talk now and Tilly would listen.

*

Northern Ireland was a snake pit for mainland cops, outsiders who could easily fall foul of the province's little ways, its occasional need for a blind eye to be turned to the rule of law in the war against terrorism.

Colleagues had told Laurie Benwell to go sick rather than undertake the commissioner's assignment. He ignored them, just as he disregarded advice about smoking and drinking. Retirement and boredom wasn't far away. Ireland offered a last chance to kick in some big doors – those of the British Army and the Royal Ulster Constabulary.

Theirs was a world of covert operations – wire taps, spies, informants and double agents inside all the terrorist groups. Yet despite this deep penetration, some murders – like O'Brien's – remained unsolved.

Benwell's brief was to go where the evidence led and to hell with anyone who tried to stop him. Not all the enemies he'd make would carry Armalites. Some would smile, wear suits, offer help.

But dirty wars meant dirty tricks. Evidence could disappear, premises burn down. Every scrap of paper, every witness statement and exhibit gathered in Ireland was duplicated and couriered to Benwell's main office – not in a Met Police station but a secure and anonymous industrial unit near Heathrow Airport.

Roach was waiting for him as he arrived in their shared office.

'Good session with the man upstairs?'

'Good enough,' Benwell said. 'Anything for me?'

'There's a message on your answer machine. It's some woman… seems to know you.'

Benwell pressed play and heard Tilly Brown's voice.

Laurie, something weird's happened. I didn't tell you before but I took some pictures when I was in Scotland of that helicopter that crashed in Wales and the negs have been cut off the reel, just the three that showed the man I'd been staying with, the guide on the course I'd been on, getting in it. I'd printed one of them off and enlarged it and that's gone, too.

Someone's broken in while I was away. It's really upset me so I'd like to see you but I know you're busy, but the crash happened only an hour or so after I'd taken the pictures yet there's been no mention of a passenger being killed or injured.

He called himself Robbo, this man, and to my mind, none of this adds up.

'Bloody hell,' Benwell said. 'That's Tilly Brown, you remember… used to be in our legal department at the Yard.'

'You've never mentioned her being mixed up in all this—'

'Because I'd no idea she was. I'll call her.'

'Before you do that, you best read your second message. It's from Big Ears.'

Roach handed his boss a note he'd copied from MI5's intercept of a call Kat Walsh had received from her man at a covert rural observation post.

He'd observed a silver Volvo estate, registered keeper one Ms Tilly Brown of North London, parked outside a cottage

313

near Lake Vyrnwy.

This was the same cottage where Target One – Robbo – was suspected of hiding after the chopper came down.

'Jesus,' Benwell said. 'We better find her before she ends up in a bloody ditch.'

29: VENGEANCE

"... the real truth is always subversive."

Zdenek Urbanek, dissident Czech novelist

If Macbeth murdered sleep, how might the Reverend Hill describe the sin that deprived him of his? It was not a crime of statute yet he held himself responsible for bringing about the violent death of Bella, the woman for whom he'd sacrificed all he held dear – or should have done.

It was akin to being both defendant and prosecutor in a Kafkaesque trial without end as he adduced the same damning evidence against himself again and again. He could offer no defence. Only a finding of guilt was available to the court over which he also presided as judge.

Martha Whitten had had to return home. She'd left hoping he'd adapt to his new life in Wells. But all the tracks on which he'd run his life until then had been torn up. He had no destination any more, only memories of where he'd come from.

At night in the empty cathedral, he would walk its silent flagstones like his own ghost or pace the empty streets of the old town, its blind shops locked and shuttered. Martha's father, the dean, understood his guest's profound need for solitude. He didn't ask questions or object to his nocturnal wanderings.

Virginia had often accused her father of being without empathy, of exhibiting only the vocational sympathy he'd learned at theological college but lacking the innate emotional intelligence to demonstrate these feelings were genuine.

Yet he had required Martha's complete understanding when he'd embarked on his overdue bout of self-awareness and humility.

*

'Why are you so hard on yourself, Ralph?' she'd asked. 'It's not as if you had any control over anything Bella was up to and yet you seem to want to punish yourself for what happened to her.'

'You haven't heard the entirety of it.'

'No, maybe I haven't, but I can't help wondering if it is easier for you to blame yourself about Bella than it is to admit how you failed your daughter.'

Ralph Hill winced. That hurt. She'd meant to hit him below the belt, not only for Ginny, but behind his contrition and piety, she still detected traces of misogyny and latent narcissism. Her patience had run out. She was relieved to be leaving next day.

They'd arranged to meet for lunch in the cathedral's cafeteria. Foreign tourists hung with cameras and carrying guide books, milled about outside even on such a bitingly cold day. The Reverend Hill looked more grey and gaunt than ever, preoccupied with inner thoughts. Martha urged him to have vegetable soup and a bread roll like her but he wanted only a glass of iced water, nothing else.

'So are you going to tell me the rest of the story?'

'About Bella?'

'Yes, about her, and why you feel so personally responsible.'

He looked uncomfortable. The cafeteria was crowded. He suggested a quieter place to talk. Martha finished her soup and led him to a vacant pew beneath a crucifix between the cathedral's great scissor arches.

'She knew they were closing in... their secret police, they were suspicious. Why had some of their operations gone wrong... fighters they'd wanted to capture or kill not being where the intelligence people said they should be. It was only a matter of time for if she'd acted on some false information they'd only given her, then they would know Bella was the double agent. She said that was called a barium meal in that deceitful world.'

'But one which you appear to have embraced, Ralph.'

'Fool that I was.'

'So what did Bella have to do to escape?'

'Several plans came up. One involved her being smuggled over the border to comrades in Mozambique, another up to Angola, but there were spies everywhere and Bella knew if she was caught, she'd be tortured.'

'For the names of other fighters?'

'Yes, or she'd be shot like a dog because she was the worst sort of traitor – a race traitor.'

So an English country vicar, his wife cooling in her grave, conspired to save his communist lover by devising a plot of his own.

A contact in the Catholic Church in Johannesburg loaned

him a nun's long dark-blue tunic and headdress, rosary beads, bible and a silver ring for the left hand to show the wearer had taken perpetual vows. Thus disguised and carrying the same nun's South African passport to be returned later, Bella was transformed into a bride of Christ.

Soon, she'd be on her circuitous way to Europe, and the savage death that awaited her.

*

What was it with red-headed women that shorted the wiring in Robbo's head? Even before Kat, he'd taken uncharacteristic risks with his cover to get them into bed. One of them had even become his wife, and he still felt bad about that.

He'd infiltrated the London HQ of an Irish protest group his handlers saw as IRA sympathisers. Sally was an activist with access to membership records. He'd have wooed his way into her affections for that alone. But it went further. Against all advice – from her family and his boss – they married.

The first few weeks were fine. Then she began to get suspicious. He'd money but no apparent job, would disappear for days at a time, never use their phone, only the public kiosk at the end of the street. When she questioned him, he blanked her.

Sally had a librarian's ordered mind and a leftie appetite for conspiracies. Basic elements of his story – name, date and place of birth – could be checked. Somerset House sent her his birth certificate. But she'd read *The Day of the Jackal* and knew about setting up a fake ID, so had also asked for any death certificates in the same name, Robert Ellison.

And there it was, printed in black and signed by a superintendent registrar – the Robert Ellison he was claiming to be was a baby who'd died eleven hours after being born in Chatham, Kent on 7 March 1948.

The row that followed was loud and violent and tearful.

'You're a spy, a snake in the grass,' she'd screamed. 'You've used me, raped me night after night.'

She spat in his face, beat him with her fists.

'Who are you working for?' she'd screamed. 'Tell me, you little bastard. It's MI5, isn't it? MI5 or the Special Branch. They're your masters, aren't they?'

Robbo left and never saw her again. She could've exposed him to the group, to the media. But the military stuffed her mouth with pound notes and though the affair died a death, it must have left Sally badly scarred. If his defences had a weakness, she was the gap in the curtain wall.

The game moved on and he'd fallen for Kat. At least she was Army and knew the rules of engagement. With her, he could almost be himself, whoever that was. Yet for all his intuition and nous, Robbo's flaw was never to see beyond the coppery golden hair and the smile that promised him all he'd never known.

Had he done so, he would not have agreed to her caper in Bolivia, which he now saw as beyond insane. It had turned him into a murderer.

He was ashamed of much in his life but his loathing was reserved for what she'd made him become.

Now, as he prepared to bow out as Brennus, the Iron Age farmer, he was lining up another auburn-haired female. But Mags was young enough to be his daughter if he'd ever had one. That unfathomable alchemy of blind attraction was working on him again.

The roundhouse door opened and Mags entered with a blast of cold air.

'Hi, Robbo. I'm back.'

'That didn't take long. Managed to get everything, did you?'

'I did, but that clergyman—'

'Yeah?'

'Well, I rang round a few churches in Herefordshire like you said and it seems he's retired.'

'The papers haven't mentioned that. Did you get an address or a contact number?'

'Not as such, but I gather he's gone to Somerset, to the cathedral at Wells.'

That was all Robbo needed to know. Mags emptied out her shopping: dark brown hair dye, bottle of whisky, scissors, tube of lip balm, toothbrush and pain killers for the migraines he said he'd been having.

'OK, shall we make a start?'

'Right, but listen Mags, are you sure about all this? You're happy to help me?'

'I've said so, haven't I?'

'I appreciate it, honestly, I really do.'

Mags allowed herself the hint of a smile and began cutting his hair short and trimming his straggly Brennus beard. She put lip balm close to his hairline front, back and sides so the dye wouldn't run, mark his skin and give the game away. Mags then dipped the toothbrush into the dye and began applying it from his scalp upwards. When she finished, she said no one would recognise him.

'You look ten years younger.'

'You're a star, Mags. You'll get your reward when we get to where we're going.'

'And where's that exactly?'

'Just a little place to escape the madding crowds.'

'But where is it? Give me a clue.'

'We'll be there soon enough,' Robbo said. 'Now come on, we need to get going. Where's your car parked?'

*

For all the long drive south and his overnight stake-out, Christian Moreley had learned nothing meaningful about Sir Frazer Harris's death from the cop he'd doorstepped on the waterfront at Itchenor.

Research time was running out. The news organiser in London needed Moreley back in Manchester covering the North. There was barely concealed sarcasm in her voice when she'd asked when his big exclusive might drop. It was all his own fault. He'd sold Eamon's tip too hard before he'd even a sniff of corroboration. But he hadn't come away from Itchenor entirely empty-handed.

Detective Inspector Roach of the Met's Major Crimes Unit had given him his card and direct phone number.

So Moreley rang him and now walked through Soho, between the shouts of competing fruit and veg stallholders in Berwick Street market and towards the Blue Posts pub on the corner. This was where Roach suggested they meet. Much hung on the next hour or so. Moreley could have murdered for a drink.

Roach was a few minutes late. With him was a shorter,

older man, dark-haired, face potholed by the acne that must have plagued his youth. He was introduced only as Laurie, a colleague from the office. The cops made for a table by the loud jukebox. It was their way of not asking – or caring – if he was wired up. Moreley bought pints of bitter for them and a non-alcoholic lager for himself.

'Why are you drinking that piss?' Laurie said. 'There're more fucking hops in a dead frog.'

Moreley said he was taking strong tablets for a bad back and not allowed alcohol.

'Right,' Roach said. 'Here's the deal. You want information, we want information. Are we agreed, are you happy to do a trade?'

'Sure, up to a point,' Moreley said. 'I've got some difficulties, though… you know, sources. If I break their confidences, you'll not trust me with yours.'

'We understand where you're coming from, Christian,' Roach said. 'But look, when we met, you mentioned something about the gun Sir Frazer had used, some Irish connection. Tell us more about that.'

'OK, and if I do, what will I get in return?'

'What is it that you really want?'

'Some steer from you that there's a definite Irish or terrorist link to Harris's death.'

'Talk to us and it'll be worth your while,' Benwell said. 'Trust us on this.'

Moreley drank from the bottle. His options were clear: lose the story and lose face; cough a bit, lead the evening news and stand by for a herogram from the director general.

'It's like this: a guy rings me every once in a while and gives me the nod on something I'm not supposed to know.'

'And this man, it's him saying the gun that killed Sir Frazer has a link to Ireland?'

'Yep, that's right.'

'Are you prepared to say who he is, what his job is?'

'No… that would be a trade too far.'

'But you know his name?'

Moreley nodded, took another swig of his lager.

'Are we right to assume he's something to do with the world of intelligence?'

'Right again, yeah.'

Benwell went to the bar and came back with two pints and a large Scotch for Moreley.

The cops were initiating him, testing him. Fuck your bad back, son. We're having a session. Join us if you're man enough.

One Scotch wouldn't kill him. It'd be a heart starter. But God forbid he got the taste again.

'Cheers,' Moreley said. 'Your health.'

He was on his way. The cops gave him the benefit of their viperine smiles and raised their pint pots.

'OK, right,' Roach said. 'As we see it, you've got problems with this story. Your informant can't know anything about the gun because it's not been found and tested and we've no idea where Sir Frazer went into the water, so where the hell do we look for it?'

'But is it significant that his body was found across from Thorney Island where the Special Forces have a base?'

'Is that what your source is suggesting?'

'In a roundabout sort of way, yes.'

'Well, he's talking bollocks,' Benwell said.

'Maybe he is,' Moreley said. 'But if Harris just topped

himself plain and simple, what are you blokes from the MCU wasting your time investigating it for?'

'Because he was an ex-Minister of Defence, wasn't he? It's political. Everything has to be squared off for the man upstairs.'

It was Roach who went to the bar next. He brought back pints and chasers. Moreley should've made an excuse and left. But he was starting to feel good again. His old confidence was returning.

Benwell leaned in closer to Moreley. They were becoming mates.

'Here's what I think, Christian. Your tout is a spook and he's using you in some little rat-fucking battle you'll never know anything about. His intelligence isn't evidence.

'These guys never have to stand up in court like we do, they don't have to prove anything. It's OK for them just to believe something to be true and hey presto, it is.'

'So what are you driving at?'

Benwell fixed Moreley with a stare heavy with menace.

'You run with this Irish angle and you'll leave your arse out of the window,' he said. 'But if you back off it, we'll give you the leads for something every bit as tasty and with proof.'

And so they told him about Sir Frazer, owner of Woodside, the house in Bognor split into rented apartments where a failed actress and would-be glamour model, Miss Poppy Nelson, provided sexual services to men in her basement flat.

Thus her landlord was living off her immoral earnings and the police in Sussex had begun a formal investigation with the operational name Rosebud.

'Rosebud's the reason the old bugger killed himself,'

Benwell said. 'His secret was out, nothing to do with Ireland and everything to do with being a fucking pimp whose own weird fantasies Miss Nelson was only too happy to see to.'

'But where did the gun come from?'

'I tried asking him that,' Benwell said. 'But the bastard's gone no comment.'

*

An hour later, Moreley was in the gardens of Soho Square, sipping nips from a half bottle of Scotch. He'd fallen – or been pushed – off the wagon. At least now he had an exclusive to put his news organiser back in her box then burn across to Fleet Street.

First, he had interviews to arrange, library footage to order up and a camera crew and a producer to organise for the morning, then he'd set off for Sussex.

But how the gods splice together the lives of those they might wish to destroy is beyond computation. So Christian Moreley wasn't the only one heading for Sussex.

Tilly Brown was already in a hotel within the Roman walls of the cathedral city of Chichester. She lay on her bed, planning how best to approach Robbo's wife when she knocked on her door next morning.

And Robbo himself was leading Mags through the darkness and along a beach of pebbles eight miles south with sleet whipping off the churning sea and soon to turn to snow.

'How much farther, Robbo?'

'Nearly there. Keep hold of my hand.'

A hundred yards further on, Robbo pushed open a gate in a wicket fence. He took them down a concrete path with overgrown bushes on either side. At the end amid a screen of winter bare trees was an ancient railway carriage, long since converted into a holiday home. Beyond were others, bungalows and shacks, dark and empty.

Mags didn't know what to say. Part of her was starting to feel afraid. Robbo had only said they were going to his bolt hole. She thought he'd meant a house.

'What's this, Robbo?'

'It's a place of memories... happy memories.'

The old compartments had been stripped out to make way for a tiny kitchen with a Calor gas stove, a central sitting area heated by a pot-bellied wood burner, and a bedroom. Robbo lit candles then the fire. The smell of damp remained.

'It's possible to feel at peace again here,' he said.

Once more, Mags was unsure how to react.

She thought of the retired policeman who'd been suspicious of Robbo at the settlement. Why was that?

It was directly after she'd told him this that Robbo decided he must change his appearance and leave straight away. And she'd gone along with him, didn't even think to ask him why.

Going off with an alluring older man who might be a criminal on the run was exciting for a young woman who felt herself unattractive and whose life she pretended wasn't dull.

She sat across the small pine table from him. He'd made tea and apologised for having no milk. Mags sensed his mood change, that he'd become sad, reflective.

'Robbo?'

He looked up. In the candle light, he seemed older despite her best efforts to groom him, not at ease and somehow diminished but by what, she couldn't begin to guess.

'Are you going to tell me what's going on, why we're

here?'

He put his hand on the back of hers and tried to smile but failed.

'I had to come... see it again, just this once,' he said. 'And there's something here I've got to get and deliver to someone.'

'What is it, Robbo? Please tell me what this is all about, please?'

'You mustn't worry, it's just some business I have to finish.'

'Robbo... your wife didn't die in a car crash, did she?'

'No... I haven't got a wife.'

'What is it that you're running away from?'

'Lots of things, Mags, lots of things.'

'But you've got to tell me... you're not a terrorist, are you? Just tell me who you really are.'

It took a moment for him to answer and as he did, he looked away, looked away so she couldn't see into his eyes and what they might reveal.

'Dear trusting girl. My heart says I should tell you everything but my head knows I mustn't... for your own good, honestly.'

And so she lay in his arms all that cold night, fully clothed on a narrow iron bed, the storm of her Renaissance hair on the pillow, in his face, in his head.

He remembered the smell and feel of it from long ago from the one who was mother to all the children in that big and frightening place. They would gather on the lawn by the cedar trees and listen to her stories as she sat with her back against the rough stone plinth of a sundial.

And etched into its round bronze face were words he

couldn't understand… not then: *Thus we pass on to the Halls of Light or to the Dwelling of the Shades*.

30: FUGITIVES

"First mend yourself,
then mend others."

- Jewish proverb

A passenger train slowly clanks and shimmers through the heat of the Great Karoo, a semi-desert of blood red earth and brown hills known as the land of thirst. Bella sits by herself, dressed as a nun. She has a head start – if only for the moment – on the National Intelligence Service and its assassins from Z Squad.

These people she knew... knew they killed to order. They targeted influential fighters who were then found shot or maimed by letter bombs. Her knowledge of chemistry had been sought about poisoning others. The law, morality, religion, none of these meant anything to such men. Putting her in a morgue would be a satisfying day's work for them.

Bella had been summoned to a meeting with her handlers for no apparent reason. She'd suspected a trap and believed only torture and death awaited her so she fled. If the NIS needed confirmation of her treachery, this vanishing act was proof.

She and Ralph are now in the same carriage but apart. They behave as strangers. She carries a hessian bag with a flask of tea, sandwiches and biscuits. Nuns are poor and cannot afford shop prices. They always take their own provisions on long journeys.

Knowing little details like this, convincing communists and fighters that she was one of them, had made Bella an effective and reliable infiltrator.

But her record worked against her, too. Why hadn't so able an agent warned the NIS of the ANC's audacious bombing of the nuclear power plant at Koeberg eighteen months earlier?

Bella claimed not to have known about it beforehand. Privately, she wasn't believed – and she sensed it. Other NIS operations hadn't quite come off, either. And when she failed to deliver the English vicar to give the NIS the honey trap propaganda coup they'd planned, they must have realised she'd gone native.

For now, Bella's borrowed passport, issued nine years before, shows she is Debra Steyn, born in Pretoria, a nun with the Missionary Sisters of the Assumption. The photograph inside its green cover is hardly a perfect likeness. If questioned, Bella will say time hasn't been kind.

Two seats behind her is the NIS's would-be patsy, the Reverend Ralph Hill. Other passengers, seven or eight of them, respect his privacy and keep clear. They reach the major railhead at De Aar to wait for a connection to Windhoek in South West Africa.

The NIS will not be so active there. Bella's chances of getting on a plane to Europe will be greater. The Reverend Hill buys himself a coffee at the kiosk on the platform, stretches his legs. He'd been hours on the train.

Across the oily black shunting yard are the hulks of ten

worked-out steam locos, dumped like the carcasses of great animals to be scavenged under the pitiless sun.

A troop train clatters by. It's taking South African soldiers across the border to the war for independence in SWA. Enemy fighters lie in wait for them in the bush, trained in Angola by communist forces from the Soviet Union, Cuba, East Germany. The scramble for Africa is still not over.

The blur of faces staring back at Ralph Hill from the windows of the grey and maroon coaches seem young and immortal and are gone in a flash.

Their connection to Windhoek arrives. He and Bella board a carriage coupled to the rear of a train of goods wagons. They sit either side of the aisle this time. Each needs the discreet reassurance of the other.

A man comes aboard. He takes the seat opposite Bella. Maybe he's thirty, muscled beneath his sandy brown suit, which he wears with a white shirt and striped tie. He appears not to have any luggage.

He glances at Bella for longer than she would like but doesn't smile. Fear and suspicion stalk the land. Who is he? What is he?

Bella fingers the plain wooden beads of her rosary. She begins to pray. Ralph Hill opens his bible but finds it difficult to concentrate on God's message of peace and love.

*

There was nothing for breakfast in Robbo's hideaway. He found another teabag and boiled water on the Calor gas stove. His mood was as preoccupied as the night before. Mags went to pee in the chemical loo in the outside shed. More snow had

331

fallen overnight. The sea sucked at the bank of pebbles on the shoreline and far in the distance, clouds the colour of lead loomed over the bridal white hills of the South Downs. She asked him where they were.

'This is Pagham Harbour,' he said. 'But listen, we need to leave soon.'

It wasn't yet seven o'clock.

'Where to, now?'

'You'll see. Bit of a drive but not that far really.'

Mags went to the bedroom to change. She heard a scraping noise and looked round the partition. Robbo was kneeling by the wood burner, which stood on a slate slab. He'd forced up the square stone hearth in front of it to reveal a hole in the wooden floor beneath.

From this he took three packages, each the size of a bag of sugar. They were wrapped in layers of plastic. She couldn't see what was inside. Robbo reached back into the space and brought out a thick roll of banknotes, fivers and tenners, held together by an elastic band. He returned the stone to its original position and scattered wood ash over it so it didn't look as if it'd been disturbed.

'Robbo, what are you doing? What's going on?'

'I don't trust the banks.'

'Yes, but all that money—'

'It's just my savings.'

'But those packages, what's in them?'

'I've been minding them for their rightful owner... not for much longer, though.'

'Robbo, you're worrying me, you really are.'

He peeled off two hundred pounds.

'There's no need to be worried,' he said. 'Here, take

this… it's what I owe you.'

'No, I can't. I don't want it.'

'Please, Mags… you've been so kind and I never leave a debt unpaid.'

But she wouldn't accept it. Theirs was a sullen walk from the beach to her car. Each had thoughts they couldn't – wouldn't – share with the other. Robbo led the way to a narrow track overhung with alder and stunted oaks and up to a small car park serving an ancient church and graveyard. Nearby was a great earthen mound on which a strategic Norman castle once stood.

More snow began to fall. Only the skirling gulls and the distant sea broke the silence. It was difficult to imagine such a deserted place ever having been a seat of power and activity where laws were enforced and wrongdoing punished. But a thousand years later, actions still had consequences.

*

The funnies of MI5 guarded their intelligence jealously, even from senior police officers like Laurie Benwell. They might be on the same side but empires, once built, had to be maintained. Only after political pressure from Met Commissioner Silvey did the spooks pass on a critical piece of information for Benwell's unsolved murder inquiry from their gold asset in the IRA, the agent codenamed Navoi.

He'd sworn on the curly heads of his many children that the car bomb that killed Kat Walsh's Int Cell driver, O'Brien, was not a Provo operation.

Given that Navoi's hands must be deep dyed in the blood of those that were, the funnies believed his version of events.

For Benwell, this disclosure wasn't enough. Commissioner Silvey lobbied hard for him to meet Navoi's handler and ask for more background.

'They didn't quite laugh in my face,' Silvey said. 'But I was told they'd be selling coats in hell before that happened.'

But not long after, Benwell had a call on his mobile from a man with a cultured but weak voice revealing no discernible accent.

'I hear on my grapevine that you would like to talk to me.'

'Who is this? Who's calling?'

'Someone who knows the number of the phone you were only provided with yesterday.'

'So? You could be from the phone company.'

'Then I wouldn't share your interest in the untimely end of a certain Mr O'Brien, would I?'

Benwell clicked his ancient Zippo to light his first cigarette of the day.

'How about if you tell me who you are.'

'I'm someone who could fill in some of the gaps in your knowledge and I think, could add to it as well.'

'OK, but if you're in a position to do that, why aren't you making this contact through our usual channels?'

'Because there are those in authority who want this contentious matter swept under the office rug and forgotten about. Isn't that your reading of it, Mr Benwell?'

'Maybe, maybe not, so are you suggesting something more informal then, unofficial?'

'That's rather the reason for my phone call, yes.'

Benwell said he didn't understand why his caller was prepared to take the risk of talking out of turn to someone he didn't know. A moment of silence followed before the reply came.

'It's my experience that the lives of men and their beliefs, motives... they're so complex, all of them, and facing death even more so but there it is. My offer stands if you wish to take it up but I'll not be offended if you prefer to proceed without it.'

They both knew he wouldn't. He gave Benwell the number of an apartment in a mansion block near West Hampstead tube station and said he'd expect him for tea at four thirty.

A Land Registry search showed it had been owned by one Adam Ian Dearden for twelve years. The latest voters' list had him down as the flat's sole occupant.

An old friend in the Home Office told him Dearden recently retired from K4 (A), the MI5 section that identified intelligence officers from the Soviet Embassy in London and tried to suborn – or blackmail – them into spying for Britain.

'Christ,' Roach said. 'How come a Cold War spook knows about dirty deeds in Ireland?'

'I'll not bother answering that. I don't need another damned headache.'

The block was Edwardian, solidly built in red engineering brick, four floors high and with a secure entry system. Benwell pressed the bell for Flat 6. He was asked his name then he and Roach were electronically admitted to a communal lobby.

They walked up a flight of white marble stairs to the first floor where a man was waiting. He looked skeletally thin, leaned on a stick and was still in his pyjamas. He held out a blue-veined hand to Benwell.

'Ah, I see you've brought a witness,' he said. 'How very wise. Do come in and I'll set another cup and saucer.'

*

Martha knew all too well how bitterly upset Ginny had been after Bella moved into the vicarage at All Hallows.

'Daddy told me she was a political refugee from South Africa,' she'd said. 'There were death squads after her and I wanted to say well, they'll never find her now, not in the bed you shared with Mummy.'

However complicit Bella had been, she was not the one to blame. But Ginny now knew what had been going on as her mother was dying. Her relationship with her father, never truly close, didn't have far to fall.

'How could I ever trust him again, Martha?' she'd said. 'I mean, the flowers on Mummy's grave had barely wilted, for God's sake.'

Martha had tried to comfort her and now, in the presence of the parent responsible, it was difficult to remain neutral.

'So you and Bella got to Windhoek and out of Africa, Ralph,' she said. 'But meeting Bella for the first time can't have been easy for Ginny.'

'No, how could it be? But I wanted to believe she had some understanding of my predicament.'

'But what about your understanding of hers... did you give that some thought?'

'I tried, of course I did, and I thought in time the two of them would reach some sort of accommodation, one with the other.'

'That didn't happen though, did it?'

'Not as much as I'd hoped, no. But in the end, what did it matter? I lost them both.'

The letter bomb that tore into Bella had another purpose beyond causing her death. Within the pages of the Afrikaans bible in which the explosives were hidden was a wider message to South Africa's enemies: whoever they may be and wherever they might hide, they could be traced and their treachery repaid with interest.

Those were bleak days for the Reverend Hill, besieged by reporters and camera crews, interrogated by anti-terrorist detectives, deeply hacked off that South Africa's dirty war had come to an England already being blown apart by the IRA. And in all this, he received only lukewarm support from his bishop. But even harder to bear were the parting remarks of Bella's son who came to take her body home to Johannesburg for burial.

'Do not ask me or your God for forgiveness,' he'd said. 'I hold you and you alone responsible for my mother's death.'

'Please, you mustn't say that.'

'You took her out of our country, it was you who made her an enemy of the state.'

'She was that before I ever met her. I loved your mother.'

'But not as much as you loved yourself, priest.'

Within the anger of the young man's bereavement was a truth Ralph Hill could not deny, not then and not to Martha now.

They were sitting towards the back of the cathedral. Martha was about to leave him and drive home when one of the volunteer guides approached her.

'Miss Whitten, I've just left a man by the entrance,' the guide said. 'He seems pretty insistent that he must speak to the Reverend Hill quite urgently.'

'Did he say what it's about?'

'No, he didn't give me his name or anything. He's rather poorly dressed but he's with a young girl and he keeps saying he's got some information that's very important and the Reverend Hill should know about it. Shall I bring them through?'

31: SECRETS

"Eshajori"

- Japanese word for the transient nature of all human relationships.

An actor whose face Tilly thought she recognised from television answered at the address she had for Sally Tobin. He'd never heard of her. The house was rented by the Festival Theatre a few streets away for performers in their productions.

Snow blew about Tilly's head in a bitter southerly wind from the English Channel as she knocked at other doors. No one recalled Sally or suggested others who might. Residents in gentrified Victorian terraces were no longer close to their neighbours.

Tilly's other option was a possibly fruitless trawl through Chichester's latest voting list for someone who may already have left the area.

A postman turned into the street in walking boots and a padded jacket. He remembered Sally's soft Irish accent, her coral-coloured hair. He didn't know where she'd moved to, but it couldn't have been far.

'By the library in town, I've seen her several times,' he said. 'I've a mind she works there.'

Ten minutes later, Tilly stood outside a circular glass and concrete structure in the shadow of the cathedral's great free-standing bell tower. And stacking a shelf with books was the connection to Robbo she sought: a woman in her early forties, attractive if stern-looking, wearing a navy bib and brace boiler suit, which Tilly – prejudicially – always associated with militant feminism.

She wouldn't interrupt her. If she did and they made an arrangement to meet later, she'd have time to think up reasons to cancel.

Best to wait until her shift finished, catch her off guard in the street. That's what Laurie would do. Thinking of Benwell prompted her to cross to a phone box and ring him.

'He's out at a meeting,' the office manager said. 'Probably not back till early evening.'

'Will you tell him Tilly Brown called?'

'Sure, any message?'

'Say I've got some fascinating new information about the helicopter crash.'

She left her hotel number then went to the café on the corner to warm up with a coffee and a pastry. It was still only mid-morning. Laurie always said surveillance was ninety-nine per cent tedium, then you blink and the bastard's away on his toes.

*

A poignant image of the Reverend Hill looking lost, gazing round her father's spare room for a place to hang his dead wife's painting of Ginny, wouldn't leave Martha on the drive home. He was all that Ginny ever said – dogmatic, totally lacking empathy, egotistical – but he'd been broken on a wheel of his own devising.

Whatever time remained to this maddening priest, he would never shed the guilt weighing him down. For this, she could only pity him.

The answerphone in her hall was blinking with messages when she opened the front door. She made herself a pot of coffee before listening to them. Kat Walsh had rung twenty-four hours earlier.

'Hi, Martha… just a welfare call. I'm wanting a sit-rep on the Reverend Hill… how he's doing and all that. Get back to me when you've a moment.'

She'd left a contact number in Belfast. But Martha knew that in Kat's line of work, it could be automatically diverted and ring out anywhere. It took a good twenty seconds before she answered. Martha told her Ginny's father was only just about coping.

'He's had a lot to bear,' Kat said. 'Losing his daughter… terrible for him, being on his own.'

'Oddly enough, he had a visitor just before I left him, someone who knew Ginny.'

'Really? Who was that?'

'I think he said his name was Rob or Bob, something like that. Had a young woman with him but she didn't say anything.'

Kat tried not to sound too interested.

'What did this guy look like, Martha?'

'Looked like he works out, dark brown hair, about forty I'd think… and he had a beard.'

'Did he say if he'd been in the Army? Was that how he knew Ginny?'

341

'I was just leaving,' Martha said. 'All I remember him saying was he had something really important he had to tell the Reverend Hill about.'

Kat stayed quiet for a moment then went for broke.

'Martha, think back… this is really important. Could his name have been Robbo?'

'It might have been but I really can't be sure. Sorry.'

For Kat, this was confirmation that Robbo had risen from the dead and was on the move. She could guess what he'd told Ginny's grieving father – and why. But what would the old boy do with the information? And how long before she got a tap on the shoulder?

Even as she tried to compute what might overtake her in the coming hours, her phone rang again. A female asked if that was Mrs Laurel. Kat stiffened at this mention of her code name on undercover jobs with Robbo in Northern Ireland.

'Who is this?' she said. 'Who are you?'

'That doesn't matter,' the girl said. 'I've got a message from your good friend, Mr Hardy, that he's asked me to read to you.'

Kat could almost hear her heart thumping.

'And what is this message?'

'He says I've got the material you've always wanted and I'll do a deal with you for it at ten tonight by the boathouse on the north side of the place where I went swimming.'

The caller then rang off. Kat knew exactly where was meant and gathered documents and other possessions she wouldn't want to fall into the wrong hands. She'd five hours to get to the RV. There was a trade to be done, but she'd want it on her terms. Then it would be Kat's turn to disappear.

On the fifth floor of MI5's offices in Mayfair, one of a bank of recorders clicked off. Two specific tapes were ready to be transcribed by an audio typist in Section A2A. She was told they were urgent. An officer who liaised with the Met's Major Crimes Unit waited for her to finish.

Then he'd have a phone call to make. In the freemasonry of that closed world, he would know the two detectives whose office needed to be told they had a couple of important transcripts waiting to be read. What he wouldn't realise was that at that moment, they were having tea and cakes with one of his most revered former colleagues.

*

In his pomp, Adam Dearden's manner would have been that of the penurious owner of a large country house and estate who, despite obvious signs of dilapidation, remained courtly towards tenants, even while creditors were at his gate and bankers at his throat.

He'd present as an archetypal pre-war Englishman, one who put value above price and saw the moral purpose in loyalty, duty and personal sacrifice. Yet behind this benign facade was a talent to prey upon human weakness to serve his country's ends.

Dearden had occupied one of twelve desks in the large open-plan office of Section K4 in MI5's grey stone headquarters at 140 Gower Street. He targeted Soviet diplomats and staff in allied outfits like Aeroflot and Novosti, to persuade them – most often using the three-card trick of blackmail, money or sex – into working as agents for Britain.

But he'd had to retire after being diagnosed with pancreatic cancer.

'We're most grateful for your time, sir,' Benwell said. 'We'll treat anything you tell us in the strictest confidence.'

'Yes, please do. There's much at stake.'

'We gather that talking to us isn't what your service wants.'

'No, but Navoi is my creature and I'm greatly troubled by how that source is being run.'

He stood up suddenly and excused himself.

'I'm only just out of hospital,' he said. 'Can't be too far from the blasted bathroom. Please, help yourself, more tea, whatever you want.'

Dearden's sitting room had a high ceiling and large windows giving a view over the traffic in West End Lane. One entire wall was hung with oil paintings of naval battles at the Nile, Copenhagen, Trafalgar, Cape Vincent and beyond.

Much of the furniture was antique and most likely came from a larger, older house. The soft furnishings, the matching decor, all had a cultured feminine touch, though there was no obvious sign of a woman's presence.

Dearden returned and sat down cautiously in the wingback opposite them.

'Forgive my absence but we have to deal with what's in front of us in this life, don't we?'

'True enough, sir,' Benwell said. 'Maybe you could help us understand our rather sensitive situation a little more by explaining how someone with your particular function in your organisation came to be running an agent in Northern

Ireland.'

Dearden took a breath. He leaned forward, both hands on the rounded handle of his cane.

'This is somewhat painful for me,' he said. 'But you're right – context, background, motive all need to be scoped in serious matters like this, even if it means breaking what our French friends call my *devoir de réserve*.'

'Sorry, sir, I don't—'

'My duty of silence, Mr Benwell, of confidentiality.'

He said his wife had been killed in a car accident fifteen years earlier in 1975. Her major organs were donated for transplants.

'I asked if I could meet some of the recipients,' Dearden said. 'I suppose it was part of my grieving process... I wanted to believe her existence hadn't been for nothing and to see for myself that her death had served some positive purpose.'

Mrs Dearden's kidneys had saved the life of a woman in Belfast.

'This lady had been on dialysis for years but somehow brought up several children,' he said. 'The gratitude of her and her husband knew no bounds.'

Dearden, ever the spook, checked the husband's name against files in MI5's registry. The man was an IRA volunteer and close to its decision-makers on the Army Council.

'My elders and betters had concerns about me meeting this fellow but this was my field, you see... spotting those I could turn around for queen and country.'

They eventually met in the first-floor lounge of the Europa Hotel in Belfast.

'Was he suspicious of you, sir?'

'He might have been at first but he seemed more anxious to know how he could repay me and I said it was enough for me to know his children still had their mother.'

Benwell wondered if this had brought a tear to the eye of a murdering terrorist bastard, but kept the notion to himself. Other meetings had taken place and Dearden met the man's wife.

'Who did they think you were?' Roach said.

'I told them I was a tutor of Russian in London and did translation work on the side, but by the look of me and my clothes, they could see I wasn't doing very well.'

'But you gained their trust?'

'Over time, yes. They felt sorry for me… my loss had been their gain and through this, I literally had a stake in their family.'

'But what an extraordinary reason to become a spy for you,' Roach said.

'Indeed, especially when there's graffiti all around Belfast proclaiming, with deadly accuracy as it happens, that touting can seriously damage your health.'

Benwell asked how long the man had actually been passing over IRA secrets to him.

'No, you misunderstand,' Dearden said. 'Navoi isn't the man. Navoi is the wife.'

*

It was going dark by the time Sally Tobin left the library. Tilly saw her from the doorway where she'd sheltered. Snow was still falling by the brightly decorated windows of houses thereabouts.

346

Sally wore a silver fox Russian hat, a crimson coat and long black boots. She walked up Tower Street and made for the cathedral on the other side of Westgate. Young choristers from the Prebendal School were rehearsing a performance of carols.

Several teachers and parents sat watching the boys in their red blazers and grey shirts. They took the choirmaster's cue and filled the nave with their angelic, unbroken voices.

'Be near me Lord Jesus, I ask thee to stay
Close by me forever, and love me, I pray.
Bless all the dear children in thy tender care
And take us to heaven, to live with thee there.'

Tilly sat slightly to the left of Sally in the row of seats behind. She could see her side-faced, enjoying the performance.

One of the boys seemed to look across at her every so often. He might be ten or eleven with thick brown hair, solidly built and tall for his age. Was he Sally's son? Could Robbo be his father? He'd told Tilly that he hadn't got any children. But Robbo and the truth rarely lay in the same bed.

The choir finished *Away in a Manger*, sang three more carols then took a break. Sally got up and went to the boy. She would've kissed him but he was embarrassed and turned his cheek away.

Sally's smile was loving and proud. Tilly heard her say something. It sounded like, 'I'll see you later' but she couldn't be sure. The boy waved her away and went to his boisterous friends joshing around the piano. They pushed and shoved for they were excited but irreverence, even in a holy setting, was forgivable at that time of year.

Sally left and didn't look back. Tilly kept a few paces

behind her, into the street and by the gaudy windows of department stores, shoppers with bags and parcels and office workers waiting for buses delayed by the weather.

A Salvation Army band played in the swirling snow by the medieval market cross. Children queued by a brazier to buy roast chestnuts. It was like being in a cheap Christmas card, a commercialised vision of an arcadia that never was. Tilly wasn't given to sentimentality or maternalism, yet in that moment, felt a twinge of both. She was aware of an emptiness in her life and experienced a sudden yearning for that which she'd consciously chosen not to have.

Even as Tilly tried to push the thought away, Sally stopped abruptly outside a coffee shop. She turned quickly and took a determined step towards Tilly.

'You're following me,' she said. 'Who are you? What do you want?'

*

Death, observed Dearden, concentrates the mind like nothing else.

'I should know,' he said. 'I am a dead man talking.'

He looked away, stared into the cannon fire and raging seas depicted in his paintings.

'Mrs Navoi would lie awake imagining her own funeral, the grief of her children, her family, at losing her... then the gods roll the dice and a car and a lorry collide in a village in Surrey and Mrs Navoi can live but my wife must be taken in part exchange.'

Benwell nodded his head in what for him passed as sympathy.

'When we were on our own, she told me this second chance at life had altered her in quite profound ways and given her an insight into human suffering she hadn't had before.'

'Didn't she know her husband was in the IRA, then?' Benwell said.

'Of course she did. That's what was eating at her Catholic conscience.'

'But she'd just about managed to turn a blind eye, had she?'

'As many must do, yes. But being on a kind of death row for so long then being released from it affected her and put her at one with the families of the victims on all sides.'

'So there's a road from Belfast to Damascus, is there?'

'And Mrs Navoi found it with a little help, yes,' Dearden said.

'Plus a few thousand quid, I don't doubt.'

'That's where you're wrong. Money was never her prime motivation. I always felt part of it was her making amends for the husband, trying to wash the blood off his hands.'

'But how did she obtain intelligence about the IRA's activities?' Benwell said. 'The husband was the terrorist and he'd not be talking out of turn.'

'No, but members of the Army Council met in Mrs Navoi's house. They felt they were amongst friends so they talked and she listened.'

'And so did you, presumably?'

Dearden smiled at this.

'On one of my early visits, I took Mrs Navoi and her children to the zoo while one of our people did some minor adjustments to a light fitting in their front room.'

'So where was the husband when this was happening?'

'On his shift at the abattoir… animals by day, humans at night.'

And herein was Dearden's ethical and legal dilemma.

Mrs Navoi's husband was being allowed to get away with killing not just loyalist enemies but alleged informers in the IRA's own ranks. But if they arrested him, the security services would lose an invaluable source of inside information.

'Gathering intelligence is now deemed politically and strategically more important than solving crime,' Dearden said. 'We are colluding with our agents in terrorist organisations to kill and cause chaos in breach of the guidelines we're supposed to follow. We may have no alternative, but the very word "collusion" suggests a moral equivalence between terrorists and the state's lawful entities, and this will ultimately undermine public confidence in the authorities when peace comes. We cannot murder our way out of Ireland, though heaven knows we've tried. The law may be an ass but ignoring it is out of harmony with the moral law and the law of God.'

Benwell hadn't signed up for a tutorial. He looked at his watch and thanked Dearden for his assistance.

'Is there anything else from Navoi that would help our investigation, sir?'

'Just this, I think,' he said. 'That helicopter that crashed in Wales, in that lake. The media has it that it was sabotaged by the IRA but I can tell you that though Navoi confirms the comrades were delighted that it happened and wished they'd done it, they were not, repeat not, responsible. You must look elsewhere for those who were.'

*

Christmas decorations could hardly be more out of place than in MI5's other bunker of a building in Curzon Street. Spooks didn't do goodwill at any time of year; they dished out FUD – fear, uncertainty, doubt – to those deemed enemies of the state.

Benwell and Roach ignored the streamers and were taken to a secure office to make notes from the transcripts of Kat's two tapped phone conversations. It was logical to assume from these that Robbo had broken cover and set up a meet with her, but where was the place he'd gone swimming?

'We've got to bring her in,' Benwell said. 'Hit the phones. Get the team to call anyone in our system who might have a steer where she might be.'

'Trouble is she's already way ahead of us,' Roach said. 'It's nearly six o'clock now and their meet's at ten.'

Their office manager then called to say that Benwell's friend, Tilly Brown, had some information about the crashed helicopter. But she wasn't in her hotel room when Benwell rang. The woman on reception took his mobile number and promised to say he'd been in touch.

'Just you tell her it's bloody urgent, do you hear?' he said.

32: TRUTH

"If three people know a secret,
it's not a secret any more."

- Irish saying

'I'm not allowed to talk about him or anything to do with that whole affair.'

'Sally, I'm only trying to find out what's become of him.'

'But that's no business of yours or anyone else's. Anyway, how did you find me?'

'Look, my hotel's just down this street,' Tilly said. 'Please listen to what I have to say.'

'Why should I?'

'Because strange things have happened which have alarmed me and you need to know about them for your own sake and for your family's.'

Sally shot her an icy glance through the falling snow, as suspicious as it was defensive.

'You've no right coming into my life like this, raking up the past. You could be from a newspaper.'

'I'm not from a newspaper. Like I said, I'm a lawyer and I worked in the legal department of the police in London until a few months ago.'

Tilly took out her Met security pass. Sally looked at the

photograph on it then at Tilly.

'Why's any of this of concern to you?'

'Hear me out then you'll understand.'

'If I'm to do that, these are my terms,' she said. 'I'll listen to what you have to say then that's us done, finished. Robbo doesn't know my new address or anything about me and that's how I want to keep it. Is that understood?'

*

Two cars had headed north on different minor roads that night, through the same treacherous conditions and towards the same bleak destination. Neither driver could travel fast. Snow was drifting in places. Some vehicles had slid into ditches or through hedges. Kat Walsh didn't want hers to join them.

There was a desperation about her, the sweaty edginess of a gambler who'd bet the farm on the turn of a single card. She had gone for broke big time and was now absent without leave. None of her Army colleagues or the funnies with whom she liaised knew where she was. But what option did she have?

She knew all about criminal investigations, the gathering of evidence, the circling around the suspect, then the target's door gets kicked in and it's goodbye career, freedom and the future.

And if that's what was planned for Kat – and she'd read the runes – those who'd connived with the dirty work she'd done for the state would shake their grey heads and wave their clean hands as they led her up the steps to the dock. Well, fuck them… fuck them all. She'd only put into practice what gutless politicians wanted.

Robbo's plea for a truce was her stay-out-of-jail card. She still had the connection in Liverpool who'd wanted their Bolivian marching powder. Profit from that would buy her time, a new identity, a new life.

She'd many a hurdle to clear first. It was a racing certainty that Benwell had an ear on her phone. He would know by now that Robbo had surfaced and set up an RV at ten that night. But Benwell wouldn't see a transcript immediately. And by the time he did, distance and the weather would be against him making it from London to the lake before her.

Robbo would've had a head start and arrive first. So what? He'd want to do the business in pretty short order. Even if he'd figured out why the helicopter had ditched, he'd not wish to stick around and risk arrest any more than Kat would.

In truth, each had a gun in the mouth of the other. But where was the benefit in mutually assured destruction? For all their differences, it made sense for the man who'd wagered his life for the love of her, to do whatever deal he proposed then for both to disappear.

But in the parallel moral universe wherein Kat and Robbo had dwelt so long, the wise tended to take out insurance. She'd meet him in good faith – or her interpretation of the concept – but she'd have more than just a lace handkerchief up her sleeve.

*

A waiter came across the hotel lounge to the alcove by the open fire where Tilly sat head to head with Sally.

'Miss Brown, there's a phone call in reception for you,'

he said.

'For me? Who is it, did they say?'

'No, but it's the same man who rang earlier when you were out.'

The interruption wasn't welcome. Sally had listened to what Tilly was saying but was she onside? If Tilly took the call, would Sally still be there when she returned? She ordered two more mulled wines from the waiter then went to the phone. It was Laurie Benwell and he sounded harassed.

'Tilly, you left me a message about the helicopter crash. What have you found out?'

'That the man I photographed, Robbo, was definitely on board. I knew I was right, Laurie. Robbo survived and a squad of soldiers came looking for him, armed to the teeth.'

'How do you know? Who's telling you all this?'

'I interviewed the woman who hid him in her cottage not far from the lake.'

'What's her name, Tilly? All this has become very important.'

'She's called Florence Rossiter and according to what Robbo told her, he'd crawled out of the lake half drowned and she found him next morning, bleeding and semi-conscious at her back door.'

Tilly heard Benwell turn to someone and say he now knew where Robbo had been swimming.

'You still there, Tilly?'

'Yes, anyway he wouldn't let her call an ambulance so she nursed him and bought him a lot of second-hand clothes because he told her he had to escape in disguise because someone was trying to kill him.'

'Did he say who that was or why they wanted to kill him?'

'Not in so many words but he warned her about a woman with fiery red hair, not to trust anything she said if she came looking for him.'

'Bloody good advice,' Benwell said. 'I'll bear it in mind if I get to meet her tonight.'

Tilly quickly returned to the lounge. Her coat was still on the back of her chair, the two glasses of untouched wine on the table. But of Sally, there was no sign, just the aroma of cinnamon.

*

It wasn't until eight thirty that the pilot of the Met Police helicopter felt the intermittent snow across central England no longer posed an unacceptable risk for a flight from his air support base at Lippitts Hill in Essex to North Wales.

Benwell, Roach and three other detectives had assembled there to wait for the weather to clear. Lippitts Hill also doubled as the Met's firearms training centre so they knew it well.

Only a chopper gave them a chance to make the RV and mount any sort of surveillance. Police in Wales had been asked for support but Benwell's faith in others hadn't always been repaid.

Besides, Robbo and Kat Walsh were his collars. He was buggered if anyone else was going to feel them. His nervy anxiety began to show.

'For Christ's sake, if we don't get going soon, the bastards will be back in their fucking beds drinking cocoa while we're stuck here building fucking snowmen.'

The pilot was ex-military, a dry and understated man, not

unduly cautious but governed by an overwhelming, if selfish, desire to live another day.

'You make valid points, Commander, but conditions aren't what I'd call ideal,' he said. 'But if we keep to three thousand feet, we shouldn't bump into anything and I'll be putting you down in two hours from now.'

'Praise bloody be,' Benwell said.

The pilot led them from the briefing room to the airstrip. A midnight blue Aerospatiale 355F1 stood fuelled up and ready to leave. Instrument checks took a few more minutes then they lifted off into the darkness, set on a course for Lake Vyrnwy.

*

Sally's long crimson coat wasn't too difficult to spot, even at a distance and in a street crowded with Christmas shoppers. But it still took Tilly a few minutes to catch up.

'Sally, please,' she said. 'That was a police officer on the phone, the one who's trying to find Robbo.'

'Then I wish him all the luck in the world because I never did.'

'Just give me five more minutes, Sally. You don't owe him or me anything but something's not right about all this. I want to understand what's happened.'

'Then let me help you,' she said. 'Robbo is not what he seems. Never has been and never will be.'

'But why, Sally? Why's he like this?'

'Because he's a servant of the secret state, one of their hidden hands, a spy, a plant, a liar, a cheat, anything you want, that's why. He lied to me from the moment we first met. He stole all my confidence, my sense of who I was, and I can never forgive him for that.'

There was anger in her face and tears in her eyes. The emotion of the moment took over. She began to sob. Tilly pointed to a café across the street.

'Come on, Sally, you need a coffee and a shoulder.'

*

Smoked salmon, scrambled eggs and champagne were brought up to their room in the Lake Vyrnwy Hotel, which Mags had registered in a false name – as Robbo ordered – and paid for with his cash. As she told the receptionist… my father is very old fashioned and doesn't approve of credit cards. From the eccentric cut of his hair and charity shop suit, he might not have approved of barbers and tailors, either.

Mags was warming to her role, to its intrigue and excitement and the danger of the unknown. Part of her was nervous, too. But Robbo hadn't forced her to be his accomplice. He'd asked for help and she'd given it, a willing Bonnie to his Clyde. All he made her do was to feel wanted.

For most of the journey from Wells Cathedral, he'd sat in concentrated silence except for telling her which roads to take, especially after they crossed the border into Wales. A few miles before the hotel, he'd told her to park outside a remote cottage. Its two downstairs windows were lit but he didn't knock at the door.

Instead, he pushed something through the letter box. Mags was sure it had been money. She'd seen him take a wad of notes from his inside pocket just before they'd stopped. He came back to the car and told her to drive away quickly. Yet again, he offered no explanation, no reason for what he had done.

Their room had two single beds. They ate at a small side table beneath the window. Somewhere far beyond was the lake, black and brooding and sly. Mags turned off the lights except for the lamp between their beds.

Robbo opened the champagne. It frothed down the bottle as the cork shot towards the ceiling. Mags laughed. They clinked glasses, which were quickly refilled. She smiled coyly but feared he was somewhere else, somewhere with another woman in a world that had come to an end as this one surely would before the dawn.

'Please, Robbo… please.'

She began to unbutton her blouse. What was she wanting from him that he could possibly give in that place on that night of all nights? Was it her reward for services rendered or some deeper, unfulfilled impulse, a desire to be desired?

How pale her nakedness, her unsuckled breasts; how innocent the slope of her virgin belly down to that tight little triangle of ginger curls. Robbo stood and took her head in his hands and kissed her. It was a long, slow kiss, neither of love nor lust, just the instinctive act of a man familiar with both.

Had he known Japanese, he might have remembered the phrase *pikit mata*, which translated as "with eyes closed", meaning an acceptance that something against one's innermost wishes must be done.

But he didn't and in a minute more, he entered her body as he had entered her mind, without a word, for Robbo had nothing to say.

*

359

'How did you first come to meet him?'

'Through the Troops Out Movement in the late seventies, '79 I think,' Sally said.

'So you were active politically back then?'

'Absolutely. Anti-Internment League, Big Flame, anything to protest at British rule in Ireland and I was there shouting the odds.'

Sally's tears in the street had been the first indication of pent-up emotions bursting. For years she'd held back her feelings, the bitterness at being used and abused by an agent of the state. They'd paid her off, bought her silence. But circumstances change. For whatever reason, Robbo was now being sought by the police. New facts may emerge for there was more than one truth in any story. She would talk to Tilly despite not quite understanding how she fitted into the affair. But she could yet be an ally in whatever lay ahead. Tilly said there'd been many IRA murders in the 1970s.

'Yes, there were,' Sally said. 'And this is why the Special Branch and the military infiltrated movements like ours, to get intelligence about their opponents on the streets.'

'But you didn't have any links to the IRA, surely?'

'No, but we often had republican speakers from Belfast. Maybe they did, I don't know.'

Robbo had given his name as Robert Ellison and said he was a van driver appalled at British Army brutality in Ireland. He'd come across as friendly, politically non-sectarian and happy to do boring admin.

'I was updating our membership list,' Sally said. 'He offered to help but of course that gave him access to every activist we had – phone numbers, home addresses, work, everything.'

'But you obviously liked him as a person, though?'

'Yeah, he could be funny, irreverent, always had that glint in his eye. We had a drink, a meal, then after a while, we inevitably ended up in bed. What is it they say... act in haste, repent at leisure. Well, I certainly did.'

'Was nobody suspicious of him, did no one check where he lived, worked, anything?'

'I suppose so and his cover story must've held up because I went and married him, didn't I?'

'Did his family come to the wedding? Did you ever meet any of them?'

'No, he said he'd broken off all contact with them so just a few of his mates came.'

It wasn't long after that Sally's own suspicions were aroused. She told Tilly how she uncovered the truth about Robbo and the name he'd stolen from a dead baby.

'Worst time in my life. I don't know how I got through it... still don't.'

'You must have confronted him, though. How did he explain all that deception?'

'He couldn't, not really,' Sally said. 'He denied he was a spy. Just kept saying he was on the run from the police and he'd used a fake name to protect me in case he got lifted. It was all baloney, made no sense, not then, not now.'

She looked at her watch. They'd finished their coffee and little remained to be discussed. Tilly had a final question.

'Tell me, Sally... the boy in the choir... he is your son, isn't he?'

'Yes, he is.'

'And Robbo is his father?'

'Yes, but he doesn't know he's got a son nor must he ever find out.'

33: ENDGAME

"Alas, I ha' lost my heat, my blood, my prime,
Winter is come a quarter 'ere his time,
My health will leave me; and when you depart,
How shall I do, sweet mistress, for my heart?"

- Ben Jonson, 1572–1637

'Why do you have to go out, Robbo? Stay here, stay with me... come back to bed.'

'I can't,' he said. 'There isn't time.'

He was writing what looked like letters on hotel notepaper and didn't look up. When he finished, he sealed whatever they were in envelopes. Next, he put the three parcels from his secret bolthole in the same plastic bag in which Mags had carried the Irish whisky and the other items he'd wanted from the shop near the Iron Age settlement.

'I'll see you later, won't I?' she said.

'Sure, course you will.'

Robbo then pulled the sheet from his bed and folded it into the bag. He buttoned his coat to the neck and paused at the half-open door. He looked across at her. She sat up and held the duvet to her bare breasts.

'There's a note for you,' he said. 'There's no need to open it till tomorrow, OK?'

363

That was it... no kiss, no fond adieu. He just closed the door quietly behind him.

Downstairs, a party of overdressed farmers' wives at a noisy pre-Christmas celebration were as frisky as cows let out in a field.

They milled around the bar and foyer, drinking wine and shrieking at bawdy jokes they'd never tell in chapel. Husbands stood in market day groups, faces like polished apples, pint pots small in their fists.

Robbo slipped away unnoticed. There was no moon, no shadows. Everything was dark save for the flakes of snow that had started falling again. The wind gathered strength. It funnelled down from the Berwyn Mountains to drive through the wooded banks on the far side of the lake and piled up waves to slap against the dam's huge stone ramparts.

Somewhere in the blackness beneath, in the drowned streets and ruined houses of the village that died for the dam, Kat would've had him sacrificed with that sad old vicar's daughter. He thought of her, trapped in their sabotaged helicopter. Please God, she was dead before it sank. All this to punish him for not handing over the cocaine he'd risked his life to get and to rid herself of a witness who knew enough to put her fingerprints on O'Brien's corpse rather than those of the IRA.

Their past as lovers was of no account nor bonds formed during covert operations against an unforgiving enemy in Northern Ireland. Whatever she'd said at the time, Kat can't have returned his feelings, still less his blind devotion to earn her favour. Behind what he'd always taken as ambition was the narcissism of a psychopath.

Maybe Ginny's father might raise a stink with what he'd

told him. But Robbo knew how these things worked. Somewhere in Whitehall, near the Home Office or the Ministry of Defence or even amid the roses in the garden of 10 Downing Street, was a large patch of grass, never to be cut.

And into this untended wilderness was kicked every awkward tin can that the state would prefer to have rust away to nothing. Robbo feared that when weighed in the jeweller's scales between public interest and political expediency, justice for Ginny would lose out every time.

*

Kat parked her hire car by the side of the B4393 on the north side of the lake.

Music could just about be heard from the hotel in the distance. Its lights came and went through the wavering branches of trees shielding it from full view. She moved with speed and stealth as she'd been trained. Knowing Robbo, he'd be dug in already, watching for her to pitch up by the boathouse. But what was the deal he had in mind? It couldn't just be a con. He'd not take the risk.

Whatever it was, it'd best be done quickly. The possibility of her car being snowed in was real. She had a plan and it didn't involve hanging round Lake Vyrnwy. Kat would be heading to where its water was piped – seventy miles away to Liverpool – and the smart offices of a churchgoing lawyer who bent more than just the knee on Sundays.

*

Covert surveillance in the open requires an almost Zen-like state of stillness and focus. Robbo lay beneath the bed sheet from the hotel, undetectable in the swirling snow, his eyes fixed on the boathouse twenty yards away. This is where he'd swum to after the chopper ditched. He'd scrambled onto the bank, bleeding and disorientated, and fallen amid some old skiffs, dumped in the undergrowth.

Another ten minutes and Kat should arrive, lured in as he intended. He'd see what she did, gauge her body language. His own mood was detached, head and heart chilled and numb but not by the weather. That strange depersonalised sense of being outside himself returned, of being an observer of the action, not a participant.

It was like being back in Ireland, on a stake-out or in an ambush where someone could die and most likely would. But not him. He wasn't really there. Robbo was always just looking on.

What manner of person was Kat on such operations? If she had nerves or fear, they never showed, not to Robbo. Hers was the instinct of a killer before the Army refined it, put it to use. But where it came from – inherited nature or nurture – who could say? As with Robbo, she'd been abandoned and raised in council homes, by foster parents or in temporary shelters.

Hers had been a chaotic, uncaring world. Like Robbo, she'd assumed identities as garments to clothe the nakedness of the self. Both could be understood, even forgiven, for lacking any sense of who they really were.

The Army became a family of sorts and Robbo her pretend husband on intelligence-gathering missions. In this she flourished, ensuring Army agents in loyalist death squads assassinated the right republicans, not just any Catholic passing by.

Kat saw no legal or moral contradiction in saving the lives of some for the greater good by bringing about the murders of others for the same reason. But such killings begat revenge and retaliation so the wheel of hatred forever turned and crushed all in its path.

In the wild mountains of Albania, feuds between families lasted down the generations. Robbo had read that if a man was shot dead, his bloodied shirt hung outside his home until the stain turned rusty yellow. That indicated it was time to find and kill his killer. And so the madness went on, shirt upon shirt, grave upon grave.

Another minute ticked by. Then he saw movement by the boathouse. The silhouette of a figure emerged against the white background. Kat had taken the bait. She looked around before finding cover in the trees.

He crawled out from under his hide. As he drew closer, she heard him and turned. Did she smile or was that a smirk at bringing him to heel once more? Kat guessed what was in the bag he carried and thus she glimpsed her future. She touched his bearded cheek with her fingers and affection and said it was good to see him again.

'It suits you, Robbo… handsome, it really is.'

'A bit late for flattery, isn't it?'

'Maybe, but you'll forgive me. We've travelled a long way, you and me.'

'Yeah, good times, bad times… mainly fucking awful times.'

'No, that's not true,' she said. 'Come on, lover, let's have no hard feelings.'

That was rich, he thought. Still, what did it matter now? Kat kept looking back to the road, obviously anxious to be away. She wanted to know about the deal he'd mentioned.

'Simple,' he said. 'Just take this Bolivian shit and go on your way then we can be at peace.'

'That's it? Seriously, that's all you want?'

'I'm weary, Kat, so fucking weary, tired of living with myself like this. I want it over with.'

'If you'd stuck it out to the end and done what we planned—'

'What you planned.'

'OK, but what you went along with, then you'd have been set up for life.'

'Yeah, but even the asking price was enough to break me.'

Kat looked at him, looked into his defeated eyes and saw a sense of an ending to all that he was, all that he had been. She knew then she'd won.

'The police are after you. You know that, don't you?'

He shrugged, made no reply as if this didn't matter, it wasn't important.

'No one can run and hide for ever, Robbo.'

'You don't have to tell me.'

'Then what are you going to do?'

'Nothing that you'll have to worry about.'

'But I do worry.'

'About what I might say or do, you mean?'

'No, not that. We were close once… that's the reason.'

'So did you worry about me when I was blown out of the sky?'

'Christ, of course I did. I thought those IRA bastards had done for you.'

Robbo's expression didn't change.

But in the gauzy night, it was too dark for Kat to notice that he'd seen right through her.

'Strange that the papers never said there was a passenger on the chopper.'

'Yep, but that was kept quiet for your own sake. The media would've crawled all over you and you're not without enemies, are you?'

That much was visible to a blind man. Kat checked her watch. Time was running out.

'Listen, Robbo. I need two clear days from now to pull off my disappearing act.'

'You take all the time you need.'

'Sure, but if the cops get to you first, what then?'

'I'll not be talking, not to them or anyone else.'

At that, he dropped the cocaine by her feet.

'Here, this is what you've always wanted, it's what it's all been about, isn't it?'

Before she could reply or pick it up, he held her for one last embrace. Her tongue was in his mouth, her hands around his backside pulling him towards her. Robbo felt her breasts against his chest, and the gun zipped in her pocket. Theirs had always been the deadliest of games. He held her head in his hands, ran his fingers through her blood orange hair. And in that long goodbye, he felt himself back in a country far away, kissing a girl with no name, a girl with no hope, no future, for Robbo was to trade both for the contents of the plastic bag by which he now stood.

And as with the girl in Bolivia, the moment between existence and eternity was but an exhalation of air, the blink of an eye, and so Kat also went limp. Her head lolled unnaturally as he laid her down in the snow. The living are only ever the dead on leave.

For Robbo, the books were almost balanced, now.

There must always be a reckoning however crude and atavistic, a kind of justice in lieu of anything else. If sins required penance, evil demanded its own settlement. Vengeance wasn't the Lord's alone, whatever His adherents said.

Robbo felt neither guilt nor remorse, just the detachment of the retributive stranger Kat had caused him to become. Snow fell on the freckles of her puzzled face, still warm but not for much longer. He edged back up through the trees and brambles to his hiding place. The bed sheet would be her shroud. There was still much to do before he, too, might make amends and rest.

*

That night, three women were each preoccupied by thoughts of the same man. In a hotel in Chichester, Tilly Brown now knew that the intriguing, alluring Robbo was an amoral, double-dealing agent of the state, purblind to the emotional havoc he'd caused. What, if anything, would she do with this information and why was Laurie Benwell breaking a gut to find him? But whatever Robbo had done, did he deserve to be punished by not being told he had a son of whom he could be justly proud?

Not far away in a townhouse by the cathedral, his ex-wife, Sally Tobin, remained in turmoil. Despite the anguish Robbo had put her through, she would never want him to come to harm. Tilly Brown seemed to think him in danger but didn't know why or from what quarter. For all his faults, Robbo was still the father of her child.

At some point in the future, the boy would want to know his own backstory, even to meet his dad. What could be more natural? But then what? Did her hurts outbid the child's rights? The divorce, her non-disclosure Army pay-off, time passing – in all this, she thought she'd boxed Robbo away. But he was out and about and in her head once more, and Sally would struggle to sleep that evening.

Barely a quarter mile from where Robbo was sidling down through the trees at the edge of the lake with Kat's body to the boathouse, Mags – Margaret Anne German aged twenty-two – should have felt a degree of satisfied contentment at finally losing her virginity.

But lying in the bed where she'd entered womanhood, hers was a state of uncertain agitation. Should she defy Robbo and open the note he'd left her?

Or would this simply confirm he wasn't coming back, that he'd lied to her, used her as she suspected he'd done to others before? Inside the envelope, she felt a key... a small, Yale-type key. What might that open and why would he give it to her?

He had to be a criminal. The clues were there: the hidden parcels he wouldn't explain, all that money squirrelled away in a hiding place. If her mother found out – God forbid – she'd insist that Mags should report what she knew to the police.

She would be right, of course, and yet Mags had never felt more alive or as desired, grown-up and trusted with the secrets. Mags would keep them, would stay loyal and breathe

371

in the sweat and scent her lover had left behind, on the bed, on the pillow and on the very body of her.

*

It took strength and patience to manoeuvre Kat's shrouded form into the skiff. Robbo, still detached from the sacrilegious indignity of what he was doing, pushed and dragged until she was wedged tight beneath the rower's seat. He looped the handles of the plastic bag containing the cocaine around her ankles.

All that remained to do was heave the boat into the lake. Even as he did this – and exactly as he wanted – water seeped in through a split by the keel. Then he launched her into the dark, through the blizzard to a point above the drowned village to which, in her wickedness, Kat had consigned Ginny Hill. Justice would be done.

Robbo watched the little craft settle deeper and deeper in the water then vanish. He felt nothing, not guilt or remorse, just empty, and imagined looking down on his lone self, a slow cinematic pullback from an actor in a final bleached-out scene over which no credits would ever appear.

*

Flying was Laurie Benwell's idea of a cruel and unusual punishment. It was why he never took foreign holidays.

If a destination couldn't be reached by ship or train, he didn't go. But on this investigation, buttocks clenched, knuckles pale, he'd no choice but to cadge seats on a Met helicopter if he and his team were to get a result.

They were flying at one hundred and ten knots on a direct route to Lake Vyrnwy using a police call sign with air traffic control and had an estimated time of arrival of ten thirty, half an hour after Kat Walsh's RV with the wanted man. The droll pilot had smiled disarmingly when Benwell asked can't you go any fucking faster?

'Tired of life, are we?' he'd said. 'I'd sit back and think of England if I were you.'

*

Robbo sat motionless, his penitente's back against a tree high above the boathouse. Snow continued to fall soft and silent. He had neither wish nor intention of finding shelter. His coat and outstretched legs became ever more covered. He found it quite spiritual.

By reason and experience, it was far better this way than a lingering death locked in a cell. He drank from his bottle of Tullamore Dew. In between each swallow, he took six or so painkillers. If his thoughts had free rein, his questions had no answers, not about his mother or why she'd abandoned him or who his father had been. He was, after all, but a manifestation of chance intermingling down through the ages, a collision of DNA and genetics, of the savage and the civilised, all long dead and gone to dust.

Another swallow of whisky, another handful of pills.

Breathe in, breathe out, breathe in, breathe out.

How tired he felt, how fatigued his body and soul. And still the snow fell. Such whiteness, all that purity. He thought he could hear the sea and children playing. And what was that music in his head, that song? He knew it. Clair de Lune. Yes, that was it. Clair de Lune. Someone would play it on the piano in the hall of the big house. That was where he'd lived. But why there?

And how was it that the girl from the jungle was standing before him, a ghost in the snowstorm, holding out her hand?

More whisky, more tablets. Please make the pain go away.

The opiate slowly began to depress his breathing. It became shallower, his heart starved of all it needed to pump in and out, in and out. The urge to lie down, to sleep, could be resisted no longer.

Then above him, a clattering din like the end of days had come. A great brightness shone from the leaden clouds and swept over the lake then him. He was blinded and deafened. And it occurred to Robbo in these final confused moments that he'd been forgiven and was to ascend to heaven on this beam of light as they had in bible pictures at Sunday school.

But it all went dark once more.

The noise faded into the night.

Silence returned to the lake.

And the snow continued to fall on the quick and the dead alike.

34: DISCOVERY

"Let no one weep for me or celebrate
my funeral with mourning;
for I still live, as I pass to and fro
through the mouths of men."

- Quintus Ennius, Roman poet

Life, like death, can be a messy affair – dramas without scripts, players stumbling around, the gods mocking from the wings. And in all this, disappointment abounds. It is not only political careers that end in failure.

Laurie Benwell, barely three weeks from retirement, was having to confront what could be the inglorious conclusion of his own, albeit in the warm embrace of Tilly Brown's brandy and Christmas pudding.

'Missed the buggers by minutes, both of them,' he said. 'Bloody helicopter... could've got there quicker by bus.'

Tilly pushed the Courvoisier across the table to him. She'd some sympathy for his debacle in Wales but not much. He could be impetuous, arrogantly so, operating on the fly more often than was wise. Good fortune inevitably runs out, even for the luckiest of generals.

But she now knew why Robbo and Kat Walsh were central to Benwell's investigation. She'd earned the right to be trusted with his secrets. Her insights into Robbo, the man, had helped and she'd made it her business to schmooze the old lady who'd safe-housed him. Better still, she'd combed out sensitive background from the missing man's ex-wife.

But if Tilly had a detective's nous, she remained an unsentimental prosecutor at heart, seizing on any weakness in a defendant's position.

'Why didn't you arrest Walsh when you had a chance much earlier?'

'I should've done just that,' he said. 'Big mistake, big mistake.'

'You wanted a double whammy, didn't you, the glory of lifting the conspirators together?'

'Yeah, can't argue with you there. Wish I could.'

Matters had got worse when the pilot said the helicopter had to return to base the next day. Benwell and his team had a choice: stay in snowbound Wales or hitch a ride back to London on the chopper.

'The local plod were with us by then,' he said. 'They got a search party out so my blokes looked at the weather and thought of home and said we should leave it to Taffy.'

'Have they found anything significant yet?'

'No, just Walsh's car.'

'Anything useful from that?'

'No, it was hired by another Army bod but he was a waste of rations, knew nothing.'

'So you know how she got to Wales but Robbo didn't arrive on a magic carpet, did he?'

'Well, if he did, he's taken Miss bloody Walsh away on it somewhere.'

'So what do you conclude about all this so far, Laurie?'

'That I'm being given the runaround, not only by those two bastards but the rat-fuckers in the shadows behind them.'

'OK, but who's the female who rang Kat Walsh on Robbo's behalf?'

'You'll have to ask Roach.'

'Your bagman?'

'Yeah, Roach. It'll be his job to trace her soon enough.'

'So no going out in a blaze of glory for you, then?'

'No, dammit. Close but no cigar.'

*

It was as if the 1950s had never ended in the house where Mags German was raised. The brown leatherette three-piece in the neat front room had lace antimacassars. There was a gas fire but no radiators. The rose and trellis wallpaper matched the curtains in the bay window, and the kitchen had a plain utility-era table and four wooden chairs.

Her mother's only nod to modernity was a TV and a fridge. Washing was still done by hand then put in a spin dryer and hung out in the garden.

Becoming a widow hadn't noticeably grieved Mrs German. Her dead husband, a clerk in their council's finance department, had been fifteen years older. Mags was a late child, the product of a rare coupling in a marriage where passion wasn't encouraged.

Mags had never brought school friends home, not that she had many to ask. Mrs German was a private person, uninterested in the lives of others.

On that Christmas day afternoon, they sat on the settee letting their dinner go down, as Mr German would've said.

Mags hadn't eaten a great deal nor had she explained why she'd been several days late returning from her university project at the Iron Age settlement. Neither had much to say to the other but it was ever thus.

'Shall I put the television on?' Mags said.

'If you like. I've got the washing up to do.'

Mags didn't volunteer to help. Her mother took herself and her grey, brooding presence to the kitchen. A cathedral choir appeared on the TV. Their joyous voices were as those of angels awaiting the arrival of the infant Jesus. But Mags was unmoved.

She felt only sorrow; the man she'd not wanted to leave her bed would probably never return. The Lord takes as surely as He gives.

Fixed in her mind were those dark figures setting out across the snow. They said at the hotel it was a police operation, all very hush-hush. A dangerous man was on the run. But she'd read his note by then. His words didn't fit that description.

Mags, you've been a great support and I owe you big time for that. The key is to my little place of safety in Pagham Harbour. It's yours now, and everything inside. If you can find it in yourself to forgive my cavalier treatment of you, for how I've been, that would be a comfort, but whatever you do, mind what you say to anyone who comes calling. It's always best to say nothing and trust no one. I've valued our friendship, Mags. You just take care of yourself and don't pray for an easy life, pray to be a stronger person. R.

She willed herself not to weep, not to display any outward sign that might cause even her mother to ask questions to which Mags could provide no answers.

378

Everything – happiness, success, failure – now seemed a matter of chance, not personal action. How cruel for her and Robbo to be cast together for so brief a time. What purpose had it served save to leave her with an overwhelming sense of loss? But of what and of whom, she hadn't had chance to be sure.

Before breakfast at the hotel, she'd seen a policeman dressed only in black taking a long gun from what could've been a sports bag. The manhunt was underway. They would kill Robbo if they had to.

Mags had driven off with her guilt before she could be questioned. She would go to Pagham Harbour soon, escape to the refuge he'd bequeathed her and once there, think and reflect and reassess all previous thoughts about what her future would be. Time would pass and she would sleep to the sound of the murmuring sea and remember what she had lost and what she had gained.

Another heavenly voice brought her back into her mother's austere front room. A boy soloist was singing *In the Bleak Midwinter*.

The carol told of snow upon snow, the earth like iron, water like stone.

Mags looked into the child's face, into its purity and innocence, yet to be corrupted by the world outside. He seemed strangely familiar, though for no obvious reason. The TV caption over his angelic performance said he was Robert Tobin of the Prebendal School, Chichester, but that meant nothing to Mags.

*

The street light came on outside Tilly Brown's house in North London. Snow streaked through its yellow halo as she drew her sitting room curtains.

She lit scented candles on the mantelpiece and along the cupboard beneath shelves of biographies and escapist titles from a book club.

Laurie might think she was dressing the set for seduction. Maybe she was, maybe the solitary life was losing whatever appeal it once had. Laurie Benwell was a good man, flawed like everyone, but Tilly wouldn't object to them becoming closer companions, friends with benefits... if that was his wish, too.

For now, he was stretched out in an armchair, tie loosened, eyes closed, supposedly listening to her CD of Christmas music from King's College. It had been a long lunch. Tilly stifled a yawn and could've nodded off herself but for her front door bell. It was Giles Worth, pink-faced and affably, volubly drunk.

'Got you a present, old girl,' he said. 'Seasonal greetings and all that.'

He stamped the snow from his brogues onto the bare boards of Tilly's hall, handed over a bottle of Château Rauzan-Ségla and kissed her on the cheek.

'Giles, you shouldn't—'

'Not another word, dear lady. Your good health is beyond rubies.'

He made for the sitting room unbidden but stopped mid-stride when he saw Benwell.

'Goodness, what's this? Another gentleman caller?'

Tilly, embarrassed but annoyed, introduced them. Both already knew of the other through her, if only by name.

They shook hands, smiles fixed, mutual suspicion barely disguised. Worth fetched a corkscrew and glasses from the kitchen, demonstrating his familiarity with both the house and the host.

'Cheers to all,' he said. 'And may good fortune attend all your investigations, Mr Benwell.'

Benwell made a non-committal reply. He wanted Worth a little more pissed before engaging the enemy.

Tilly brought in mince pies and offered coffee, which Worth declined.

'Tilly tells me you work at the Ministry of Defence, Giles.'

'Yes, Whitehall pen-pusher, that's me.'

'You're too modest. How would a mere pen-pusher know about that dear old lady in North Wales who gave bed and breakfast to a man I'm trying to find and arrest? How so, Giles?'

If Worth sensed an ambush, he didn't show it… not then.

'I just snuffled around in the department,' he said. 'I only did what she'd asked me to do.'

'And no one thought to share this rather relevant information with the police?'

'Police liaison, not my role.'

'So what exactly is your role, Giles? In the MoD, I mean.'

Worth said he was an analyst, a writer of reports and, if asked, the giver of advice. Benwell sucked air through his teeth.

'OK, I'll buy the MoD having an interest in my runaway because he's ex-military but what do your informants say about the death of Sir Frazer Harris?'

Worth wrinkled his brow as if perplexed.

'I'm sorry, I don't understand you. In what respect do you mean?'

'In respect of your former minister topping himself or being murdered.'

'Phew, steady on old man, that's way above my pay grade.'

'Not if you're in the loop enough to know where an undercover agent was hiding, surely?'

'I know nothing about Sir Frazer's death,' Worth said. 'Didn't the BBC and the tabloids have him running a brothel? Maybe he couldn't face the scandal.'

'So it's just a coincidence that for reasons not yet understood, he'd been hand in bloody glove with the woman from Army intelligence who's been running my missing man?'

Worth shrugged to convey complete ignorance. But he was noticeably less cocky, uncomfortably so.

'Do you know, I don't think you're being straight with me, Giles.'

Worth stood up and said he should be going.

'No, sit where you are. There's a little mystery you can help me with.'

Tilly hadn't seen this sharkish side of Laurie before – predator scenting the blood of its prey.

'This is the scenario, Giles,' Benwell said. 'An amateur photographer takes three pictures, nothing important at the time, just a man getting into a helicopter. She tells only one other person about them, a neighbour of hers. By then, these pictures have become important, evidence in what could be an act of terrorism. But you'll never guess what happened next, Giles… a burglar breaks in to her darkroom and steals the three negatives and a blow-up of one of them. Nothing else is taken and not a trace of a break-in can be found.'

Benwell fixed Worth with a stare that could strip paint from a door.

'Now, Giles, in my position, how suspicious of this neighbour would you be?'

'Again, why are you asking me such a question? You're the detective.'

'Yes, Giles, I'm the detective, and do you know what I think?'

'No, but I'd be delighted for you to tell me.'

'Right, smart arse, I will. You're a spook and at some point, I'm going to bring you in for questioning. Breaking into people's houses is a crime, you know.'

At this, Worth rose again, smiled at them both then took Tilly's hands in his.

'Always a pleasure to see you, dear one. I'll call again soon but I have to be off now.'

She and Benwell followed him into the hall. They watched as he put on his coat.

'Bye, Tilly, bye, Commander Benwell,' he said. 'Enjoy the rest of your evening together.'

Tilly forced a grimace out of her face. Benwell was much more cheerful.

'Happy Christmas, Giles,' he said. 'I'll be in touch.'

*

Three days after arriving at the Lake Vyrnwy Hotel, Denny Debbaudt still felt naked without the .38 five-shot normally strapped to his ankle. But this was Wales, not Detroit.

Debbaudt, tall and languid with an easy smile, played bass with a band in the Soup Kitchen, a smoky blues joint on North Franklin.

He was also a private detective but kept that quiet. Not all the Soup Kitchen's clientele led blameless lives.

After breakfast on Boxing Day, Debbaudt and his wife, Gay – touring Europe for their wedding anniversary – pulled on hiking boots, waterproof trousers and anoraks and set off to take photographs of the lake. Snow still lay thick on the ground and on the surrounding hills. But it was starting to thaw, dripping from the branches of fir trees under a Mediterranean blue sky.

They needed elevation to get the reservoir's distant ramparts in the same frame as its Gothic straining tower, built in stone with a conical verdigris roof. Gay shot the pictures she wanted. Then they slid and slipped down a steep bank towards a stretch of woodland between them and a bridge out to the tower itself.

Debbaudt described what happened next in a statement to the police.

We were a few yards along what seemed like a sheep path through the undergrowth beneath the trees when I saw some smears of red in the snow where it had drifted. Then we came across what looked like a bundle of clothes but on closer examination, was obviously a body.

It was facing away from us so we could not see if it was male or female. I have a background in law enforcement and have attended many scenes of crimes.

I turned the body on its back and saw that the person's face was unrecognisable because it and the neck had been bitten away, possibly by an animal or animals. There were many paw prints in the snow and blood, too.

We took several photographs at the scene, the negatives of which I now produce and which, among other things, should show that the body had been partially dragged to the point where we found it, a bottle of whisky that was half empty and left nearby, a box of pain killers and a buff-coloured envelope protruding from the overcoat pocket.

My wife returned to the hotel to call the police and I stayed where I was to preserve whatever evidence might be found later.

*

Benwell was in the shower and Tilly still in her nightdress when she answered the door to Inspector Roach. His boss came downstairs with a white towel wrapped around his middle.

'Best get your clobber on, guv,' he said. 'Robbo's been found and we've got a helicopter to catch.'

35: REALITY

"The truth is never as dangerous
as a lie in the long run."

- Ben Bradlee, *The Washington Post*

Robbo had spent much of his military life whistling past many a graveyard. He was now on his circuitous way to another – the last – and by his own hand, too. Not many would have predicted that.

It was with difficulty that his disfigured corpse was manoeuvred down the treacherous hillside, slushy with melting snow, through forestry and scrub to the road where the undertaker's blacked-out van was parked. He was then driven the fifty miles or so across the English border for a post mortem in Shrewsbury.

A pathologist put the age of the deceased at between thirty-eight and forty-two. His general health had been excellent. Death was due to an overdose of opiates consumed with alcohol. Foxes had caused his subsequent physical injuries. This summary was phoned through to the Powys coroner, Esther Radcliffe, with a fuller written report to follow later.

This wasn't the only phone call she'd received about the body by the lake. A man who said he was a liaison officer at the Ministry of Defence had already been in touch.

'Sorry, but this particular inquest won't be a run-of-the-mill one,' he'd said.

'Really? It seems straightforward enough from what I've been told so far.'

'No, the background here is terrorism and Northern Ireland.'

'Ah, so the authorities want a lid kept on it?'

'Not the way I would put it,' he said. 'National security is involved so please, as foul play is not an issue, open the hearing for identification purposes but do so late one evening then you can release the body for burial. We'd much rather you avoid any publicity on this one.'

'And what about the full inquest? Who will take that... me?'

'I'm afraid not, no. You haven't been through the developed vetting process, have you?'

'No, I haven't.'

'Well, given the sensitive nature of the intelligence material which might be well adduced, a judge assistant with the relevant security clearance will be appointed in your place.'

No coroner likes having a case taken from them. But she hadn't a choice. The full inquest would be held in private some time in the future with press and public excluded. If nothing else, this told Esther Radcliffe that the man with no face had secrets some would wish buried with him.

*

'Is that Commander Benwell?'

'This is he, yes.'

'It's Commissioner Silvey's secretary, sir. He wants to see you.'

'Sure enough. When and where?'

'Eleven this morning, in his office.'

Not his club then, Benwell thought. He didn't know why but this summons to the fifth floor seemed unduly formal. Then again, they were both about to complete their thirty-year stretches so maybe he wanted to talk about a joint retirement party.

It took an hour to get into central London. Sir Graham stood at the bulletproof windows in full uniform, hands behind his back, looking out across the city. He'd obviously just come from a meeting.

'Laurie, good to see you,' he said.

'I only got back from Wales last night.'

'I know, so what's the situation now the missing agent's been found?'

'Yeah, selfish sod. He was a potential key source in the murders we're looking at, now he's done the dirty on me.'

'No confessional suicide note, then?'

'Only a letter saying where he wants to be buried.'

An aide brought a tray of coffee and biscuits and set it on the commissioner's uncluttered desk.

'What about his handler,' Sir Graham said, 'that woman, Kat something-or-other?'

'Kat Walsh. Still no sign and she remains AWOL as far as the Army is concerned.'

'So the state of play with your inquiry now is what, exactly?'

'You're not going to like this—'

'Try me.'

'I think MI5 knew that elements within military intelligence had gone rogue and were killing IRA men but they looked the other way because it served their own purpose.'

Benwell paused to let the legal and political implications of this appraisal sink in. The commissioner's face remained impassive.

'MI5 have copies of every Army document that might implicate Army agents and personnel in these murders. Kat Walsh has weeded out the originals from their system but MI5 won't let me have their copies, not even sight of them. Why would they do that if they weren't in cahoots with the killers?'

Sir Graham sipped his coffee, didn't answer.

Benwell told him about Giles Worth, his real function as an MI5 officer and his suspected role as the instigator of the burglary at Tilly Brown's house. The stolen negatives and picture had direct relevance to the helicopter crash in Wales, which a copper-bottomed MI5 source alleged was not an IRA job. Benwell wasn't finished.

'While Worth was operational in Northern Ireland, I've got information that he panicked and as a result, the police who were with him shot dead two IRA men and one of them was their own informant. And guess who helped the police to cover this up? MI5.'

At this, the commissioner of the Metropolitan Police went to the window and surveyed his vast and troubling manor once more.

'One last thing on the subject of killings,' Benwell said.

'My gut tells me there's something very convenient about the untimely passing of Sir Frazer Harris.'

Sir Graham seemed not to be listening any more.

'Look down there, Laurie,' he said. 'All those people it's our sworn duty to protect. Do you think they give a monkeys if a few terrorists get slotted before they carry on bombing the blazes out of innocents like them?'

'The law is the law. Try as we might, we can't murder our way out of Ireland, can we?'

Sir Graham chose not to answer the unanswerable. He turned to Benwell and spoke softly as if he didn't even want the walls to hear.

'Look, Laurie, now we've got a body, this man, Robbo, it's considered the best option if we assign responsibility for these killings to him.'

'Do a cover-up, you mean?'

'Put it how you like but this is bloody Ireland, Laurie. There're moves on the backstairs, peace talks between us and the bad guys. Even I don't know the half of it but Downing Street, the Home Office, they want all this talk of the Brits running death squads finished. It's not helping anyone politically and now we've got the suicide of this rogue agent, it's a chance to put everything down to him and draw a line.'

Benwell didn't reply immediately. He crunched through another Rich Tea biscuit then finished his coffee.

'I will do as I'm instructed,' he said. 'If you want to wind up this inquiry, that's fine. But don't think this won't come back and bite your bollocks off at some point because it stinks.'

'I'm aware of that, Laurie,' he said. 'But I've got no choice. You're not the only one with orders to obey.'

Benwell had no need to ask who was giving them. It wasn't ministers or Downing Street or the Home Office. High-fliers in post there might think they ran the country but Benwell would disrespectfully beg to differ.

*

It was midday when Tilly Brown walked into the library in Chichester. The sixty-mile drive from London was delayed by a lorry crash on the icy road over the South Downs.

Sally Tobin saw her but was busy with an elderly borrower. Tilly sat and waited until she'd finished.

'Is something wrong?' Sally said. 'Why are you here?'

'When's your lunch break?'

'Now, I'm due to have it now. What's happened? Is it Robbo?'

'Come on, let's get a drink.'

Sally fetched her coat and bag. Nothing was said until they found a corner table in the Dolphin & Anchor on West Street. A waiter brought tonic waters and a menu.

'So go on, tell me the worst,' Sally said.

'They've found Robbo... I'm sorry, Sally. He'd taken an overdose.'

Sally looked out of the window, out at the blur of passing people whose lives she felt must surely be enviably neat and ordered, their backstories without shame or remorse, their futures uncomplicated by truths that could not be told.

'You all right, Sally?'

She nodded, took a drink, didn't weep. She'd no tears left, not for the past.

She'd never wanted their son to know his father and now

391

he was dead and never could.

'Where was he found?' she said.

'In Wales, North Wales, by a lake… very peaceful, beautiful place… just after Christmas.'

'Why in God's name did he do it? What was going on in his head?'

'I can't say. I know he was a wanted man. Maybe he couldn't face being locked up.'

'But we're all locked up, one way or another. There's never any escape.'

'Not sure I understand what you're saying, Sally.'

'I'm saying we're all locked up with our mistakes, the decisions we've taken. What's the option but to live with them? We can't all kill ourselves; there'd be no one left.'

The waiter returned and asked if they wanted lunch. Neither did and he went away. Weak winter sunshine streamed in on their sadness – not grief – at what might have been and what still was.

'Sally, there's one other thing I need to mention. Robbo left a note but it only says where he wants to be buried.'

'And where's that?'

'Oddly enough, not far south from here. Church Norton near a place called Pagham Harbour. Do you know it?'

'No, but why there? He'd no connection this way any more than me. I only moved here to start again when Robert was born, somewhere no one knew me.'

'Be that as it may, you do realise there will be a full inquest, don't you?'

'Oh, God… really?'

'Yes, but not for a long time yet and it probably won't be in public.'

'That's a relief I suppose, but why not?'

'I'm guessing, but the authorities probably won't want whatever he's been doing for them to become public knowledge.'

'He didn't remarry, did he? Am I still his next of kin, even though we're divorced?'

'Your son certainly will be, so legally, you can arrange the funeral on his behalf.'

'God, it's all going to come out, isn't it? Robert's never going to forgive me about his dad.'

'It won't be easy, that's for sure,' Tilly said. 'But if you want any help, you only have to ask.'

*

The Shiv was a discreet wine bar in a cellar near Bond Street. Senior detectives like Benwell would huddle and gripe in its dimly lit alcoves with those they trusted, plotting until the early hours when cabs would be called and sleeping wives woken in suburbs across the city.

Roach had been summoned to the presence. Bad news was anticipated. His boss was already halfway down a bottle of house white. He ordered another and carried it over to Benwell at the upturned barrel that doubled as a table.

'I've seen you looking happier,' Roach said.

'No bloody wonder. The bastards are pulling the plug on our inquiry.'

'You're kidding me. They can't do that, not after all the work we've put in.'

'Damn well can. They want everything dumped on Robbo... all of them, the funnies, the Army, fucking politicians. Robbo's the patsy so they're going to lift the carpet on the fifth floor while we get stuck in with a big fucking brush.'

'Christ. They'll never get away with a stroke like this.'

'Won't they? Just watch this space.'

'But what about all our leads... that young girl at the hotel, false name, paid in cash?'

'They'll not want her traced any more than they'll want Kat bloody Walsh turning up.'

'No but it'll be the girl who ferried Robbo to the RV. What couldn't she tell us?'

'For sure but by topping himself, he's given the grown-ups their get-out-of-jail card. That's the one the buggers'll play so we're out of the game, matey. We've lost.'

*

In the year AD 681, an argumentative Northumbrian bishop called Wilfrid, a man whose life was framed by dispute and turbulence, built a cathedral church on the coast near Selsey to convert the pagans of Sussex.

Thirteen centuries later, a chapel bearing his name still stands at Church Norton. It's at the end of a long, narrow lane off the road to Chichester, cutting through farms and plough land where the wind blows and trees bend and the battle between man and the sea never ceases.

Mags drew into the parking area by the lychgate into St Wilfrid's churchyard as a funeral was about to start. It was more respectful to stay put and look on from her car. The coffin was pale oak with brass fittings, hoisted on the black-suited shoulders of six pallbearers. It was late January and their faces were pinkish purple with cold. They made their slow, steady way to a newly dug grave, by ancient tombstones leaning this way and that, pockmarked with lichen, orange and yellow in the sombre light of the afternoon.

A clergyman stood hands inside his white cassock, ready to conduct an outdoor service. The deceased could not have had many friends or a large family. Only two women and a boy stood by the graveside, and some distance away, three men in dark coats waited and watched.

Mags took the groceries she'd bought in Selsey from the boot and left quietly. A few of the vicar's words carried on the chill air: 'For my soul trusts You and in the shadow of Your wings, I will make my refuge.'

More than this, she didn't hear. She walked down a muddy path to a shingle beach and from there, turned right for another half mile or so to Pagham Harbour and the womb-like warmth and security of the shack she'd been gifted by Robbo. It had been almost a month since she first arrived. Now, she'd no wish to leave. Her mother knew where she was but disapproved.

Mags wasn't far from her door when she began to feel nauseous, just as she had the previous day. A gale was whipping up whitecaps that crashed onto the pebbled shore. It was going to be a rough night.

*

It would've bordered on rudeness had Benwell and Roach not invited de Lanerolle for a drink after the funeral. Besides, he might let something slip. Funerals – and wakes – can loosen tongues. All three were staying in the same hotel. After dinner, they had a session in the bar.

De Lanerolle was cultured, politically astute, a man always with an eye to the next rung up the ladder. He could hold his drink, too.

Not once did he stray from the Army line that Kat Walsh had become a lone wolf, running in the shadows and covering her tracks brilliantly – and those of her partner in crime, the late Brian Oliver Roby, aka Robbo.

'We're still working on the basis that she met Robbo as arranged,' Benwell said.

'At the reservoir?'

'Yeah, that's where the car you hired for her was found, but then she disappears from the radar. So what happened? Did she have another accomplice, a second car? What?'

'We're as stumped as you, Laurie,' de Lanerolle said. 'We'd turn her in if we could.'

'You Army blokes... very pragmatic, practical lot, aren't you?'

'How do you mean?'

'Well, there's a military way of thinking in my experience,' Benwell said. 'Here's a problem, here's the solution. You just get on with it, don't you?'

'I suppose we do, yes.'

'So if the loyalists are going to kill republicans, the military mind would think OK, let's make sure they take out the right ones... you kill a snake by chopping off its head, don't you?'

'Look, I know where you're driving with all this, Laurie, but honestly, you're talking to the wrong guy. I've got the mop and bucket on this one. I'm just helping to clean up the mess.'

Roach ordered a nightcap for them all.

'Cheers,' de Lanerolle said. 'Here's to a result.'

'We'll drink to that... well, Roach will 'cos I put my papers in next week and that's me as good as done.'

They went to bed. Roach rang his wife, de Lanerolle called his lover and Benwell got no reply from Tilly. He was too sloshed to talk to her anyway, too uncertain about the future, how empty it might be, if she would save him or not.

His sleep was shallow and unsettled. He knew he was about to finish as a failure. Cops like him were never short of enemies, above and below the fifth floor. His would smile and pat him on the back and all the time be rejoicing that he'd fallen at the last fence.

If he did but know it, Benwell would be there for the last act of the drama, but he'd have to wait a while. The gods had yet to roll the right dice.

36: CLOSURE

"I want to leave you something,
something better than words or sounds.
Look for me in the people I have known or loved,
and if you can't give me away,
at least let me live in your eyes and not in your mind."

\-   A meditation for mourners

Police investigating the lonely death of the Reverend Ralph Hill took a while to establish why he'd been in Temple Meads station in Bristol. It emerged that he'd travelled from Wells by bus then paid cash for a single ticket from Bristol to Hereford. But the icy weather of late February had frozen points along the route so his train was delayed.

He'd found a bench to sit and wait, wearing only his black suit but neither a coat nor scarf. No one took any notice of him. He was elderly, unimportant.

All was noise and bustle anyway. People coming, people going, doors slamming, whistles blowing and above everything, the rolling thunder of engines arriving into Brunel's great cathedral of a station. At some stage, he'd lain along the seat, knees drawn up towards his narrow chest, face turned to the red brick wall, as cold as he would be soon. And gone from his eyes at last, that irreducible pain of every

398

parent who'd outlived a child.

In these last remorseful moments, did this man of God pray, if not for salvation then for absolution? Maybe he'd stopped believing by then, maybe his faith had died with all the other certainties that perished with his daughter. No one could know, no one could say.

So he was buried between Virginia and his wife in the churchyard of All Hallows in Herefordshire, and they became at one with the earth if not with each other.

*

Benwell was moody and distracted during the first unstructured weeks of his retirement. He'd also given up smoking, at Tilly's urging. But what gnawed at him most was how his career had fizzled out. Few others knew he'd been leaned on to shut down his own investigation, more or less ordered to tidy away unpalatable truths for some higher cause, and one that required state-sponsored murders for it to be attained.

'Come on, Laurie,' Tilly said. 'You know the people in that quarter well enough. They never like the lights on so don't be surprised when they switch them off.'

But his professional pride, admittedly rough and ready, was wounded by any hint that he'd been a willing party to a cover-up. It was galling that Kat Walsh still hadn't been traced, not by the police or the Army.

'Dangerous to be around, that woman,' Benwell said. 'Old Frazer Harris, that man, Robbo, the helicopter pilot. All linked to her and all dead... what a coincidence.'

'Didn't some old spy once say there's no such thing as

coincidence in their world?'

'Damn right there isn't. So where is she, Tilly? Why hasn't she been found?'

'You don't believe she acted alone, do you?'

'No, she can't have done. She was getting her hands dirty for the Army but who was behind her? The funnies, that's who, all doing a Pilate with the soap and bloody water.'

'But you can't change anything about any of this now, Laurie.'

'No, but it still rankles and I don't doubt the bastards who shut down my investigation aren't breaking sweat to find her. Last thing they'll want is her forgetting the script.'

'Laurie, love, don't forget that the beginning of wisdom is the realisation of how little we know.'

*

Not long after, the satirical magazine *Private Eye* ran a story in its news section about how a bizarre MI5 intelligence-gathering operation in Northern Ireland ended in a deadly shoot-out, which was then covered up.

An inexperienced MI5 officer got into a key IRA man's empty home to photograph his kitchen table so a leg might be replaced with one fitted with a bug.

But he panicked when the terrorist unexpectedly drove up with an accomplice.

The spook ran out of the house, blowing the mission. Both terrorists were shot dead by MI5's back-up team.

But one of the dead IRA men was a registered informer. His loss is described as "devastating" in a report by the Metropolitan Police that we have seen.

It alleges: "MI5 pressured the Royal Ulster Constabulary into misleading the public by saying the firefight was a chance encounter. The deployment of an untested officer on a high-risk operation was a total failure of management."

When Tilly Brown walked to Holloway Road for her newspaper, Giles Worth's house was being staked-out by journalists and camera crews. Neighbours said they had no idea he was a spy, only that he was a man who kept himself to himself.

Benwell had coffee waiting for when Tilly returned. He'd moved in and they were happily adjusting to their late flowering affection. She told him what she'd seen.

'So who's been leaking secrets to the press, Laurie?'

'Haven't a clue,' he said.

'Not you, then? Not you risking the Official Secrets Act to settle a grievance?'

'Me? God, no. But it's good to see those tricky bastards getting paid out, isn't it?'

Tilly and her smile went back behind her paper.

*

The full inquest on Robbo – Ginny Hill's passenger who never was – took place in secret in a community centre near the lake one evening in front of a judge. Robbo's Army psychiatrist gave telling evidence.

'What was extraordinary about him was his complete lack of fear,' he said. 'He had been in situations where his life depended on the next word he uttered or the next move he made.'

The judge asked how Robbo was able to maintain his

401

cover under such pressure.

'Because he had the rare ability to inhabit or become different characters, rather like an actor I suppose, though his audiences consisted of people who might kill him.'

'Living under such stress as that cannot have been without psychological cost, can it?'

'No, sir, it can't. He often suffered paralysing flashbacks, reliving some gruesome event or other he'd either witnessed or taken part in as an undercover agent.'

'What would be the likely consequences to his mental health in the longer term?'

'In my opinion, sir, the nature of his work in the Army will have resulted in significant post-traumatic stress disorder later on in his civilian life.'

'Enough for him to consider suicide?'

'Yes, sir... without a doubt.'

The judge reached the only conclusion possible: that Brian Oliver Roby intended to take his own life and did so.

And there the story would have ended, but for a heatwave four years later.

*

July and August of 1995 were gloriously, dazzlingly hot. Road tar melted, green hills turned brown, clouds were a rarity in cobalt skies. Drought dried up the land, left it hard and cracked and caused water levels to fall in rivers and reservoirs.

Rick Cater and his wife, Chrissie, recreational divers from the Black Country, planned a weekend exploring the lost village of Llanwddyn, sunk far beneath Lake Vyrnwy. As with others, they'd smiled on hearing the local legend of its church bells ringing under the waves. But swimming through the ruins would be more interesting than diving in flooded quarries.

They parked near the lake's boathouse. The sun lit on the red, blue, white canvas triangles of small sailing boats tacking between the sloping banks where tourists were picnicking in the shade of trees. The Caters, architects in the same practice, put on wetsuits and orange buddy jackets holding air tanks and regulators, then hoods, fins and masks.

The water was warmish so they didn't need gloves. Visibility was good, too. It didn't take long to locate the tumbled stones of St John's Church – sans bells – and the houses and shops of its dead congregation.

It felt weird to be floating above cobbled streets, peering into rooms wherein people once lived and loved. Close to what had been the Powis Arms Hotel, Chrissie saw something out of place.

She signalled Rick to follow her down. It was a skiff. Lying within it was something the shape and size of an Egyptian mummy wrapped in what had been a white sheet. The material had rotted in the water and ripped when Chrissie pulled at it. She rather wished she hadn't.

Inside were the remains of what had been a man or a woman, dressed in a camouflaged Gore-Tex jacket. In one of the pockets was a handgun. And when the jacket hood was pulled back, there wasn't a face any more, just a skull.

*

The tabloids inevitably went big on the body in the lake

mystery. A preliminary examination showed the remains were female. Death had been caused by a broken neck. Benwell, now drafted on Tilly's hill-walking, birdwatching weekends, rang Roach, who'd been promoted to Detective Superintendent.

'Fifty to one it's our girl,' Benwell said. 'I knew we should've sent a bloody frogman down.'

'Yeah, but you'd blown the budget by then.'

Welsh police transmitted pictures of everything recovered with the skeletal figure to Roach. Army dental records proved Benwell right; it was Kat Walsh. Sensationally, the pistol in her jacket – a nine-millimetre Browning Hi-Power – was the weapon that killed Sir Frazer Harris. His death wasn't suicide. He'd been murdered.

But if Kat killed him, who killed her? The answer was blindingly obvious. It had to be Robbo. And though his motive might never be known, it had to be connected with the second sensational find – three kilos of uncut cocaine, still in its original packaging and stamped with a Bolivian cartel's mark. It was found in a white plastic shopping bag, still attached to Kat's ankles. Just about visible were the fading words Bell Hill Stores, Petersfield, Hampshire, printed in blue on either side.

On Roach's recommendation, the Met Police lured Benwell out of retirement with a six-week contract to pursue this new lead. He was given pictures of the two items found with Robbo's body: the bottle of Tullamore Dew whisky and the box of painkillers.

Benwell set off for Petersfield next morning, feeling happier than he'd been for years. Country walks and wagtails suddenly had less appeal.

Bell Hill Stores began as a small family business then grew into a busy supermarket. It sold everything from wines and spirits to newspapers, gardening equipment and hardware.

Benwell had trouble locating the manager. He was harassed off his feet by deliveries, staff problems and demanding customers.

Yes, they kept daily sales records back five years but no, he didn't have them on the premises – they'd be with the accountant in Havant. Benwell headed south on the A3, unknowingly driving close to the Iron Age settlement where Robbo had hidden.

The accountant was a humourless, self-important little man. He wanted Benwell to make an appointment for later in the month.

'Do you realise how much work getting these records will entail?'

'Not really, sir, no,' Benwell said. 'But do you realise this is a murder inquiry?'

'And so?'

'And so if I have to, I'll get a warrant and take every sheet of paper out of here and back to London and study them at my leisure. What'd suit you best, sir?'

Within an hour, Benwell was trawling through a heap of till transactions from the days before Robbo died – Friday, 7 December 1990 – looking for any sale of a bottle of Tullamore Dew. It was hardly a gripping scene from Inspector Morse but it was real detective work, tedious and methodical.

He found two quite quickly but the purchases didn't include all the other items. But on 4 December, there it was – details of the whisky, the painkillers, various hair products and household items bought on a credit card.

Benwell called the company's head of security and read out the details printed on the receipt. Back came the card holder's name, Margaret Anne German, and an address thirty miles away in Romsey. The door wasn't answered by Margaret but her mother, a nervy, sad-eyed soul, thin and mouse-like.

'She's not in trouble,' Benwell said. 'But she can help the police with an important inquiry.'

'My daughter isn't here. She moved away.'

'Was that to get married?'

'She might have got married,' Mrs German said. 'I wouldn't know.'

'Things not good between you, then?'

'I haven't seen or heard of her for a long time now.'

'Sorry about that,' Benwell said. 'So can you tell me where Margaret works?'

'She could be doing anything for all I know about it.'

'I see, then what about an address for her. You must have one, I take it?'

'If I do, I can't say she'll still be there. You'll have to wait here while I see.'

She left the door on its chain. Benwell shuffled in the porch, a contaminant from a world Mrs German kept at arm's length. It was getting late. He was looking forward to a lager and a *Ruby Murray*. There had to be a decent Indian restaurant thereabouts.

Margaret's mother came back with an address book.

'She'd her whole life and a good career ahead of her,' she said.

'She was quite young when she left, then?'

'Yes, a student. So clever, everyone said so. Then something got into her, she gave everything up, and for what, I ask you?'

Benwell took a note of Margaret's last known address, and it immediately registered. It was close to the churchyard where he'd watched Robbo being buried. He'd never had any doubt that the young female who'd used a false name and paid cash at the Lake Vyrnwy Hotel was in cahoots with Robbo. Now it was confirmed.

But how had she fitted into the rest of his jigsaw of a life? And why had she upped sticks and dropped out? Maybe she realised she was in trouble but he doubted if she knew just how much. Either way, a prosecutor could view her as an accomplice of a probable drug runner and a murderer.

But he'd need to tread cautiously. With Kat Walsh dead, Margaret was a crucial link to Robbo while he was on the run and immediately before he died. What might he have told her about his life, about Kat and whatever else they were escaping from? Everyone had secrets. So what were Margaret's?

Benwell would find a guest house then drive down to the seaside in the morning and give her every chance to tell him.

*

The man was a distant figure when Mags first saw him through the heat haze rising from the pebbled beach, picking his way through clumps of pale green sea kale. She knew by some primitive instinct that he was coming for her.

Mags stood at her gate, didn't move, didn't attempt to hide. This was a day she'd long anticipated. As he got closer, she saw he was wearing a dark suit and black shoes. His face was blotchy, damp with perspiration.

'I'm looking for a place along here called The Refuge,' he said.

'Then you've found it. This is it.'

'So you're Margaret, then? Margaret German?'

Mags nodded and smiled. She never thought she'd be this calm when the time came.

'You're a policeman, aren't you, a detective?'

'That obvious, is it?' he said. 'Lovely spot you've got here, not easy to find though.'

'That's one of its attractions.'

He dabbed a receding hairline with a blue handkerchief and apologised for not ringing to make an appointment.

'I don't have a phone so you couldn't have rung me.'

'No, anyway, my name's Laurie Benwell and I've got some questions I need to put to you.'

'Then let's go inside. It'll be cooler and there's coffee if you'd like some.'

It took a moment to adjust to the dusky light. He sat in an American rocker with a moquette seat and turned wooden arms, worn smooth from use.

The shelves above were heavy with volumes on archaeology, palaeontology, natural history. On a desk under the window were reference books and an A4 pad of handwritten notes. Whatever her mother claimed, Margaret was still studying.

She set cups, milk and a glass coffee pot on the low table

408

between them.

'You haven't asked me why I'm here, Miss German.'

'I don't need to,' Mags said. 'I already know.'

'You do? How come?'

'Because it'll be about Robbo, won't it?'

*

Any estate agent would have wanted The Refuge on their books. It was a one-off; a quirky holiday house created from an old railway carriage.

When Mags had turned eighteen, she banked a twelve-thousand-pound inheritance from her paternal grandmother. She'd now used some of it to improve Robbo's parting gift. A small bathroom with a shower and loo was built on the back. The main roof was re-felted, rotting timbers replaced and treated against the salty sea air.

Mags had a collector's eye and bought furniture, pictures and ornaments from antique fairs and flea markets and painted the inside walls Dorset cream and tallow.

To all that had been neglected and chaotic during Robbo's ownership, she gave colour and form for this was now her place of safety.

'You must realise, Miss German—'

'I'm Mags. Call me Mags.'

'OK, but please understand, this is an informal conversation. You're not under caution or anything like that but I need the truth about you and Robbo, everything, OK?'

'Of course.'

Benwell thought he detected a look of relief in her guileless eyes. In the end, secrets weigh heavy so confession was invariably good for the soul.

He asked if she knew what'd happened to Robbo.

'No... but I've always felt that he's dead. I'm right, aren't I?'

'Sorry but yes, he is dead.'

'So I was right. How did it happen?'

'With painkillers and a lot of whisky.'

'Oh God, that would've been the stuff I got for him.'

'Probably, but don't blame yourself. He'd been planning what he did for quite a while.'

Mags went quiet. She flattened an invisible crease on her long white cotton dress. The sea broke against the beach, but gently and with barely a whisper.

'You OK, Mags? Are you sure?'

She gave him half a smile and poured more coffee for them both.

'I suppose Robbo must have meant a lot to you.'

'I'd feelings for him, yes... don't know if they were returned, though.'

They carried on talking. Benwell didn't make notes. He was there to prompt and observe, to look into her face and watch the body language of this plain, impressionable young woman as she laid out her part in Robbo's life on the run, from their first hello to the last goodbye.

'He was like no one I'd ever met before in my dull old world,' she said. 'He was like several people in one, charming on the surface yet dangerous, too. That's what drew me to him.'

'That morning you left the hotel so hurriedly, you must have connected all that police activity with Robbo.'

'Most likely I did but if I'm honest with you, I was really

410

afraid by then.'

'You mean the reality of being with a wanted man caught up with you?'

'It had all been a big adventure till then, exciting.'

'Exciting? Being with a drug runner?'

'I didn't see any drugs until he brought me here.'

Benwell leaned forward. He was hearing new information. Here was red meat.

'You mean this place belonged to Robbo?'

'Yes, it was his bolthole, somewhere to hide.'

'How did you know he kept drugs here?'

'Because I saw him take some packages from a hiding place and they had to be drugs because I've seen stuff like that on the TV and Robbo said he was going to give it back to its rightful owner.'

Good cops think like bad people. Robbo and Kat had both seen service in South America. The coke found with her remains was from Bolivia.

What if she and Robbo were topping up their Army pensions with one they'd kept off the books?

'So whereabouts did Robbo stash the drugs, Mags?'

'Under the hearth stone but it's not been moved since he put it back.'

Benwell got on his knees and began to prize it up. Lodged between the floor joists beneath was a scuffed biscuit tin, nine inches square, four deep – big enough to have held three kilos of coke. The lid had a silvery diamond pattern and a red panel between two cartoon bakers saying Peek Freans were supplied by Royal Appointment to Her Majesty the Queen.

Benwell took out a thin gold ring, a first birthday card to my little prince from Mummy, a pair of chamois leather baby

411

boots and a large brown envelope. Inside this were five birth and five death certificates, a black and white photograph and with it, three bundles of disused white five-pound notes still in wrappers from Coutts Bank in The Strand. He spread everything across the carpet. Mags knelt beside him.

'What is all this stuff?'

'Not sure yet,' Benwell said. 'Some more of his secrets, I suspect.'

There was a noise by the front door. Benwell looked round and into the room ran a little boy, barefoot and brown, dark curly hair, laughing and shouting and holding a dead crab.

'Look, Mummy, look what I've got.'

But she was looking at Benwell and he knew exactly why.

37: FINIS

"... endings are also beginnings.
We just don't know it at the time."

- Mitch Albom, writer

Lunch was spaghetti hoops for Robin and a sardine salad with iced water for the grown-ups. The boy had intelligent eyes, an impressive vocabulary and a quiet confidence in the presence of a stranger. He would be four in September. The gestational maths was not hard to figure out.

After he went back to play with his friend next door, Benwell sat across the table from his mother and asked if Robin was like his father.

'Absolutely, he is,' Mags said. 'He's got his self-control, that ease within himself, but missing nothing at the same time.'

'Does your mother know she's a grandma?'

Mags sipped her water. She'd probably never made friends easily, hadn't anyone to whom she could reveal her inner self without fear of jeopardising the life and home she'd so carefully built to protect herself and her child.

'Yes, she knows all right,' Mags said. 'But she's never seen him and she doesn't want to. She wanted me to get rid of him when I could.'

413

'That can't have been pleasant to hear. Why would she say something like that?'

'Because of the shame of it, because of me not having a husband, not being the perfect daughter she would've wanted.'

'So I take it she doesn't know anything about Robbo?'

'Too right she doesn't but then again, I don't know much, either.'

He helped to clear the table then dried the plates and glasses as she washed them in the little galley kitchen. She went to check that her neighbour was still happy to look after Robin. When she returned, Benwell was going through the contents of Robbo's tin box. In all probability, the birthday card was to him and the baby shoes had been his. It wasn't possible to assign the ring to anyone. But it was the documents that were intriguing.

All five birth certificates were of children born in the early 1950s. One was for Robert Ellison born in Chatham, Kent on 7 March 1948. Stapled to it was a death certificate. He'd succumbed to pneumonia ten days later. But as Tilly had found out from Robbo's ex-wife, he'd stolen Robert Ellison's name as the basis for a fake legend for himself. He'd then infiltrated the Troops Out Movement, and fraudulently married Sally Tobin.

The second birth certificate revealed even more. All Robbo's official paperwork, from school days through to joining the Army and beyond, had him down as Brian Oliver Roby, born in Warrington on 4 September 1951.

But paper-clipped to this birth registration document was a death certificate, for Brian Oliver Roby who'd died from gastroenteritis at just eleven weeks old.

Someone had fitted Robbo with this dead baby's identity very early on in his own life. Here was irony: the person he'd genuinely thought himself to be was no more real than the characters he'd assumed for his undercover roles. At some point, possibly while combing through child mortality records for new names, he'd discovered the truth about himself.

'So his whole life was a lie from the very beginning,' Mags said.

Benwell didn't answer. Three questions immediately struck him: who was Robbo before he became Brian Oliver Roby, why did his true origins need to be disguised, and for whose benefit?

'And all this money,' Mags said. 'There's three hundred pounds. What's the story here?'

'No idea, but white fivers haven't been legal tender since I was in short pants.'

The photograph from Robbo's box of secrets was six by four, creased and cracked with age. It showed an instantly recognisable, but much younger, Queen Mother, smiling, coming out of a stately home in a long pale coat, cuffs trimmed with bands of fur, three strings of pearls at her neck and carrying white gloves in her left hand.

Written in ink on the reverse were the names of her less well-known companions: Her Royal Highness, the Princess Royal, with Lady Harewood and Lady Jane Rankin following behind.

Of far greater interest to Benwell was a young woman only partially visible in the shadows of the hallway. A circle had been drawn round her face in pencil and above that, the one word: ME.

'She's pretty but she looks like a maid in service, a servant of some kind,' Mags said.

'It's obviously someone who meant something to him or he wouldn't have kept it.'

'Maybe she was a relative.'

'Could be... but how close a relative, Mags? That's what we don't know.'

The look between them suggested they'd both had the same thought at the same time.

'You mean really, really close?' she said. 'No... that can't be the case, can it?'

'Well, if it is and she's his mother, then who was the father?'

Mags, the lone parent, went quiet at this.

Had Robbo's mother been in love and if so, with whom? Or had she just been used, abused, deserted? Again, if so, by whom? She asked Benwell what he thought. He held her gaze as he answered.

'This photograph doesn't make the puzzle any easier to solve,' he said. 'It's got to be from the early fifties, in other words from around when Robbo was born. But these banknotes from Coutts complicate matters.'

'Why? What do you mean?'

'Because Coutts are the royal family's bankers and only millionaires bank there, so I'm wondering how Robbo had that amount of cash from Coutts which, if it's also from the early fifties, would've been worth about five grand in today's money.'

'So you mean it doesn't prove anything?'

'All it suggests is that someone close to him was in royal service and was either given the money or stole it.'

'But either way, the servant would've spent it, surely?'

'Most likely yes, but then again, what if it was a bribe, hush money, and she was too proud or offended to take it, then she wouldn't spend it, would she?'

Cops like Benwell knew the protective instincts of large organisations in the eye of a crisis. They deny, dissemble then cut the best deal – for themselves.

If the servant was Robbo's mother and had been made pregnant by someone in the extended royal family, they'd certainly want to buy her silence.

Benwell had no wish to encourage Mags to think that Robbo – and through him, her own son – had a trace of royal blood. Only madness lay that way. But he could see how she was already thinking.

'I could find out who she was, couldn't I?' she said. 'It wouldn't be that difficult.'

'Don't kid yourself, Mags. You don't know her name, where she was in service, who she might have slept with, and what you can't do is ask everyone from the Duke of Edinburgh down to take a DNA test for you.'

'But seeing all this, it just makes me want to know more, for my sake and for Robin's.'

'Leave it, Mags. You'll get nowhere and if you carry on and if what you're doing gets out, this place'll be crawling with reporters and you'll not stop them digging up stuff you really, really won't want to become public.'

'So where does that leave me when the day comes and Robin asks me about his dad?'

'Can't help you there,' Benwell said. 'But my advice would be to keep as far away from the truth as you can.'

Benwell's childless marriage had ended in a rancorous divorce. His wife would've cited the entire Criminal Investigation Department of the Metropolitan Police as co-respondent had she been able to. Instead, she won that miserable day, claiming – rightly – unreasonable behaviour, innumerable burnt dinners, drunkenness and broken promises.

Suspicions of infidelity were taken into consideration. Living with Tilly had brought him to the late realisation that fulfilment wasn't just a car chase and a collar then an all-nighter in the pub later.

However involuntarily, some latent paternal feeling had manifested itself in him during his few hours with Mags. A chance meeting with a charming man had capsized her life. Yet it had given her meaning and purpose – and a child. She'd coped, adjusted, was managing on a student grant and benefits. And all this by herself and in a shack she'd turned into a home. Mags was no criminal, and his report would say as much.

For now, he sat in her front garden with a glass of cordial made from elderflowers Mags had picked herself. She'd fed Robin cheese on toast for his tea and after a shower, he was going for a sleepover with his friend.

Sitting in her small front garden in the early evening sun, Benwell felt like a visiting uncle, content and not in the way. The sea was mirror flat and might be all across to France as far as he knew.

Benwell thought he could live in this place, that here was a peace he'd never known. The tides and the trees would have their seasons and he, his. Every man needs a dream.

Mags returned from her neighbour's. She smiled, no longer a suspect in his eyes. She drank her cordial; he finished his then said he had to leave.

'First, there's something I think you ought to see,' he said. 'It's by where my car's parked.'

He led her over the pebbled foreshore, the sun still warming their backs, and up by the graveyard of St Wilfrid's at Church Norton. Nothing was said between them. Even the gulls were quiet. He opened the lychgate for her and they walked to where the newer graves were.

Benwell stopped at one marked only by a white wooden cross on which the initials BOR and the numerals 7.12.1990 had been cut.

'It's where he wanted to be buried,' Benwell said.

Mags put her hand to her mouth then dropped to her knees. Benwell moved away. If she prayed, if she wept, he didn't hear. He wondered if she would bring her son here one day, explain that she couldn't tell him about his father because no one knew who he was. But might it not be better for his cross to rot and the grass to grow and the past to moulder with his bones?

Mags came across to him. There was grief in her eyes but acceptance, too.

'Thank you,' she said. 'Thank you so much for showing me. I'd no idea.'

'No reason you would. No one told you.'

'I feel close to him again... reunited, I suppose.'

'Good, I'm glad because I'd say that's what he wanted himself.'

'Was Robbo a bad man, Mr Benwell?'

419

'I wasn't his confessor, Mags, nor did I ever have to walk a mile in his shoes, thank God.'

They touched cheeks at his car. In an odd way, each felt close to the other.

'There is one thing you should keep in mind,' Benwell said. 'Not all questions have answers and not all mysteries have solutions. Just remember, don't do anything to risk all that you have here, OK?'

He drove away, out of her life and a little reluctantly, back into his own. She walked slowly towards The Refuge. The sun would set soon and the day would end.

As she made her way home, a boy in his mid-teens carrying a wreath he'd made of yellow sea poppies and purple sea lavender left his bike by the lychgate. He laid the flowers against a simple wooden cross with a square of white card on which he'd written: To my dad with love.

Then he had to leave. It was eight miles back to Chichester. He'd an exam in the morning for the Royal School of Church Music. He was tipped for a medal and wanted to do well for his mum – and the man he never knew.

ACKNOWLEDGEMENTS

The poem *Nearing An End* by Norman MacCaig in Chapter 3 is quoted by kind permission of the Norman MacCaig Estate and his son, Ewan.

The excerpt from the song *Strange Affair* by Richard Thompson in Chapter 17 is quoted by kind permission of Richard Thompson and Vector Management, Nashville, USA.

*

I am always amazed by people's willingness to give of their time and expertise when I've pestered them for research help on this book. I am really grateful to Pat Prentice, a veteran foreign desk man in Fleet Street, who subbed and edited my efforts and made so many constructive suggestions. Similarly, I benefitted hugely from Anne Loader's subbing and proofreading skills.

TV producer Virginia Hill allowed her name to be hijacked. She also provided me with fascinating insights into female thinking on so many sensitive topics, and all with humour and candour.

The actor Graham Seed and his wife, West End theatre

producer Denise Silvey, were content to morph into Sir Graham Silvey, my fictional Metropolitan Police commissioner. Ex-Army pilot Alan Calder was endlessly patient in dealing with my queries about flying helicopters.

I'm indebted to John Thorne, former BBC foreign correspondent; Nicholas Light, Paul Calverley and Catherine Mainstone, ex-colleagues from TV; Colin Dunne, a star writer in Fleet Street's great days; and the Rt Reverend Ian Brackley, retired Bishop of Dorking, who advised me with great courtesy. Also Martha Linden of the Church of England Press Office and David Curran, an expert in classical music. The late Rick Cattell schooled me in training methods for Special Forces and another contact, Paul Acda, provided further background.

Professor Ian Linden let me plunder his brave experiences as a secret courier to the ANC during the murderous years of apartheid in South Africa. I am hugely grateful to Penelope Schofield, HM Senior Coroner, West Sussex, and Nicholas Rheinberg, archivist of the Coroners' Society of England and Wales. Similarly, Anne Marie Aherne, deputy head of the Chief Coroner's Office.

I received guidance from undertaker Phil Ellis of Llanfyllin, Powys. Jane Linden read the manuscript and gave me invaluable notes. I am in considerable debt to Lt Colonel Kearn Malin (retired) for technical advice. Medical help came from Dr Peter Jones. Adrian Bradshaw helped with railway links between South Africa and Namibia in the 1980s, while Peter Ball and his son James, editor of The Heritage Portal, generously assisted on the same subject. Language guidance in Swedish, Welsh and Spanish-English came from Josie Jones, Glyn Evans and Gerard Coffey, while

John Ford provided further help with specialist terminology.

My thanks also to Gaynor Richfield, co-founder of the Tanat Theatre Club in mid-Wales; Gareth Sandham, Collections Manager at the National Trust's glorious Welsh property, Powis Castle; Richard Craven, Harbour Master at the Chichester Harbour Conservancy; Anya Frampton of Mulberry Divers, Selsey, West Sussex; and Butser Ancient Farm near Petersfield, Hampshire. Denny Debbaudt, a friend and former private detective in Detroit, happily figures in the story as himself with his wife Gay.

My good friend from our newspaper days, Peter Reece, has been a constant source of encouragement for which I am really grateful.

Others have helped but are professionally averse to publicity. I am grateful for their friendship and permission to use some of their hairier moments in this story. To all the above, not least my uber tolerant and supportive wife, Ann de Stratford, I offer my most sincere thanks. Any mistakes in the narrative are mine, not theirs.

BV - #0071 - 210323 - C0 - 197/132/24 - PB - 9781803781044 - Matt Lamination